More Praise for K[illegible]
Some Quiet Place

"An utterly original, compelling story—with maybe the most irresistable love interest of all."

—Claudia Gray, *New York Times* bestselling author of the Evernight series

"Chills and goose bumps of the very best kind accompany this haunting, memorable achievement."

—*Kirkus Reviews* (starred review)

"Sutton sets the bar high in her YA debut."

—*Publishers Weekly*

WHERE SILENCE GATHERS

kelsey sutton

flux®
Woodbury, Minnesota

First Edition
First Printing, 2014

Book design by Bob Gaul
Cover design by Ellen Lawson
Cover image: "Reaching for Clouds"/©Brooke Shaden Photography

Flux, an imprint of Llewellyn Worldwide Ltd.

Library of Congress Cataloging-in-Publication Data
Sutton, Kelsey.
Where silence gathers/Kelsey Sutton.—First edition.
pages cm
Summary: Since her family was killed by a drunk driver six years before, Alexandra Tate, now eighteen, has seen emotions personified—especially Revenge—but now that the driver is out of prison, surprising discoveries about her father's past make choosing between Revenge and Forgiveness a struggle.
ISBN 978-0-7387-3947-2
[1. Emotions—Fiction. 2. Orphans—Fiction. 3. Conduct of life—Fiction. 4. Uncles—Fiction. 5. Aunts—Fiction. 6. Choice—Fiction. 7. Youths' writings.] I. Title.
PZ7.S96828Whe 2014
[Fic]—dc23

2014009914

Flux
Llewellyn Worldwide Ltd.
2143 Wooddale Drive
Woodbury, MN 55125-2989
www.fluxnow.com

Printed in the United States of America

Acknowledgments

It turns out that writing a second book isn't any easier than writing the first. First thanks must once again go to my agent, Beth Miller, although I'm fairly certain she's a superhero in disguise. Her patience and dedication are definitely not human.

To the entire team at Flux: Brian Farrey-Latz, for his guidance and continuing faith in me. Mallory Hayes, for being just as enthusiastic the second time around about getting the word out. Sandy Sullivan, for her sharp eyes and determination to get the story absolutely perfect. Ellen Lawson, for yet another gorgeous cover. And everyone else who worked on this that I never got the chance to meet. I'm eternally grateful to you all.

To my critique partners and cheerleaders: Stefanie Gaither, Gabrielle Carolina, Amber Hart, Tanya Loiselle, Tessa Edevold, and Bailey Hammond. These women urged me on and listened to every question or problem I brought to them. What would I do without you?

To all my fellow students, who went to so many of my events and encouraged me during the deadline crunch: Jordan Shearer, Joe Stusynski, Devan Bierbrauer, Mark Duret, Andrea Nadeau, Zach Hanson, Meagan Brault, Sarah Barott, Dezaray Thoen, Matt Lavrenz, Morgan Bartlett, and Tia Massar. Even when the time comes to part ways, I know this group will come back together again.

To my professors themselves, for being yet another support system: Larry Swain, Carol Ann Russell, Lauren Cobb,

Maureen Gibbon, Jeanette Lukowski, and Rose Weaver. I can't thank you enough for letting me barge into your offices every other day.

To my Caribou crew, for reminding me to laugh in the midst of writing such a solemn book and having such enthusiasm for this world I've created: Grace Slaubaugh, Randi Georges, Liz Burnard, Becca Johnson, Katie Ogden, Liscia Oines, Tiffany Pierce, Mikaela Boyd, and Hana Kim. Someday I'll put your names in a book, like we're always discussing!

To all of my friends and readers online: Your passion for these characters is what pushed me to finish their stories.

And last but not least, to my incredible family, for being there every step of the way. Thank you.

For my grandparents, Lyle and Corby,
who have shown me by example how to
face down the difficult choices.

ONE

Revenge finds me on the bridge.

He sits down just as I finish my uncle's bottle of rum. His legs dangle off the edge. I don't look at him, and for a few minutes neither of us says a word. Plumes of air leave my mouth with every breath. It's still too cold for crickets, so the night is utterly silent. If I listen hard enough, I can almost hear the stars whispering to each other. Cruel, biting whispers.

"Saul's not going to be happy with me," I finally slur, watching moonlight quiver over the creek. "He didn't even try to hide this, because he trusts me. But you know, if he *had* hidden it, I can find anything! Anything, I tell you!" I lift my finger in the air and almost topple over. Revenge doesn't reach to steady me. That's one of his rules, after all: no touching. I giggle, reaching for the bottle again. Oh, right. Empty.

There's a pause, and then Revenge turns his head to look at me. "I like the eyebrow ring."

I touch the silver loop, almost surprised. I'd completely

forgotten about it. Now I notice the pain. "Georgie did it for me earlier."

My friend studies it for a moment, then faces the water again. "There are better ways to deal with this, you know," he tells me. His usual grin is missing, which means that something is wrong. Swaying, I give him a questioning look. He shrugs. "We can talk about it tomorrow."

"Screw that. Tell me."

A few more seconds pass, and I start to think he's ignoring me. He doesn't take his attention off the water. Then, suddenly, his gaze meets mine. Revenge's eyes always manage to make me feel things, no matter how much I try to pretend otherwise. Some days they're hazel, some days they're green. Once in a while, like now, they're a mesmeric emerald. Tonight, though, it's his words that are the most powerful.

"They let him out today, Alex," Revenge says.

Instantly I open my mouth to ask who he means. Then comprehension slams into me with all the force of a hangover and my spine goes rigid. "No. No. He's not supposed to be out for another—"

"He was released on good behavior. He's already home."

I lurch to my feet without hesitation, scraping my palms in the process. My car is parked just a few feet away. Revenge doesn't protest, doesn't help, doesn't encourage me. He just follows.

"That's where you were today, wasn't it?" I mutter, struggling to open the door. "I bet you're loving this."

There it is, the thorn that's always made our friendship bleed. Once again Revenge doesn't answer, so I get in. After a moment he follows, tucking his body inside and somehow managing to make it look graceful. His hair glints, the color of spilled blood.

The keys are in the ignition. Revenge knows better than to offer to drive, so as I struggle with the gear—forgetting that I haven't started the car yet—he just settles into the passenger seat and waits. Usually I can't get him to shut up. His voice is a constant sound in my ears, at school, at home, with my friends. Everything is different now; the dynamic has shifted.

He's excited.

There's an animation to his expression that's never been there before. His time has come. My jaw clenches as I finally start the car. *I'm not ready for this, I'm not ready for this.* The engine whines into the stillness, but I don't move. Seconds pass and I think of another night, another drunken mistake. "You have to drive," I finally mutter.

The Emotion—it's not quite what he is, but I don't know what else to call him—grins. As I climb back out and circle the car, he slides behind the wheel. Before my door has even shut completely, Revenge slams onto the gas. The tires squeal. He can't hold back a loud whoop.

Resentment appears in the backseat, a bald Emotion who talks almost as much as Revenge. Yet now he just touches my shoulder, sending his essence burning through me, and vanishes. They know, they all know, that something is happening.

I'm clenching my fists so hard it hurts. Nails. I haven't clipped my nails lately. "It's too hot," I say through my teeth. As a response, Revenge leans over me to hit the window button. His familiar scent teases my senses: chocolate. I adore-despise it. "Get off me."

Those green eyes gleam in response. "It could all be over tonight," he murmurs, leaning closer than he ever has before. The car swerves, nearly hitting a tree. It doesn't even faze him; he just corrects us. "I'll help you, Alex."

"I don't need your help," I hiss. The road lines keep flying past, white blurs, and it's so disorienting.

"Come on. Who are you talking to?"

"I *thought* I was talking to my best friend. But I keep forgetting what you are." I laugh bitterly. "Ironic, right? Forgetting something like that?"

At this, Revenge's expression darkens and he leans away. Which is exactly what I wanted: him to feel as unsettled as me. Still smiling tightly, I focus on the signs, knowing that the turn is coming up. The house we're looking for is two towns over from Franklin, an hour away if we drive fast. And we are. So fast that it almost feels like I'm leaving everything behind. Almost.

That's what I like about Revenge most, I think. He doesn't feel the need to slow down; he thrives on the speed just as much as I do. With the taste of rum in my mouth and the sting of remembrance in my heart, I set my sights on the man who killed my family.

I lose track of how much time passes. The glowing numbers on the dashboard don't exist; there's just what's coming. I can't stop myself from picturing the moment, the instant Nate Foster sees me.

"What was he like?" I ask. My voice is quieter now. Like that hushed moment just before everything implodes.

The trees continue to rush past as we drive down the mountain. A line deepens between his eyebrows as Revenge considers. Again, uncharacteristic. Revenge is impulsive and wild.

"Tired," he decides. "He looked tired." I don't say anything to this, and I feel him watching me. "What are you thinking about?" he asks.

I'm thinking that I can't hear the whispers of the stars anymore, but Revenge wouldn't understand that. Instead I answer, "The day we met."

He grins again. His grip is relaxed on the steering wheel. "You were so chubby back then. I'm glad you turned out nice."

How can he sound normal? Apprehension materializes and reaches for me. I resist the urge to recoil. He pokes my shoulder rather than resting his hand on it, like the others do. He's one of the odder Emotions, with tangled hair and clothes that are baggy from him tugging at them so much. He's nearly identical to Worry, as if they were born as twins. Creatures from the other plane aren't born, though, and Apprehension smells worse.

Revenge notices our guest, but he wisely chooses not to comment. As always, I pretend not to see him. I do this with all the Emotions, even though they must know about my Sight. It's an instinct born from habit and a deeply rooted hatred.

Hatred for all of them—except him.

Apprehension disappears. I hardly notice; I'm remembering that day for real now. I was twelve. There was a newspaper on the coffee table, and the headline caught my eye. Saul must have forgotten to hide it. *Drunk Driver Kills Family.* I was young, but even then I was capable of darkness. The sight of those words caused it to spread through my chest.

That's when Revenge came into my life.

"You're small," he said to me that afternoon. He was dressed in a simple long-sleeved shirt and jeans—a tame choice for him, I'd learn—yet I still knew he wasn't like me. By then I'd learned how to discern them from humans.

I glanced at my aunt, who was busy in the kitchen. Dishes clattered in the sink. "Who are you?" I asked, turning back to the stranger in our living room.

Revenge smiled, and the breath caught in my throat even then. "I'm your new best friend."

"You're one of them," I said, frowning.

He shrugged. "So? You're a fat little human. You don't hear me complaining. That's what friendship is, right?"

I thought about this. "Why would I be friends with you?"

"Because I'll be here when you need me, and I'll help you get what you want."

"And what do I want?" I asked suspiciously.

Revenge wasn't smiling anymore. He straightened, looking down at me with an intense expression. "That's the question, isn't it, Alexandra Tate? What do you want?"

What do you want?

The question still echoes through my head six years later. I find myself looking away from the twists and curves of the road to study Revenge's profile. He's not beautiful in the traditional sense, but he is striking. Sometimes I have trouble tearing my eyes away. His coppery hair is cropped short, and his features are sharp and flawless. Every time he grins, dimples deepen in his cheeks.

Feeling my stare, Revenge turns his head. I quickly look at the road, biting my lip.

Has he stayed with me all these years because he wanted this moment so badly? Or did he stay because... he just wanted to? I've never let myself ask. I didn't want to ruin it, ruin us. My entire life I've chased after the things that scare me most—maybe because it feels like a punishment, or maybe because I can. But Revenge is one of my greatest weaknesses. As things are, he feels safe. Dependable. If I change this, there won't be any going back.

It's my fault, really, for falling in love with my best friend.

A love that's unorthodox, impossible, and worst of all unrequited.

To escape the black hole of my thoughts, I turn on the radio. Revenge glances at me with an indiscernible expression. We don't get reception up here, though, so all that will come through is Joe's local station. And he only plays Elvis. A song I've listened to a thousand times drifts through the thick silence of the cab.

"My dad hated this," I say suddenly. "He grew up here, you know. Joe refused to play anything else back then, too, so the entire town has always been stuck driving around with Elvis in our cars. It's either that or tapes. No one exactly has a car made in this century. But where are you going to find tapes?" I smile.

"You don't talk about him much," Revenge comments.

He's playing with me. I'm aware that it's what he does, but it still hurts. Revenge knows everything about me. What happened the night I lost everything, what's happened since then, why I don't talk about it. He wants me to remember, and he wants me to get angry. For the first time, I wish Revenge wasn't here. But there's no point in telling him to leave; the only thing creatures from the other plane listen to are their summons.

SANDERSON ROAD.

The sign appears suddenly, a flash of color in the blend of black and brown. Revenge slams on the brakes so hard the smell of burnt rubber permeates the darkness. My nostrils flare as I take in the illuminated words. Every road on and around the mountain is named after some old miner from the very first crew.

Revenge's smile is back. He's forgotten to hide it, or maybe he doesn't care. Deliberately, he turns onto the street Nate Foster lives on. Elvis keeps singing, oblivious to everything that's unfolding. We're slowing down now, and I reach to flip the headlights off. I don't want him to know I'm coming. I want the moment we meet to be devastatingly unexpected.

Gravel crunches beneath the tires and moonlight guides us around the curves. There are only three houses down here, and they're miles apart. No witnesses.

Nate Foster's driveway is marked by a single mailbox.

Plastic, beige, the number 36 stickered on the side. I've stared at it so much that the image is embedded into my brain. There's a *FOR SALE* sign next to it, which has been there for months.

Now I hesitate.

Sensing this, Revenge stops the car.

The only sounds in the entire world are Elvis, my breathing, and the rumbles of the engine beneath us. For a few minutes I concentrate on that, on the air flowing through my lungs. In. Out. In. Out. Then, as if I'm moving through an ocean of syrup, I lean forward, open the glove box, and take out the gun. It's cool in my hand.

Revenge says nothing.

"It's Saul's," I whisper. He knows this, of course, but I feel an overwhelming need to speak, to say something. "He keeps it in his nightstand drawer. It was tucked under a Bible, shoved in the back, but I can—"

"Find anything," Revenge finishes. The sound of his voice is jarring.

"Go," I say.

He hits the gas and spins into the driveway, abandoning subtlety. Emotions flood the car and reach for me. Their hands brush my cheek, my hair, my shoulder, my back as Revenge parks and I jump out. The spring air tries to soothe me, but all I'm aware of is the wide window to the left of the front door. Yellow light spills from a chandelier and over the ground outside. The dining room. Two people sit in chairs, eating and drinking. Wine quivers in their glasses. Somehow they haven't seen me. I dart to the side and edge closer, using the shadows of the trees to hide me. Closer. I still have the gun.

And there he is.

Over all these years, I'd built him up. He became this monster, this thing made of thorns and red eyes and hisses. But all I see now is a man. An ordinary, weary-looking man. He takes a bite of his food and chews like a cow, his jaw going around and around. There are bags under his eyes, and he's lost hair since I saw his picture in the paper. Nate Foster.

"Alex," Revenge breathes from his place beside me.

He must feel the way my insides go still. "So that's who killed them, huh?" I ask, barely recognizing my own voice. It's flat, empty. My grip loosens on the gun. "I almost wish he was a monster."

"Just because he looks like an accountant doesn't mean he isn't capable of murder." Revenge is standing so close I can feel the heat rolling off his skin. That scent of chocolate coaxes me. *So good, so easy.*

For some reason, I choose this moment to imagine that empty bottle I left on the bridge. It rolls across the gritty surface, clinking over the rocks and dirt. Then it falls. It makes the smallest of sounds when it hits the water, and all its pain and toil is behind it. The water carries the bottle down the mountain, to new and different places. I could do that, couldn't I? Float away and never look back? Just... move on?

Something flickers out of the corner of my eye.

No, not something. Someone. The newcomer stands in the shadow of a pine tree, too far away for me to make out the details of his face. All I see is a white T-shirt.

"Who is that?" I ask Revenge, not taking my eyes off the newcomer.

Oddly enough, Revenge's jaw is clenched. "No one," he growls. "Alex—"

"Don't." I'm still staring at the stranger. He stays where he is. Somehow, as always, I know he's one of them. It's the way they move, I think.

Eventually, I tear my gaze away from the stranger and focus on the gun. It's so light, so small. Strange that something this insignificant could cause such damage. I glance at Nate Foster again. He's listening to the woman speak. His wife.

I could do it. I could walk up to that window and shatter their lives the same way he shattered mine. I could.

Instead, I walk away.

"That's it?" Revenge calls after me. He doesn't follow this time, and I see that the stranger is gone. Feeling as if my soul is made of the heaviest iron, I head for the car. I'm not drunk anymore. No, I'm more sober than I've ever been in my entire life.

"For tonight, yeah."

Just as I reach the driver's side, I hear, "Hey, Alex." I turn to face him, and Revenge musters one more smile. If I didn't know any better, I'd think he looks sad for me. "Happy birthday."

TWO

Saul is waiting for me when I walk through the front door.

He sits at the tiny kitchen table. It's round, placed right in the center of the room. One lone light bulb dangles from the ceiling and casts a soft glow over him. I pause in the doorway, flattening one palm against the wall to pull my boots off. They leave dirt on the floor.

Uncle Saul watches for a moment. "Are you drunk?" he asks calmly. He looks at me with my father's eyes, rich and brown and knowing. They flick to my eyebrow ring, but he doesn't comment on it.

I hesitate before going to stand behind the chair opposite his. My finger trails the wiry path of some blue river on the wall; every room in the apartment is decorated with the contours of a continent. "Not anymore."

"There's cake in the fridge."

His tone is still even, but the implication is clear: they

had plans for tonight. They wanted to celebrate the day that I dread most.

"Is Missy asleep?" I ask, trying to sound as controlled as him. We're both frozen lakes, everything hidden beneath a layer of ice.

Saul finally cracks. He rubs his eye with the heel of his hand, revealing just how worried he was. Even if the Emotion has left, their essence always lingers. But all he says is, "I told her there wasn't a point to both of us waiting up."

"Look, I'm—"

"Give me your keys." I toss them onto the table and open my mouth to try apologizing again. "Just go to bed, Alex. We'll talk in the morning." Saul heaves himself up, wincing. He must have been sitting there for hours. Guilt appears and puts her heavy hand on me. That's how they come, almost every time; one moment there's nothing, and the next they're reaching for you with too-hot or too-cold hands and forcing you to feel everything.

Without another word, Saul lumbers down the hallway and disappears into their room. The door clicks shut. I stay there for a few seconds, wishing I'd done everything differently tonight. Regret joins Guilt and both of them torment me with their existences. I slip out of their grasps, giving them no time to enjoy it.

We live above Saul's piano tuning shop, in one of the three apartments. The one to our left is empty; it's where I used to live with my family. I haven't been inside since the day of the accident. The one to our right is occupied by a little boy and his parents. Angus. The moment I enter my room and sit down on my bed, the springs squeal and Angus knocks on the wall our rooms share. It's a language we invented a couple years ago, something to connect our uncertain worlds. I listen and decipher. *You okay?* he's asking.

I smile and knock back: *Fine. Sleep.*

His reply takes a few minutes. *Happy birthday.*

The simple statement pierces me even more than when Revenge said it. Angus reminds me of my little brother. Or at least, what my little brother might have grown to be.

Exhausted, I don't bother with pajamas or brushing my teeth or even the mascara caking my eyes. I just crawl beneath the covers and curl up. The sheets are cold. Light from the hallway spills toward me, reaching. I stay in the shadows. Still, it's comforting. That light never stops trying, never fades.

Alexandra.

My name is so faint I wonder if I imagined it. Frowning, I sit up and listen. The fridge hums in the kitchen and the wind blows against the window next to my nightstand. I don't hear the voice again. "Uncle Saul?" I shout-whisper.

No answer.

Glancing warily around the darkened room, I lie back down and close my eyes. Eventually I fall asleep and dream of the figure in the white T-shirt.

Voices drift down the hallway. I open my eyes a slit and hover in that place between full awareness and the straggling images of my dreams. They were all about the accident, of course. There are spaces of white in my memory, but every night I see a doctor's droopy eyes, a ceiling rushing past. Blood. Always blood.

As I wake, those images slowly fade. Gray light pours through the window and rain splatters against the glass. Another day.

I can hear the giant clock on Main Street marking the hour. *Dong. Dong. Dong.*

"... just think we need to nip this in the bud. If we give her any leniency, it'll only get worse."

Uncle Saul. I sit up, rubbing my eyes. The hangover isn't as bad as I thought it would be; my head aches rather than pounds. Mascara smears my hands. I'm still wearing the clothes from yesterday. After sniffing everything else lying around, I just leave them on. Then I leave the comfort of my bed and tiptoe toward the kitchen, trying to ignore how cold the floor is. I get close enough in time to hear Missy reply, "You don't know that, honey. She's never done anything like this before."

There's a *thud.* "You may not see it, but Alex is exactly like William. I won't let her go down the same path he did."

My aunt takes her time in answering. She must be frying something, because there's the distinct smell of grease in the air and the sound of sizzling. "She might be like Will in some ways, but she does have her mother's qualities too, Saul."

"Maybe." He sighs. That single release of air contains the weight of all our sorrow. "But if we come down hard on her now, maybe she'll think twice next time she wants to steal our rum and come home drunk."

"When you put it like that . . . "

I don't want to hear any more. Pretending to yawn, I shuffle into the room. Both of them instantly stop talking. Missy stands at the stove, attempting to make scrambled eggs from the looks of it. She can't cook anything without burning it—she always gets distracted by other tasks or her own thoughts—but that doesn't stop her from trying.

"Want some?" she asks, glancing briefly in my direction. She must have been warned about the eyebrow ring, because she doesn't look surprised.

Saul is at the table again, this time with a paper and a cup of coffee. Steam rises from the black surface. He doesn't look any less severe than he did last night. I smile at my aunt and shake my head, going to sit down across from him. He doesn't look up, and my keys glint in front of my seat, along with a wrapped gift.

"It's cold today" is all Saul says. Meaning, I have permission to drive. The present gleams and beckons, and I know they expect me to open it, but I can't bring myself to touch it.

Not when I don't deserve to.

Another apology sticks in my throat, but Revenge decides to show up just as I'm about to speak. The sight of him makes my mouth go dry. He's chosen to dress in modern clothes again—today it's a brown leather jacket, form-fitting jeans, his typical glinting hair, and that cocky grin—yet I can't control the way my entire body ignites.

Another Emotion comes up behind my chair and leans down, putting hands on my shoulders and a mouth by my ear to whisper, "You don't know what you're getting into, girl." I don't turn around or acknowledge the words, but her scent overwhelms me.

Oblivious, or maybe choosing to ignore her too, my friend settles into one of the other chairs. It doesn't creak or even move. "Better eat something," he drawls. "You've got a test in American Lit, right?"

I freeze, forgetting to be disappointed that he doesn't seem as affected by my presence as I am by his. "Shit."

Saul and Missy stare at me now. Recovering, I clear my throat. "Uh, sorry. I just meant … I just realized that I have to be at school early today. I'll see you guys tonight, okay? I'll open your gift then." Standing, I scrape my hair into a ponytail and use the hair binder around my wrist to secure it. The gathered strands brush my lower back.

A line deepens between Saul's eyes as he begins to stand, too. Worry twitches into reality behind him, a frizzy-haired Emotion who avoids eye contact. "Alex—" my uncle begins.

But I'm quicker. I snatch a piece of toast from the plate on the counter, grab my keys, and dart back down the hallway. Missy says something I don't catch. My teeth sink into the burnt bread as I yank my boots on—no socks—and I'm out the door before my left heel slides into it completely. The keys jangle in my hand, and once I've hurried down the stairs and reached the car I spare a moment to look up and wave at Angus, who's watching me from their front window.

Revenge materializes in his spot in the passenger seat. "Smooth," he says, eyes light with amusement.

I roll my own eyes in response and start the car, an ancient Saturn that Saul fixed up for me. "Shut up."

But my heart doesn't feel like a hot coal while I say it, as it did a few hours ago. Everything feels normal again, like all the shifting and changing that happened yesterday was just another dream. Nate Foster is still in his tiny jail cell, Revenge is here because there's nothing for him to do but wait, and the gun in my glove box hasn't been touched. There are no decisions, no uncertainties, no memories slamming at the inside of my skull.

Then Revenge has to ruin it.

"Are you going tonight?" he asks.

I could pretend confusion. I could act like I didn't hear him. Yet his simple question destroys any pretenses of normality I've managed to achieve. Elvis mourns into the sudden stillness. I turn the radio off, gritting my teeth. The clouds have relented just a little, but the light drizzle makes the world the darkest of greens.

The few businesses in Franklin crawl by on our right. The gas station, the diner, the general store. Everything else has *OUT OF BUSINESS* signs propped up in the windows. Ever since the mines closed, we've been fading away. The only people left have nowhere else to go. Most have lost hope. A group of kids play on the street, their faces dirty and their clothes ragged. They should be in school. But they aren't. It makes me think of futures and families... or the lack of them.

Naturally, this leads to thoughts of Nate Foster.

"Will you come?" I ask Revenge, even though I already know the answer.

"There's nowhere else I'd rather be."

He's looking at me. I can feel it. I focus on the road, unable to ask my own questions. *But why? For me? Or for you?*

Fear—an Emotion I meet more often than I'd like to admit—wraps his arms around both me and the seat. His skin is so cold, and his smell is sickeningly sweet. "Five seconds," he whispers in my ear. "That's all it would take to face your fear. Maybe less, if you can talk fast."

My eyes meet his in the review mirror, and the blond creature flashes me a quick grin. Revenge watches him with obvious dislike. Hopefully he thinks Fear's summons stem from the idea of facing Nate Foster tonight.

Then I blink and we're alone again—nothing to prove that Fear was even here other than his lingering scent. Revenge visibly relaxes. "So, why are we going in early today?"

The school rises up against the horizon. Back in the 1800s, it was a huge courthouse. Despite the conversion, it still has the gold plaque next to the door. The town clock towers beside it. I guide my old car into a parking space next to the curb and still avoid looking at Revenge. I'm afraid he'll see the truth in my eyes. "I had to get out of there" is all I say.

Rather than climbing out like a normal person, Revenge vanishes and reappears at my side. "I understand that," he says, shrugging. "There isn't a species more annoying than humans."

"No, it's not that." I study the cracks in the sidewalk as we make our way to the front steps. There isn't anyone around to notice me talking to the air. "I just hate making them worry. My father wasn't the most well-behaved kid, I guess. The sheriff was always arresting him and Dad didn't get to graduate, which is why he went to work in the mines. Saul and Missy probably think I'm going to end up the same way." And I probably will, in most ways.

Revenge looks speculative. "You made him out to be so perfect."

I picture my dad. I was twelve when he died, and already it's hard to remember the exact details of his face. We had the same thick eyebrows, the same clear skin and wide eyes. I got his hair, too, a caramel-like shade of brown that has a slight wave to it. Maybe the similarity is why I haven't cut it in years, and now it's become a thick, unmanageable curtain. What does Missy think I inherited from my mother, exactly? When I look in the mirror, all I see is Dad.

Realizing I still haven't answered Revenge, I shoulder my bag and start to climb the steps. "To me, he *was* perfect. I never saw that side of him."

"Wrong," Revenge says, startling me. "Don't you remember what—"

A familiar perfume—sweet pea—surrounds me just before someone slams their shoulder into mine. "Can someone please tell me why I have to stick around here for another year? Is a diploma really that important? I mean, I have a plan. Move to L.A. and become a star. Who needs high school for that?" My friend eyes me and tosses her curls over one shoulder. "You look like shit, by the way," she adds. "That birthday dinner with Missy and Saul must have been exhausting. Did you get in trouble for the eyebrow? I have to say, I did a great job."

"Hey, Georgie," I say dryly. Revenge wrinkles his nose

in distaste. He's never liked her. Probably because they're so alike. "Why are you here early?"

"I told you, it's Georgiana now. Georgie is just... amateur."

"Oh, excuse me. Georgiana." We reach the front doors and I open one of them for her.

She sweeps past. "Make fun of me while you can. You won't be laughing in a year."

The air in our school smells like mold and disinfectant. Though her locker is on the other side of the building, Georgie walks with me toward mine. "A year is all it will take to rise to fame, huh?" I ask her, trying not to smile.

"Again, I've got a plan." She sniffs. "Don't you ever listen to me when I tell you things? First, I'm going to—"

"We listen to you, Georgie. There's no need to go through it all again." The third member of our little group appears beside us, holding her books and fixing her gentle smile on Georgie. Briana Brinkman, who's been a part of my life for as long as I can remember, shifts her clear gaze to me and her smile grows. "Hey, Alex. We came early to work on Georgie's essay. It's due first hour, and all she's written is her name."

"Essay... " I repeat with a sinking sensation in my stomach. "I completely forgot."

Georgie eyes me. "What's going on with you lately?" Her expression changes and she grabs my arm. "Oh my God, I can't believe I forgot to tell you!"

Grateful to avoid explanations, I indulge her. "What?" We all start to walk toward the library.

"Billy and his friends were down by the mines the other night and they heard *moans* coming from the tunnels. Pretty freaky, right? Maybe the ghost of Sammy Thorn really does exist." Georgie doesn't try to hide how thrilling she finds this.

Briana responds, her tone solemn, but I don't hear what she says. I'm thinking of the Sammy Thorn legend, a bedtime tale for wayward children. Decades ago, little kids were disappearing from their beds. It became a national issue, and Franklin turned into a place of closed curtains and locked doors. Somehow it was discovered that a miner called Sammy Thorn was the culprit, but only one of the children was found when they searched his house. Thorn was chased into the mines and never seen again. Things went back to normal in our town, and so many years passed that people began to feel safe again. Thorn became a story.

Mid-sentence, Georgie turns to me again. "Don't think you're off the hook, by the way," she adds.

They're both staring at me, waiting, and I falter. "There's nothing to tell. Personally, I'm more interested in finding out if Briana finally asked Rachel Porter out."

At this, Georgie scoffs. She doesn't give Briana a chance to respond. "Of course not. She's too much a chicken. Now, spill. How did the birthday dinner go? Were they mad about the piercing?"

Damn it. "Uh, well, I—"

Alexandra.

I freeze, forgetting how to breathe. All the nerve endings in my body flare to life. This isn't like it was last night, some faint whisper in the distance. It sounds close, right in my ear. I lean against a locker to steady myself. What's happening to me?

My friends are staring. Even Revenge. "Did you hear anything?" I demand, still breathless.

Briana puts her hand on my arm, and an Emotion presses close to her. I don't let myself look up; her concern only makes things worse. Am I going crazy?

"I have to go," I say, taking a step back. Then another. My glance flicks to Revenge. He's frowning. For the first time, he doesn't understand me.

Something has started, and I'm a leaf in a current, helpless against it. I turn away from them and face the light pouring through the front doors. I think of Nate Foster and empty rum bottles and mysterious strangers wearing white.

Georgie swears. "Is she high or something? Alex? Alex!"

I run.

THREE

"Shouldn't you be in class?"

I turn away from the bookshelf and meet Andrew's concerned gaze. In case there was any doubt about what he's feeling, Worry stands beside him. I'm sick to death of this particular Emotion. He ignores me, and I ignore him as I say to Andrew, "They cancelled school today. A meteor fell and destroyed all the classrooms."

What I don't say is, *Oh, I think I might be losing my mind, and I can't be in Franklin right now.*

My godfather, who was my father's best friend, sighs and lowers himself into the chair behind the desk. His glasses flash in the weak lamplight. "You need a diploma, young lady. Life will be much more difficult without it."

Despite knowing how much he hates it when I touch his things—I've never been to his office before, but I've been to his house a hundred times—I pick up a plaque in front of him and read the engraved words: *PROFESSOR ANDREW*

LOMENTA. I drove over an hour to get to Green River Community College.

"Life, difficult? How so?" I ask flatly, putting the plaque down.

Worry's body gives a particularly odd twitch. It draws my attention to him, and as I watch he flickers again, like a channel with bad reception. I frown. It takes me a moment to remember what's happening and how Revenge once explained it: Beings from the other plane are able to be in multiple places at once. In order to address each and every summons, they do what Worry is doing right now—create another copy of themselves to send.

After another moment, Worry vanishes completely, his summons from me answered. Yet his effect lives on.

Andrew purses his lips and leans forward, imploring me with both his expression and his words. He can't resist readjusting the plaque so that it's exactly where it was before. His fingers are long and elegant. "Well, what about college? You want to go to college, right?"

I swing away and stroll along the edge of his office, feigning interest in the wall of books again. "Is that a trick question?"

"Missy asked me if I gave you a recommendation. She thinks you applied."

Anger appears and lays a heavy hand on my shoulder. I resist the urge to shake him off. His touch burns, right through my skin and into my bones. Just when I think I can't take another second, he vanishes.

Andrew types something on his computer while I struggle

to respond, but I'm clenching my jaw so tightly it's nearly impossible to get anything out. "Can we not talk about my aunt, please?" I say finally.

Another sigh. Andrew always gives in eventually. "Fine, Alex. You can hang out here for a while. But promise me you'll go back for your afternoon classes, okay?"

I pluck a textbook from its place on the wall—the one I'd been looking at earlier—and plop into the plushy chair by the door. My legs dangle off the armrest. "Of course," I chirp. I flip through the pages, stroking the ridges with my thumb.

Andrew pauses in his typing. His expression is strange. "What made you pick that book?"

I shrug as if the answer doesn't matter, as if it's nothing. "I figured it wouldn't be boring." But I can feel the embossed title against my palm—*Creatures of Myth*—and it matters more than he can know. Almost as much as getting the nerve to face Nate Foster matters.

"You didn't used to be interested in myth," Andrew says.

His tone is light, conversational, but no one can ever suspect. The other plane wouldn't like it. So I lift my head and snap, "I don't see any gossip magazines around here, so . . . "

The professor raises his hands in a gesture of surrender. Behind him there's a wide window, and the newly grown leaves of an oak tree sway in the breeze. "I didn't mean anything by it. I just thought it was interesting. Your father read that book too."

At this, my stomach flutters and I stare at him. "He did?"

"Cover to cover. He used to ask me questions about . . .

other dimensions. Or planes. I can't remember the exact way he phrased it."

"What did you tell him?" I try to sound casual, but my grip is too tight on the book. Excitement and Confusion lean over me.

Andrew picks up a pen and frowns at a paper on the desk. "I'm not really an expert on the subject, since my specialty is economics. But I gave him access to the college's library, and the number of an old friend who used to dabble in the subject."

Without thinking, I open my mouth to demand the name and number, and I'm saved when a student fills the doorway and ventures, "Professor Lomenta? Do you have a minute?"

Andrew hesitates, glancing at me.

I stand up, still clutching the book. "I better go, anyway."

"Can you wait in the hallway for a moment, Jenny? I'll be right there."

The girl nods and leaves. Andrew focuses on me again. "Alex ... I know you're having a difficult time, especially lately, considering ... " He stops and clears his throat, fidgeting with his pen. *Click. Click. Click.* "But your parents would have wanted you to be happy."

I force a smile, studying this awkward man that my father loved. Trusted. "I know, Andrew. Thanks." A hug is a bit too much, so I just move to put the book back.

"You can borrow it, if you want," he says.

I hesitate, but I already know there isn't anything in this

book that can help me. "No thanks." The book slides back into its place with a soft sound.

"Alex." When I turn yet again to meet his gaze, Andrew hesitates. He stuffs his hands in his pockets, and I'm surprised to see Apprehension appear behind him. Andrew's eyes flick toward the window, toward those quivering leaves, and then he says, "Don't come to my office again. If you need me, call, and we can meet somewhere. My house or a coffee shop. All right?"

He's always serious, but there's something different about his voice, a shadow that clings to the words. So I don't argue. "No problem. See you around, Lomenta."

This time he doesn't stop me from reaching the doorway. I feel him watching me go, and he probably thinks whatever issue I had is resolved with his simple assurances. But it will take more than concern or kindness to make everything right.

What will make everything right? a little voice in my head asks me. *Nate Foster's death?*

Maybe.

But that's not what's most important right now. No, what matters most is this new discovery, this burning knowledge that yearns to expand and grow. Something I should have known. It may mean nothing; it might mean everything.

My father saw them too.

Angus sits on the bench outside of Saul's store, holding a jar in his hands.

The town clock is going off again. It does that every single hour, on the dot, no matter how annoying we find it or how much we complain. Just like Joe and his damn radio station, playing all that Elvis. *Dong. Dong. Dong.*

I slam the car door shut and approach my small neighbor. "What are you doing out here? Are your parents fighting again?" Angus just nods. I squat in front of him. "Is that a new jar?"

"Found it," he mumbles, swiping at his nose. His sleeve leaves behind a streak of dirt. I smile a little, watching him use the edge of his shirt to clean the glass. He does so with a painstaking dedication that I've never given anything.

"How many jars does that make, now? Fifty?"

Angus shrugs. It's strange, the fact that he's more talkative through a wall than here, where the sun makes everything bright. Then again, maybe it does make sense. It's easier in the dark, sometimes, with a barrier between you and everything else.

"Have you decided what you're going to do with them yet?" I press.

Nothing.

I stand and let Angus revel in the silence we don't get in the apartments.

The moment I step through the front door I smell dinner. Well, I smell dinner burning. I set my bag on the floor and tug my boots off. With a heavy sensation in my chest, I wander down to the kitchen. The maps look older in the lamplight, and the harsh lines of the world seem softer. Saul has even more in his office, framed maps that are worth more money than anything else we own. They're ancient and yellowed and treasured, and if looking at something could make it fade, Saul would have had lost his maps long ago. I've never asked him what he finds so fascinating about them; I've just accepted it. Same with Angus and his jars. We all cling to something.

Missy and Saul wait in the kitchen, talking in low voices. Once again Saul is at the table, his silver hair shining in the dusk. Missy is leaning against the edge of the counter with a bowl in one hand and spoon in the other.

"Hi," I say, going to sit beside my uncle.

In unison, they focus on me and put on their smiles. "Hi, honey," Missy says. She's mashing potatoes.

"About time you showed up." Saul wraps his arm around my shoulders. Guess he's not mad at me anymore, or at least he's doing a better job of hiding it. He smells like cigars and… garbage. I wrinkle my nose. Saul notices and pulls away, sighing. "Damn animal got in the trash cans again," he says. "Had to clean it up."

My aunt pours a glass of water and slides it in front of me. She picks her spoon back up and starts mashing again. "How was your day?"

"Fine. Yours?" I take a drink so I don't have to come up with anything else to say.

Missy and Saul exchange a glance, probably without meaning to. I see it and clench my fist under the counter. If Saul feels the tension in me, he doesn't comment.

"So are we going to do this or what?" I ask, trying to sound flippant.

Silence. I attempt to interpret their wordless conversation. *Do you want to take this? No, you do it. Are you sure? I'm sure. Okay*. Looks like Missy draws the short stick.

"The school called," she says, brushing a stray hair out of her eyes. Her black hair has gray streaks it didn't used to. When did she stop dyeing it? "You missed class today."

I study the designs in the wooden table, losing myself in the thick and thin lines. They wait patiently for me to respond. But what can I say? What can I tell them? It feels like any words would only cause more damage.

"Do you need help with anything? Dishes? Dinner?" I offer when the silence becomes too long. "Or I could run to Ian's and pick something up." He's the owner of the general store.

As soon as the words leave my mouth, it's not just the three of us in this small room. Worry, the Emotion I seem to bring out the most in people, appears. He touches both Missy and Saul, and the sound of his foot tapping is something only I can hear. I grit my teeth.

Oblivious, Missy sets her spoon down once more, and it clinks against the side of the bowl. Her dark eyes try to find the secrets in my own. "Alex, we need to talk about this. Where did you go today? Do you need to talk about anything? I know that Nate Foster—"

"Don't." I slide off the stool so violently that it scrapes over the floor with an ear-splitting squeal. That name can't exist outside of my head. He can't be anything other than the monster. I head for the door.

"Where are you going, Alex?" Missy calls after me. Then

there's the *thud-thud-thud* of her pursuit. "Honey, you can't just—"

"Nowhere, Missy. Just out." Hating myself, hating the pretenses even more, I shut the door on her concern.

She doesn't try to follow me.

Guilt walks beside me as I make my escape into the trees out back. She towers over my head, her greasy hair shining yellow in the twilight. It takes the last of my self-control not to shake her big hand off. The emotion oozes through my veins.

But Guilt doesn't linger, and I stop when I reach the trail. I stand there for a minute, concentrating on the push and pull of air in my lungs. The haze ebbs from my vision enough that I can see the ground, so I make my way down to the ditch and search the long grasses for a flash of color, the glint of an object. Over the years, I've searched miles of the woods that surround the store.

Nothing.

After a few minutes, I climb back to the trail and squint at the horizon. I hear dirt crunching behind me, and then Uncle Saul's voice drifts into the stillness: "It hurt your aunt when you talked to her like that."

At first, I don't respond. Because they deserve better. The thought calms the storm raging within me. Calms it but doesn't stop it. My lungs are clouds and my blood is a torrent of rushing rain.

"I know." I shove my hands in my pockets. "I'm sorry. And I'll tell her that too. I just …"

Uncle Saul gives me a chance to finish. When I don't, he

does it for me. "Being young isn't as easy as everyone makes it out to be, huh? Especially when life has dealt you some rough cards."

My nostrils flare. It's been six years, but I can still taste blood in my mouth, hear the screams, feel the heat of breaking glass and twisting metal. "Is that what you call it? Rough cards?"

He chooses not to respond to this, but I see the way his mouth tightens. Remorse grips my stomach; sometimes I forget that when I lost a father, he lost a brother.

Saul puts his back to the sun and faces me. A tuft of hair sticks up on the back of his head, making him look younger. "What are you doing out here?"

I wasn't expecting that. Part of me was steeling myself for something about Nate Foster, about the unfairness of his release, how it would be best for me—for all of us—to move on. I let out a breath, and the truth comes out along with it. Maybe to make up for last night.

"I'm looking for something," I tell him. "Dad used to talk about it. He said that one Fourth of July, you guys shot off this giant rocket he built and he always wanted to find it. He didn't exactly get the chance, so I'm ... " I swallow.

In the distance, a flock of geese honk as they cross the sky. Winter really is behind us, despite the chill in the air.

Uncle Saul steps closer. "Don't stay out here too long, okay?" He kisses my temple. His lips are dry. "Oh, and you get to clean the attic. As a consequence for taking my rum. We'll give you a pass on school. This time." With that, he leaves.

He doesn't look back. But I do. I watch him return to the apartment, return to Missy, and feel the darkness rise inside me again. The rocket isn't here. It's been years since that summer. Dad couldn't find it. What makes me think I can?

I can find anything that's been hidden ... but I can't find what's been lost.

The sun is nearly gone now. The moon is a faded crescent, struggling to emerge. There's the sound of that damn clock again, unstoppable and unapologetic. *Dong. Dong. Dong.*

Time to go.

FOUR

The car vents breathe into the stillness. I sit in the driver's seat, tapping my finger against the steering wheel. I can't seem to get warm no matter how high the heat is set. My body is ice, and my mind is a frozen lump that can't let go of the sound of that voice I heard earlier today: *Alexandra.*

"Am I crazy?" I whisper, mostly to the stars.

Revenge turns toward me, the leather creaking beneath him. "Probably not. If you're crazy, what does that make me?" He winks.

It's impossible not to notice his outfit. Revenge has been alive for a long time, and sometimes he gets nostalgic. Today, it seems, he misses the Civil War era. The uniform of a Union soldier gleams in the glow from the radio. His hair looks gelled. Did he dress up for this?

I smile faintly and adjust the vents again. "You're a raving lunatic, Revenge."

"True. You still like me though."

He doesn't wait to see what I'll say. After all, Revenge is confident in his place and where he stands. We both focus on the house. Nate Foster isn't home, but his wife is. We watch her through the dining room window again. She's in the kitchen, in front of the sink. A curtain of brown hair falls over her shoulder as she leans over and puts a plate into the dishwasher. Jennifer Foster looks ... sad. As if she's lost something in all of this, too.

My smile dies. Something in my chest hardens, and an Emotion shimmers behind me, touching me with tender fingertips. I reach for the door handle, and Revenge instantly begins to fade so he can reappear beside me.

"No. Stay here," I say. I don't know why. All I know is that I want to go up to that house without him.

Now a frown tugs down the corners of his generous mouth. "Alex—"

"Please."

Something in my voice must be different, because Revenge studies me for a moment, then nods. He doesn't look happy about it, but he nods.

I leave the warmth of the car, slamming the door behind me. The road sparkles with frost and wind whistles through the trees. I cup my elbows and slink through the shadows. That wide window watches me come closer, closer, as if it can see all the pain I try so hard to keep locked inside. I stop inches away from the glass, off to the side so Jennifer can't spot me. My heart pounds. I want to touch the pane, to prove that I'm capable of doing more than waiting and thinking and hurting.

A sound rips through the quivering hush. It takes me a moment to realize what it is.

Sobs.

Disregarding caution completely, I stand on tiptoe to peer in. Jennifer is right where she was before. In this moment, though, her hands grip the edge of the counter as if it's all that's keeping her up. Her head is bowed. Her shoulders shake.

I ease back and press against the house, fixing my gaze on a tree a few yards away. There's a new sensation spreading through the center of my chest now, a tightness, like there's a hand reaching through the skin and bone and muscle and trying to crush my heart.

Compassion.

The Emotion herself must have arrived without my noticing, and if Jennifer Foster weren't within hearing range, I would tell this creature how much I loathe her. Her expression is pained as she brushes a strand of hair out of my face. She's a dark-skinned Emotion with disquieting eyes.

Twisting away, I focus on Jennifer again. Compassion steps back and slowly diminishes. Jennifer isn't crying anymore. I watch her take a breath and straighten her shoulders. I can't help but think that she wasn't in the car the night Nate Foster shattered my family. She didn't make the mistake. He did.

Seconds later, something else moves out of the corner of

my eye. I jump, facing the threat. The instant my eyes meet his, though, I forget to be alarmed and just stare.

"You," I whisper after a long, long pause. Every thought about Jennifer Foster flaps away into the night until there's only him.

The Emotion stands there, hands shoved in his pockets. "Hi, Alexandra."

For a few seconds neither of us speaks. I keep staring, and he just waits patiently. "Who are you?" I finally demand, careful to keep my voice low. But a part of me knows exactly who he is—has known since the first moment I saw him across the clearing. And if I'm really honest with myself, he's part of the reason I came back tonight.

I'm not feeling particularly honest right now, though.

A lock of dark hair falls into his eyes. Where Revenge would grin or wink or offer some brash statement, this Emotion just smiles. His skin is pale in the moonlight. "I'm Forgiveness," he says.

I smile back disdainfully. "Of course you are." And it's only fitting that he'd be just as tempting as Revenge. Even more so, because he possesses both that magnetic force and the beauty to go along with it. His eyes are darker than mine, but they're blue—what I would imagine the deepest part in the ocean to be like. His features are noble, with that square jaw and a slight indent in his chin. His hair is brown and wild, curling around his ears and neck. He's wearing the same clothes as the last time I saw him: jeans and that colorless T-shirt.

I refuse to let how much his presence affects me show.

"Picked a hell of a time to show up," I comment, transferring my attention back to Jennifer. I almost prefer Compassion.

He regards me with an unfathomable expression. "I've been waiting for you to let me show up, actually."

"What's that supposed to mean?" I frown and turn to face him against my better judgment.

Forgiveness doesn't answer, and all I can think now is that he had such a sad countenance. We're standing closer than I realized. Unlike Revenge, he doesn't smell like chocolate or anything sweet and tempting. His scent is distinctly … minty. Yet still alluring, somehow.

I grit my teeth and take a deliberate step back. "So, what, you're here to save me?"

He doesn't move. "Only one person can do that," he answers. His meaning is all too clear.

Scoffing, I swing away and start for the car. I've had enough of Jennifer and her pain, Compassion and her touch, Forgiveness and his disturbing eyes. "Franklin already has a pastor. Granted, I haven't been to church in years, but if I was interested in sermons or saving, I'd go there." Leaves quiver in the wind, and moonlight filters through the trees to guide my way.

Forgiveness is walking beside me, unfazed by the pace I've set. His long legs match my short strides. He doesn't respond, and this infuriates me further.

"What do you know about any of this?" I make a vague gesture at the house. A branch snaps beneath my foot and I falter, glancing back to see if Jennifer heard it. She's back to loading the dishwasher, still looking lost in her own home.

There's an Emotion behind her, half-concealed so I don't know which one.

Forgiveness doesn't reply, but a breeze stirs his hair and I remember him.

"What do you know about anything?" I add, scowling.

He steps closer. My traitorous heart picks up speed. Forgiveness's eyes are pits I could fall into and never be able to climb back out of.

"I know that you feel an emptiness inside of you, Alexandra Tate, that you're trying so hard to fill," he says quietly. "I know that you cry yourself to sleep sometimes, but you're always careful to make sure your aunt and uncle don't hear. I know you pretend that the boy next door really is your little brother. And I know that Revenge—"

"Stop." I'm shaking. Resentment flashes and fades, his palm cool on my back. "If you were trying to persuade me to do something, that was the wrong technique."

"I'm not trying to persuade you to do anything." A familiar silhouette appears on the ground beside us—Revenge—but Forgiveness doesn't take his eyes off my face. "I'm trying to help you."

"I don't need any help." With that, I walk away from both of them.

This time, Forgiveness doesn't follow me. Strangely enough, Revenge doesn't either. I hear their voices, low and indiscernible.

Seething, feeling as if my insides are going to explode from some chemical combination that's not supposed to blend together, I get into the car. The two of them are still standing there. I grip the steering wheel and glare at their profiles, despite the fact that neither is paying attention to me. It's strange, seeing Revenge and Forgiveness together. Like the brightest dawn and the darkest time of night. Whatever they're talking about, they disagree on something. Revenge's fists are clenched in a rare display of aggression, and though Forgiveness seems relaxed, his stance also has a tense quality to it.

They're talking about me.

Nate Foster's release has opened a door that can't be closed. Voices. Forgiveness. Change.

As I reach for the keys dangling from the ignition, I allow myself one more glimpse at these creatures who are tearing me apart. I think I know what I'm going to call them now. They're not Emotions, or Elements, or anything else literal and simple.

They're Choices.

The cold wakes me.

I turn on my side and frown at the open window, ignoring the present on my nightstand that's still unopened. The filmy curtains Missy picked out flutter in the breeze. Did I leave it open? Blearily, I stand and shuffle over to it to pull at the frame. It sticks. "Damn it," I swear under my breath. Shivering, I stand on tiptoe and put my weight on it. Nothing.

Alexandra.

This time it comes on a gust of air. I leap back, tripping

on the edge of the rug. Pain radiates through my bones as I land, and then I'm scrambling back as if something is crawling through the window after me. My back hits the edge of the mattress.

Fear bursts in front of me, tapping my nose before I can recoil, and then he's gone again. I stare at the sill, half-expecting a hand to clamp around it. Nothing appears.

"No," I moan, clutching my head. This isn't real. I'm dreaming. I tell myself that monsters don't exist, that Sammy Thorn is nothing but a story fabricated to frighten children into staying in their beds.

Alexandra.

Again, right in my ear. I close my eyes and focus on breathing. "Where are you?"

The mines. The mines.

This isn't happening. It isn't. "Leave me alone." A whimper escapes me, and I despise how weak it makes me feel.

Enough. On trembling legs, I stand. My boxers are sticky with sweat. Every instinct in me shrieks to hide under the covers or run to Saul and Missy. Instead, I take one step after the other toward the window that I didn't open. The voice doesn't speak again, but there's a thickness to the air, a sense that I'm not completely alone. I pause a foot away, cursing the stars in all their safety up there when I'm trapped here.

Yet another Emotion appears in my room. I jump, ready to scream, but the sound halts in my throat when I see his kind face. The touch is equally gentle, almost encouraging. "Real courage is embracing the fear," he says quietly. He reminds me of Forgiveness in his solemnity. No games, no facades. Just the truth of who he is.

Then Courage pulls away, offering me a small smile before vanishing.

I shut the window.

FIVE

The light above my head hums. It's faint, the brightened wires flaring and fading uncertainly. In hopes of letting some more light in, I pull a stack of boxes away from the round window above our heads. Dust flies up and I sneeze.

"I didn't think cleaning the attic was much of a punishment, honestly," Revenge remarks from the other side of the room. "But now I totally get it." He slides a pair of spectacles on and grins at me with huge, magnified eyes.

I give him a dirty look. I'm a little annoyed with him; so far he's refused to answer even one of my questions about Forgiveness. Like whether he has the same rules as Revenge does, or why he's never appeared before, or why he's appeared at all.

"A little help would be nice, you know," I snap. My friend doesn't grace this with a response, and I kick at a crate full of yarn. "There's so much junk here. Their entire lives can be summed up just by looking around." I pick up an ancient children's book and flip through it. The yellowed pages rustle in the stillness. "Neither of them has ever been out of Franklin."

Revenge tosses aside a gigantic hat. He bends, rooting around in a different trunk. His back is to me. "And you?"

"Me, what?" I pull the flaps of a box open.

There's a *thud*, then the sound of something shattering. Hurriedly, Revenge slams the lid of the trunk down and turns around. "Do you plan on getting out? Like Georgie does?" He mock shudders as he shrugs an ancient coat on. "Can you imagine her in Hollywood?" Next he stoops to retrieve the hat and plop it on his head. He looks like some eccentric bag lady.

I smile a little, peering inside the box. Just old photo albums. I reach for another box. "I've thought about it, I guess. But where would I go? It's not like I'm good at anything. I can't play piano like Saul or get perfect grades like Briana." Dust covers the top of this box. I use my sleeve to wipe some of it away. All it says on it is *WILLIAM TATE*. My pulse quickens.

But the contents are just odds and ends—his old mining helmet, some folders and tax records. There's an ancient newspaper with a front-page article about Sammy Thorn. Dad was always a bit fascinated with the stories about Thorn, since all of it happened when he was a little boy.

Despite my own prick of interest, I keep digging. At the bottom of the box I find a square Ziploc bag, holding what looks like a pair of jeans and a shirt. I frown, touching the plastic. Why would these clothes be—

The realization knocks the air out of me. The truth is

shown in the plaid pattern of the shirt, nearly camouflaged by the red squares. Stains. Speckles. Blood.

This is what he was wearing the day he died.

"... think you could figure something out," Revenge is saying, his tone dry. "You're not exactly a delicate flower."

I don't answer. I lean back, still on my knees, just staring down at the shirt. Why would they keep this? As if my fingers have a mind of their own, I find myself opening the bag and pulling the shirt out. The material is still soft. Where the dried blood is, though, it's hard. I touch it and my insides quake. *Dad.*

"Hey, Alex. Look at this."

I lift my head, dazed. Revenge is grinning again, standing beside a short, shining box. Standing up, I move toward him, the floorboards moaning beneath my weight. I peer in and see it's an old record player.

Revenge has already figured out how to work it... or maybe he was there when it was invented. He expertly slides a record out of its paper case, flips it over with the tips of his fingers, and places it in the center of the player. There's a brief sound, like static on a radio. Some old song comes on, the words so garbled I can't make them out, but it's better than Elvis. Revenge backs away, moving to the rhythm. There's a mischievous glint in his eye.

"What are you doing?" I frown, loosening my hold on the shirt. Revenge raises his brows at me, still bobbing his head and snapping his fingers. Then, as I watch, he begins to swing his narrow hips.

"Oh, my god." Forgetting what's in my hands, I take a

step back and stare. Revenge smirks and lifts his arms, giving it all he's worth.

Then he reaches for me. I clap my hand over my mouth to smother a shriek of laughter. "No!" I dart away. "I won't!"

But Revenge advances. He looks utterly ridiculous, still wearing his Civil War coat and twitching to the music.

"Weren't you around when the first human danced?" I taunt him, using a rocking chair as a shield. "Shouldn't you know how to do it?"

He growls. "I won't tolerate insolence from a little human!"

"Not so little anymore," I retort.

We run toward the window, and the space is so confined there's nowhere to go. Revenge lunges for me and I squeal, sidestepping him. My back hits the wall. Revenge quickly plants his hands on either side of me, panting. I could escape, duck under his arms and run again, but I don't. I smile up at him, tracing his familiar features with my gaze. I ache to trace them with my fingers. To quench the impulse, I clench them into painful fists around the shirt.

As if he can hear my thoughts, Revenge's eyes darken. The space between us suddenly feels thick and hot. Electric. Neither of us seems to be breathing. Images race through me, something that only happens when Revenge is this close. A girl with a fierce expression stuffing a note in a locker, a man in bed with a woman while the picture on the nightstand depicts him with someone else, a boy just a little older than me loosening the spokes on the wheel of a dirt bike.

"You're right," Revenge says, bringing my attention back

to him. To us. "You're not little anymore." Is it my imagination, or is there a catch to his voice?

I've stopped laughing.

"Alex! Breakfast!"

We both jump. "Coming," I manage. It comes out hoarse, barely more than a whisper. I clear my throat and say it louder. "Coming!"

Even from up here, I can smell the familiar aroma of burnt toast. But I don't move. The record crackles. Silence creeps through the attic. Distantly I wonder if I somehow missed hearing the town clock. Revenge lifts his hand, like he's about to touch my cheek. Every thought about clocks or breakfast evaporates. My heart stops.

"Better get down there," Revenge says. And he backs away. He doesn't stay long enough to see Disappointment—a stick-thin boy with a head of wild curls—pat my arm, almost in sympathy. I don't acknowledge him. Instead I leave him there in the shadows of a thousand wasted memories and creak down the narrow stairs.

It isn't until I reach the kitchen doorway that I realize I'm still clutching my father's shirt.

"This is pointless."

"Just try, Georgie."

"No one is going to care about my crappy artwork when I'm a star!" She lifts her head to glare at Briana. "And it's not like UW will take back your acceptance if you make anything less than perfect either, you know."

Briana doesn't respond to this.

Outside, it's raining. It sounds like a stadium full of people are tapping their fingers against the windows on the other side of the classroom. Briana, Georgie, and I sit around one of the tables in the art room. Each of us has a pile of clay—unformed, simple, just an idea of an idea. I still haven't touched mine.

"Alex." At the sound of my name, I lift my head. Our eyes meet and my friend smiles. Briana, always smiling, even when there's nothing to smile about. "How are you? We've been worried. You didn't respond to any texts."

Georgie snorts. She punches her clay and the table shakes. "Worried? Try freaked out. You totally lost it."

"Georgie." Briana's voice is uncharacteristically sharp.

"What?" Georgie glances at me. "It's true, isn't it?"

I envy her view of the world. Black and white, right and wrong, truth and lies. And the way she's scowling at me is justified; after all, I've told them nothing. Given them nothing. They don't know that I found my father's blood-speckled shirt and slept with it last night. They don't know I'm hearing voices or seeing Revenge and Forgiveness. And they don't know I go to Nate Foster's house and sit in my car with a gun in the glove box.

Silence has fallen over our table. Across the room, our teacher walks from student to student. He'll reach us last.

The floor suddenly rumbles. Briana turns toward the window. The gray light of sky slants over her face, highlighting freckles I never knew she had. "It's the first real storm this spring," she says softly. Her clay is already becoming something. A bird, it looks like. "Kind of nice, isn't it?" Rachel Porter is at a table across the room from us, and I see Briana glance at her.

Lightning flashes as I'm about to answer, illuminating the entire room. Freckles, expressions, corners. No, not just corners. I blink, and suddenly I'm remembering. Remembering something I didn't know I'd forgotten.

Thunder rumbles through the tiny apartment, and I almost miss the sound of the front door opening. "Dad!" I exclaim from my place on the rug. I'm about to drop the book in my hands and jump up when I see his face. I pause, and Apprehension kneels next to me. Worry appears a moment later. I look at their faces as their hands settle on my head, my shoulder.

Watching them with narrowed eyes, Dad loosens his tie. "Don't touch her," Dad slurs, stumbling toward us. His foot snags the edge of the rug and he stumbles. He stays there, leaning against the wall as if he doesn't have the strength to stand.

"Honey? What's wrong?" Mom touches his arm but he shakes her off, muttering. It sounds like he's saying, "Get off of me." But Dad would never say anything like that. He lurches again, tripping over a chair. Mom is quick and she catches him, even when he keeps trying to push her away. She whispers something in his ear, something she doesn't want me to hear. But I do: "Alex."

Dad lifts his head and focuses red-rimmed eyes on me. "I'm doing this for you," he says. I tremble and open my mouth to ask Mom what's wrong with him. Before I can, she's guiding him out of view, toward their room at the end of the hall. All the while he's still talking under his breath. I stay where I am and clutch my book so hard the spine creaks. I can't hear the words. No, I can't hear any of them but one. He's repeating it over and over. My name.

Alex. Alex. Alex.

Then the door clicks shut, and everything is quiet.

Lightning flashes again, but this time it does nothing, doesn't reveal answers to the questions this memory brought to the surface.

I see movement out of the corner of my eye, a familiar flash of red, and I turn. Revenge is sitting on top of a vacant desk, his eyes on me. *You knew*, I want to say. Maybe not everything, but I must have told him something when I was younger. When I said that I'd never seen the wild, non-perfect side of Dad, he'd asked, *Don't you remember?*

I want to force Revenge to tell me what I should remember. I want to leap up and drive ninety miles an hour until I get to Andrew's office so I can ask him what he knows about any of this.

But Briana is here, her shoulder pressed to mine as if she senses that I'm cracking inside. Georgie says something that I don't hear, and Briana responds. Then, "Do you want to come over tonight?" she asks me. "I could help you with that essay." Neither of them seems to have noticed that they lost me for a few seconds.

"Tonight?" I repeat faintly. Tonight I'd planned on going to Nate Foster's. On watching him through that window and thinking about that gun. Maybe it isn't such a bad idea to escape everything for a few hours. "Yeah, okay."

Before Briana can answer, Mr. Kim is stopping beside our table. He surveys our work and of course sees that my clay is still just a square. "What are you making, Alex?" he asks with a smile.

I'm doing this for you. Slowly, I focus on Mr. Kim's face. His smile begins to fade as the seconds tick by. Georgie waits, Briana waits, Revenge waits. Everyone's waiting.

To avoid them all, I stare down at the clay. "I haven't decided yet."

SIX

It's still raining as I drive to Briana's. The driver's window is stuck open an inch—I keep forgetting to ask Saul to fix it—and drops slip inside, trembling on the ceiling and falling. My hair and clothes stick to me. The windshield wipers do their best to clear the way, hurrying back and forth on the glass. *Thump-thump. Thump-thump*. The sound makes me think of another rainy day, another car. Mom's scream echoes through my memory. *William!*

My hand flies to the radio knob, and I crank it so loud it's painful. Elvis drowns everything out.

Behind me, another car inches along. Raking my hair out of the way, I frown as I study it in the rearview mirror. Despite the downpour, the color and model are obvious. A brown Taurus. I don't recognize it, which is strange in Franklin. What's even stranger is Revenge's absence; I haven't seen him since art class. What is he up to? And why hasn't he ever—

Alexandra.

I stiffen.

Lightning flashes again, and Fear's face looms in the mirror. He winks at me, tucking a damp curl behind my ear, and then he's gone again. I slow down, trying to calm my racing heart. The Taurus's headlights brighten in a signal of irritation. I try to tell myself none of this is real, I'm just imagining things, but it's not working. I can *feel* something in the car with me. The air is warmer somehow, and suddenly it's harder to breathe.

Panicking, I guide my car to the side of the road and stop. I lean my forehead against the steering wheel and concentrate on inhaling and exhaling. Something is wrong with me. This is all in my head. Did this ever happen to Dad? Did he ever go crazy?

I'm doing this for you.

Driven by some instinct, I lift my gaze. The Taurus is still there. I roll the window down further and wave, indicating it should go around. It doesn't move. "I don't need help," I mutter, jerking my hand harder. Rain pelts my skin like needles. *"Go around."*

The headlights are blinding, reflecting off all my mirrors so that I can't see whoever is behind the wheel. They just sit there, the engine rumbling. Watching me. What the hell?

Another Emotion appears in the backseat. I ignore his touch as I reach for the handle and pull. The wind intensifies as the door begins to open.

Suddenly the Taurus lurches forward.

I yank the door shut just in time. The car roars by, and my side view mirror shatters. I scream. The Taurus smirks at me with its red taillights, then it's spinning onto the dirt turn that will eventually meet the county road.

For a few seconds all I'm capable of is sitting there, panting and staring at the splintered, plastic stub where my mirror used to be. Did that really just happen? After another minute I fumble for my phone and dial the first number that takes no thought or effort. There's a *click*, a female voice in my ear. My brain recognizes it. "Briana," I whimper, pressing a hand to my face just to prove that this is all real.

"Alex? What's wrong?"

The sound of her voice brings me back to myself. She's worried. I realize I'm trembling and I close my eyes. "N-nothing. I just c-called to tell you I'm on my way."

There's a pause. I can practically see her, analyzing the words and deciding the best course of action. She must decide to accept this. For now. "Okay," she says finally. "I just got home myself, so I'll be in the kitchen. Do pizza rolls sound good?"

I swallow. The idea of food makes me want to vomit. "They sound great."

"See you in a little bit, then!" she chirps.

We hang up. But I don't immediately move to change gears. *Thump-thump. Thump-thump.* My gaze falls on my backpack, hiding in the crevice under the glove box. The zipper is undone, exposing a glimpse of plaid. Without thinking about it, I lean down and grab it. A button snags. I tug at it, strangely desperate, and it comes free. The rain continues to soak me through the opening to my left, so cold I'm losing feeling, but that's okay. I slump in the seat and hold Dad's shirt. It smells like mildew and attic. What did Dad use to smell like? I should know this, I should know this…

I'm clutching the material so tight that I feel it. Something in the pocket. Hard, rectangular, small. I dig it out and frown. A flash drive? But if it was in Dad's pocket this entire time, it means that he had it on the day he died. He was a miner. His business was in dirt and machines and darkness. Not computers or files. Why would he have this?

I need to know what's on it.

Fear's essence still hasn't entirely left me, but now the desire to find out all the secrets of Dad's flash drive pushes me into motion. I shift the gear into drive and slam on the gas. Mud and rocks spew from beneath the tires, and as my car picks up speed, the voice doesn't come back. I pass the turn that the Taurus vanished on and allow myself one glance. Trees lean over the road and angry clouds roll above it. The Taurus—and whoever was driving it—is long gone.

I face front, clenching my jaw. A few miles further, Briana's driveway appears on the right. Their crooked mailbox greets me, along with those faded letters on the side: *BRINKMAN*. Already I feel the tight sensation within me loosening, relaxing, unfurling. I don't bother with the blinker and guide my car into the narrow space.

Her house is as familiar to me as my own. It's tiny, the siding yellow and rotting, and the shingles on the roof are quietly disappearing with each year that goes by. The best part about it is the four-season porch attached to the front. During the summers, when it's so hot and muggy we feel like we're going to melt, we lie in there and turn a fan on. Bugs battle the screen while we drawl long words into the spinning blades, enjoying the effect it has on our voices. As kids, we'd pretend we were aliens visiting this strange and frightening planet.

Briana and I never had one of those memorable meetings or significant first words exchanged. She's just always been there. Our mothers were best friends. They went to high school together, they married around the same time, and then Briana and I were born two weeks apart. She arrived first, of course. Our friendship was preordained. It's the only thing I haven't fought against in the course of my life. Then Georgie moved to Franklin with her mom in third grade and we accepted her into the fold.

I park, turn the key, and jump out. The rain has let up, but not much. I wipe more water from my eyes and make the bolt to the door, backpack thumping against my side. There's no truck in the driveway, which means Briana's dad isn't back from the general store yet. After the mines closed, he was one of the lucky few who managed to get a job in town. Almost everyone else drives the fifty miles to the tire factory in Pasco. No one can move, though, because property in Franklin doesn't sell anymore. Foreclosures are another story.

There's a beat-up Buick parked next to the garage, which means Briana's brother Ethan is back from one of his frequent trips. Everyone knows he's a dealer, but people love their vices in these parts, so he doesn't get turned in.

I enter without knocking. A *whoosh* of air announces my presence. Or at least, it should. Dropping my bag—*thud*—I shut the door behind me and pull off my soaking jacket. Someone comes out of the kitchen and walks toward me. Ethan.

"Hey," he says around a mouthful of food, a bag of chips in his hand. He looks like his father, with ruddy skin and heavy-lidded eyes.

"Hey," I say back. He goes into the basement without another word.

Sounds drift out of the living room, a combination of clicking and voices that must be from the ancient television. I put my jacket on one of the hooks on the wall and wring my hair out on the rug, craning my neck to catch a glimpse of whoever is watching. Francis, Briana's mom, is standing in front of the wide window. She doesn't seem to notice me as she bends over a pot of dirt. The wheel on the show she's not paying attention to spins again, emitting noise that's almost similar to the rain outside. *Click-click-click-click.*

Francis must sense my presence, suddenly, because she turns around and straightens. "Oh, Alex," she says in soft surprise. "I didn't hear you come in." It's strange how much she and Briana look alike, yet how drastically different. Time and hardship have marked Francis.

"How are you?" I ask, smiling.

Sighing, she flaps a hand at the pot. "Still can't keep a plant alive to save my life. Otherwise we're all fine, I guess. What about you? How are Saul and Missy?"

Something brushes against my leg, distracting me, and I glance down at their tabby cat. Einstein cries for attention so I bend to scratch his chin. "They're—"

"Hey," Briana says from behind. I start. Standing in the shadows, my friend inclines her head in the direction of the kitchen. "I'm set up in here."

Before I can say anything, she walks down the hallway. "Maybe try giving it less water," I suggest to Francis. She purses her lips and looks at the pot again, contemplating this. Quickly I grab my bag and follow Briana. The sounds of the television fade away.

I wait until we're alone to ask, "So, did you talk to Rachel Porter today?" The smell of something spicy fills the kitchen.

Briana goes to the oven and opens the little door to peek inside. She shrugs, but the light that heats the pizza rolls illuminates her tight expression. "I didn't have a chance" is all she says.

That's not what's bothering her, though; I saw how she was looking at Francis. I don't know what to say. Their relationship has always confused me. All I know is that sometimes, when Briana looks at Francis, Fear materializes. And I wonder if she's terrified that she'll end up like her mother.

I used to think that inheriting traits from our parents wasn't real. Now, though?

I'm doing this for you.

To occupy my hands, I take out everything I need for the essay. But I can't wait; the flash drive rests in the center of my palm, dry and warm. The last key to Dad that I have. I pull Briana's laptop toward me from where it's been humming on the counter, and I uncurl my fist.

There's a clatter—Briana pulling the pan of pizza rolls out—and then she notices what I'm doing. "What is that?" She takes a spatula out of a drawer and begins transferring the rolls onto a plate. Crumbs scatter across the surface of it.

The laptop was asleep. I tap the touchpad and impatiently wait for the screen to come up. "A flash drive," I mutter, distracted. My knee bounces. Impatience, short-haired and stocky, gives me a hard shove. Briana doesn't seem to see the way I jerk forward, scowling. No point in whipping around and punching him in the face, though; he's already vanished.

"... on it?" Briana is asking.

"I don't know." The computer is still waking up, and I watch the screen intently, but then I realize Briana is waiting for me to go on. "I found it. I think it was my dad's."

The laptop finally finishes. Without waiting to see what my friend's reaction will be to this, I plug the flash drive into the jack. It takes another minute to load, and then a message pops up on the screen. My heart sinks. "There's a password," I say, perplexed. Why would Dad put a password on anything?

"Oh, well, that's easy." Briana circles the counter to lean over me and types *ALEX*.

The computer thinks for a moment, then the box quivers and erases the dots. Wrong. I try my mother's name: *TRACEY*. Next, my brother's: *HUNTER*. My dad's birthday.

Our first and only dog's name. Wrong, wrong, wrong. "Maybe ask your aunt and uncle?" Briana suggests.

It comes over me without warning—a fierce ache to be in motion. Acting on impulse, I unplug the flash drive. "Look, sorry to make this so short, but I better go. I haven't been home yet, and Saul and Missy have been on edge lately." The pizza rolls are still on the plate, untouched.

"Oh, okay." Briana watches me pack up my things. "What about the essay?"

I shove the flash drive in my pocket and shrug. "I can work on it later. Thanks for offering to help."

"Of course. See you tomorrow?" Her anxious eyes follow me to the door and I mumble a vague response. It feels like I'm always leaving someone. Funny, since I was the only one who stayed six years ago.

Outside, the rain has stopped. I plunge into the cold, forgetting my jacket. "Alex—" Briana calls. She wants to ask questions, demand answers that I can't give. Almost as expertly as the Emotions, I disappear.

There are two missed calls on my phone. Both Missy.

The drive home is less eventful. No voices, no Taurus, no Fear. By the time I get to the apartment, it's dark. The woods around the building are full of swaying shadows, and the only lights on are coming from Angus's window and the one over the shop door. Fear stalks me up the stairs, all the way to the narrow deck and around the corner. His hand tangles in my hair, brushes the tender skin of my neck. I yank free and reach the door, slamming it in his face.

Just like at Briana's house, noise blares from the living room and a blue glow covers everything. I set my bag and keys on the floor next to my boots. Missy sits on the couch, her knees covered by a blanket. One hand clutches the remote and the other rests limply in her lap. She's not wearing makeup and her hair is in a ponytail. She looks... weary. And alone. I try not to make comparisons to Francis.

"Where's Saul?" I hover in the doorway, shifting from foot to foot.

"On a job. Someone's piano needed tuning in Othello."

I hesitate. Once, I might have gone and sat beside her. Watched *Who Wants to Be a Millionaire* with her. She always managed to kick my ass. Now, though? "Well... good night." I turn my back on her and head for the relief of my bed. Maybe Dream will be kind tonight.

"Alex." Halting, I keep my gaze on the floor. I can feel Missy fixing her worried eyes on me, though. "What can we do?"

"What?" I can't do this right now. I can't.

"What can we do?" she repeats, more forcefully this time. "You know, I thought it was strange that Briana got her acceptance letter from UW and we still hadn't heard anything. So I called the school to check on your application. They informed me that they'd never received one... which means you've been lying to us for months. We could take your car away, we could ground you, we could make you clean the entire building. We could even revisit counseling. But none of that's going to help you, though, is it? I'm not delusional, Alex. Everyone has secrets, especially teenagers. I just wish you would *talk* to us. So I'm asking. What can we do?"

"Missy, I . . . " She waits. I angle my body toward her, making a helpless gesture. "I'm not trying to hurt you. I just . . . I have some things to figure out."

One side of her face quivers from the light of the TV. It matches her voice when she asks, "Like whether or not you want a future?"

"No." *Like whether or not someone else should have one.*

But I can't say that. I can't offer her any promises or tell her things are going to change, either. All I can say is this: "I'm sorry. I am."

My aunt just looks at me for what feels like a very long, long time. Then she whispers, "Destroying yourself isn't going to bring them back, Alex."

Silence. She saves me from having to answer by getting up. Slowly, she walks past and creaks down the hallway. Into her room. *Click.*

The stench of Guilt fills my nostrils. Her hand settles on my shoulder and it feels as if she's made of concrete, it's so heavy. I walk away. Without showering or brushing my teeth—again—I go to bed. I stare at nothing. Soon, Angus knocks on the wall.

For the first time, I don't knock back.

Saul comes home around ten. But he doesn't come up to the apartment. Instead, I hear him tinkering around in the shop below, playing the instruments no one wanted anymore. After a while, I recognize the melody: *Swan Lake.*

It was one of my dad's favorites. He'd been teaching it to me before he died. Saul plays it over and over again, and a lump forms in my throat as I listen. The voices of those sad pianos eventually lull me into dreamland… the music of something forgotten, something aching to be remembered.

SEVEN

I dream of my family.

We're laughing, teeth glinting in the sunlight. The grass is green and birds sing. A circle of Emotions surround us where we sit in the park. Joy, Love, Anticipation, Hope. All the good ones, whose touches are like a drug. Enthralling, thrilling, addicting. I sit between my parents—twelve years old again—with Hunter in my lap. He's sucking on his thumb.

"William, don't," Mom suddenly says, her voice high and frightened. The sun ducks behind some clouds, casting shadow over all of us. I turn my head to look at Dad, but he's cut off from us now, surrounded by a different group of Emotions. Anger, Despair, Desperation, even Hate. All I can see are the backs of their heads.

"Mom? What's happening?"

She covers my eyes, holding me close as if to shield me. "He's doing it for you, he's doing it for you," she starts chanting. I'm a quiet hole of fear. I want to run to Dad and I want to run away all at once. Mom's smell wraps around me just as securely as her arms. Honeysuckle.

Then the sun brightens.

I open my eyes, and I'm utterly alone. Mom and Hunter are gone. I turn to where Dad was, but he's disappeared too, along with the Emotions haunting him. The only thing left in his place is a single, glinting flash drive.

The town clock is sounding, over and over again. *Wake up, wake up*, it says. I want to take a hammer and smash it into silence.

My eyes flutter open, and even before I see her I know she's here. "I hate you," I rasp.

Dream blinks, the movement slow and deliberate. She's a new Element that—for some reason—replaced the old Dream. There was something especially disturbing about him, anyway, so I accepted the change without bothering to ask questions. She stands next to my bed. She's one of the strangest-looking Elements there is: black hair and eyelashes, skin so pale I should be able to see veins, long limbs that are almost unnatural. Her lithe body is draped in a gossamer gown of more black. Her feet are bare and her toes peek out at me. Long, bony toes.

"No you don't," she replies, in a voice that's made of feathers. Then it's my turn to blink, and my room is empty.

She's right. I don't hate her. Twisted as it is, she gave me back my family for one night.

I must be running late; the air smells of burnt bacon and the clock struck eight times. Missy didn't wake me up. I fly out of bed, stumbling over clothes on the floor. The window is tightly shut, exactly as it should be. Relief blooms in my chest and I dart to the bathroom, ignoring the Emotion hurrying after me.

Fifteen minutes later I'm tentatively poking my head into the kitchen. My wet hair drips, and my eyebrow ring must be getting infected because it hurts. Saul is in his usual spot, chewing loudly. There's a bowl of cereal in front of him and Missy is nowhere to be seen. He doesn't even look up when he asks, "What happened to your car mirror?"

Hesitating, I dare to take two steps closer. Is he going to mention the application I lied about? "Some freak broke it. He came so close I was lucky the mirror was all he hit."

"What?" Saul's head jerks up. An Emotion appears. "You don't know who it was?"

I take a banana out of the fruit bowl and shrug, leaning against the counter while I unpeel it. "Must've been someone passing through." A glance at the clock on the wall tells me there's no possible way I'll make it to my first class. I take a bite and a bad taste greets my tongue; I didn't see the bruise. Making a face, I toss the banana into the trash.

"No one passes through Franklin." Saul turns his attention back to the paper and shovels more cereal in his mouth. "I'll talk to Frederick about it. And you should pay a visit to Erskine about the mirror. He always gives us a good deal. Shouldn't you get going?"

Crunch. Tick. Crunch. Tick. I watch my uncle and—

though there aren't any Emotions around him now—know that he's disappointed. And hurt. And angry. That clock won't stand still long enough for me to attempt to bridge the distance between us, and I'm already late. I move to the doorway again. Just as I reach the threshold, I pause and think about saying something meaningful. But, like with Missy, all I have are lies. So I slip away without saying anything and Saul doesn't try to stop me.

I wish he would.

Angus watches me leave again. He doesn't wave or smile while I drive off into the fog. Saul must have fixed my car window, because it's finally shut.

I'm halfway to school when the urge to run consumes me again. Briana will be there, probably wondering about the flash drive I haven't been able to unlock and looking at me with those troubled eyes. The teachers will drone about times and things and places I don't care about. And Emotions will be there. So many Emotions. Disorienting and constant, relentless and meddlesome.

I think of Missy's face in the glow of the television last night, and how Saul avoided my gaze this morning. They've already lost hope, and Franklin High eventually stops bothering to call when a student skips too many times. That's how things work here. Why keep fighting when I'm not sure I want to fight at all?

Of their own volition, my hands yank the steering wheel to the side and I'm turning onto Halbrook Lane. No one comes this way anymore, but the dirt remembers when men rolled over it in their trucks every morning and night. Grass doesn't grow. Trees surround the road, green-brown blurs as the miles pass. Then the signs begin appearing. Bright, rusted warnings. *DANGER. MINE SITE. NO TRESPASSING.*

There it is.

The opening is black, empty, expectant. There's more than one entrance to the mines, but this is the biggest and the safest. Someone put up a fence and another sign, both easy to ignore. I park and get out. Despite the mist, it's warmer today. Spots of sunlight touch the ground and birds call. I stay by the car, staring at that wide mouth and remembering when Dad took me down there. The damp walls frightened me and the low ceilings were terrifying. I lasted twenty minutes before crying and begging him to take me back up to the surface, where everything was bright and safe and familiar. He did, and he never expressed any disappointment or impatience. I didn't see the Emotions, either. In many ways, Dad really was perfect.

And then he was taken from me.

The quiet is too loud, so I tap an erratic beat on my thigh. After a few minutes, I know I can't go in there. My movements jerky, I yank the passenger door open to grab the gun. The handle is freezing on my skin. The door slams shut again with a hard kick from my boot. I spin around, close one eye, and pull the trigger.

Bang. The thunderous echo vibrates through the woods. The bark of a tree explodes. My ears ring.

"Your aim could use a bit of work."

I jerk at the sound of Revenge's voice. Before I can turn,

he comes up behind me and I feel the furnace of his skin as he plays with my hair. My limbs lock into place.

"Relax your grip," he whispers. He's careful, so careful not to touch me. But he could. He's just a inch away, so close. He could. I could.

Once again Lust sidles up next to me, a creature with full lips and yellow hair. She's not the one I want, but her touch has all the same effects Revenge's would. She taunts me with that vicious mouth, brushing them over my cheek, my jawline, my ear. "My, my, Revenge," she purrs. "This one really wants—"

"You've done your job. Now get lost," I hiss, breaking my own rules by acknowledging her. She smirks at me before leaving.

In the silence that follows, a blush ebbs through my face; there's no way Revenge didn't see her. Hear her. I close my eyes and breathe. Parts of me still quiver and tingle. *Talk about something,* instinct urges. *Anything.*

"Revenge . . . " I make myself face him as if nothing has changed. His expression gives nothing away. I clear my throat, silently telling my pulse to calm. "I've been . . . I think I'm going crazy. I just thought I should warn you. In case I start going rabid or something." How does the gun feel so hot now, when moments ago it was so cold?

Revenge's eyes soften in a way that makes the breath catch in my throat again. "You're not going crazy, Alex." His voice is strangely tender.

"How do you know?" I manage to ask.

He shrugs, as if it's so obvious. "Because I know you."

Overhead, a bird calls to another. The canopy of leaves—still recovering from the long sleep of the past few months—struggles to hide them. Then one bird takes flight, flitting to another branch in a flurry of brown feathers. It hops to a different tree, this one close to the entrance of the mine. I stare at it again. Mom's voice haunts me. *William, don't!*

"My dad worked down there. He knew those mines better than anyone," I say. The bird lifts into the sky and soars to better places.

"Is that why you came here? To feel closer to him?"

It would make sense. A pretty lie, tied up with a pretty red bow. But no, that isn't why I really came here. *The mines. The mines.* "Just needed to clear my head," I mutter, raising the gun. Revenge doesn't respond, and he steps away. I fire off another shot.

Bang. Smoke billows from the muzzle. The action feels empty. I imagine the bullet putting a hole into Nate Foster. But with thoughts of him comes thoughts of someone in a white T-shirt, who speaks of redemption and hope. Things I'll permanently leave behind when I actually do face Nate Foster.

"What do you know about my dad?" I ask Revenge without looking at him.

He shrugs. "Not much, honestly. Once, years ago, you told me your father was frightening. When I asked you why, I couldn't get anything else. I figured you just didn't want to talk about it."

This raises too many questions that have no answers. My mind goes to the next topic that's been bothering me. I try to think of a careful way to bring it up.

"So are you going to tell me about Forgiveness?" I blurt. I don't know if I say it because I want to know or because some part of me wants to drive Revenge away.

His countenance darkens. Like with Saul, the space between us doesn't feel like inches or feet or yards; it feels like miles.

"You won't give up, will you?" he snaps. "What do you want to know?"

"I'm just curious." Now I shrug, but I can tell it hardly convinces him. The truth is something I won't say out loud. As infuriating as he was, I found Forgiveness . . . interesting. The way he looked at me has been impossible to forget. It wasn't like I was a dealer selling the drug he wanted or just another duty to be carried, though. No, Forgiveness stared at me as if I was *someone*.

And that's a drug all its own.

Revenge picks up a fallen branch. He stoops and plucks a pine cone from the ground, too. Then, with one swift movement, he throws it into the air and swings. The cone shatters. I wait.

"We've been doing this dance for centuries, Forgiveness and I," he says finally. "Sometimes it's over within minutes. Sometimes—like with you—it takes years."

"What takes years?"

He looks at me. A breeze toys with his bright hair. "The choice."

For so long, I'd thought of the other plane as something inhabited by feelings and nature. It's still difficult to wrap my mind around the knowledge that all this time, there's been something else. "Are there more? Choices, I mean?"

Now it's his turn to shrug. "A few. Not as large a group as the Emotions, or even the Elements. Choices only exist if they're significant enough that they change the course of a human life. And sometimes the choice is made so quickly that even you, with your Sight, can't catch them. Truth and Lie, for example. Now those are some slippery characters." Revenge grins, expecting me to smile back. When I don't, he expels a breath that sounds infinitely resigned. "What else?"

I bend and pick up the shards of the pine cone, even though it's fruitless to try to put it back together. They nestle in the center of my palm, permanently broken. Revenge waits. "How does this work, exactly?" I finally ask.

I've never wanted to hear the answer before, and we both know it. Maybe because with Nate Foster in jail, there wasn't really anything I could do about it. Or maybe because I wanted to cling to something that wasn't mine to have.

"The same way it works for everyone else, even with your Sight," Revenge answers after a long, long pause. "You won't be picking *me* or *him*. You'll be picking what we *are*. You can't just decide to grab my hand one day and that's it. When you've really made your choice, I'll know, and that's the moment I'm free to touch you."

The pieces of the pine cone fall to the ground. I don't know what to focus on. The gun, the mines, him, the sky. Clenching my jaw, I decide on the tree I've just decimated. "How many times have you been picked?"

"Does that really matter, Alex?"

"I guess not." Because I can picture them—those people who were stronger than me. Who made their choices while here I am, using the forest as target practice and hurting the family I have left. That's not the only reason I back down so easily, though. More questions are crowding into my throat, questions I won't ask: *Did you befriend all those others, too? Or am I just another game?*

I twist so I can see Revenge's face again. But he's gone.

Wind whistles through the woods. No, not just the wind. *Alexandra.* "Shut up," I growl. I turn and shoot the tree so many times that it's more holes than bark.

EIGHT

SAUL. FRANKLIN. SWAN LAKE. Every time, the computer rejects my words. I sit in a booth in the diner, inhaling the scents of grease and sweat while I try to unlock my father's secrets. The weekend has come and gone and still I haven't been able to find the right word.

Loretta Roan—Georgie's mom—walks over, glowering. She has big platinum curls, staggeringly red lipstick, and one too many buttons undone. There's no mystery as to where Georgie gets her flair. "Anything besides the coffee, darlin'?" she asks. *Shouldn't you be in school?* her tone really asks. I shake my head. After a long look, she moves to pour the town pastor another cup. I take a drink from my own mug and my lip catches on the chink of missing glass. It seems like everything in this town is either chipping, rusting, or breaking.

The front door opens and a gust of wind blows a stack of napkins off the long counter. A moment later someone slides into the seat across from me. Her perfume tips me off before her voice does. "Considering there aren't any mines to work in anymore, graduating high school is more necessary than it used to be."

"Not now, Georgie."

"When, then? When it's too late? When you finally decide to get your head out of your ass?" She smacks the table to get my attention. "I'm not Briana. I'm not going to bake you cookies and tell you nicely that you're ruining your life."

"I'm not—"

"Sorry, not in the mood to listen to bullshit right now. We can finish this later. Come on. A bunch of us are going to the lake. Some of the guys are going to build a bonfire. Should be fun, right? Oh, and we already called Saul and Missy." Georgie scoots out of the booth, adding "Hey, Mom" as Loretta hurries by. She lifts her coffee pot in a quick greeting.

There's only one reason we build bonfires in Franklin. "The last time I got drunk, Saul gave me the job of cleaning our attic. No thanks."

"Good. Someone has to drive me home. Which reminds me, we're taking your car, since mine conked out again and Briana's brother stole hers. Now get up."

Sighing, I allow Georgie to pull me out of the booth. I grab the laptop, still thinking of possible passwords, and follow her to my car. Briana is already sitting in the passenger seat, reading a book. They must have walked here from school. Georgie steals the keys out of my hand and sashays to the driver's side. As she opens the door Briana lifts her head. That bright smile stretches across her face, blinding me, and Shame squeezes my shoulder while I get in the backseat. His touch makes me remember how I left her the other night.

"Hey, you," Briana says, twisting, completely unaware. "I brought your jacket. You forgot it at my house." She tosses it to me.

Alexandra.

Neither of my friends notices me stiffen. My grip makes the jacket bunch up. Georgie starts the car, and we leave the diner behind.

"Are you sure you want to go tonight?" Briana asks, marking her page with her finger as we squeal down Main Street. Really, the town's only street. "I mean, we don't have to. We could just stay in and make a—"

Georgie snorts. "As if. We're going to have fun tonight, even if I have to force you guys. Plus, I need someone to protect me from Billy. He's been more persistent than usual." She grimaces. The rest of the way to the lake, she talks about L.A. and how annoying the boy from school is. Briana nods and makes noises of agreement and I watch the world pass us by.

Then we're bumping down a back road, and water glints in the distance. "Ready, girls?" Georgie demands, practically bouncing. She's pulling my jacket onto her bony shoulders. A group of kids are already here, teeth glinting in the twilight as they laugh and talk and pretend that this life is enough for all of us. The bonfire reaches for the sky with quivering orange fingers.

We get out. I wrap my arms around myself. The Bentley twins wave at us. Rachel Porter stands beside them, the violet streaks in her hair glinting in the firelight. A muscle tightens in Briana's jaw, and when she leaves to talk to her, she's followed by Apprehension and Longing.

Georgie must have disappeared without my realizing it, because a few seconds later she hurries back and puts a beer in my hand. She ignores my protests as she abandons me again. Billy Jenkins stands by the flames and greets her with a wide grin. I don't need to see her face to know she's grinning back. Protect her, indeed.

"Hey, Alex."

A shadow falls over me, and I tense before seeing who it is. "Oh, Mark. I didn't know you were in town." My fists unclench.

Georgie's cousin smiles. He graduated from Franklin High a year ago, but like most people from this town, he seems unable to leave it completely. He towers over me, and my neck begins to hurt from looking up. Mark has the friendliest face, though. I don't think I've ever seen him frown.

"Just for the night," he replies, running a hand through his thick curls. "Georgie invited me. How have you been?"

"Fine," I lie. "And how are classes at Green River going? Is Andrew still your advisor?"

"Classes are great, and yeah, Andrew is the best. Just one more year to go and I'll have my degree. I'm actually thinking of moving back up here and—"

"Mark! Get over here!" Georgie, of course. Mark turns toward her and holds up one finger.

But I'm already retreating. "Actually, go ahead. I'm going to get another drink."

"Are you sure?" A wrinkle deepens in his forehead. "I mean, we can talk. I haven't seen you in a while, and I was hoping we could catch up."

"Find me later," I say. Before he can say anything else, I slip away.

Someone else calls my name, and I just wave. Blue coolers rest by the water. Faith Carson—the pastor's daughter—lifts the lid and digs out a bottle. Georgie is surrounded, and her hands move as she talks animatedly. Briana is off to the side, a quieter force, but still a part of the hum in the air. Even though they have secret pains like Francis and unfulfilled dreams, they manage to act as if it's okay. They can exist with the shadows.

But how do you exist in the darkness?

Smoke curls through the sky. Resentment materializes at my side and wraps his arm around me. "How's the pity party going?" He squeezes. I don't shake him off or respond; I just pop the lid of my beer and take a long swig. A bitter taste greets my tongue. The Emotion says something else that I don't hear, and then I'm alone with his lingering essence and the contents of all those coolers. An antidote to the poison of the past.

Georgie will have to get another designated driver. Tossing aside the empty beer can, I walk to the coolers and get another one. The ice numbs my fingertips. Too bad it can't numb the rest of me. I glance around and grab another beer for good measure, then slip away to the edge of the beach. I lean my back against a tree and watch the bonfire. It grows brighter and bigger when Billy adds more wood, and more cars pull up, their headlights sweeping across the lake. I drown my sorrows. Laughter drifts through the air. Marty Paulson suddenly leans over to puke, and Faith shrieks.

Time loses meaning. Maybe it's a minute, maybe it's an hour. I pull some blades of green-brown grass out of the ground and watch the breeze carry them away, thinking about how easy it is for something to be firmly rooted one moment and gone the next.

"Alex! Where's Alex?"

Briana's voice. She'll be looking for me. Letting out a loud belch, I haul myself up. It's dark now. How did that happen? I start to make my way toward her. Halfway to the bonfire, though, I stumble and fall. Briana calls my name again, but I just roll over. The damp sand clings to me. For a few moments I stare up at the starless sky, tapping my fingers against my chest so some part of me is still moving. Clouds drift in front of the moon. I wonder if Nate Foster is looking at the same black expanse.

A face fills my vision. It takes me a moment to recognize it in the dim. When I do, though, my heart beats harder and faster. "Oh. You again."

"Hello, Alex."

The sound of his voice lurches me into motion. We've

only spoken once, but I know what's coming. He'll start talking about Nate Foster, and mercy, and letting things go when all I'm capable of is holding on tight. I push myself up, swearing, and stumble through the trees to escape him.

He follows me effortlessly. "Alex. Alex, stop."

Briana calls my name again, though her voice is fainter. My breathing becomes ragged and my head swims, and part of me realizes it's fruitless to try outrunning a creature that isn't human. That doesn't stop me from trying. But I'm not holding my liquor too well tonight, and soon I'm having trouble remembering why I should be avoiding Forgiveness in the first place. He isn't even attempting to stop me anymore. Instead he just keeps up with my pace, a silent presence.

"Help me," I snap after a while, tripping over a branch. Forgiveness doesn't reach for my arm, but I move away as if he has.

"Help you with what?" he asks finally.

Pine needles crunch underfoot. "To find it." I stop in a circle of trees and look up again, straining to see in the faint moonlight.

"Find what, Alex?"

Forgiveness is next to me now, so close I can feel the temperature of his skin: warm, like the lake after the sun has reached inside the depths with its bright fingers. I hate how this creature says my name. Hate it, and like it.

"The damn rocket!" I snarl at his exquisite features. "What else?"

The Choice doesn't answer, and I don't wait for one.

I'm whirling again, rushing through the night, trying to forget and remember at the same time. Then the tree line suddenly breaks and we're on the edge of a playground. My chest heaves and I stare at the red plastic slide. A memory flashes, an image of Mom waiting for me at the bottom. *Come on, honey. I promise I'll catch you.*

I throw up.

Gentle hands hold my hair back while I cough and gag. Forgiveness is careful, so careful, not to actually have contact with any other part of me. Shuddering, I make my way to the swings and settle on one. The chains whine.

"Why don't you just touch me?" I sigh, resting my forehead against the cold links. I close my eyes again. Everything would be so much easier if the choice was just taken from me.

"You know why." Forgiveness surprises me by sitting in the other swing. It's an odd sight, such an unearthly being doing something as mundane as swinging.

At this, I meet his gaze. Maybe it's the beer, or maybe it's the part of me that likes to dangle off bridges and hold guns, but I hear myself saying, "I think you want to."

"I think you're drunk."

Nothing seems to rattle him. I push my feet against the ground to make the swing sway. The cries of the rust-covered chains are the only sound between us. "If you're not going to help me, then leave," I growl when the silence becomes too loud.

Forgiveness angles his body toward me, and now his expression isn't so detached; his dark eyes burn and brand my soul. I wait, thinking I've finally gotten to him, but after a moment he only tilts his head back and focuses on the struggling moon.

It's strange to think that all this time, Revenge was my only companion while someone else waited on the sidelines for a weakness to show. Now that Nate Foster has been released, and I finally have a chance to right the wrong that was done to my family six years ago, that weakness has revealed itself. Forgiveness is water through a crack in a dam, the sensation of fear on a stage when all the lights are shining down, a beam succumbing to all the earth's weight in the mines. I open my mouth to once again tell him to get out of my life—

"Alex." There's something different about his tone, a razorlike edge when before it was soft as a cloud. Tensing, I follow his gaze to the road. A car is parked by the curb, lights and engine off. There are abandoned cars all over Franklin; that's not what's unusual. What's unusual is the fact that there's someone sitting behind the wheel, a dark silhouette turned toward us.

Whoever it is, they must see that I know I'm no longer alone. Without warning, the engine roars, the lights flare, and the tires squeal. I stand and watched the taillights disappear—the two glowing red squares look like angry, accusing eyes. It reminds me of what happened on the road with the Taurus. I shiver, rubbing my arms. Within seconds, the car is gone.

There's an irritating, flicking sensation at the back of my mind. That silhouette seemed so familiar...

"Do you know who that was?" Forgiveness asks.

I keep staring at the empty road. Unease stirs in the pit of my stomach. How much did they see? To anyone else, my conversation with Forgiveness would have looked like I was talking to air. This town is full of crazy people; I'm not worried about being locked away. But once again I think of the Taurus from days ago, the shattering mirror. These aren't coincidences. Someone is watching me.

Someone knows.

NINE

"Oh, say can you see! By the dawn's early light!"

"Just get in the car, Georgie," Briana sighs. Together, she and Mark lower our friend into the backseat. Georgie nearly stumbles into him during the process. I would offer to help except I'm not entirely sober myself just yet, so I get into the passenger side and shut the door.

"What so proudly we hailed at ... something, something!" Georgie hiccups and leans against the window. Rolling her eyes, Briana digs into Georgie's pockets for the keys, her arms jutting at awkward angles to reach them.

"If you wanted to get in my pants, all you needed to do was ask," Georgie slurs. Ignoring this, Briana gets in. She's our designated driver tonight, since she only had half a beer. Smart and good to a fault, that's our Briana.

Mark is still in the back, helping Georgie lie down. His eyes meet mine. "Are you all right?" he asks.

"Fine." I force a smile.

"Well, if you need anything, call me. Okay?"

"We will, Mark," Briana says. After another moment of hesitation, Mark eases out and shuts the door. Then he stands back, hands shoved in his pockets. As Briana settles behind the wheel, she lets out a breath. Her bangs lift and fall. "So, did you have fun?"

The engine comes to life and Briana smiles at me, but it looks strained. When I hesitate, she adds, "You weren't around for most of the night. Did you meet up with someone in the woods?"

We reverse, and then we're heading home. Mark disappears into the darkness. Listening to us, Georgie giggles. She's always been a happy drunk. "Rendezvous in the woods, huh? Go, Alex! Living life to the fullest. Was it Mark? He was really excited to see you, you know."

Neither of us responds, and Georgie starts singing again, drowning out Elvis. Even drunk, she has a nice voice. We don't speak for the rest of the way, me because I'm thinking about that silhouette watching me and Briana because silence is more natural to her. Then my apartment is towering over us, blocking the moon, and stillness fills the small space. The engine idles and Briana leans across me to open the door. Good thing, since I would probably have trouble with the handle. "We'll pick you up tomorrow," she says, giving me a meaningful look. *No arguments*, it says.

I flap my hand at her. "Yeah, yeah. Just don't let your brother touch my car. Love you, nerd. Later, skank."

Georgie blinks, trying to look indignant and failing. "I don't know what you're talking about," she slurs.

"Tell that to Billy Jenkins." I slam the door before she can come up with a response. Briana gives me one last wave. Georgie has her face flattened against the window, smearing the glass with her saliva as she tries to convince both of us she doesn't like Billy. The taillights vanish when they turn the corner.

Quiet.

Something crashes in the distance. The sound echoes as I whirl to face it. One of the garbage cans in the alley is tipped over, its insides spilling out onto the ground. The light at the top of the pole flickers. My heart skips a beat and I remember shattering plastic and lurking shadows.

Fear is already beside me, of course, his elbow brushing mine. "What kind of person are you?" he muses, head tilted. "Are you the type to go look for the source of that noise ... or will you run?"

He doesn't know me very well.

A hand touches my back as I stalk toward the trash cans, and resolution leaks through the dread. Still, I forget to breathe while I dare to peek around the corner ... and catch sight of a tail. Relief is in the sound of my exhale. I step into the alley.

In another life, it must have been a lab. In this one, its fur is so matted and full of forest debris that it's nearly unrecognizable. "Well, you're not a raccoon," I mutter. The dog freezes. It raises its eyes and spots me, a glob of drool falling out of the corner of its mouth. Ribs stick out beneath its once-brown fur. Before I can do anything, the dog bolts. I stand there and watch it vanish into some bushes. The quivering leaves are the only proof that it was real.

Just then, a breeze stirs my hair. A familiar scent of mint encircles me. I look around, searching for Forgiveness, until I realize that it's coming from me. From my skin and clothes.

I need to wash his smell off. Need to wash off that brief moment of vulnerability on the swings. Glancing around—for once I'm alone, no Emotions, no mysterious strangers—I shoulder my bag and hurry around the back. The stairs shudder loudly under my weight, but Angus doesn't appear in the window; it must be later than I thought.

Inside, there's a note taped to the mirror that hangs above our shoes. *Missed you. Dinner is in the fridge.* I touch the scribbled words with my fingers, assuring myself that these are real, too. I haven't ruined everything. Not yet. I can still turn back if I choose to.

Choices. Revenge. Forgiveness.

I find my way through the darkness and shut myself into the bathroom. Seconds later steam fills the air and I climb into the ancient tub. Soap runs down my body and I scrub so hard my skin might come off. The hot water pounds onto every part of me and it isn't enough. Forgiveness haunts my thoughts, so much that there's not enough room for Revenge or Nate Foster. I won't let this happen. I can't.

I'm doing this for you.

"No. I'm doing this for you," I whisper, closing my eyes. There's no answer, so I turn the water off, wrap myself in a towel, and tiptoe to my room. Uncle Saul snores so loud it's a wonder the walls don't tremble.

As soon as I open my bedroom door, I'm aware of a distinct scent of chocolate in the air. It takes my eyes a moment to adjust, and then I see him, lying on my bed in a slant of moonlight. Wearily I tighten my grip on the towel. "You missed one hell of a party," I say.

"I wasn't in the mood tonight."

There's something strange about his voice, something different. For that matter, he's never been in my room before. Growing up, it was always one of his boundaries, another unspoken rule. Yet here he is, lying there as if it's the only place he wants to be.

Instead of asking him about this, I ask instead, "Since when are you not in the mood for a party?" I open the folding closet door and step behind it. Revenge doesn't answer. Once I'm wearing a big T-shirt and some underwear, I step out again. He hasn't moved. He's just staring up at the ceiling, hands folded beneath his head. His profile is sharp and luminescent, beautiful in all its strange solemnity. I frown. "What's up with you?"

Again, no response. Sighing, I ease into the space beside him, careful not to brush his arm. The springs in the mattress squeak. For a few minutes we simply exist. There's a stain in the upper right-hand corner of my room. I focus on it, wonder when it happened. It's round, yellow. Water leaking through the roof, maybe? I've never noticed it before. I tap my finger against my thigh, counting the seconds. No, not the seconds. Though there's a breath between us, I can feel it, steady as the town clock.

"If you're not human, why do you have a heartbeat?" I whisper, turning on my side to face him.

Revenge turns, too. He frowns as if he's never thought about it before. His eyes are still clouded with thought. "I don't know." He finally concentrates on me. "Did you go tonight?"

Did I go to Nate Foster's, he means. I swallow, the sound audible. "No."

"Did you . . . did you see him?"

There's an unexpected shadow of uncertainty to his voice, and I know he means Forgiveness now. Maybe that's why I lie. "No."

My best friend closes his eyes. Yearning overtakes me. There's so much unspoken, so much undone. I should be used to it, because that's the way it's always been with us. This time I want to tell Revenge that everything is about to change. But he already knows that. Change is inevitable. So all I say is, "Do you remember when I was thirteen and I broke my arm?"

"Yes." He turns his head to look at me again.

I smile at him. "It was on the first anniversary of the accident. I climbed that tree because I wanted to escape everything. Maybe some irrational part of me wanted to just disappear into the sky. Missy and Saul kept telling me to stay on the ground, that it was dangerous. You didn't. You just stood there and watched me go higher and higher. Maybe it was because you didn't care, or because you can't interfere with human affairs. But I don't think so. I think you hoped I would reach the sky, too."

Another silence gathers. "What made you think of that?" he asks eventually. He doesn't confirm or deny it.

The truth? Being with Forgiveness. It has to be his essence getting to me, because when I'm around him, all I want to do is be. Be with the people I love, be better, be more than what I am or will be. I want to touch the sky again, after all these years.

It's my turn to evade. Rather than answering his question, I tuck my hand under my chin and grapple for the covers. Tug them over me. "I'll see you tomorrow, Revenge."

The heat of his breath—chocolaty, of course—thaws the ice of my heart as he murmurs, "See you tomorrow, Alex."

After a few minutes, my eyelashes turn to steel, so heavy they won't stay open. I dare to lean closer to Revenge... and I pretend. Pretend that he's a normal boy, that I'm a normal girl. It won't last, but nothing ever lasts. For now, it's enough.

He doesn't move away.

My car struggles to awaken.

I turn the key in the ignition again, and this time the engine catches. As it growls into the morning, I don't let myself look toward the school doors. Briana and Georgie have no idea that I'm leaving. They'll be waiting for me at lunch.

A sharp pain pierces my chest, as though someone has shoved a shard of glass into my heart, and Regret looms in the rearview mirror. My eyes meet his. We don't exchange a word, but we understand each other. His touch elicits images of others: a girl clutching a positive pregnancy test, a man standing over a grave, a boy clutching a paper with an *F* on it. I'm alone, but I'm not alone in this. I clench my jaw and guide the car onto the county toad that will take me to Green River.

Andrew is on his phone when I get to his office. He startles at the sight of me in the doorway. "Yes, I'll have them to you by this afternoon," he says, waving me in. He tugs at his necktie. "Uh-huh. Yes, I have it."

There's a clatter when he puts the phone back into the cradle. The moment he's finished I march up to his desk and slap the flash drive down. "I need to know what's on this," I say.

"What's . . . " Andrew frowns. He adjusts his glasses and leans forward. I'm watching his face carefully, and he's always been a horrible liar. First, recognition flickers in his gaze. Then panic. The office floods with Emotions. "What—" Andrew begins, rising. Before he can touch it, I grab the flash drive again.

"It's Dad's. I found it in the pocket of the shirt he was wearing on the day he died."

Silence. Andrew's breathing changes, and he looks over his shoulder as if someone might be pressed to the window, peering inside at us. But there's only the peaceful oak tree and its swaying leaves, and the empty road beyond.

"Let's go outside," he says finally, gesturing for me to follow him. He walks past me to the door.

I stay where I am. "No, I want answers, and I know you have them. You were his best friend. He told you everything."

Andrew's eyes dart to the hallway. I've never seen him so unsettled. No, not unsettled. *Scared.* He lowers his voice and says through his teeth, "Not here, Alex."

"Why not? What are you afraid of?" I cock my eyebrow challengingly. Something tells me I'm more liable to get answers in here, where he's so unnerved, than wherever he wants to go.

As an answer, Andrew opens the door wider. "I don't know why Will had that or what's on it," he says. "But I can find out." He holds out his free hand. His eyes are almost manic in their desperation.

Lies, a voice in my head whispers. Faltering, I take a step back. There's a sour taste in my mouth. *This is Andrew*, another voice protests. *Your dad loved him. Your dad trusted him*. It's true. This is my godfather. This is the man who helped me with my math last year when I was flunking the class. Not that grades matter now.

Yet my instincts are telling me that something isn't right here. "I should get back," I hear myself say.

"Alex—"

Suddenly it clicks. I see it. And I wonder how I ever missed it. "It was you," I whisper. Time stops.

Andrew is still holding his hand out, but now it seems less for the flash drive and more to stop me from going. "What?" he asks. Confusion links her arm through his and shares his puzzled look.

The shard of glass is still there, wedged into the flesh of my heart. This truth drives it in deeper. I look my father's best friend in the eye and say, my voice hard, "You were watching me last night. On the playground."

Surprise pops into the room, joining the others. Andrew continues to stare at me. Five seconds tick by. One. Two. Three. Four. Five. After a pause that feels like years, Andrew lowers his hand to his side. He must have gotten a manicure recently, because they're perfectly trimmed and filed. Andrew has a touch of OCD when it comes to his appearance. And his things. Somehow, remembering these tiny details makes the moment hurt even more.

I keep waiting for him to answer. When he does, the words are weak. "I… I'm trying to protect you."

A few more second pass while I absorb this. He's not even going to deny it. I'm used to lying to people… but I'm not used to them lying to me. I feel what they must feel, a feeble hope for more, of a reasonable explanation for this betrayal.

"Protect me from what?" I ask, striving to keep the question even. When he doesn't respond, my nostrils flare and I lose the last of my control. "*From what?*" Still he remains silent. "Does this have something to do with my dad?" I ask next, hoping to get *something* out of him. Anything.

At the mention of Dad, Andrew's entire body tenses. He clutches the doorknob so tightly it seems like it should shatter. "Please. I'm begging you. Leave this alone."

Leave this alone? I'm not capable of that. And I especially hate the feeling that I didn't even know my own father. "You might as well tell me what's on the flash drive, Andrew. I'm going to find out eventually, with or without your help." I shrug, as if it's so simple.

He lunges for me.

I'm so shocked that I react too late, and my back slams into his bookshelves. He's crushing my hand, grappling with my fingers and trying to pry them apart. There's a frantic gleam in his eyes that I've never seen before. Calm, logical Andrew is gone, leaving this stranger in his place. I try to shove him away, screaming, and when he only presses closer I kick his shin as hard as I can. Andrew cries out and jumps back, holding his leg. I start to run past him, but he recovers and yanks me back. I swing around and punch him in the face. Something *crunches*. Now Andrew is the one screaming, recoiling and cupping his face.

I rush for the doorway. A woman nearly collides with me, and her eyes widen when she sees Andrew. "What on earth—"

Blood runs down his mouth and chin and he stretches his hand in my direction again. Gasping for breath, I jerk into motion again and dart around the woman. "Alex! Alex, wait! *Please*!" Andrew keeps shouting my name, but I'm already gone. His cries are so loud that they echo down the hallway, ricocheting off the walls.

But the sound of my heart breaking is louder.

TEN

Nate Foster has been sitting in his car for seven minutes.

He doesn't notice me on the street, parked in the shadows. I watch him with a frown. He doesn't move, just stares straight ahead at the garage door. As though he sees something there that I can't. Before the end, I want him to see my family on that blank surface. The same way I do.

His wife is waiting for him, I can tell; she keeps pacing through the house and glancing at something out of sight. A clock, probably. Sometimes I wish I could destroy every clock in the world, just so I can't keep track of how much time has passed since I heard my brother's laugh.

It doesn't make sense, that Forgiveness appears beside me a moment later. I can't deal with him tonight. Not after what happened with Andrew. Tonight I'm just fury wrapped in skin and muscle, about to explode any second. The gun feels warm in my hand, like an old friend.

Forgiveness must sense this, because he doesn't try to talk sense to me. For six more minutes we exist in silence. With Revenge, the wordlessness is painful and thrilling, full of maybes. With Forgiveness, it's just painful. Like I'm being torn in half or pulled toward something. I don't have to look at him to know that he's gazing at me with those eyes of his. Wide, blue, fathomless. Shining, as if he understands my pain.

"Hunter was four," I whisper suddenly. The words just slip out, as though they've been waiting under my tongue, patiently biding their time for the right moment. I'm helpless to stop them. "I remember he was going through this phase where he was just absolutely obsessed with airplanes. I would get so mad at him, because he'd leave these plastic models all over the floor, and I'd step on them all the time."

After I've spoken, a stillness surrounds us, and it feels as though my heart has finally stopped its painful beat. I don't let myself wonder what the cause of this is: speaking of Hunter after all these years . . . or Forgiveness.

The stars don't exist right now. Clouds hide them, and even the moon struggles to be seen. I shift so I'm closer to the windshield, trying to find that faint glow so at least one person can acknowledge it. Then Forgiveness ruins the quiet by murmuring, "Tell me more."

The sound of his voice makes my blood quicken. "No." I focus on that door.

"Why not?"

"I'm not playing this game with you."

"It's not a game, Alexandra."

"Then what the hell is it?"

"It's a conversation."

"Not now. Not with you." My grip tightens on the gun. Of course the Choice would show up now. It's a test, a temptation, a splash of ink on the page I've already written. In front of me, Nate Foster waits. It would be so easy. I close my eyes and imagine doing it. *Bam. Thud. Blood.* I could. I should. I will.

I stiffen when Nate Foster finally gets out of his car. He tugs at his tie—I don't know where he works now, but before the accident he was a manager at the factory—and walks toward the front door as if his shoes are lined with lead. There aren't any Emotions to give him away. Yellow light slants over the lawn as the door opens, and I reach for my own door handle. This is my chance. Here it is. Going, going. Why can't I *move*?

Then the door is closing, and Nate Foster is gone. Missed my chance. Again.

Damn it. Exhaling through my teeth, I ease away from the handle and go back to tapping that erratic beat on my thigh. My hold loosens and tightens on the gun some more. Loosens and tightens. I feel Forgiveness's gaze. "Do you ever just sit still?" he asks me, sounding genuinely curious.

"Nope." I glare so hard at the door now that I don't understand how it hasn't burst into flames. Where is Revenge? Why isn't he the one beside me, urging me to choose?

Inside, Jennifer whirls, probably hearing the door. Her flowered skirt twists around her thighs. Foster brushes past her and enters the kitchen, heading straight for a cupboard next to the fridge. Jennifer makes a sharp gesture, Frustration and Worry hovering around her. Foster responds by pulling out a bottle, brown liquid sloshing within the glass. He walks past her again. Jennifer is still trying to get a response from him—she's one of those people who talks with her hands. I don't like that I know this small detail about a Foster.

Forgiveness inclines his head, shifting slightly. The leather seat creaks and mint drifts over me. "May I offer you some advice?" he asks. When I don't respond he continues anyway. "You can't trust my kind. We're volatile . . . and we're not human. We don't have the same laws or instincts you do." His voice is always serious, but there's an extra gravity to the statement.

Not human. As if I didn't already know that. A bitter smile curves my lips. "And what are those laws and instincts?" Finally I look at him.

"To protect the ones we love." His gaze is unwavering. "Our ideas of right and wrong are too different."

My jaw clenches, and somehow it becomes a battle of wills. Whoever looks away first is weakest. What Forgiveness doesn't know is that I adore-hate his eyes. They're so sad they make me remember what I've lost, but they're so bottomless I could fall forever. I lied; being around Forgiveness is thrilling, too, no matter how much I want to deny it.

"You're talking about Revenge," I comment, hoping my face doesn't betray my thoughts. Picturing him, I put my finger on the trigger. My best friend wouldn't tell me what to do, of course, or let me touch him—that would be interfering—but just the proximity to him would be enough. Just enough.

I'd have the strength to walk up to that door and finish it. Why doesn't he come?

"You don't have to do this." Forgiveness's voice is gentle, just like everything else about him.

"Yes, I do," I hiss. It's unfair, how my stomach flutters when he moves his hand closer to mine. He really is a beautiful creature, no matter how much I want to deny it. Too bad he's such an ugly concept. "I didn't summon you. You don't belong here."

Forgiveness doesn't relent. "Part of you wants me here." He leans toward me, as if to prove this point. His eyelashes, long and dark, brush against the tips of his cheekbones when he slowly blinks. As usual, he's wearing that white T-shirt. It's an obvious effort to seem human, to appear touchable and pure. And even the knowledge that he's anything but doesn't make resisting him easy. I know that if I choose him ... the shifting tectonic plates within me might finally go still.

I can't let that happen.

So I turn away again, gritting my teeth, and resume glaring at the bright window. Forgiveness doesn't sigh or try to pull me back. He just eases into his seat again and watches me while I watch them.

"Do you want to know what Nate is doing right now?" he asks after another pause. I don't respond. He tells me anyway. "He's in his study, drinking a glass of brandy. He's tired. His wife yelled at him for being so late and not calling. The real reason she's angry, though, is because she's scared she's lost the man she knew. The man she loved."

"Shut up," I spit. "Just shut up." My finger curls around the trigger even more, and I'm shaking.

"But she'll forgive him. She always does. I usually feel her summons sometime in the middle of the night, when she's cold and lonely."

"If I could put a bullet through your head, I would. Gladly."

The threat doesn't affect Forgiveness. He rests his hand on the gear shift, a silent way to let me know that all of this could be over and behind me if I would just give in. Let go of the anger and summon him for real, let that hand touch my shoulder or my cheek or my fingers.

My phone is next to Forgiveness's wrist. It's off now, since I got tired of dodging Andrew's calls. He's been calling nonstop since I left the college.

"You've never killed before, Alexandra," Forgiveness reminds me. "Do you really think you want to?"

It's my name on his lips that does it. *Alexandra*. My mind goes back to another place, another time, another person who used to call me that. Dad's voice echoes through the stillness. *No, Alexandra, this is C-sharp. Put your finger there. Yes, good. Okay, now, do you remember the scale?* No, not anymore. Those black and white keys no longer represent music; they represent what should have been. Everything that was ripped away on that rainy night.

I turn to stone as I say, "Yes. I do." The intensity of Forgiveness's presence wanes as my fierce longing for revenge increases. The Choice himself finally appears in the backseat.

"Alex." Revenge greets me in silken tones. Finally. Defiant

and desperate, I stretch out my hand toward him, willing him to hear my thoughts. *I choose you. Touch me. Take this unbearable uncertainty away. Help me.*

But instead of ending it, Revenge draws back. Out of reach. Shocked, I stare at him. My friend avoids my gaze and whispers, "You're not ready yet. You haven't really decided."

Another silence ebbs through the car, this one so thick it clogs my throat. My breath comes in jagged pieces. In. Out. In. Out. Forgiveness and Revenge just wait, and they don't even bother to acknowledge each other. They want me to choose? I laugh. "Fine!" A gust of warm air shocks me; I've opened the door. I choose neither. I choose my family.

"Alexandra, don't." For the first time, Forgiveness's expression seems strained; his mouth purses. I'm rigid now, my vision blurred as the urges tear each other apart. I can see myself opening that door and going in. Hunting down Nate Foster's study, finding him behind a large oak desk. He'd see me, and he would drop that glass of brandy in shock. It would shatter on the floor, into a thousand glittering pieces. The same way he broke me. I'd raise the gun, and I wouldn't waver. Maybe I'd say something. Words that had meaning, about poetic justice or vindicated retribution. A single moment. That's all it would take.

"Alexandra," Forgiveness repeats. I'd nearly forgotten him. His lullaby voice jars me from my thoughts. Involuntarily, I look at him again.

There's no chance to prepare myself. Whatever sharp response I had dies as those melancholy eyes manage to pierce my armor, and I'm falling into him again. His beauty is a net that ensnares. His wild hair, his nose that's long and noble, his jaw elegant and defined. And his lips...

I will never, ever feel those lips.

What's happening to me? It must be the choice. I'm going crazy. "Get out," I manage. "Both of you."

The order isn't so effective given the breathless quality that clings to it. I hate my weakness. I despise disappointing my family. But I keep hearing those words, and they stop me from taking the next step and walking up to that door. *The real reason she's angry, though, is because she's scared she's lost the man she knew. The man she loved.* Bile burns my throat.

I shut the door, lean over, and shove the gun back into the glove box. My glance flicks to the rearview mirror, where Revenge regards me with an indiscernible expression. Then he fades into nothing.

Somewhere in the trees, an owl calls. It reminds me that it's late. I try to summon Anger now, anything to keep the pain away, but the Emotion doesn't appear. There's only a small, wistful twinge in my chest.

The being in the passenger seat shifts. I'd almost forgotten he was here. Before I can think of something to say, Forgiveness's form begins to go transparent; he's preparing to leave, too. Which means that he's concluded I'm not going to use the gun tonight. Maybe I'm just not strong enough to do this.

I don't realize I've spoken out loud until Forgiveness says, "Maybe you're stronger than you realize."

I wilt like a flower, still trying to hate him. "Why won't you just leave me alone?" I whisper. The moon disappears among the wisps of clouds and condensation creeps across the windshield from my breath.

No, not only from my breath. From his, too. I feel the heat emanating through his clothes as Forgiveness comes closer than he ever has before. I refuse to give him the satisfaction of turning, so when he answers me, the words are puffs of air on my cheek.

"Because you keep calling for me," he whispers back.

Instant denial rises up, and I jerk around to argue.

But Forgiveness is gone.

There are no other cars when I get home. At first I'm worried that my aunt and uncle went out looking for me, fed up with the missed calls and unexplained absences. It takes me a moment to remember Missy's earlier text, informing me that Saul is playing poker with his buddies and she's doing a late shift answering the phone at the sheriff's station. Relieved, I get out of the car and climb the rickety stairs to the deck. Just as I'm about to turn the corner, though, something whines.

I jump and spin, pressing a hand to my chest. Fear stands next to me already, and he snorts when he sees it's just the stray, standing at the bottom of the steps. His form shimmers as he leaves, but I hardly notice. The starving dog gazes at me with those big eyes, and I clear my throat. "Hey, girl. What are you—"

She retreats. That's when I realize her hackles are raised and her teeth are bared. Before I can move or speak or blink, the stray bolts, and once again I lose her to the forest. After she's gone, I squint at the shadows.

Strange.

Mentally shrugging, I turn back around. At the door, my phone goes off. A text from Briana. *WHERE DID YOU GO TODAY?* She always spells every word out. Smiling wistfully, I text an empty apology back. There's also a text from Georgie. It isn't so polite. I don't respond.

I wrap my hand around the doorknob and the hinges let out a whine; the door is ajar. *Not right*, instinct whispers. Missy may burn things, but she doesn't forget things. Frowning, I step inside.

The apartment is dark and quiet. Moonlight cascades over the kitchen counters and the rug in the living room. Nothing seems to be amiss. No reason for my instincts to be bristling like a threatened porcupine.

A sound reaches my ears. Faint, but I know I didn't imagine it. Wood sliding on wood. The drawer to my desk. I freeze.

Someone is in the apartment.

It can't be Missy or Saul. Angus would have waited for me on the steps. I can't breathe. I can't breathe. Rational thought is suddenly impossible.

Slowly, I retreat. Step by step. Back toward the door. Almost mockingly, Fear tiptoes beside me, his hand on my arm. I don't acknowledge him. My lungs begin to shriek. Doesn't matter. All that matters is getting outside, to the car, and away.

Wait. Maybe it's just Andrew. No, not *just* Andrew. He nearly overpowered me in his office today. He wanted that flash drive. Enough to bring him to this? How do I get him out of here before Saul or Missy come home?

The gun.

I need to get to the gun in my glove box. Then I can confront whoever is stupid enough to break into the apartment where the only family I have left sleeps and eats and lives. I take another step, my heel high off the floor. Only a few more feet—

Creak.

For the second time today, time utterly stops. I feel my heart leap into my throat, and the stranger isn't opening the drawers anymore. The silence quivers. Then there are footsteps. Coming for me. *Thud-thud-thud.*

I dive for the open doorway.

The intruder is faster. A rough hand hauls me back, wrenching my shoulder, and slams me into the wall. That same hand covers my mouth, eliminating the chance to scream. The stench of unwashed body assaults my senses. I struggle, still trying to shriek, but every part of me is pinned. Heavy breathing heats the back of my neck as the person laughs.

"Wow, you're pretty," a voice purrs against my temple. Definitely not Andrew. "Would be a shame to scar that smooth skin."

I retort, the words muffled by his big palm. He's male, without a doubt; I can feel him against my thigh.

Before I can think of a way to get free, the voice adds, "Where is it?"

Where's what? I start to ask. Then it occurs to me. Of course, the flash drive. What else could it be? The hand falls away, giving me a chance to answer. I should call for help; Angus might be home. I should shatter the night with a scream. Instead, I hear myself growl, "I think it's where your balls should be."

Pause. I steel myself for a blow, and in the instant of silence there's another sound, not at all faint. An engine. There's no mistaking whose car it is, because that tell-tale pop of the exhaust bursts through the night. Horror washes over me and I'm slow to react, to comprehend.

No.

Missy, coming home early. My attacker must know time is running out, too, because he presses even closer. Outside, a dog begins to bark.

"Tell anyone about this, we go after your precious Saul and Missy next," he hisses.

I try to speak again, this time to beg him not to hurt my aunt. Before I can, there's a flash of movement and a moment of searing pain against my skull. I fight a wave of dizziness, but it's no use. The darkness swallows the darkness.

ELEVEN

Dr. Norris shines a light in my eyes. Back and forth, back and forth. I study him and remember a time when his hair wasn't so white and his eyes weren't so watery. We're in his kitchen, since Missy rushed me right to his front door. His office is on the other side of the garage, but I guess that was too far to walk before doing the examination.

"Are you feeling dizzy at all? Nauseous? Or anything out of the ordinary, really?" the old man asks. His bones creak as he flattens his palms against his thighs and stands.

Out of the ordinary. Right on cue, that voice penetrates the medicinally induced fog around me. *Alexandra*. I force a bright smile, looking our town's only doctor in the eye as I chirp, "Nope." My head has stopped throbbing, at least.

"You need to be more careful." My aunt rests her hand on my shoulder, as though to assure herself that I'm really solid and sitting here. She's been doing that a lot since she found me on the floor of our apartment—after I tripped on the edge of the rug and hit my head. That's the story she knows, at least. The truth would put her in danger, and I need Saul and Missy to be safe. "It's late," she adds, sighing. "Let's go home. It's safe for her to sleep, right?"

Dr. Norris nods, and Missy follows him into the other room, checkbook in hand even though we can't afford this. My new pills rattle in her purse. They leave me in the kitchen. I stay there to gather my composure. Across from where I sit, there's a window. Something moves in the glass. My pulse picks up speed again before I realize it's just a reflection.

I stare at the girl. She stares back with wide, fevered eyes. I don't recognize her. She must be me, though, because we lift our hands at the same time. Blink at the same time.

"Alex? Are you okay?"

"Yeah, I'm fine. Coming." I turn my back on the stranger.

They're both waiting for me by the door. Dr. Norris winks and presses a sucker into my hand, just like he did when I was little. I manage to thank him, and the old man pats my cheek as Missy pulls me into the night. He smells like cigarettes, which he shouldn't, because everyone knows he was diagnosed with lung cancer last year. Still, I understand. Even when we know something is bad for us, we depend on it anyway, because it's easier than acknowledging how broken we are.

Missy and I get into the truck and head home. We don't speak. As always, Elvis is oblivious to the strain filling this space like Dr. Norris's cancer, unseen but devastating. When Missy first found me, Fear hounded us all the way to the doctor's.

Now Worry appears behind her, his hands fluttering over her. For the first time, he addresses me. "She's wondering if you told the truth about your accident," the Emotion mutters. "She's worried that you won't survive this."

"This?" I repeat, so quietly that Missy doesn't hear. She's immersed in the road, lips twisted in thought.

Worry begins to disintegrate. His answer drifts to me. "Grief."

The brakes squeal when Missy parks. We both get out and climb the steps. Missy goes right in, but I hesitate at the threshold, remembering what happened just a few hours ago. *Wow, you're pretty.* Somehow, I know the intruder won't be back tonight. He'll be back, no doubt, but not tonight. *Would be a shame to scar that smooth skin.* My stomach quakes, and I make myself step through the doorway. I turn the lock, something we haven't done in years. Saul has a key.

It isn't until we're completely inside the apartment that Missy finally breaks the silence. She takes a breath and faces me, her expression unfathomable in the darkness. "Don't you ever scare me like that again," she says, holding my face in her rough palms. My aunt's scent is a combination of soap and laundry detergent. It's one of the best smells in the world, but I can't tell her that. The words just won't come.

For once, though, I close my eyes and let myself enjoy her warmth. "I'll try not to," I whisper, tightening my hold on her wrists.

"It was strange." She frowns. "When I got home, I was going to straighten the trash cans. But there was a dog at the bottom of the stairs, and it wouldn't stop barking until I went up. Maybe someone is watching out for you, huh?" Without waiting for a response, Missy gives me one last troubled smile. Then she pulls free to lumber down the hallway into their room. The door shuts.

The moment I hear the click, I go to the kitchen and rummage around in the fridge. There isn't much here; we survive mostly on cereal and microwave dinners. But I find something that will work. Something that will give me a semblance of control, that makes me feel the tiniest bit powerful and able to make a difference in this place of so much sameness.

Something that will express my gratitude.

Bowl in hand, I slip back outside and down the stairs, around the corner to where the garbage cans are lined up. I leave the cold broth on the ground and wait for a minute, hoping to see the creature who's just as damaged as I am. The shadows stay empty. After another minute, I give up and go back up the stairs.

In the morning, the bowl is licked clean.

A fly buzzes past my ear.

Around me, everyone's clay has become something. While I've been away confronting the past, my peers have moved forward. Georgie is making an ashtray. Briana's bird has spread its wings, straining to break free of the base its feet are molded to. As always, she aims for perfection; while others are just creating basic shapes, Briana is using a sharp tool to create tiny feathers. I sneak glances at her, thinking about how she won't be in Franklin much longer. She'll move on to bigger and better things, like college, and it makes me happy. It does. Once I find the strength to face Nate Foster, at least I'll know that my friend will be living enough for the both of us.

It's impossible to concentrate; dreams assaulted me throughout the night. I tossed and turned and the blankets tangled around my torso, trapping me like a seat belt. There was the sprinkle of broken glass. Pain. Silence. The wail of distant sirens. A limp hand. A river of blood. Someone sobbing. When the alarm clock went off, I floundered in disorientation. Surrounded by rain, glass, metal. It still feels like I haven't woken up completely.

In a vain attempt to appear like I'm doing something, too, I keep flattening and twisting my own block until it looks like some kind of lagoon monster. Mr. Kim already expressed the need for productivity, since I'm so behind. I can feel him keeping track of my progress. No one at the table speaks; it's been this way since I first found Briana and Georgie by the lockers. They're angry. Understandably so; I'd be irritated with me, too. Vague excuses and hollow apologies aren't enough. But they're better than the truth, and they're better than any of the lies, so now I just accept the silence and wait.

Finally, Georgie can't hold her curiosity back any longer. "What did they call you to the office for?" she mutters, pinching the edges of her ashtray.

This morning, just after first hour, Principal Bracken

hunted me down and gave me one of the severest lectures I've ever gotten in my life. And that's saying something. I sum it up for her: "I've been informed that if I miss any more school, I won't be able to graduate." I keep my attention on my clay, but I sense Briana stiffening.

Georgie, on the other hand, just snorts. "No surprise there."

Any other day, I might snap back, but my head aches too much. I forgot to take a pill this morning. Missy did her best to convince me to stay home—ironic, her actually encouraging me to skip school—but the idea of lying in bed with nothing to distract me from my thoughts wasn't exactly appealing, so here I am. What's bothering me most, though, isn't what happened with the intruder, or with Andrew, or the fact that the flash drive is still locked. Or even that my friends are beginning to see my holes and shortcomings. No, what's uppermost in my thoughts is that I haven't seen Revenge yet today.

Ever since we met, that afternoon in my living room when I was twelve, he's been a constant presence. Waiting at the kitchen table in the morning, sitting beside me on the way to school, offering commentary on every little thing throughout my day. My best friend. Of course, his nature pulled him away sometimes, but never for more than a few hours. This is different, now. Somehow I know that he's avoiding me, and it's even stranger considering this is the time he should want to be near me most.

Something about last night unsettled him. He'd been so quiet. I wish he would appear so I could demand answers. Or at least tell him to get over it.

That fly darts by again, and my gaze follows it around the light on the ceiling.

Briana leans toward me. "Alex? Are you feeling okay?" She touches one of my ragged nails. The touch is so gentle, so concerned, that I want to run.

I study our hands and try not to think of my mother, how she used to squeeze my fingers and tell me I was going to change the world. "Just tired is all," I say, trying to sound dismissive. "Think I'll go to the bathroom and splash some water on my face." Before she or Georgie can respond, I slide off my stool and leave the room. Mr. Kim doesn't notice.

The bathroom is empty. I head straight for the last stall and shut the door. Pressing my back to the opposite wall, I search for the words that always bring me here. There it is, among all the others. *FOR A GOOD TIME, CALL ANDREA. PENELOPE IS A SLUT. TRACEY LOVES WILL.* I touch the letters of her name, picturing her in this same spot, carving the truth of what she felt. "Mom," I whisper, desperately wishing she could answer.

She doesn't.

It's become instinct, to leave school when it becomes unbearable. Today, though, there's no Andrew to visit and no Revenge to pull me away from the edge. If I went home, Missy would only hover, and Saul would either scold me or try to talk about Nate Foster. Neither of which I can deal with right now. So I wipe my eyes, lift my chin, and go back to class.

Relief touches Briana the moment I walk in. Georgie just raises her brows as if to say, *Wow, you're still here?* Making an effort at normality, I glare back and sit down. The clay waits expectantly. All I can think of molding it into is a flash drive. Or a gun. Somehow I don't think Mr. Kim will be impressed by either of these.

"... making that for, anyway? I thought everyone in your family quit," Briana is saying, adjusting her bird's beak so it's not quite so sharp.

Georgie sighs. "Mom started again. I know I shouldn't be encouraging her, but it's kind of pathetic when she uses a Pepsi can for the ashes."

"Must be that time of year. My mom has also been wanting to start again." Briana sighs too.

Mom. Maybe it's the head wound, or the time of month, or I'm just losing it, because that's all it takes. Georgie still has her mother—to make things for, to worry about, to mock. Another Emotion shimmers into view, this one meant for me. Sorrow. He has a scent similar to what I imagine the ocean would smell like. Salt and wind and the vastness of the unknown.

Mr. Kim says something as he walks past us, but I don't hear the words. Sorrow brushes my cheek with his pale fingers, and it takes all of my strength not to let the tears spill from my eyes. I don't stop myself from looking at his face. He doesn't seem surprised that I can see him. He doesn't say anything, and I don't either. His touch evokes a dozen images. Me and Mom at the lake. The two of us curled up with a book. Making cookies together in the kitchen. I want to tell Sorrow how much I despise him, but it sticks in my throat; he's crying for me. As if he feels the wound Mom's absence left behind.

Maybe he does.

Georgie pokes my arm. "Hey. Back to earth, Alex. I feel like you're going to start drooling any second."

I force myself to glance away from Sorrow and stare at the lump in front of me. Right now it's nothing. Like Nate Foster's front door, it's just potential. Its fate is my decision. A fan hums in the corner, sending cool air over my skin. For a few minutes I'm not sure I can make a choice even as simple as this. But then Sorrow kisses my cheek—something he's never done before—and walks away.

My mom will never kiss my cheek again.

The thought jolts me into motion. Of their own volition, my hands return to the clay, which has cooled in my absence. It becomes warm again. I work with a mindlessness that consumes. Sorrow has opened another door I can't close—not today—and all I'm capable of is remembering. My hands move without guidance. The fly darts by again, ignored.

"Who is that, Alex?"

The question jars me. The light pouring through the window is suddenly too bright. More time must have passed than I realized. I look at Briana blankly, and she's frowning at the clay in my hands. I follow her gaze.

He looks up at me with those eyes that see everything. See my weakness. See me. I'm no artist, and to anyone else it probably looks like no one, but I know who it's supposed to be.

Just like last time, my friends wait for an answer. I swallow, clenching my jaw so hard it hurts. How can this be? I'd meant to sculpt something else entirely. *Someone* else entirely. "No one. He's no one," I mutter, wishing I meant it. That's the biggest lie of all, though. My friends just stare.

I crush Forgiveness with my fist.

TWELVE

Progress in the attic is slow-going. One wall of boxes is finished, organized and labeled. I washed two old chairs and put them under the window, a small table between them. Some of the books and knickknacks from the boxes are on display along the shelves behind it. An old snow globe, the record player, a dollhouse. Things Missy didn't think worthy of keeping but couldn't bring herself to throw away, either.

My phone vibrates in my pocket—Andrew, no doubt. I ignore it and bend to open a new box, coughing when dust flies up. A spider skitters out of the sweater on top. An instant after I spot it, something touches my shoulder and I shriek, recoiling. Fear laughs before vanishing.

The spider is gone, too, hidden beneath the untouched boxes in front of me. I eye them warily, wondering if there's any way I can get out of doing the rest.

"See, that's one thing I've never understood about you.

Guns and fights and your aunt's cooking don't faze you, but one little spider ... "

The sound of Revenge's voice doesn't startle me; I've been expecting him ever since I got home. "Shut up," I grumble, turning. He sits in one of the chairs, hands folded between his knees. His hair is longer today, artfully gelled so it curls and glints. He's wearing what looks like a designer jacket. Most creatures from the other plane don't bother changing their appearances, but Revenge has always been a little vain.

I don't bother with small talk. "Where have you been?"

Imitating my brusqueness, Revenge shrugs. "Helping mankind exact his vengeance."

Which is exactly what I haven't allowed him to do here, with me. Maybe that's why he's pulling away. He's frustrated. Maybe he's given up. Out of all the people I expected to give up on me, it was never Revenge. The idea terrifies me more than any spider or declaration of love. But instead of voicing my thoughts, I say, "That's sexist. What am I, chopped liver?"

He laughs, and it's as if nothing strange between us has happened. That odd pensive look in his eyes is gone. I'd been about to tell him about the attack, but I don't want to bring it back. "It's an expression," my friend tells me, grinning.

"Well, I've never heard it before," I lie, because I have nothing else to say, and dig through the rest of the box. Just clothes. The marker is next to my knee. I yank the cap off and label the cardboard side, then close the flaps and push the whole thing away.

Revenge stands and moves to the record player. There's that scratching sound again as he puts the needle on it.

"You've never left Franklin. There's a whole wide world out there, my friend, with many expressions and places and experiences you've yet to discover." Soft music ebbs through the room.

Surprisingly, him being here isn't improving my mood. I'm almost violent while I root through the next box. "You sound like you're writing a pamphlet for a travel agency."

"Those are pretty much extinct now. See how cut off you are, on this mountain? I bet you don't even know who the president is." I don't have to look at him to know Revenge is smirking, thinking he's so clever. I don't feel like humoring him. *TEA SET*, I scribble. My handwriting is illegible, a fact that my aunt and uncle seemed to have forgotten when they assigned this task to me. Revenge watches, twitching. He's bored. I can tell. Some things don't change.

That's when I realize that I'm twitching, too. My fingers tap the wood floor. Forgiveness's words break through my barriers. *Do you ever just sit still?*

Fortunately, I won't have time to think about him tonight. I lean back and look at the ceiling, counting under my breath. "And three, two, one… "

"We haven't gone out in a while," Revenge says suddenly.

There's no way Saul and Missy will let me go anywhere. Not with my head wound and the way I've been acting lately. And things are different now. Before, Revenge would suggest some party happening in another town or just a long drive.

"What did you have in mind?" I snap. "The bridge? No, wait, let me guess. Nate Foster's?" Revenge starts to answer, but I laugh, cutting him off. "Forget it. We've established that all I can do is sit in that damn car and stare at his house. I don't have what it takes. Okay? So you can focus on the people who are actually worth your time."

Turning my back on him, I rummage through yet another box. A long, long pause cracks our friendship, threatening to shatter it completely. Desperation kneels beside me, her expression strained as she strokes my hair. Maybe Revenge thinks she's here because I want to confront Nate Foster so badly—and I do—but in this moment all I want to do is ask him what we are. Or, at least, what we could be. It's on my list of fears, after all. Small spaces, spiders, confronting Nate Foster, and asking Revenge for the truth.

Desperation leaves us to our stilted silence. We've never fought before, not like this. It's my fault. I've been unraveling ever since art class, the knots of sanity and reason so far undone it will take hours to tie them back together again.

The music screeches to a halt, probably sensing the tension. I don't know how to fix this, and I'm not sure I want to. It begins to seem like the damage is permanent when Revenge finally says, "I know what will help."

I rub my eye, sighing. Suddenly I'm so, so tired. "Oh, yeah? What?"

"Kiss me."

At first, I wonder if I imagined the words. They're so faint, just a whisper. Slowly, I face Revenge again. "W-what?"

As an answer, he gets up from the chair, and my breathing becomes uneven. His essence burns through me, almost painfully. More images of vengeance flicker through my mind, but I'm so shocked that I barely notice them.

With an expression I've never seen on his face before—one I can't even define—Revenge advances. I'm so startled that I instinctively get up and retreat. He doesn't stop, and suddenly my back hits the wall, as it did the last time we were in this attic. Only now, there are no interruptions. Now, Revenge doesn't hesitate. Like before, he plants his hands on either side of my head and puts his mouth so close to mine that I can feel his breath. That chocolate scent torments my senses. "Kiss me," he repeats. "Choose me." I wait, but even though he's breaking the rules, he still won't take the choice from me.

"Revenge," I manage, my voice strangled, all my irritation forgotten. His eyes close, like his name on my lips is a dose of morphine and he's in the throes of oblivion. Still he waits. Still I hesitate. Lust is sliding her finger up my arm.

This is the moment I've daydreamed about since I first realized how much I love my best friend. It seems so perfect. The light is serene, falling over us as if from a lantern. Silence floats through the golden space. And Revenge is here, so close I can smell his skin. I've never touched his skin. Would it be hot? Would it burn me, even deeper than I already burn? I look up at him, wondering if he can hear the way my heart thunders. *So perfect*, I think again.

But it's not.

"Why?" I whisper back.

He opens his jade eyes and frowns. Already the haze around us begins to fade. Lust flips her hair and disappears. "What do you mean?" he asks.

I put my hand over his chest, wishing I could let myself

close the distance between us. It hovers just over his heart, trembling, and I remember how his heart beat that night in my room. "Why do you want to kiss me?" I clarify, forcing myself to meet his gaze.

Finally, the question is out. Yet I don't feel relieved. All I feel is . . . dread. Maybe Fear himself does have some tact, because he doesn't stay after answering his summons.

It seems I have good reason to be afraid, though, because Revenge isn't answering. He takes a step back. I feel myself blanch, and another fracture splits between us. It's never been this way. There are always words or debates or laughs. Not this. "Revenge?" I bite my lip so I don't cry. I will not cry.

I've never seen him so . . . cold. He's a stranger, with his tight mouth and darkened eyes. He takes one more step. "Stop," I say through my teeth. He does. Remaining against the wall, I clench my jaw so hard that it aches, but it's nothing compared to the pain of losing my best friend. I can't look at him anymore, so I study the floorboards, all the ridges and stains. Revenge doesn't speak, and after a few seconds my broken whisper echoes into the stillness. "Please . . . please don't give up on me."

Exactly three more seconds tick by, and I feel his shock. Then he's back, his hands cradling the air around my face. "I will *never* give up on you," he growls.

A sound escapes me, part-hiccup, part-laugh. I raise my hands to finally touch him.

Too late. He's gone, off to another part of this spinning planet where I can't demand answers to questions that never should be asked. I don't move. Downstairs, I can hear Missy singing and frying something on the stove. The record player is stuck, making a faint clicking sound I hadn't heard before. Just as I start to walk toward it, there's movement out of the corner of my eye. I spin, and my heart sinks when I see it's just the spider. The tiny creature has emerged from its hiding place, daring to scuttle across the floor toward another stack of boxes.

I step on it.

After dinner, I try to help Missy with the dishes. She waves me off, saying I need to rest. That's the last thing I need; now, more than ever, I need to avoid the turmoil of my thoughts. So I drift downstairs, into the shop. Shadows fill every corner, but moonlight illuminates the area around the front door. It reveals the dusty, tiled floor. I never come down here; the pianos remind me too much of Dad.

One of them calls to me more strongly than the others. It waits in the corner, black and ancient. Probably untouched for years. Reluctantly, slowly, I approach. For a few seconds I just look down at it. Then, gently—despite how much I want to destroy it—I lift the lid. The black and white keys greet me. I run my fingers over them, steeling myself against the images it brings. The ring on my thumb glints. *Concentrate, Alex. I know you can do this. Remind me, what's this note again?*

I slam the lid down.

Averting my gaze, I swiftly walk to the office door, which is behind the long counter with the old register. Saul is sitting at his desk with a map laid out in front of him. A single lamp casts a glow over everything. First I look at the file cabinets, which hold all the customer and tax records for the shop, then I turn my attention to the piles of maps. Some old, some obviously new. Finally, I focus on the man who collects them all. The top of his balding head gleams.

"Saul?"

Once again, I bring Surprise to Franklin. The Emotion settles his hand on my uncle's back. Saul recovers quickly and seems genuinely pleased to see me. "Hey, beautiful." He smiles. His glasses are perched on the end of his nose. Looking at his maps always puts him in a good mood. "Couldn't sleep?"

More like I never tried. Revenge, dreams, and voices make sleep impossible. Thinking of the voice must give it strength; I hear it in my head again, louder than ever. *Alexandra.* Wanting a distraction—any distraction—I leave the doorway and sit down across from Saul. It's the first time I've been in this room since I was a little girl. Nothing has changed, not even the smell.

Saul must sense something isn't right, because he actually sets his map aside. My eyes follow the movement. It's a night of asking what's never been asked before, because I blurt, "Why do you love maps so much?" *Distract me. Please.*

Saul tilts his head and appraises me. I wonder what he sees. After a moment he pulls the map back toward him. It rustles. He traces the lines with the tip of his finger. He and Dad had such different hands; my uncle makes a living tuning pianos, while my father spent his days beneath the ground.

Now he spends all his time there.

Stricken by the thought, I almost miss it when Saul says, "... guess I like the organized chaos of the world." He looks at me, smiling sadly. Somehow I know we're both thinking of Dad now. "I like knowing how things begin and end."

His pain is unbearable to witness, because it only reminds me of my own. Focusing on the map instead of his face, I walk forward and put my fingers next to Saul's, touching an ocean. The light slants across our wrists.

"If only everything could be like that, huh?" I murmur, swallowing.

Maybe Saul wants to avoid the pain too, because he leans away. "If only." He takes his glasses off and rubs his eyes. "It started when I was a kid. Your dad and I used to have this dream. We talked about exploring the Amazon. So I studied maps, to figure out our route."

I open my mouth to respond, but suddenly it clicks. My spine goes rigid. An Emotion puts a hand on my back and I don't even care. "I better get back to the attic," I say hurriedly, backing away. "Uh, thanks for the talk."

Obviously puzzled, Saul watches me go. I'm too excited to make a better excuse for my abruptness. I run back upstairs, digging the flash drive out of my pocket.

I know what the password is.

THIRTEEN

A single word. Without Saul, I never would have guessed it. Some dreams are too unbearable to share when it becomes evident they'll never come true. They become so much to us, just as important as family and friendship. Georgie might talk about getting out of Franklin, but Dad always said he'd die here. As if he knew. I remember how the light was fading from his eyes day by day. But some part of him must have kept hoping. We always hope, even when we know we shouldn't. I sit down at my desk, ignoring Angus's nightly knock once again, and boot up the laptop. Plug the flash drive in. Wait for it to load. The password box pops up and my hands tremble as I type it in.

AMAZON.

The computer thinks for a moment. My pulse hammers. My cell phone goes off yet again and for the hundredth time I let Andrew go to voicemail. I wait for that little box to jiggle and tell me I'm wrong. But then . . . it works.

A list of files lines up, a scroll bar to the right of them. There's so much that I know it'll take me *days* to get through everything. I let out a long breath and get to work, reading as fast as I can—which isn't very fast. The titles are vague, things like *SUBJECTS* and *TEST ELEVEN* and *COMPONENT ATTEMPT SIX.* Some of the files are videos. When I double-click on the first one, the clip shows rubber-gloved hands putting drops of liquid into a petri dish. The substance reacts, expanding in different colors. An accented voice narrates in scientific terms I don't understand. There's nothing that links to Dad, so I keep going, frowning.

"Alex?" A knock on the door. "Are you all right?"

I jump but don't take my eyes off the screen. *Don't open the door, please don't open the door.* "Fine, Missy! Just . . . working on an essay." The laptop begins to cool itself down, humming into the stillness.

"Oh, okay. I'll leave you to it, then." She sounds pleased. Ignoring Guilt's heavy hand and the prick she causes in my chest, I click on another folder. A few seconds later, I'm alone again.

There are what looks like dozens of documents, full of formulas. I go back to *SUBJECTS* and open it. There's a list of people's names. Some names have been marked with the strikethrough tool: Emily Knowles, Greg Lick, Cornelia Hass. The labels beside them read *Found* or *Failed.* Next to the untouched names—Travis Bardeen, Christine Masters—they become *Found* and *Submitted.* There are more, but I'm too eager to find information on my dad to scan all of them.

Then I find it. A mention of him. There are emails

between Dad and someone named Dr. Felix Stern. Each one is short and to the point: *My office today. Bring samples. Meet me at the lab. Pick Emily up at six o'clock. No research today. Doing the next test.* The dates occur every single day for three years, and then they abruptly stop just before the accident.

How did Dad know this man? What were they doing? And why wouldn't he tell his family about it? I rack my brain, trying to recall any conversations I overheard between him and Mom about this, but there's nothing.

I put Dr. Felix Stern into a search engine.

Results fill the screen. He's the only Felix Stern in the area . . . and he's a chemistry professor at Green River Community College, where Andrew works. Coincidence? Probably not. His office number is on the website. It's too late to call, so I rummage in my desk drawer for a pen, then scrawl his contact information down on my hand for tomorrow. Before I've even finished writing the last digit I'm back on the laptop, opening another one of the videos.

This one is different. It's in the lab, but there are shots of other people standing around the table. They watch as those gloved hands drop something red into the petri dish. One girl is holding a bandage against her upper arm. She raises her gaze, obviously anxious. The camera moves on to the boy standing beside her. His attention is glued to the table. Whoever is recording moves on again . . . and my stomach drops. This person I recognize. This person I've already learned not to trust.

Andrew stares back.

Throughout my classes, I'm so distracted I may as well have skipped. The lectures are barely a sound in the background, my friends are dull blurs in my peripheral vision, and for once the Emotions don't bother me. I keep going over it again and again: Andrew standing at that table. Andrew knowing about the flash drive and lunging for me. Every instinct I have urges me to drive to Green River and demand the truth, but all that gained me last time was bruises and betrayal. I could take one of his calls, but this isn't a conversation I want to have over the phone, and the sound of his voice would make me nauseated. The only person who can help me is the mysterious Dr. Stern, but he doesn't pick up any of the times I call.

After the last bell, Georgie finds me at my locker. Exasperation trails after her, a creature with rat's nest hair and permanently pursed lips. "We're meeting at the lake again," Georgie says, leaning her hip against the locker next to mine. She watches my movements with narrowed eyes, probably sensing the instant denial that rises up inside of me.

I sigh, leaving all my notebooks and textbooks because I know there's no chance I'm doing homework tonight. "Isn't there an easier way not to see Billy while actually seeing Billy?" *Slam.*

She ignores this, scanning the kids walking past us. I know the instant she spots Billy, because her entire face brightens. "The lake in ten minutes, or we'll hunt you down!" she tosses over her shoulder, flouncing away. Her perfume lingers even when she's gone.

Scowling, I start to compose a text to Missy. Halfway through, a new message comes in from Mark, saying he won't be able to make it to the bonfire but do I want to grab a cup of coffee next week? Resolving to respond later, I let my glance flick back to Georgie, at the end of the hall. Billy has his arm wrapped around her and she isn't fighting him. I wonder what changed. Just a couple weeks ago, her only interest was L.A. It seemed like nothing would distract her from that. Is attraction so inevitable? Or just that powerful?

Yet Revenge seems to have no trouble resisting me.

Text forgotten, I yank my jacket on so hard that the teeth of the zipper catches the skin of my palm. I suck in a breath. "Are you coming?" someone asks, rushing past. Briana. I nod, forcing a smile, and she beams. "Good. Meet you there in a little bit." Once again I have no chance to respond, because she's already at the doors, pushing them open, walking into the sunlight.

I stay where I am, watching the Emotions and my classmates hurrying by like some ocean made of limbs and hidden pains. I close my eyes... and when that familiar scent of chocolate washes over me, they snap open again.

Revenge smiles. "Hey."

That's all it takes. Just the sound of his voice. Suddenly I'm transported back to the attic, and those words he said surround me: *I will never give up on you.* For the thousandth time I lose myself in the fire of Revenge, and for the first time since I opened the flash drive, I forget about the shroud of mystery hanging over my father and the past.

"Hey," I say back, softly. Never before have I been so

tempted to touch him, to finally give in to wanting him. Images come hard and fast—us facing each other on my bed that dark night, the sweat beading our skin when we moved to the music on the record player, the way his eyes glowed that first night at Nate Foster's.

He thought I would choose him. Instead, I torture him. I'm a yo-yo, a metronome, a pendulum, everything vacillating and restless and infuriating. Maybe I've known all along why things have been changing between us. By not making a choice myself, I've left him no other choice.

Choice. My fingers twitch, just moments away from reaching for him. But then Forgiveness's face flashes in my mind, and I stop.

I tell myself there's no way Revenge can know what I'm thinking. It must show on my face, though, because his countenance darkens. A third chance to speak slips through my fingers like sand. Before I can repair what I didn't mean to break, he vanishes.

"Damn it!" I swear. Faith Carson gives me a funny look as she passes. She doesn't know what it is, to have someone and then begin to lose them. To believe that nothing can ever come between you, only for it to actually happen. Sighing again, I head for the parking lot.

Gray clouds gather above the mountain, great frowns in the sky. Wind flattens my shirt against my front. Hopefully it will start raining soon and Georgie will let me slip away. I point the unlock button at my car and the headlights flash. The smashed stump where the mirror used to be reminds me that Franklin isn't as safe as it once was, so I make sure to lock the doors again when I settle behind the wheel. Briana and Georgie are in Briana's car, already pulling out. Georgie leans out the window, her bright hair flying, and whoops. Billy honks his horn, and an amused smile tugs at the corners of my mouth.

One by one, like some kind of parade, they all get onto the road. I'm slower to follow. Every instinct urges me to turn the opposite way and find Dr. Stern. There's a line behind me, so I eventually turn, but once I'm on the county road I keep glancing in the rearview mirror, in the direction of Green River. The horizon has darkened even more. Is there really a point going to the lake?

There's no sign of the others; they must have sped ahead. Briana and Georgie are probably standing around the fire, talking and drinking and enjoying being young and alive. Maybe they wouldn't even—

In the mirror, something glints where before there was only trees and road. Frowning, I do a double-take.

There's a brown Taurus following me.

My heart stops. Once again Fear pays a visit, his freezing hand brushing the back of my neck when he tugs at my ponytail. As usual, he's there and gone in the space of a few seconds. Quickly I reach over and take the gun out of the glove box, my hand shaking. Then I press on the gas. Gravel spews under my tires and dust flies, filling the mirror and hiding the Taurus from view. My best chance is to get to the lake. Everything else is too far away. Distantly, I'm aware that Elvis is singing on as he always does. The world could end and Elvis would still be singing.

A sound rips through the chaos, a smattering of rocks against the side of the car. I jerk my head and see the Taurus alongside me, dangerously close. The man behind the steering wheel is wearing a ski mask. All I can see are his eyes, crinkled and bright as though he's smiling. I go faster, and he does too. Suddenly the Taurus veers and slams into me.

I scream, clutching the steering wheel tight. Some part of me realizes that my hands are empty; I must have dropped the gun. There's no chance to reach down and feel for it, because I know he's going to try to push me off the road. There's no ditch to cushion my fall, only hard, merciless trees. For a wild moment I consider slamming on the brakes or trying to surge ahead, but there's no time. The Taurus swings away and comes back with all the force of a battering ram.

I grit my teeth and yank the steering wheel back, just barely managing to stay on the gravel. Metal screeches on metal, and the inside of my door has begun to fold in. What do I do, what do I do? Can't call anyone, I'll be dead before they can—

The Taurus hits me again, and now he stays against my car. It takes all my strength to keep the wheel straight, and I'm not screaming anymore. Instead, another Emotion appears in the seat beside me. A hard, tiny smile flits across his thin lips as he tightly grips my shoulder. Rage crackles through me, making the blood boil in my veins, making me see red.

The man in the Taurus pulls away, readying for another strike. He thinks I'm weak. He thinks I'm content being a victim. Not this time. I do what I couldn't the night of the accident: I fight back.

I see Surprise touch my attacker just before I jerk the steering wheel to the left and shatter his world.

Maybe it was because of our ever-increasing velocity, or maybe my anger gave me strength he didn't have, but the damage is far more substantial from this collision. Those eyes behind the mask scrunch in pain just before he slams on the brakes. Without thinking I stop too, flying forward to search for the gun. It's next to my heel. Then I'm jumping out and swinging the barrel in the attacker's direction. He hurriedly shifts into reverse. Running at the Taurus, I fire off three shots. The sound of them is distant, as if someone else is pulling the trigger. *Bang. Bang. Bang.*

My aim is terrible. One hits his headlight. Glass sprinkles to the ground. One hits the grill. One hits the windshield, just to the right of the man's head.

Then another sound joins the gunshots, coming from him, but I'm so removed, so blinded by fury, that I don't know what it is. The Taurus, now whining, continues reversing and spins in a circle. Dust gets in my eyes and throat. I keep the gun raised. There's no point, though, because once the dust clears, he's gone. The wheeze of the engine fades. I stay where I am, the clouds still roiling above me. Geese honk and flap across the somber expanse, then they're gone, too.

There has never been a silence like this. So devastating, so confusing, so painful. No, that's a lie. There was one other silence similar to now. Though I try not to remember that night, I do remember being in the hospital room after, when Missy tearfully told me I was the only one left. I lay there beneath those mint-colored blankets, listening to the sound of my heart beating on the monitor, and I existed. I didn't absorb or process or think. Alex Tate was gone, and in that moment there was just a girl with skin and blood and bones and organs. I didn't recognize myself, and I don't now.

The adrenaline is leaving my veins, and soon I hear that sound again in my memory. The one coming from the man in the ski mask as I shot at him.

He was laughing.

Slowly, I return to my car. I get in, close the damaged door. Grip the steering wheel tight, as if I'm still fighting to stay on the road. The normal thing to do would be to call the sheriff. But those words are ringing in my head, paralyzing me: *Tell anyone about this, we go after your precious Saul and Missy next.* The threat probably applies to this situation as well.

So I don't call anyone. I don't cry. I just take a breath, shift gears, and drive the rest of the way to the lake.

At least now I know that I'm capable of using the gun.

FOURTEEN

Someone left their car doors open and the radio blaring, so Elvis is crooning to the entire lake when I get there. Joe must be in a wistful mood, because it's one of the ballads. I park and get out, thankful that my legs aren't shaking anymore. It's dark enough now that no one will notice the damage to my car unless they're looking for it. Georgie spots me right away. She's well on her way to getting drunk, because she leaves Billy and gives me a fierce hug.

"We won't give up on you, you know," she whispers in my ear. Her breath smells like beer. I pat her back and start to respond, but she's already flying away, back to her flock. A few of my classmates greet me, and I nod. Briana stands near the fire, the orange and black lights flickering over her face. She smiles and waves. I wave back and find the cooler. Just like every other time, I take out a can and go to a place empty of conversations or people. This time it's the shore. The sand is cold and damp, but I sit down anyway. I pop the lid on my beer and take a sip.

To keep myself from reliving what just happened on the road, I picture Revenge. The lyrics to the song echo across the still-thawing waters. Images of my friend change to memories of sitting outside the Fosters' house with him beside me. All the expectations, all the promises.

Suddenly Forgiveness is here, wrists dangling on his knees as he looks out over the lake. It's my fault, really, for thinking about Nate Foster and how old he looked hiding in his car that night.

"Change is the law of life," Forgiveness says. Usually he lets us have a few moments of quiet. "And those who look only to the past or present are certain to miss the future." Finished, he looks at me and sees my questioning frown. "John F. Kennedy."

I focus on a house in the distance, old man Holland's place. There's a local myth that he's really a ghost, but the stench surrounding him when he visits the diner says otherwise. Like me, Holland has lost most of the family he had left in the world. Just his bottle and his bitterness. Am I on my way to becoming him?

"Never had something from the other plane quote a president at me," I comment, hiding my thoughts as best I can.

"Someone."

I frown and turn my head toward Forgiveness again. "What?"

"You said 'something.' The correct term is 'someone.'" He meets my gaze, unflinching.

Suddenly my rage awakens again. It wasn't gone, it was just waiting for an opportunity. "Well, to quote *you*, nothing from the other plane is human," I counter, forgetting my own convictions that Revenge is different. Too late, I realize that I'm raising my voice, and glance over my shoulder to make sure no one has noticed. Billy is telling a story, and everyone is laughing. The only one who stands apart from them is Briana, and she's looking up at the sky. Probably searching for constellations despite the approaching storm. She loves finding meaning in something as vast as space. Watching her, the anger within me dims again. The world can't be entirely bad with someone like her in it.

Forgiveness's voice brings my attention back to him: "... is that dog you've been leaving food for," he says. "But you don't think she's just an animal, or you wouldn't be—"

"Have you been watching me?" I demand. No one knows about the stray, not even Revenge. Sometimes I wonder if she's real or just something I conjured up so I don't feel so alone.

The Choice doesn't answer, which is answer enough. He sits there concentrating on the lethargic waves as though they're speaking to him, telling him just how to get under my skin.

I don't know what to say, so I let out a breath and hug my legs tighter. "Prove it. Prove that you have some kind of... individuality. Come on."

For the first time, he hesitates. He doesn't respond. The pause stretches and thins and I start to think he has no answer to give, but then he leans forward. His voice drops and he looks out at that house across the water. "Sometimes . . . I get tired of being what I am," he whispers.

I'm so surprised that I forget to be annoyed, and our gazes collide. "Really?"

"Really. Sometimes I envy you humans. Your ability to choose, your chance to leave marks on the world, your opportunities to become more." There's a wistful note to the words, making it impossible to doubt him.

I want to say that it's not as wonderful as he makes it sound. Instead I hear myself say, "You leave marks on the world, Forgiveness."

At this, he smiles. There's a pleased light in his eyes and something in my chest flutters, as though my heart has become a butterfly in a jar. Once more I check to make sure no one is observing our exchange. No; we're alone, even with a crowd just a few yards away.

Feeling reckless, I turn my body toward Forgiveness. Somehow the mood between us has changed, and I don't resent his presence so much. Forgiveness shifts closer, too, his palm sinking into the sand. Pictures touch my mind. Two old women clasping hands over a bingo table, a child kissing a baby on the forehead, some teenage boys roughing each other up on a basketball court. Sobering, I huddle into myself again. It's getting colder, and now faint plumes of air leave my mouth. I polish off the last of the beer. Thunder rumbles.

Finished, I wipe my mouth off with the back of my sleeve and toss the empty can to the sand. It doesn't make a sound. Time is running out; I can feel it. Soon the sky will open up and drench the mountain with its tears, and everyone will run for their cars. They'll go home to their families, make hot chocolate, and remain blissfully unaware. I could go back to Saul and Missy, I really could... but I know I won't. The call of Nate Foster is too strong.

"I feel like you've already given me the speech a million times," I murmur to Forgiveness, a lump swelling in my throat. Maybe tonight will be the night. "Aren't you getting sick of it?"

"Never."

The word makes me remember, again, that moment in the attic with Revenge. My stomach flutters as I picture how close his mouth was to mine, how our bodies were a breath away from touching. It hardens me against Forgiveness.

"How long have you been around?" I ask, without turning my head. "A thousand years? A million? You've watched us, and changed us, but have you really learned anything about us?"

It seems like no matter what I say, I can't ruffle him. "Yes," he replies, so simply that I know he believes it. His dark eyes radiate sincerity.

I hate it. I want him to be as uncertain as I am. To be as lost as me, as lost as my father's rocket. "What could you really know about losing your family?" I challenge. "You've never had one."

Forgiveness sighs and looks away. The wind toys with his curls. "I know what it is to lose someone I love, Alex."

"Really? You're capable of love?" I ask, trying to sound mocking. The words come out as cautious things, though. Then Hope betrays me, squatting next to us and smoothing my hair back. She's an Emotion I rarely let close, a plain creature who is somehow beautiful, even with the unexplained scars on her face. Her eyes are sympathetic. She knows how I think of Revenge, and how hopeless it is for us to have any kind of future. I wish I could shove her away.

"I'm capable of everything you are," Forgiveness says, nodding politely to Hope. She smiles just before disappearing. "Pain, longing, anger. Even more so, because I exist on the same plane as all of them."

The imprint of Hope's hand lingers, a sensation like someone put a branding iron on my skin. I clench my fists, and if I had nails they would leave marks. I've been chewing them lately. "But you don't know what it is to watch your father die," I say through my teeth. "Your mother. Your brother." There's movement in the distance, something small and dark. Loons. They came back even when spring didn't. I focus on the ripples they create in the frosty water. One of the loons suddenly releases a mournful cry into the night. "I can't let myself remember that day. I think I'd lose what's left of my sanity. I can remember everything else, though. The sound of Dad's laugh. The smell of my mom's perfume. My little brother . . . " I swallow. "My little brother . . . "

Alex! Alex! The exact details of his face may be slipping away, but I'll never forget the sound of his voice the first time he said my name. He was sitting in his high chair, Cheerios stuck to his chin. He beamed at me, and Mom gasped with wonder and pride. The memory causes a sharp pain to grow in my chest, as though a knife protrudes from the inside, and I blink rapidly. One of the loons stares back at me, drifting close enough to the shore that I can see the droplets glistening on its black feathers.

"Tell me about them," Forgiveness says. He's asked before, without success, but something has changed. This time I don't lash out. I don't try to get a rise out of him or push him away. Instead I do it. I talk. About my father's booming laugh, my mother's gentle hands, my brother's first steps. All the while the loon draws nearer, as if it wants to hear, too.

When I'm out of breath, out of words, Forgiveness continues to look at me instead of the bird. I don't look back at him, but I can feel the weight of his gaze. "You have Saul and Missy. You haven't lost everything," he tells me gently. It doesn't matter; the words could be made of air and they would still feel like fists.

"When you say things like that, it's just a reminder."

"A reminder of what?"

I get up, sand sticking to my clothes. Forgiveness remains seated and tilts his head back. "That you really aren't human, no matter how easy it is to forget," I tell him.

Briana starts toward me but gets waylaid by one of Billy's friends, Dylan. Even with the wind in my ears, I can hear the slur in his voice. I turn around so they can't see my face. This is the part of the night when I should walk away, or shift gears, or end the conversation. Yet I don't move. Why do I stay, when every part of me insists I should go?

Because I always stay.

Now Forgiveness stands, his white T-shirt flapping against his torso. He's so close I can feel his breath on my cheek again.

Maybe he's more human than I thought. Heartbeats. Lungs. Those are for the living. Aren't they?

No, not always. Because I have them.

The Choice bends to say the words directly into my ear. "You can blame it on Nate Foster, you can blame it on my kind, and you can even blame yourself. But none of it will bring them back."

Missy said almost the exact same thing once. My jaw works, and the knife isn't stabbing now—it's tearing through me. My soul bleeds. "Don't you think I know that?" I ask, trying to keep my voice even.

"Do you?" He waits, but this time I'm the one who doesn't respond. I cross my arms as a weak shield against the wind. Behind us, the bonfire crackles in a desperate attempt to remain bright and burning. Seconds pass, and the only ones who speak are my friends, their conversations empty and light. Their universes are planets of homework and routine and somedays. Someone is yodeling.

"You can't trust him," Forgiveness says suddenly. There's no need to clarify who he means, but he does anyway. "Revenge has been among us longer than anyone realizes. *The Count of Monte Cristo* isn't entirely fiction. And he was at the center of the St. Bartholomew's Day Massacre. He was there at the beginning of the War of the Roses, and when the Roman Empire—"

I feel my nostrils flare. "I get it, okay? He's selfish and impulsive and dangerous. But he's not as bad as you think. He's my..." I stop, start again. "He'll always be there for me, no matter what I choose."

At this, Forgiveness falters. He never falters. I know I'm not going to like what he's about to say. For a moment I think about bolting. But then he's opening his mouth, and words are coming out, and it's too late to escape them. "The thing about choices is that they only exist as long as there's one to make," he says slowly.

Briana has managed to disentangle herself from Dylan and is coming toward the shore again. She's smiling, and the space between us shrinks. Forgiveness and I are out of time. Though I want to see his eyes when he answers, I focus on the loon while I force myself to ask, "What are you saying? That you'll vanish the instant I choose one of you?"

Again he hesitates, and I swallow the hysterical scream that wants to demand the truth *right now*. More seconds tick by, marked by the teeth-grinding silence. Just as I'm about to let the scream out—damn whoever hears—Forgiveness sighs. "Essentially, yes," he says, his tone reluctant. He rakes a hand through his dark hair. Is that regret in his expression?

I don't have a chance to find out; Briana is nearly upon us, and I finally turn to her. But Forgiveness isn't done. "Unlike Emotions, we are only allowed near a human before and during the summons. Afterwards, we're gone. It's just the way things are." The words should be hard, absolute, yet there's a shadow of imploring in them.

I don't—can't—acknowledge it. All I can do is think, *Revenge didn't tell me that*. No, he *lied* to me. He said ... he said ... what *did* he say, exactly?

I'll be here when you need me, and I'll help you get what you want.

I will never give up on you.

When you've really made your choice, I'll know, and that's the moment I'm free to touch you.

But each of those statements could apply to the choice itself. Revenge never actually promised to stay with me once the choice was made. Suddenly everything has a new, darker meaning. *Why do you want to kiss me?* He never responded. Well, I have my answer now. Best friend? No. Revenge? Yes. That's what he is, that's what he's always been. I was an idiot to let myself believe otherwise. Once I make this impossible decision—even if I choose him—he'll leave my life forever.

"Hey, you."

Though I've been expecting it, the sound of Briana's voice still makes me jump. My blood pumps faster and harder as I open my mouth to greet my friend, attempting to hide the fury that's reared it's beautiful-hideous head again.

" . . . think it's a good idea, Billy," Georgie is saying, the wind carrying the worried statement to us. Briana reaches me and turns at the same time I do.

"I think it's a great idea!" Billy slings his arm around Georgie's neck and steers her toward his truck. She's so drunk she can barely stay standing. How long was I talking to Forgiveness? Everyone is suddenly running to their cars. Someone trips and no one helps him up. There are a few Emotions among the group, but not as many as usual; alcohol numbs us. Maybe that's why we like it so much.

"What's going on?" I ask Briana, momentarily forgetting Revenge and his betrayal. I take one step in Georgie's direction, wondering if I should intervene. She hates it when we do that, though. Worry is here, twitching between us and touching our backs with hesitant fingers. The wind is getting stronger and the sky is even darker.

Frowning, Briana just shakes her head, but Faith is grabbing the cooler and overhears me. "They've got it in their heads to go to the mines," she answers, glowering. Her cross glints in the dying firelight. "See who's brave enough to go in."

The door to Billy's truck slams, and then the headlights flick on. Too late, Briana starts to run toward them. "Georgie, wait!" she calls, her voice rising in panic. Billy just laughs and reverses. I can see Georgie's silhouette as she drapes herself over his shoulder. He must have rolled down the window, because the sound of her drunken "Star-Spangled Banner" drifts through the air just before the truck drives out of view.

Seething, Briana runs back to the shoreline and seizes my wrist. "Idiots!" she hisses, tugging at me. We head for her car. The interior smells like pot when I get in. Ethan did just borrow it, after all. Usually Briana tries to cover up the smell with perfume, but tonight she just starts the engine and follows the parade, a line deepening between her eyebrows. "This is so stupid. The boards are probably rotting in there. Even when the mines were functioning, they never let us—"

"It'll be okay. We'll get Georgie." I may not have drunk much, but it doesn't really sink in until right now how badly this could go. Suddenly a new fear presents itself. I stare at the taillights ahead of us, trying not to let it show how anxious I am. Everyone left in a hurry; there are probably a lot of drunk drivers on the road. Wobbling, squinting, slurring. A vile taste surges up in the back of my throat and I turn my head to force it back down. And in that moment, the rain begins to come down. It doesn't begin with the gentle pitter-patter it usually does, the gradual increase of ferocity. The downpour lashes at the side of the car. Briana switches her wipers on, swearing under her breath. She never swears.

While I'm watching her, trying to think of how I can stop the night from spiraling out of control, I hear it again.

Alexandra.

I'm looking right at Briana when it happens, and she doesn't even blink. The voice really is entirely in my head. There's something so familiar about it, so infuriatingly out of reach. Gritting my teeth, I twist away and concentrate on the rivulets of water quivering down the glass. Revenge said I wasn't crazy, but I can't trust anything he says. Not anymore. Maybe this unraveling isn't just because of Nate Foster or the choice.

William, don't.

Madness has touched my family before.

"They probably won't do it," Briana says, almost to herself. "They'll chicken out."

Thunder shudders through the mountain again. We're getting closer. Even if the sign wasn't there, announcing the truth of it in glowing letters, I would know. There's a sensation in the marrow of my bones, not just dread or fear or worry—it's like I'm about to step onto that rickety elevator myself and plunge into the darkness.

The mines. The mines. I'm remembering that moment in my room again, when I heard something besides my name.

I've tried to convince myself it was one of those waking dreams, something that felt real but couldn't be.

But in this moment, I know the mines aren't empty.

My best friend is chewing her lip so hard her teeth are taking skin. To fill the black hole of silence sucking us in, I blurt, "Billy's dumb enough. He might. He won't get far, since the elevator is shut off. But there is a ladder beside it, for emergencies. It's made of metal. It'll probably hold his weight. My dad took me down a couple times, so I might be able to remember the tunnels if someone gets lost." I keep babbling, managing to distract one of us, at least. My words are only making things worse for Briana.

Fear is sitting in the backseat, eyes closed, nostrils flaring as he inhales the scent of our mutual terror. One corner of his mouth tilts up in a tiny smile. Images flit from Briana's mind to mine. She's picturing Georgie on the ladder, the whites of her eyes bright in the gloom as she clutches the bars. Then her foot slips. She falls. The sound of her scream echoes in my ears.

"Briana," I breathe, wanting it to stop. "Don't worry. Nothing bad is going to happen."

"How do you know?" she whispers. Her grip on the steering wheel is as tight as mine is when I'm sitting in front of Nate Foster's house.

Fear is gone, yet it's still difficult to speak. My tongue feels thick and dry, as though it's made of cotton. "I promise. Okay? You know I never break a promise."

She glances at me. "You don't."

"So you have to believe me. I'll take care of everything.

I'll make sure. All right? You just stay in the car and wait for me to bring Georgie back." I take one of her hands off the wheel and lace our fingers together, wishing that strength was something that could be shared through air or skin.

Briana opens her mouth to protest, but the mines come into view and we both go silent, trying to assess the situation. Her grip tightens painfully as we park behind the chain stretched over the road. The others must have lifted it and gone under; I can see fresh tire tracks in the mud. Though it's hard to tell through the glittering curtain of rain, there are dim shadows moving next to the mines. Billy is really going to do this.

A fresh sense of urgency surges through my veins, and I secretly welcome the distraction from the choice, the unknown, the past. With one last, reassuring glance at Briana, I get out of the car. She says something I don't hear just before the door closes.

The downpour is relentless. It pounds at me, making my clothes stick to my body in a sopping mess. Ducking beneath the chain, I shield my eyes and slosh through a puddle toward the entrance. There they are. Billy and his friends parked right by the mouth. They all have flashlights, beacons that guide me to where they stand. Georgie must have lost her enthusiasm when the storm started, because she's still in the truck, watching us.

I go up to Billy and resist the urge to shove him into the rock wall. "This isn't funny!" I yell, pushing my hair out of the way, snagging my eyebrow ring in the process. They all turn to me. "Let's just get out of here and go to the diner. My treat!"

"Yeah, right!" Billy grins, and a drop of rain slides into the gap between his front teeth. "We're going in. Dylan dared me to touch the pick!"

The pick. It's on display in one of the tunnels, the very first tool ever used in these mines. Dad took me down to see it once. It was so rusted and moldy I hadn't wanted to touch it.

"Are you insane?" I snap, swiping at my nose impatiently. "The pick is on the other side of the mines, by the entrance they closed up. Even the workers didn't use that tunnel anymore!"

This just strengthens the gleam in Billy's eyes. He brushes past me and starts for the entrance. I stay where I am, trying to decide what to do. Then lightning flashes, illuminating everything for a moment. But it's long enough to see it, to realize what I'm looking at.

Someone is standing in the entrance to the mines.

Instinctively I blink, convinced it's a hallucination or a dream. But it doesn't disappear. The voice speaks in my head again, louder and more clearly than ever before. *Alexandra.*

Suddenly I can move again, and I stumble back so quickly my heel catches on a rock and I fall. Dylan says my name, reaches for me. Billy has stopped, but I barely notice. "No, no, no ... " I keep scooting away, terror exploding in my chest. The palms of my hands tear on the gravel. Yet I can't take my eyes away from it. The form is broad-shouldered and tall. There's no way to mistake it for the gangly boys surrounding me. The darkness swallows his face, and though there's nothing to give it away, I *know* this thing isn't human. What is it? *What is it?*

A door slams in the distance, and then warm, solid arms are wrapping around me and helping me up. "Alex, what's wrong?" a voice shouts in my ear. This one I know. Briana. Finally I shift my gaze to look up at her and rain gets in my eyes. I blink again, and when I glance back at the entrance, it's empty. Whoever—*whatever*—was standing there is gone.

"I know you're still there," I whisper.

Briana puts her head next to mine. "What?"

That's when I comprehend that everyone is staring at me. Georgie is outside, huddling next to Billy and shivering. Even she looks bewildered, and she's accustomed to all my peculiarities. Trembling, I stand up. My wounded palms ache and sting.

"I'm freezing. Let's get out of here," I say, clenching my fists to hide the scrapes. The others seem to agree. The boys shut their flashlights off and trudge to their vehicles, muttering about me. Georgie extends her hand, her expression conflicted, but I walk away. *We won't give up on you.* They should. They will. One way or another, the pieces of me will keep falling until there's nothing left.

I get into Briana's car, and a few seconds later the two of them follow. The seats are soaking and I listen to them squeak as they settle, notes in harmony with the thunder and rain. The engine idles, adding to the noise that blocks all my thoughts.

"Alex?" Briana says, looking at me as if I'm about to detonate. Maybe I am.

"I'm not drunk," I say dully, leaning my forehead against the cool window. "You can drive me back to my car."

Still, no one moves. Georgie clears her throat. "I'm sorry I went with Billy. I-I know how you feel about... about driving when..."

"It's fine, Georgie."

She stops talking. The wordlessness becomes so thick it feels like the air itself has become solid. Nothing is distracting me now. I want to tell them everything about the other plane and the memories resurfacing about my father. I wish I could talk about the attacks and the betrayals. I yearn to reveal how I sit outside a house on Sanderson Road almost every night. But I don't. I don't say anything at all.

Briana shifts gears and drives.

It isn't until we're back at the lake that someone actually speaks again. Her voice floats from the darkness of the backseat, sounding just as broken as I feel. "You guys don't have to call me Georgiana anymore."

Then she vomits.

FIFTEEN

The flag over the shop doorway snaps in the wind. The storm may have subsided for a few minutes, but it's far from over.

I park my whining car, slam the door, and run up the stairs. The boards beneath my feet quake with every step. Angus stares at me from his window, something suspiciously like fear in his eyes. A dog barks in the distance. As I reach for the doorknob, the memory of that silhouette in the mouth of the mine presses in, along with the knowledge of Revenge's betrayal. So much is happening that I don't understand, so much is going on that I can't control. I want to take my gun and shoot Nate Foster until he can't haunt me anymore, but Forgiveness is there, hounding me every time I think about doing it. A scream is building up inside of me, higher and hotter and horrible in its intensity, but I can't let it out.

In the entryway, I sit on the bench and yank my boots off. They leave trails of water on the floor. Then I'm standing, barely aware that all the lights are on and the sound of my aunt's worried voice drowns out the television. Before I can escape to my room, Missy rushes out of the kitchen, the phone in her hand. That's when I realize that my cell is ringing in my pocket. I hadn't even heard it. Not once.

"Alex," she breathes, stopping. Saul comes up behind her and wraps his arm around her shoulders. Relief and Anger and Worry crowd around them, watching me with luminous eyes like rats in the dark. I want to launch myself at them, claw those eyes out.

" . . . can't just vanish and expect us to be okay with it!" Missy is saying. She pushes a wet strand of hair away from her forehead, and that's when I notice her clothes are just as wet as mine. They must have gone looking for me. My stomach sinks as I realize that I forgot to send the text. "We were worried. We're responsible for you, and—"

"You're not my mom."

It feels like I'm floating above us, looking down, watching the words leave my mouth. Regret and Guilt instantly appear, surrounding me with their strange scents and assaulting me with their big hands, but it's too late.

Saul's face is thunderous. His entire body tenses, and I flinch. He doesn't hit me, though. He wants to, I can tell, and I deserve it. But Saul is a good man. "Alexandra, you do not talk to your aunt that way," he growls. A vein stands out on his temple.

A fraught silence falls between us. We can hear the town clock, always ticking and marking time even when it feels like time should stop. *Dong. Dong. Dong.* The rain begins again, tapping against the window over the sink. I imagine the voice in my head speaking in the language of those taps, whispering *let me in, let me in.* Saul and Missy wait and stare, expecting some kind of reaction. They look like two mannequins, plastic and fake and unmoving. We all do. For a moment I just stare at them blankly, wondering how this has happened.

I'm the first to become human again. This time, though, instead of trying to glue the pieces of us back together, I choose to say nothing. I squeak and drip down the hallway and into my room. Missy calls after me. I shut the door on her concern and turn the lock. The carpet is drenched, and a moment later I feel the bite of wind over my skin. Frowning, I turn. The window is open again. I didn't leave it that way. But if someone was looking through my things again, I can't tell—my room was messy to begin with. So much has happened today that I can only feel an overwhelming sense of exhaustion and resentment.

The Emotion stands in front of me, touching my chin. I tilt my head back so it rests against the door and ask him, "Which is worse, do you think? Feeling everything, or feeling nothing?"

"Feeling nothing," Resentment answers without hesitation, his hairless scalp gleaming. "The most painful emotions are better than none at all. Ironically, we make you human."

Absorbing this, I brush past him to close the window. When I turn around he's gone, so I sit on the bed. The mattress springs squeak. Dampness penetrates my blankets and sheets from my clothes, but it doesn't matter. The glint of

Saul and Missy's birthday gift taunts me for the hundredth time, and I finally shove it into the nightstand drawer.

Through the wall, I can hear Angus's parents—Doug and Tina—fighting. That must be why Angus was watching for me. Another prick of guilt sends pain through my bones, and I sit with my back to the wall, looking at a jar on the floor and ignoring the current Emotion leaning over me. The jar had been in the art room at school, so vacant and forlorn; I couldn't leave it there, not when I knew someone who would want it, give it a purpose. Whatever purpose Angus has for his empty jars. Somehow, though, I know there is one. I'll give it to him soon ... as something to remember me by.

"I don't care if you've been working all day! You think I'm not tired? Just pick up your shit. I'm not a fucking maid." Angus's mom must be in his room, since her voice is closer than usual. Her husband answers, the words muffled, but it has the effect of poison: lethal and instant. She shrieks back.

Their anger is too much for me to handle tonight, so I lean over and fumble for my laptop, intending to do more research on the flash drive. But then something across the room moves, and I look up. My reflection in the blank television screen stares back. It waits in the corner, expectant.

Outside, lightning flares and fades. I get up and go to that ancient television, kneel in front of it. My fingers suddenly have a mind of their own as they turn it on and press a button on the VCR. The video hasn't been touched in months. Part of me expects it to be gone, as if the machine would try just as hard as me to avoid the memories and swallow the tape whole to do so. But seconds later there's a crackling sound, and my little brother's face fills the screen. My heart simultaneously soars and crashes.

"Mommy, tell her to stop!" Hunter shrieks. The camera is zoomed in on him, and he writhes with both agony and laughter as I dig my fingers into his side. But the camera just shakes as our mother joins us, and then it is all three of us on the bed in a tangle of arms and legs. I watch us, feeling a smile curve my lips.

For just a minute, my family is alive again. Nothing else exists. Something shimmers beside me, and I don't even care when a gentle hand settles on the top of my head. The smell of dandelions permeates the air, and the most dizzying sensation grips me. Joy. But she's not the only one that comes; Sorrow has returned. They hover, their essences unrelenting and not entirely unwelcome. The size of my room and the strength of their apathy make the gust of feeling all the more poignant. Tears sting in my eyes. Releasing a ragged breath, I reach out to brush my brother's round face, the sounds of his voice a lullaby that will help me sleep tonight. I'm so lost in them that it's jarring when my hand collides with the hard, cruel reality of the television.

As swiftly as she came, Joy is gone. All I see of her is a glimpse of red hair.

Sorrow and I look at each other. I don't tell him to go, I don't scream my hatred. Words have never seemed more impossible or inadequate. Which is why shock vibrates through me when Sorrow murmurs, "They are beautiful." The words are rough and raspy, like he hasn't spoken in years. And then he's gone, too.

Beautiful. I focus on the screen again, clenching my fists in the sheets. This is why I don't let myself watch it. The rush might be exhilarating, but the fall is devastating. I'm torn in half by conflicting urges: to keep watching or smash the television into a hundred jagged pieces.

"Do you give up?" the other me demands, static making hair cling to her forehead. Hunter manages to get out a yes and our mother kisses his cheek. The screen goes blue and the stillness rings in my ears.

Just like the night of the accident, they're here one moment and gone the next.

My first instinct is to turn on the loudest, most violent music I have, or open the window again and let the storm rip the room apart. Anything louder than the pain. Yet I don't move; I just concentrate on the blueness and see their faces. "I know I promised," I finally whisper, feeling as if something inside me has exploded and I'm bleeding, bleeding, dying. I trace the place where my mom's eye crinkles were, leaving the smear of fingerprints, and for the first time I take comfort in the fact that my family isn't really here. They're only on the screen, where they can't see what I've become.

Saturday dawns warm and bright, which is unfortunate, since I'm grounded. At least I assume I am, given last night and the fact that Saul saw my car this morning. I couldn't tell him what really happened, so I told him I rammed into a telephone pole trying not to hit a deer. He didn't say a word. He just took a sip of his coffee, dumped it in the sink, and walked out. Missy still hasn't left their room.

I sit on the bottom step outside, watching the wind stir the treetops. A bird flies past. Long weeds sway beside the railing. My cell phone is next to me, silent after another unanswered call to Dr. Stern and an ignored call from Andrew. I glance down at the screen, and the moment I do, it lights up. The caller ID won't let me pretend or avoid. His name glares up at me in bright capital letters: *ANDREW.*

"Who you dodging?"

A shadow falls over the ground by my feet, and I jump. It takes a moment for my eyes to adjust and recognize the face standing over me. "Oh, hey, Erskine. What are you doing here?"

The town mechanic spots my car and walks over to it. There's a toolbox clenched in one of his hairy fists. "Your uncle told me about your mirror. Thought I'd come out and take a look at it, since I'm having a slow day. Not much I can do about the other damage, though." He squats and opens the box, winking at me. His gray ponytail gleams and his red tank top is stained with motor oil.

"Thanks." I smile.

"So who's getting the cold shoulder, if you don't mind my asking?" He nods toward my phone, screwdriver in hand.

I hesitate, watching him take the remains of the mirror off. Erskine's always been a gossip and he'll just keep asking. So I eventually sigh and say, "Andrew Lomenta." *Please don't ask me why.* I don't have a good lie prepared.

An Emotion materializes beside the mechanic. Fear. He

grins in my direction while his slender fingers grip Erskine's shoulder. " ... know he was your old man's best friend and all, but I would stay away from that one," he's saying.

I blink and Fear is gone. Erskine's words register. "Wait, why? How do you know him?"

He doesn't answer. Suddenly, all his attention is riveted to his task as he pulls another mirror out of the box—it's a different color than my Saturn—and attaching it. Recalling something my father once told me, I frown. The details are fuzzy and slow in coming, but they do come.

"That's right, he grew up around here," I say. "Dad told me he moved away when he was a teenager, but I keep forgetting. What did Andrew do to you?"

Strangely enough, blabbermouth Erskine has clammed up. "Never mind, it was a long time ago," he mutters, his tools clattering and the lid slamming down. He's already finished. Usually it takes Erskine forever to do a job because the talking distracts him. "Just ... be careful. And come by the shop to get the rest of your car looked at." He stands and strides back to his truck, boots crunching on the gravel.

I start to stand too, still confused. "Okay, well, how much do I owe you for—"

"Don't worry about it. I'll see you around, all right?" Without another word, Erskine tosses his toolbox into the passenger seat, revs the engine to life, and roars down the road.

Strange, I think again. Maybe Erskine borrowed some of Ethan Brinkman's stash. He always gets edgy when he's on something.

Silence and boredom return. I could go look for Dad's

rocket, or plug in the flash drive, or finish cleaning the attic. Instead I stay where I am, tapping my foot and squinting. Part of me knows that I'm waiting for him. For Revenge. Hoping and hating. Friendship is a habit that's not easily broken. But the other part of me doesn't want to admit it, so this—sitting here, allowing my world to crumble around me—is nothing more than enjoying the warmth of the sun on my skin.

An ant makes its way up my leg, and I let it get as far as my knee before flicking it off. The conversation with Forgiveness goes around and around in my head like the record player Revenge found in the attic:

The thing about choices is that they only exist as long as there's one to make.

What are you saying? That you'll vanish the instant I choose one of you?

Essentially, yes. Unlike Emotions, we are only allowed near a human before and during the summons. Afterwards, we're gone. It's just the way things are.

If there was any phrase I could obliterate from existence, it's that one. Just the way things are.

The stillness is disrupted again by a bush across the road rustling. At first I think it's the wind growing fiercer, but it happens again and something darts behind a tree. Apprehension appears in the empty space beside me, staring into the forest with wild eyes and holding my wrist so tightly it hurts. My throat is suddenly dry, and I tell myself it's nothing but a squirrel or a deer; there may be shady characters in Franklin, but they act under the cover of night. Day should be safe. The sun should keep bad things away.

Another shadow moves. I begin to stand; whether to confront it or run, I don't know.

The stray dog steps into the open.

The Emotion dissipates and I release a long breath, silently instructing my heart to calm. The stray hesitates at the edge of the road, her ears flattened in fear. The food I've been leaving out hasn't seemed to make a difference; if anything, she looks worse than before. Now Compassion materializes, her dark hair tickling my nose as she presses her temple against mine. For a moment we breathe together, and I find myself yet again unable to summon hatred for a creature from the other plane.

In the distance, a bird sings. Even this intimidates my visitor, obvious by the way she tenses. Slowly, praying she won't bolt, I lower myself back to the step. The dog watches me with wide eyes that remind me of Apprehension. I try to go completely still, but the need to move, to twitch, to tap is constant, so I pretend to be interested in a rock by my shoe. I reach down to touch its smooth surface. For eleven seconds, we stay like this. Her staring and evaluating, me aching to show this damaged animal some kindness. It's a strange sensation, allowing this part of myself to shine through when I've become so accustomed to keeping it smothered in the darkness.

She takes one step closer. Then another. And another.

I barely dare to breathe. It seems like the only sound on the mountain is the skitter of dirt every time the pads of her feet touch the ground. I keep my gaze glued to that rock. Its image is imprinted on my brain now. When I close my eyes tonight I'll see it, the gray ridges and pitted texture. Then a black nose comes into view, and she's so close I could bury my fingers in her tangled fur. But I don't; the only way something can truly come to you is from its own choice.

Choice.

Before the vacuum of bleak thoughts can suck me in, my new friend cautiously sniffs the back of my hand. The beginnings of a smile tug at the corners of my mouth, and I forget Revenge and Forgiveness and all the rest. For the moment, at least. "You picked a fine time to show up," I whisper, showing her my empty hands in a slow movement. Her scent reaches me, and it's so awful I have to make a conscious effort not to cover my nose. "I would go get something from the fridge, but it's kind of a war zone in there right now. It's my fault, of course." The dog edges forward some more, ears perked as though she's really interested. I purse my lips, imagining Missy lying in bed, Saul fiddling with gadgets in a piano, just to keep their fears and pains at bay. Fears and pains I've caused.

The dog bumps her head against my wrist, probably aiming for my hand or too timid to, and I oblige by scratching her ear. She closes her eyes in pure bliss, as though no one has ever touched her before. It makes me feel... guilty. For being so consumed by losing my family when there are some who never had one to begin with. But I can't think like that, not if I'm going to keep my promise to them and make the right choice.

"Maybe it's a good thing that I'm hurting them," I add quietly, envisioning the moment when I finally open that red door. "It'll make it easier when . . . when I finally go into Foster's house. Right?"

Alexandra.

The dog lets out a yelp, and before I can comfort her she tucks her tail between her legs and runs.

She heard it, too.

This isn't happening. It's the same thing I've told myself every other time the voice rips through my head. It doesn't work now, though. Not after what I saw in the mines. Suddenly a gust of wind tries to blow me away, the strength of it out of place when there's only been a serene breeze to disturb the leaves.

Still raw from the incidents on the road and at the mines, still brittle from the realization that my best friend doesn't love me, I feel something inside me just snap. *"What do you want?"* I scream, clutching my head.

There's no hesitation. No, there's almost a sense of . . . *eagerness* in the response. *The mines. The mines.*

It's no longer a hiss or a whisper. The voice is distinctly male, and it must be gaining strength or confidence, because I've never been able to discern that before. Fear and Resentment follow me as I jump up and storm to the front of the shop. "You want me? Fine!" I yank my bike upright and swing my leg over it. Saul must be keeping an eye on the windows, because the bell over the door jangles as he rushes out, shouts my name. *There's no point,* I want to shout back. *Let me go.* But that's what love is: holding on and holding tight no matter what. Through death, through pain, through everything. There's a part of me that wants to turn back and be worthy of it. I'm standing on the edge of that bridge, though, and I'm tilting forward. Falling. There is no turning back.

It's seven miles to the mines. By the time the warnings appear on my right, my thighs and lungs burn. Hysteria bubbles up inside of me and bursts out in breathless laughter. I keep going, inexplicably drawn to this place. Then I crest the hill, and there's the entrance.

It has an air of expectancy surrounding it. I tip the bike to the side and get off violently, letting it crash to the ground. I stand a few yards away from the leering darkness and raise my voice. "Well? Here I am! You wanted this. *Now show your fucking face.*" My chest heaves.

Nothing. Seconds pass. In the daylight, the mines don't seem so terrifying or mysterious. If I tried hard enough, I could convince myself that I hadn't seen anything last night.

As tranquility presses in, making me doubt that what I saw was real, my fury begins to fade. Birds continue to call to each other and the treetops murmur and the sky is so blue it's almost mocking. What did I expect? Sammy Thorn to come sauntering out, have a conversation about his hobby of taking children? I raise a shaking hand to push my hair out of the way. Revenge was wrong—I have truly, deeply, utterly lost my sanity.

Manic laughter is rising up inside me again. It's a moment away from bursting into the clearing… but then something moves. The laugh dries up like one of Francis's flowers. I stare.

This is not a stray dog or some leaves.

The same silhouette emerges from the shadows, stopping just in front of a shaft of sunlight. And this time, I can see his face. The features have become fuzzy in my memory, but the edges become sharp and clear once again. My stomach drops, my heart explodes, my head becomes a balloon that floats up into that blue sky. Suddenly Emotions are everywhere, reaching for me, offering commentary in a blend of different voices and expressions that I don't hear or see. Disbelief, Surprise, Joy, Wonder, Denial.

When I finally manage to speak, I sound like the child I was the last time I saw him. "Daddy?"

SIXTEEN

"Alex!"

Briana smiles, surprised but happy to see me. Her smile quickly dies when she sees my face. "What is it? What happened?" Blind to the presence of the Emotions, she pulls me inside her house, her skin the only warm spot on my icy skin. I can hear Joe's station playing on their old radio. Briana stays by the doorway and waits for me to respond. It must be later than I realized, because both of her parents are home. Francis is in her chair, the one with the pink flowers and fraying edges, looking down at a checkerboard between her and Briana's dad.

"Alex?"

Her sweet voice breaks through the haze, and I focus on Briana again. She's standing so close I can feel her breath on my cheek, ready to take on any burden I'm willing to give her. And suddenly I can't tell her about anything, especially not what I saw in the mines. "What's wrong?" she repeats.

I force a smile and shrug, as though it's nothing. "Feeling a little moody, is all. I could use some girl time."

Of course she doesn't believe me—I can see it in her eyes—but that's where Briana and Georgie differ; one allows the walls while the other wants to kick them down.

"I might be able to help you with that," she says, hugging me. She must have just showered; her hair is wet and the smell of her shampoo wafts over me. Where I would normally pull away, I don't. After a few seconds she's the one who breaks free, cupping my elbows. "Come on in. I was just watching Mom kick Dad's ass."

"It's not over yet!" Bill calls from his spot. He holds his chin between his thumb and forefinger and squints down at the board. I follow Briana into the room and we settle on the floor in front of them. Einstein twines through my arms and legs, purring. I pat him absently and enjoy the sight of Francis, more animated than I've seen her in months. Strange that she should be so alive on a day consumed by the dead.

The thought yanks me back to the mines, to Dad. It happened so fast. One moment he was there, looking right at me with his familiar brown eyes, and the next he was gone. Reality is setting in again, and with each passing second I'm more and more convinced that I imagined the entire thing. How could it be real? There's no such thing as ghosts . . . is there?

One thing I know with utmost certainty: I have to go back.

"Honey, it's your turn." Francis plucks the skirt of her nightgown, studying the pieces on the board closely.

Just then, Elvis's "Burning Love" comes on. Bill claps his hands and jumps up, startling all of us. His knee knocks the game board and checkers scatter across the floor. Francis jerks back, scowling. "Damn it, Bill!"

Ignoring this, he rushes to the radio and turns the volume knob so loud that Einstein flees the room. Then he returns to his wife—Briana and I scramble out of the way—and holds his hands out to her, grinning. "Come on!" he exclaims, swinging his hips from side to side. "We danced to this at our wedding, remember? Briana, you were there, cooking in the oven. It's our family song!"

Briana laughs, and I'm smiling. Elvis sings his encouragement. Francis gives Bill another exasperated look, but he just grabs her fingers and hauls her up. Joy is here now, doing an odd little jig that makes the fat in her arms jiggle. Her orange-red hair is a fire that warms us all. Briana shouts encouragement. Francis is worse than Revenge as she dances, her movements uncertain and awkward. She doesn't stop, though. All too soon the song ends, and a gentler one comes on. Joe introduces it in his familiar drawl. Bill tugs Francis against him, and they sway there together as if Briana and I don't exist.

Now Love accompanies them. Her palms cup their backs. Their minds will dismiss the sensation as something ordinary; that's how it always works. Francis closes her eyes, the veins in her eyelids so thick and blue. Like rivers on Saul's maps. I remember the helplessness in her the last time I came here, when the pot on the sill was still only dirt. It feels so long ago.

Finished with their summons, Joy and Love stand back,

whispering to each other and grinning. All of this reminds me of that first afternoon in the attic. The laughter, the warmth, the closeness. I miss Revenge so much it's an ache in my chest, like he has his fist wrapped around my heart and keeps tightening his hold, no matter how hard I try to be free of him. "Why can't all love be as easy as that?" I murmur.

My friend sighs. She bumps her shoulder to mine. "Love isn't complicated, Alex. People are."

Bill says something in Francis's ear and she giggles. I watch the two of them, thinking that hope is always found in the places you least expect it.

When I don't respond, Briana looks at me sidelong. "You say that like you have experience. But so far as I know, you've never dated anyone." There's a question in the words.

The pause after she speaks is palpable, but without the pressure that usually pounds in from all sides like the storms that frequent this mountain. Here's my chance. I could be honest with Briana for the first time in my life. Tell her about the other plane and my father and everything else. She would believe me, she would understand. That's who she is.

But Briana's world is beautiful, even with its flaws. I don't want to be the one who puts something ugly in it. So instead I just say, "I messed up, Bri. I don't think Saul and Missy are going to forgive me." The image of Saul running after me as I sped away on my bike flashes and fades in my mind's eye. That ever-present shard of glass in my heart burrows deeper and I actually put a hand to my chest, convinced I'll feel it there.

Light from the window falls across Briana's face and

dust glints like stars. "Of course they will," she murmurs. "You just have to earn it."

She's not talking about me and Saul anymore. She's staring up at her mother, Longing and Hurt and Love surrounding her. I wish I knew what was wrong. Suddenly she stands, and every step she takes away sounds like an earthquake. Neither of her parents notices. Slowly, I follow. We reach the hallway and Briana doesn't say anything; she just focuses on another pot of soil next to the door. Past experience has taught me that she won't—can't—talk about her mother. So I touch her arm and say, "I better go. I'm pretty sure Saul has grounded me until graduation."

"*If* you graduate." Briana finally looks at me.

Another pause. The look in her eyes kills me. I feel like I'm running down a road and everyone I love is standing a mile back, calling to me and urging me to stop. To return. "If I graduate," I echo softly. She expects me to defend myself or offer some kind of explanation. I do neither. "See you later, Bri. Thanks for ... for this." When I leave, she doesn't try to stop me or say goodbye.

I lift my bike upright and get on, pedal far enough that I'm out of view. Then I stop on the side of the road. Gravel crunches beneath my sandal. I dig my phone out of my pocket and find the number in the *RECENTLY CALLED* list. Press *TALK* and hold it to my ear. Just like all the other times, it rings over and over. I have the sound memorized, so much that I know exactly when the voicemail will interrupt.

But this time the accented voice doesn't drone an apology

to me. Every vein in my body twitches when there's a click and the voice says, "Hello?"

It takes me several attempts to croak, "Is this Dr. Stern?"

"Yes, this is Dr. Stern. Who is this?"

"This is Alex Tate." I can barely breathe. "I think you knew my father. Will Tate?"

Silence on the other end. I wait for exactly four seconds, then open my mouth to say something else, anything that will get me answers to all my unanswered questions. Before I can, there's another click.

The dial tone moans in my ear.

Piano music floats through the floor. I stand in front of my bedroom window and make myself listen. Saul has been at it for hours. Every note, every key reveals the inner turmoil I've caused. Missy clatters around in the kitchen, making supper even though none of us will probably eat it. The smell of grease fills the apartment. Then Missy swears vehemently, and the scent of charred food joins it. I focus on the faint outline of the moon above me, toying with my eyebrow ring, spinning it around and around through my skin. Eventually I become aware of a hot presence at my back. Then, chocolate.

"Get out." I don't turn around.

Revenge moves around me, forcing me to take a step back. His brow is furrowed, and he's holding a bottle of vodka in one fist and some small rocks in his other palm. Our favorite things to have for a night on the bridge. We would get drunk and skip stones. He thought he could come here and pretend like nothing has changed. The time for pretending is so far behind me it's not even on the horizon anymore; it's just gone.

"Alex, what—"

"You may have to be there when I face Nate Foster, but you sure as hell don't have to be around me until then," I hiss, wishing I could shove him. An Emotion solidifies at my back. *"Get out."*

"First tell me what I did." His green eyes threaten to breach the wall of anger I've built.

"It doesn't matter. All that matters is that we're *done*." My control shatters, and I reach out to plant my hands on his chest, to push him right through the window and watch him fall as hard as I have.

The moment I'm about to make contact, Revenge vanishes. He bursts into sight again by the closet. His gelled hair glints in the lamplight and he's never been more beautiful to me, now that I know I can never have him. Not really.

"I'm not leaving this room until you—" He stops, clenches his jaw. *Until you forgive me*, he'd been about to say. Ironic. So, so ironic.

Saul's music strengthens, wrapping around us. I close my eyes. In the darkness I see Dad in the mines, the glint of Francis's teeth as she danced, the curve of Briana's shoulder when she hugged me so tight. I remember how Georgie's voice sounded when she let go of her dreams, the way Missy's chin trembled while I threw her love back in her face. There are other memories that try to overwhelm me, but I find a semblance of endurance and push them back.

"Just let me hate you. Please." I meet Revenge's gaze and know that there are tears in my own. Emotions touch me, some violent, some gentle. They don't linger.

"I-I couldn't exist in a world where you hate me," Revenge says quietly. I've never seen him desperate; it's obvious in his voice, his eyes, his face. He tries to hide it, but I know him too well.

Yet I didn't see through all his lies. I face the sky again, unable to look at him anymore. The stars have begun to emerge. Unlike the night of my birthday, they're utterly silent. I take a ragged breath. "I saw something today. I'm still not sure if it was real or not. But it made me realize something."

I don't go on, and Revenge dares to come close again. His breath tickles my ear. "What did you realize?" he asks.

My father's voice haunts me. *Alexandra*. "I'm not capable of forgiveness."

The creature I once called my best friend has no response to this. After all, it's the only thing he wanted. For me to choose him. What else is there?

Confirming it, Revenge leaves me with the moon and my thoughts. A bitter smile curves my lips.

Saul stops playing downstairs, and a second later there's a knock on my bedroom door. "Alex? There's supper if you want it." The floor creaks as Missy walks away. I'm just about to follow when something moves, drawing my attention; a spider has made a home out of the corner of my window. My skin crawls instinctively. Though it's on the other side of the glass, it would be easy to kill, just like the one in the attic. All I would have to do is push the frame up. Something stops me, though, and I just watch it. The web beneath the little creature glistens as it waits. So still, so patient.

It happens in a moment: a moth flies into the trap. It immediately struggles, but the spider is too fast. It zips across those gleaming strands. I lean closer, morbidly fascinated. The predator's movements are cold and efficient as it wraps the moth again and again and again. The winged thing is still alive, trying to break free even when it's obvious the end is near, that it's futile to struggle against it. Then the spider presses close, as if to kiss, though its intentions are far more sinister. Funny, how an act so lethal could seem like something entirely different.

For an instant I consider reaching out and saving it. Crushing the spider so the moth can wriggle out and away from this place of death. Death is inevitable, though, and it's too late, anyway.

I observe the gruesome pair until the writhing lump of web goes utterly still, and then I turn my back, letting the spider finish its meal alone.

SEVENTEEN

For the next two days, I'm on my best behavior. When all my instincts urge me to go see Andrew, or return to the mines, or hunt down Dr. Stern, or sit outside Nate Foster's house, I stay where people think I belong. I do it for them. Missy, Saul, Briana, Georgie. Maybe it was seeing my friend's parents so happy, or telling Revenge that he's the only choice for me. Ultimately, Nate Foster is the one who's supposed to suffer the most. So the least I can do is give my loved ones a respite, a few days of peace. Nothing is over, though. It feels like the stillness before a storm, when the sky is yellow and roiling and you know something is coming.

On Monday night I'm lying on the couch, putting on a show of reading a book for school. My aunt went to bed an hour ago, and Saul is on his way home from a tuning, but I still don't move. Part of me wishes this was real, the tentative surrender. The false contentment. They're starting to trust me again, I can see it. I want to have these days to remember when everything ends.

"You haven't turned a page in five minutes."

He stands across the room, watching me with his dark eyes. As usual, he's wearing that white T-shirt, and his hair looks casually mussed like he's just rolled out of bed. But that's impossible, since they don't sleep. For the first time I'm envious of something from the other plane: they don't receive unwanted visits from Dream.

I close the book, marking the spot with my thumb. "I know for an absolute fact that I didn't summon you, intentionally or otherwise," I comment. I haven't been tempted to think of Forgiveness since I saw my father.

"You didn't."

I frown. "Then why are you here?"

Oddly, Forgiveness ignores this. I catch him studying our surroundings with interest. The ancient carpet, the worn furniture, the framed photos of our family on the wall next to the kitchen doorway. It occurs to me that he's never been in the apartment before. I start to repeat the question when he asks, "What are you reading?"

If I didn't know any better, I would think that he's trying to change the subject. I appraise him as I answer, "I'm trying to read *To Kill a Mockingbird*. It's for a class, and I'm so behind I don't know why I even bother." My voice is low, to ensure Missy won't hear us over the running fan in her room.

He walks along the edge of the room, hands shoved in his pockets. I try not to compare them, but it's impossible. Where Revenge has always seemed out of place in the mundaneness of my world, Forgiveness . . . fits. He may be the beautiful one, with his sculpted lips and high cheekbones, but he doesn't have that restless energy that makes Revenge so otherworldly.

" . . . a good story," Forgiveness says. I blink, realizing that I missed the first part of the sentence.

"You've read it?"

Forgiveness smiles faintly and stops beside me. I have to crane my neck to look at him. "As a matter of fact, I have. I've read many of your world's books."

"Why?" It's awkward, him standing so close and me taking up the whole couch. But he's too polite to sit and I'm too stubborn to let him.

Seemingly unaffected, Forgiveness tilts his head and examines the cover of the book on my lap. "I find them interesting."

Silence. Telling him to leave has never worked before, and secretly I don't want him to. Tonight I find his presence more soothing than conflicting. I don't have to put up a façade or try to say the right things. So I clear my throat and tuck my legs under me, putting the book face-down by my feet. "Will you . . . do you want to . . . "

As an answer, Forgiveness picks the book up. He settles onto the cushion, which only indents slightly at his weight. That minty smell teases my senses. He adjusts his position until he's nearly slouching, then opens the spine wider. Though I try to put some distance between us, I find myself admiring the elegance of his jaw. Then I realize he's about to read.

"Wait, what are you doing?" I cut in.

Forgiveness raises his brows, as if to say, *Isn't it obvious?*

He shifts, effectively moving closer to me. And in that gentle voice, he begins.

Arguments and protests rise up within me. This is too strange, he shouldn't be here, I don't want him here. But he keeps going, undeterred by my discomfort, and I gradually realize that none of it is true. For a few minutes I remain stiff, uncertain. It's an unstoppable force, though—his deep, calming timbre lulls me into a place between reality and dreams. Any lingering sense of uneasiness around Forgiveness fades away. He smells so good, like mint and kindness and sleep. I let my eyes flutter shut. Eventually the story, the room, and the Choice fades into nothing.

The sound of voices ripples through the apartment. I sit up. Dad must be home. He sounds angry again. Mom sent me to bed a while ago, and I know I should be asleep, but I slip out of bed and tiptoe to the door, putting my ear to the wood. "If you don't stop this, you're going to lose us. Do you understand? I'm not going to be like the other women in this town," Mom shouts-whispers.

The floor creaks as they both walk by. Shadows move over the crack of light by my feet. Something clatters and I jump. They go into their room, and Dad rumbles something I can't hear. Mom answers. Brief snatches and phrases drift to me.

". . . promised it would be safe . . . "

". . . Alex . . . "

". . . rumors . . . "

". . . telling me the truth . . . "

With each word they become louder and louder. Hunter is going to wake up, and I don't want them to fight anymore. I want us to be like we used to be, happy and smiling. I don't like how much Dad scares me now. Deciding to risk making him even madder, I open the door and step into the hallway. Something glints on the floor, and I see it too late as my heel sinks onto the sharp edge. I reel back, crying out. Keys. I remember the sound from earlier—Daddy dropping them. I plop down and hold my foot. Blood seeps from a tiny cut.

Mom hushes Dad, and hinges moan. Light floods the narrow space. "Alex? What happened?"

"Alex? What happened?"

It takes me a minute to realize that it's Missy's voice slicing through the dream. I raise a fist and rub some crust out of my eyes, but the world is still blurry. I can see enough to know that my aunt is standing over me and she's clearly upset, staring down with a perplexed frown. Outside, the sky is the pink of dawn. What am I doing on the couch?

Last night comes to me in pieces. Dinner. Saul leaving. Missy going to bed. A book in my hands . . . and Forgiveness. I jerk upright, twisting, but of course he's gone. He must have laid a blanket over me before he left. I finger the green knit material, recalling the warmth of his voice.

"Alex? Are you listening? What on earth happened in here?"

I look up at Missy again, prepared to ask her what she's talking about. But something over her shoulder catches my eye: a piece of paper plastered to the wall just above the light switch. What . . . ? There's another piece of paper, just by her foot. Frowning, I stand up and look beyond her.

"What do you—" I blink, and the blurred room finally comes into focus.

The pages of *To Kill a Mockingbird* have been torn out of the spine and scattered everywhere.

Laughter echoes through the parking lot as I get out of my car. I slam the door shut; chips of paint flutter to the ground. The damage from the confrontation with the Taurus looks as bad as ever, but at least my car still runs. I turn my back on the forlorn car and walk toward the building, keys in hand. The letters over the doorway in front of me glint gold in the sunlight: *GREEN RIVER COMMUNITY COLLEGE.* I walk beneath them and grasp one of the long door handles, pulling it without hesitation. The time for uncertainty is over.

There's a group of students standing near the doorway. I brush past them. Air conditioning toys with my hair as I turn right, heading for Andrew's office. After all those avoided calls and messages, I'm ready to hear what he has to say. Apprehension stalks me all the way to the door. He disappears the moment I see that the lights are on in the room but the chair behind Andrew's desk is empty; he probably went for a coffee run.

I venture to the bookshelves like I did last time, prepared to wait, but it occurs to me that this may be an opportunity. If I've learned anything these past few weeks, it's that people don't destroy their secrets; they only hide them.

Hurriedly setting my keys down so both hands are free, I open all of the drawers in the desk, rifle through the files and papers. From swift glances it's obvious there's nothing here besides the typical academic documents. Next I jiggle the mouse to his computer, waking it up. The screen brightens and I swallow a curse when another password box taunts me. There's no way I'll be able to guess it. I stand back, looking at every corner of the room to see if I've missed an area to snoop. Unless Andrew actually writes his secrets down and tucks them into books, there's nothing.

Wait. Not nothing. I lean forward again and take the phone out of its cradle, stepping over the long cord. Praying that Andrew uses this machine more than his cell or the one at home, I jam a number with my knuckle to get his voicemail. My foot taps impatiently, anxiously. People keep walking by the doorway, but no one looks in and sees. That could change at any moment.

An electronic voice drones a greeting. Fortunately, there's no passcode here. I listen to the menu for a minute, then hit *7* for saved messages. The first one comes on immediately, just a co-worker offering tickets to some concert in the city. It's dated two days ago. The next message is older, from two months ago. Andrew, calling himself to leave a reminder about renewing his license.

There's a third message on the phone's memory, but I'm on the verge of hanging up. Maybe Andrew is the rare individual who keeps everything locked within his head, or at home where I can't reach it. Just as I pull the phone away from me, though, that electronic voice announces the date when this one was saved.

Over six years ago.

Why would he keep a message for so long? My breath quickens, and now Anticipation is beside me with a gleam in her eye. The message starts. This voice is different from the others. Deeper. It has a slight drawl to it that takes me a few seconds to recognize, and I'm concentrating so hard that I miss the words it's saying.

A jolt slams down my spine when I finally realize I'm listening to my father's voice.

He sounds ... breathless. Like he's running. "I know you took the kids, and I know you lied to me and Stern," Dad says. "But if you think—"

"Yes, I'll take another look at it and get back to you."

Andrew. Alarm slams through me, and I gasp and put the phone back with a clatter. I can hear his footsteps against the hard floor, coming closer, about to discover me going through his private belongings. There's no time to circle the desk and go to the shelf, act as though I'm doing nothing wrong.

The desk. Desperately I get on my knees and crawl into the space beneath it. It's tight, but I still manage to pull the chair in so I'm concealed. There's no time to grab my keys. Andrew says goodbye to whoever he's talking to and comes in. There's the sound of the door closing. I curl into myself, hardly daring to breathe. *Please don't sit down. Please, please, please ...*

He doesn't. I watch his shining shoes stop in front of my hiding place. The flutter of papers is louder than my own breathing. There's a thud; I guess he put his briefcase down. His cologne coils around me, and then someone is crouching next to the chair, reaching for me with a pale hand. I smother a cry. For a wild instant I think I've been discovered... until I see the shock of white-blond hair and that familiar smirk. Fear. "Great hiding place," the Emotion says.

I'm so tense that it feels as if my organs have turned to wood. Of course I don't answer, and Fear snickers before going off to terrorize someone else.

It doesn't take long to realize that my insides couldn't be wood, because my lungs wouldn't be shrieking for air. And the leg of the chair is jabbing into my calf. The pain becomes more important than the risk of discovery, and I'm about to shift when Andrew's voice slices through the stillness. "Alex."

I freeze.

"It's Andrew. Again. I'm coming to Franklin tonight. We need to talk. I haven't gotten any responses from my voicemails or texts, with good reason, but you need me right now. You probably already know why." I hear him moving away, and I dare to breathe again. The light flicks off, the door closes a second time.

I scramble out from under the desk, trembling. Part of me aches to finish listening to the message, but Andrew could come back and all my instincts urge me to run. I snatch up my own keys from where they rest behind a picture on the desk, grateful he hadn't noticed them. Just as I pull away, my gaze slides across the picture itself... and I stop. Double-take. Stare.

It's a faded image of a man standing next to a little boy. Their clothing is so outdated it must have been taken a long, long time ago. I don't recognize either of them, but something about it bothers me, flicks at my consciousness. How have I missed this before? Hurriedly I pick it up and remove the back from the frame, sliding the picture out from its resting place against the glass. I'm about to flip it over when words catch my eye, scribbled in the right corner.

Andrew and Sammy, 1985.

It can't be.

My heart stops, and I reread those words again and again as if they'll change or rearrange themselves into something else. But they don't. Suddenly I know what's so familiar about the picture. The man, his face. I saw it in a newspaper article in the attic, among my father's things. Sammy Thorn. Kidnapper, murderer, eternal mystery.

And Andrew is his son.

If he lied to me about this, what else has he lied about?

The risk of discovery has passed, yet my skin is crawling and every instinct I have is screaming at me to leave, get out, run. I don't fight it and put the picture back. Before leaving I make sure that everything looks exactly like it did when I came in. It has to, since Andrew's meticulous nature will sense it straightaway. I wipe my sweaty hands on my jeans and grasp the doorknob, pulling it shut behind me.

I'm heading for the parking lot again when I pause next to the front desk. I should go home, where it feels safe—even if it isn't. I shouldn't tempt fate again, especially in light of my recent discoveries. But I've never been very good at doing things I should. So instead of going to my car, I rush up to the receptionist. "Where is Dr. Felix Stern's office?" I ask, wrapping my hands around the edge of the counter to hide the way they're shaking.

The woman turns her head. She's on the phone. Smiling at me, she points the end of her pencil to the left. The opposite direction from Andrew's office. Nodding my thanks, I follow the way indicated by that worn eraser, rushing down the hallway and making sure to glance at each room number.

There it is. I jerk to a halt and stare.

Like all the other offices, there's a plaque on the door. I scan the familiar name several times as I lift my hand and knock. Nothing. But the paper taped beneath the plaque says his office hours are right now. He must be in there. Pursing my lips, I knock harder. The door rattles on its hinges. "Hello?" I call, listening for any movement within.

"Yes, yes, what is it?" A man yanks the door open and stands there, glaring. He's very short, almost pudgy. His suit is brown and wrinkled, and glasses wink at me in the light. Tufts of gray hair surround his ears.

The pause becomes too long, and I know he's about to lose patience again. If he has any. "Are you Dr. Stern?" I manage. Questions crowd in my throat, clambering over each other, making it impossible to go on.

Another pause. The man doesn't respond. The ferocity in his expression fades as he studies my features. Then recognition brightens his eyes, as unmistakable as the dawn. He casts a furtive glance up and down the hallway.

"You look like your father, Alexandra Tate," he mutters in that thick accent. The same one in the voicemail, the one that answered my call so briefly before hanging up. "You shouldn't be here." He shuffles back and closes the door a little, using it like a shield. Against me?

"Maybe not, but I am," I counter, thinking of my dreams, of the files on the flash drive. "I want answers."

"I can't give them to you." He starts to shut the door completely.

I jam my foot inside. Pain radiates through my heel. "My father is dead, Dr. Stern. He never spoke about you, and I know there's a reason. I'm not leaving until I find out what it is."

"You're going to get us both killed!" he hisses. "Leave this alone!"

I'm so shocked that when he moves to slam the door again, I don't stop him.

EIGHTEEN

Time loses meaning again. One moment I'm driving back from Green River, the road signs green blurs. The next moment I'm breathing hard and concentrating on the circular movements of my feet as I pedal to nowhere. The car is back at the apartment and I'm still desperate to find out what it is my father kept from me all those years ago. As if the answer will solve everything, end the war that's destroying my insides. Trees and signs go by unnoticed. All I know is the hurricane of air leaving my mouth again and again.

But then the road ends and I'm forced to stop. The bike falls to the dirt. Something scrapes my ankle and I don't even look down. I stand in the clearing, heaving, closing my eyes as I try to calm.

The sensation within—like tiny soldiers live in my stomach and keep shooting or jabbing at each other—slows. I open my eyes again. It takes me a moment to comprehend where I am, where I unconsciously brought myself when I thought my destination was unknown.

The mines.

Sunlight bursts through the treetops above, casting shivering shadows over everything. Dad isn't standing in the mouth waiting for me, and he doesn't appear when I walk closer. I pause, the tips of my boots touching the very edge of the shadow that the lip of the entrance casts on the ground. The darkness beckons. I strain to see any sign of movement. He could be waiting. Maybe he needs me to believe, to find the strength to go into that oblivion.

"Daddy?" I whisper, as though someone else is nearby, listening. He doesn't answer. Still, I hesitate. I wish Saul's maps could show me the way, could lead me to the right ending of this story. The right choice. I wish that the flash drive held the answers to questions like... is it possible for the dead to come back?

The thought clings to me like a leech, propels me forward until I can no longer feel the warmth on my skin. "Daddy?" I say again, clenching my fists. Fear's strawberry breath cools the space around us and his fingers slide down my arm, brush the edge of my top as I walk out of reach. I call for my father a third time. A fourth time. I'm so deep into the tunnel now that I can see the dim outline of the elevator farther down. Silence rings in my ears.

He isn't here.

I stop. A tear drips off the end of my nose and plops into the dirt. I don't know what I expected. Dad to come out of the shadows, arms outstretched? His voice, telling me that everything will be okay? His reassurances that the past six years have been nothing but a bad dream? Anything but this emptiness, this confirmation that I really did conjure everything. It wasn't real. Any of it. The dog must have fled because she was full or heard something else on the wind. Not because she sensed my dead father.

Suddenly my knees buckle, and I fall. A sob echoes into the blackness. Mine. I wrap my arms around myself and rock back and forth, back and forth. "Please, please," I whisper, uncertain of what I'm even pleading for. Something inside me cracks. Everything pours through that tiny opening: longing, anguish, regret, need. Emotions come like the apparition I believed my father to be. Not a single one of them speaks. I can't see their faces, I can only feel them. On my head and shoulders and back. Their scents combine and overwhelm, but one is stronger than all the rest and resounds in my mind, even in this state.

Chocolate.

I think I whimper his name. I can't speak past the pain searing through me. There aren't any words that will help me, anyway. I lift my face, and my eyes must have adjusted to the darkness because now I can see. His beautiful, familiar features stay when all the other Emotions drift away. For the first time since I've met him, Revenge looks... helpless. His hands hover over me. "Alex, Alex, Alex," he keeps murmuring, as if saying my name will bring me back.

And it does. Another minute passes, and the unbearable pain begins to retreat. Retreat, but not surrender. It never does. I put my palms on the ground and try to take even breaths now. "I wanted him to be real," I say eventually, shuddering. A hiccup escapes me.

Revenge still speaks softly, probably worried that anything louder will break me again. "He's as real as you make him, Alex."

The wetness on my cheeks is drying. I straighten, unflinching this time when our eyes meet. The truth rises to my lips and I don't try to stop it. "I've missed you."

My best friend doesn't hesitate. And I know that this is his truth, too. "I've missed you."

I push myself up and brush my knees off. In unison, Revenge and I leave the tunnel, walking back toward the light. The moment we emerge I squint up at the sky, needing something to anchor myself to as I ask the question that's been tossing me around like a violent wave these past few days. "Is it true? When I choose, I'll never see you again?"

Exactly seven seconds pass. Revenge fidgets in that way of his, and it's clear he's trying to decide whether or not to lie. There are so many lies around us, though, that I'm choking on them. It takes the last of my strength not to beg. *Please, don't lie.* Finally he meets my gaze and says, "Yes."

Hope has a way of sneaking up on you. It's a craving that ebbs back when you least expect it. Even though you know it's wrong, you can't help but want a taste of it now and then. Then you pay. There's always a price to pay for hope. I feel myself deflate.

"Why didn't you tell me?" I whisper. Overhead, a squirrel jumps through the treetops, and a branch snaps. The sound echoes.

"I . . ." More silence. He's probably trying find the right thing to say. I know what I want to hear most: that everything will be okay. Except that it won't. People move on, people live their lives day-to-day just trying to cope. But I think there's a small part in all of us that's just waiting for the next awful thing to happen. Everything is okay until it isn't.

As Revenge continues to grapple for those impossible words, I release a long breath. I need to focus on something else. I need to change the subject. Gathering my hair into a ponytail, I go to a fallen tree and sit. The elastic band snaps into place.

"A lot of strange things have been happening and I don't know what to do with any of it," I say abruptly.

My friend settles down next to me and crosses his legs at the ankles. Normally I would comment on the fact that he's wearing what looks like a bullfighting outfit, but not tonight. "Like what?" he asks.

"Well, the book, for one thing. That was a mature stunt you pulled. Really, I was impressed." I glare, thinking about it.

"Book?" Revenge repeats. He honestly seems confused. "What are you talking about?"

My blood runs cold. If Revenge wasn't the one who was in the apartment last night, then who? My instincts insist Forgiveness wouldn't have done something like that. I turn away, muttering, "Never mind."

It's already twilight. The sun has begun to lower, fusing with the horizon. Hues of yellow and orange spread over everything. Another missed day of school. "Maybe none of this matters. I mean, it has nothing to do with Nate Foster."

"Have you been to the house lately?" he asks.

"No." I sigh, picturing that front door. Untouchable, unreachable. "I don't think I have it in me, Revenge. To kill someone. Even after what he did to my family." This is a day of hesitations and pauses, because yet another silence falls between me and Revenge. It's not as uncomfortable as the others; thoughts of my encounter with Dr. Stern distract and consume me. The message Dad left on Andrew's answering machine.

Then Revenge shifts. I turn and find that he's staring at me with an odd expression. I tilt my head in questioning. Slowly, he says, "Death isn't the only revenge, Alex."

"What do you mean?"

As a response, Revenge jumps to his feet. "Let's go. Your car is at the apartment, right?"

By the time I get back, my body is aching again and all I want to do is crawl into bed and sleep and sleep and sleep, but Revenge is waiting on the bottom step. My gaze slides past him to a strange car parked in front of the shop—the same one that was hovering by the curb at the playground, that first night I talked with Forgiveness at the lake.

Andrew. I'd completely forgotten that he was planning to come see me.

Swearing under my breath, I hurry to the Saturn and hope no one saw me. Revenge appears in the passenger seat. There's a strange tightness to his mouth, like he's anticipating what's about to happen but wants to hide it. Almost as if, like me, he doesn't know what he wants. But that can't be it, since he's Revenge. Right?

"So what are we—" Someone raps on the windshield. I jump and shriek. Missy circles the hood and peers in at me, frowning, and I quickly roll down the window. Fear doesn't bother to offer commentary this time, and Revenge scowls at the delay.

"Didn't you see Andrew's car?" My aunt puts her hand on the edge of the door. Her wedding ring glitters. "He's here to see you."

"I can't talk to him right now," I say. Bewildered, Missy begins to argue. I shift gears and reverse before she asks questions I can't answer. Now Guilt joins us in the tiny space. She's so big that her head bumps the ceiling, and her face makes me think of a pig. Beady eyes, flat nose. I grind my teeth when she caresses my head. "This better be good," I tell Revenge.

Missy fades in the rearview mirror as Revenge says, "Oh, it will be. Trust me."

My headlights guide the way down the mountain. It begins to drizzle. Revenge and I don't speak again, not even when I turn onto Sanderson Road. After a minute the house comes up on the right, a structure of white. Tonight it almost glows, as though the Fosters are the ghosts and not my father.

It hasn't been long since my last visit, but somehow it feels like years. Once we get close I switch the lights off, as usual, and pull into my hiding place beneath a huge tree. It offers an excellent vantage point of the house. Only one car is in the driveway this time. "Where's Jennifer?"

"Visiting her mother."

Uncertain, I start to reach for the glove box like I usually do. My heart pounds harder.

"You won't need that," Revenge tells me, getting out. A *whoosh* of air follows in his wake. I hadn't realized how warm it is. The mountain can't seem to decide which season to cling to. Either that or the Seasons themselves are feeling fickle. Cutting the engine, I swiftly follow. Mist rolls over the lawn and we creep—I creep—from tree to tree. The chandelier above the dining room table is so bright that it illuminates half the yard. I recall the night I watched Jennifer Foster cry over her kitchen sink. This time, though, Compassion is nowhere in sight. Approaching, I grip the windowsill and dare to look inside.

But Revenge keeps going. "This way."

"What are you—"

"Just trust me, okay?"

Pushing aside my reservations, I tiptoe around the side of the house. Revenge stops and watches me expectantly, standing by a window. Through the glass I see a living room. A couch with a floral pattern, a coffee table with a bowl of fake fruit on it, lamps with beads dangling from the shades. But all of that fades away when I see people move in the shadows. Light from the hallway falls over them. Though the only sounds around us are frogs and crickets and wind, I can imagine the sounds they are making.

Nate Foster has a woman up against the wall, and they're kissing.

"See the possibilities?" Revenge breathes. Excitement—a petite creature with spiked black hair—quivers beside me while I dig out my cell phone, turn on the camera, and take a picture. Nate Foster and the woman who isn't his wife appear on the screen, forever documented in pixels and promises. My fingers tremble and I tear away from the sight to look at my best friend.

Words are impossible. As if he understands, Revenge smiles into my eyes, and we've never been more connected than in this moment. Those words from six years ago echo in the tiny space between us: *That's the question, isn't it, Alexandra Tate? What do you want?* Suddenly it doesn't matter that he's going to disappear, it doesn't matter that part of what I want I can never have. "I could kiss *you* right now," I whisper, grinning.

Slowly, the mirth dies in his garden-green eyes. We stare at each other, neither of us moving away or acting like the heat doesn't exist. We're both thinking about that almost-kiss in the attic again, the one we've both secretly agreed not to acknowledge. I study his features even though I have all of him committed to memory. His hair, the color of embers or an exposed wire, glints. His lips, generous and sober, have never been more tempting. I think of those minutes in the mines, how he was the one to come when I was most broken. I want to touch him so badly, and I can tell he does, too. The heat intensifies until we're burning in it.

"It's my turn to show you something," I say finally.

He frowns, clearly puzzled. Turning my back on Nate Foster—they're on the couch now, still oblivious to our presence—I walk back to the front of the house. Fireflies flare and fade over the grass like dying stars. Revenge trails after me. I go right up to the front door and face him again, willing him to realize that this is my silent promise. My unspoken vow that soon, I will let go of everything and choose.

Never looking away from Revenge, I touch the door. Just one touch. But it feels like so much more.

It feels like the beginning of the end.

Screams drift through the wall.

Ever since I got home there's been an idea in my head, the notion that the instant I touched the Fosters' door, the darkness I tried to contain beneath my skin was released. It now seems to freely affect everyone around me. Angus's parents, Saul and Missy. Their arguments are an orchestra coming from every side, notes and harmonies made of bitterness and worry and anger.

I lie in bed with my arm crooked above me, listening. Andrew is long gone, and Angus didn't attempt to reach me through his knocks. His parents are shouting about bills. Saul and Missy, of course, are shouting about me. He brings up discipline and consequences while she keeps insisting on patience and time. This is what I've brought them to. When I imagined myself on that road, I never thought I would drag them with me.

With each barbed word the ceiling looms closer, white and smooth. It feels like it's on top of me, and suddenly it's hard to breathe. I sit up, pressing a hand to my chest. I have to end it soon. We can't keep going like this.

"Alex."

His voice doesn't startle me; I'd been picturing him, hoping he would come and harden my resolve again. I turn and he's standing there beside my bed, ethereal in the moonlight. There's a gleam in his eyes I recognize, one that emanates from my own: a need to move, a frantic desire for action. "Come with me," Revenge whispers.

Wordlessly, I throw the covers aside and stand. The floor is cold on my bare feet. I crack my door open and peer out cautiously. They must have left the kitchen and gone into their room; I can hear the furious rumble of my uncle's voice behind that thin barrier. Revenge doesn't linger to watch me avoid the spots on the floor that will creak and give me away. It takes a few minutes to navigate through the dim apartment and out to the steps.

My best friend leans against the railing as I close the front door behind me. "The bridge?" I ask the moment the latch clicks. It's a good thing the air is warmer tonight, since I'm only wearing boxers and a T-shirt.

He shakes his head. "The lake."

Flip-flops were the first pair of shoes I found in the hallway, and they make a slight sound with each step I take. I cringe and hurry the rest of the way down the stairs. Since the sound of my car starting would doubtless alert Saul and Missy, I get on my bike. Revenge runs alongside me on the road, his shirt a splash of red in a world made of black and white. We don't talk. Before Nate Foster's release, we talked about anything and everything. Georgie's latest scheme, Briana's future, Saul's maps. I miss that ease. Yet there's something delicious about the silence between us now.

We get to the lake and the surface is eerily, beautifully

still. I stop next to the charred remains of the bonfire and push the kickstand. "So, what's—"

Without comment or hesitation, Revenge sprints to the dock. The boards don't shudder beneath his weight like they would for everyone else. Then he jumps. He hits the water and disappears for a moment. When he resurfaces, he whoops.

"Are you crazy?" I hiss, huddling on the shore. "It's still freezing!"

Revenge smirks. "Coward!" He tosses his head, hair flying. Glittering droplets fly through the air and ripples reach for my toes. I watch him bob and float for a few seconds, twisting my lips in indecision. Then Revenge makes chicken sounds. This propels me forward, onto the dock, and toward him. I don't pause to test the waters. I just leap.

The cold is shocking. For a few seconds I'm only aware of the freezing rush, the jolt of pain. But I squeeze my eyes shut and stay submerged. The discomfort subsides until I'm used to it, or maybe just numb. I absorb the sensation of a place without sound. The water is black and unending. Is this what death feels like? Just . . . peaceful?

My lungs start to tingle. Then they ache. After that, more pain. I kick my legs and reach the surface.

The moment I emerge, Revenge splashes water in my face. "Hey!" I sputter, kicking my legs to stay afloat. "Do you mind?"

"You know, you didn't used to be so boring," he says.

My eyes narrow. "Oh, really? I'm boring now?" As an answer, he floats on his back and stares up at the moon.

Though I can't shove him beneath the surface as I long to, I still manage to surprise him when I scoop water in my hands and push it over his mouth and nose. He jerks upright, coughing, and I laugh. We keep tormenting each other until my cheeks hurt from smiling. It's wonderful-strange how light I feel, like someone has blown up a balloon inside me and it's lifting me up, up. The usual sense of guilt I feel at being happy—even so briefly—when they aren't alive to feel anything doesn't come. There is only this—me and him and the sky.

No, that's not right. There's someone else nearby. "Look," I murmur. Relenting, Revenge follows my gaze.

There's a light on the opposite side of the lake, and I know from the location that it has to be old man Holland's house. Usually, when the sun sinks, he turns every light off. But for some reason, tonight he's left a single window still shining with yellow light. It feels like a silent announcement, as if to say, *Hello. Yes, it's true. I'm real. I'm here.*

Feeling Revenge's eyes on me, I face him again. "I should go home," I say. Reluctance materializes and complains about the water.

We both ignore her. "It's not that late," Revenge protests. He cuts through the waves as if to stop me from leaving.

"But Saul and Missy might check on me. I'll see you tomorrow, okay?" Shivering, I swim back to shore. My clothes drip and stick to me as I get on the bike. With my luck I'll get sick. I don't regret it, though. This is one thing I will never regret.

Revenge doesn't accompany me to the road, and I turn back. He's still there, floating by the end of the dock. From this distance he looks like something entirely mystical, a merman or a spirit. Lovely. Untouchable. He lifts his hand and waves. I wave back, then make myself pedal away.

The apartment is quiet when I creep inside. Saul and Missy aren't fighting anymore and the stream of light beneath their bedroom door is gone. I get into dry pajamas and clean up my wet tracks on the floor. Then I climb into bed and curl on my side, closing my eyes and seeing Revenge. Hearing his voice say for the hundredth time, *I will never give up on you.* Feel the heat of him even with air and water and indecision separating us.

When I finally fall asleep, the dream is different from all the others. There's still twisted metal and shattering glass, moans and pale skin and scarlet rivers. But amongst all those images is Dad, silent and staring. He doesn't speak, but I hear him in my head, whispering, *Hello. Yes, it's true. I'm real. I'm here.*

NINETEEN

"How are you doing up here?" Missy's head appears through the square door in the center of the attic floor. It's early, and dawn spills through the window. The past few days have been like that light, so swift and serene. I know it won't last.

"Fine." Smiling in greeting, I set a basket of yarn and knitting needles next to the rocking chair. I hope Missy doesn't notice the lines beneath my eyes, just as she probably hopes I don't notice hers.

My aunt climbs up the rest of the way and sits on the edge of the opening. She glances around with raised brows. "This turned out really good, Alex. Wow. I forgot what the floor looked like up here."

"Thanks. Hey, did I hear Saul leaving this morning?" I'm relieved that she still doesn't ask about Andrew or why I'm avoiding him.

"Yeah, he has another job. The drive is longer than most,

so he'll probably stay at a motel on the way back." Missy's smile is strained now, and I wonder if she's telling me the entire truth. Then again, I'm hardly one to judge. Truth is as rare and difficult to find as coal in the mines.

"... making breakfast," Missy is saying. "Are you hungry?"

"Starving," I lie.

"Good. Come down in a little bit, then." The ladder creaks and groans as she descends. Soon the top of her graying head is gone. I sit in the rocking chair, unsettling more dust. Something in the chair's frame must be loose, because it wobbles precariously. I push my toe against the floor and keep swaying. After a few seconds of this I close my eyes... and an image comes to me. My mother. Sitting in this same chair. She's not in the attic, though. She's in our old living room, looking out the window with a worried look in her eyes. The memory comes in pieces, like most things.

"Mom, what's wrong?" I stand next to her in my pajamas. Rain lashes against the window and makes the room quiver in silvery shadows.

She stops rocking and blinks, as though she'd forgotten where she was. "Nothing, honey. I'm just tired," she tells me. Her smile is tremulous and she tucks a strand of hair behind my ear. "Wow, it's getting long," she says suddenly. "We should probably cut it." She tilts her head and purses her lips, studying me. "But it's so pretty. It would be a shame. Maybe we'll just start braiding it, huh?"

"Okay." I shuffle closer and she hauls me up, sets me on her

lap even though we both know I'm too big for it. We gaze out at the storm together. "When is Dad coming home?" I murmur.

Her expression darkens again, and instantly I wish I hadn't asked. Someone appears in front of me, kneeling so he's at my level. He clutches the tip of my bare foot between his thumb and forefinger. I'm used to my invisible friends popping into the room, but I don't recognize this one. I almost open my mouth to ask him who he is, remembering just in time that Mom doesn't like it when I talk to them. The man answers the question anyway. "I'm Regret," he says, his voice raspy, like he smokes too many cigarettes or says too many words. "And I have a feeling you'll bring me back to this dying place again."

There's no chance to ask him what he means, because the brightness of headlights sweeps through the room. Dad is home. I feel Mom's heart quicken, too, and she hastily puts me down. She grips my shoulders and turns me to face her. Her eyes are so wide that I feel like I'm falling into the mines where Dad used to work. "Alex, I want you to go to bed and stay there, all right? Promise me. Honey, look at me and promise."

I tear my attention away from all the invisible people hovering around her chair, touching my mother with their hands. "I promise," I say, uncertain, wondering why she's afraid of Dad. Her eyes flicker—she must hear the waver in the words—but the sound of a door slamming outside is more important. She sends me to my room with another stern instruction to stay in bed. Stay, stay, stay. She stresses that so much that it becomes trapped in my head, fluttering like a bird in a cage.

Before I move to obey, I pause in the hallway and watch her. She's standing now, twisting her hands together as she waits.

That's when I realize there are suitcases against the wall. Are we going on a trip? The front door opens, and I forget the suitcases as I scurry into the safety of my room. Like most nights, I press my ear to the door and listen. Worry squats next to me, using my shoulder for balance. He smells like sweat.

"... had enough. I'm taking the kids," Mom says, her voice as hard as cement. "We're going to stay at my sister's for a while."

"She lives hours away! You can't take them that far."

"Will—"

"No. Listen, something happened today, and I was already planning to stop. I won't do it anymore. Just don't leave. Don't take them. Okay?" A brief silence falls. Then Mom sighs. Hurriedly Dad continues, "They can sleep over at Saul and Missy's tonight, just to get them out of here while it passes from my system."

Suddenly Mom gasps. "Is that... blood on your shirt? Will, what happened?" The rain answers. Dad doesn't. When the wordlessness goes on too long Mom finally says, her voice strangled, "If we're really going to do this, then I want them to go to Andrew's. That way they won't hear anything or try to come over."

"Yes, fine, okay. Let's go."

I blink, and I'm back in the attic again. More alone and confused than ever. To escape the hollow feeling inside me, I lurch from the rocking chair and climb down the ladder.

Smoke fills the apartment. Following the sound of the smoke detector, I stop in the kitchen doorway. "Shit!" Missy is fumbling for the dials that control the stove. There's a book in her other hand. She was trying to read and cook again.

"Let me do it," I say, coughing and rushing to her side. The pan is steaming—bordering on catching fire—and she gets out of the way just in time for me to remove it from the burner. There's no saving the bacon, so I seize the spatula lying on the countertop and stir the ruin of eggs. They look like scorched rubber. Missy stands there with a defeated slump to her shoulders while I grab the broom and wave the end of it at the shrieking detector. The moment it goes silent I open every window in the apartment.

When I return to the stove, Missy still hasn't moved. With watery eyes I scrape the eggs onto two plates, dig the bag of grated cheese out of the fridge, and sprinkle it over the mess. Two forks, and we have breakfast. "See? Some things can be saved." I bump Missy's hip with mine.

It's as if her strength has burned away instead of the bacon. "We should just move to a town where we can order pizza," she mutters.

I'm about to respond when a familiar noise drifts through the open window: a trash can crashing to the ground. Missy doesn't react, but I don't want my stray to be discovered. Animals aren't exactly pampered or sacred around these parts. "Do you mind if I eat outside?" I say quickly. "It's nice out, and I could use some fresh air after being in that attic for so long."

As an answer, she hands me one of the plates. I falter, wishing for the millionth time that there was a magical combination of words that could fix us. Since there are none, I kiss her cheek. Missy jumps. Before she can comment, I leave.

This time, the dog is actually waiting for me at the bottom of the steps. Her tail is tucked between her legs, an obvious sign of fear, but her hunger must be stronger. I slow down, taking the steps more cautiously. She watches every movement.

When I get too close, she retreats a little. Eventually I settle on the bottom step and put the hot plate on my lap. Glancing up at the living room window to make sure Missy isn't watching, I scoop some of the yellow-brown scrambled eggs onto my fork and offer it to the starving creature.

It takes her thirteen seconds to approach. After she's gulped down the food, she instantly backs away again. "You like eggs, huh?" I smile, appraising her. Trying to imagine what she would look like with a plump belly and a shining coat. "Well, you'll probably eat anything. But at least these aren't completely burnt for once, right?" She cocks her head, hoping for more. I oblige, and she's not so quick to step back. "I think I'll call you Eggs," I decide, giving her the whole plate. She eats with such force that I have to tighten my grip on the edges. "Everyone needs a name, and that one's as good as any. What do you think?"

Suddenly her eyes go wide, and she runs.

Frowning, I start to call after her. But then Angus is sitting beside me, holding a jar in his hands. Somehow I hadn't heard him coming down the steps. I put the empty plate by my feet and angle my body so I'm facing him. A tuft of hair sticks up at the back of his head, and his freckles are stark in the morning light. His bones make me think of a bird's: delicate and breakable. He's wearing a dirty striped shirt and his shoelaces are untied. He doesn't speak, and that should be normal, but there's something different about this silence.

"Sorry I've been such a brat lately," I say, meaning it. He doesn't respond. It would be better if he hated me. It would. Yet I find myself squinting at the sun and telling him, "You know, when I was a kid my dad used to tell me that the mountain is alive. He said it's a lady made of stone and trees, and she can hear and see us." I smile. "He also said that they were friends, and she would let him know if I wasn't telling the truth about something." Using the fork, I move a straggling piece of egg across the plate. "Sometimes I'd lie in bed at night and talk to her."

There's a long, long pause. Angus looks down at his jar and spreads his fingers over the glass sides. "Did she talk back?" he asks finally. He's too young for his voice to sound like rust and dust. But it does.

"Not that I could tell." I focus on him again. "But I bet mountains speak a different language than us. It was just . . . nice, feeling like someone was listening."

Quiet prevails once more. This one is kinder, not so fraught with the unspoken. The town clock echoes in the distance. I gradually become aware of the air around us growing warmer, and then Forgiveness is squatting in front of Angus. He looks at him intently. My little friend doesn't blink, doesn't speak, doesn't reveal that anything has changed, yet Forgiveness wouldn't be here unless Angus was thinking of him.

The Choice's azure eyes meet mine. I pull my legs to my chest and turn away to watch the end of the sunrise. The brightness, the illumination, is like yellow ribbons draping over the entire mountain, tangling together until it becomes something familiar. We sit in a row on that last step, me and Angus and Forgiveness. The light hits the glass of his jar, and it's smudged with fingerprints. Noticing this the same instant I do, Angus begins to clean it with the bottom of his shirt. The movement draws my attention to his arm, where Forgiveness's hand rests. A jolt goes through me.

So that's how it works? I want to ask him, unable to take my eyes off the touch. *It's that easy?*

"No," Forgiveness answers, as if he can hear my thoughts. "It's the hardest choice anyone can make."

The words unsettle me more than anything else he's said. "Mind if I help with that?" I ask Angus, tearing away from the evidence of his choice. He's still wiping the jar off. After a breath of hesitation—just a breath—my little friend gives me the jar.

And I know I really am forgiven.

I spend most of the day in the attic, and though I'm probably grounded, Georgie visits for a while and ends up helping. She talks about Billy and graduation but doesn't mention L.A. Once she's gone, I go up to my room. Instead of doing research on Dad, Dr. Stern, Andrew, and all the rest of it, I pull out *To Kill a Mockingbird.* My phone blinks with ignored texts. I read until my eyes hurt, then realize the sunlight is gone; night arrived without the courtesy of notifying me. There isn't a single star, only clouds. There will probably be a storm later.

Putting the book down, I get up and clutch the curtain with one hand. In the other I now hold my cell phone, with the image of Nate Foster and his mystery woman on the screen.

The scent of chocolate wafts on the air, and I turn, smiling. Revenge stands next to the computer desk where my open laptop glows. His expression is hidden in shadow. "What've you been up to?" I ask. He doesn't answer, and I go to the switch by the door to flick it on. Light floods the room. I turn to gauge Revenge's expression. His grin is missing, and though there's a glint in his eye, it's not anything good. My heart sinks. "What's wrong?"

"I saw you with him. Earlier."

"Forgiveness?" I clarify, trying to ignore the strange sensation in my chest, like my heart has become a rope in a game of tug-of-war. "Revenge, he wasn't even there for me. He was there for my—"

"I have never met anyone so blind." Revenge finally meets my eyes, and I almost flinch. In all the time I've known him, he hasn't looked at me that way before.

"What are you—"

He utters a short laugh, a humorless sound. We're directly under the bulb, and it casts blocky shadows over his features. "You have no idea what you've done to me, do you? You have no idea. I'm *Revenge*, Alex. I'm supposed to thirst for blood and pain and destruction. But even when I distance myself from you, even when I'm on the other side of the world, all I can think about are your lips. What they would feel like. What they would taste like. Do you understand now? Do you see how wrong this is?"

Surprise and Disbelief are the first to arrive. One laces his fingers through mine while the other wraps her arm around my waist. My mouth opens and closes like a fish that's been yanked out of the water and struggles for air. "I-I didn't… "

"There's a reason humans aren't supposed to see us," Revenge snaps, cutting me off. He swings away as though the sight of me is abhorrent. "To prevent things like *this* from happening." He runs a hand through his wild hair. No gel. "I shouldn't feel guilt over doing what comes naturally to me," he adds, gripping the edge of the closet door with white fingers.

The Emotions are still here, still touching me, and it takes a moment for his words register. "Wait, guilt? For what?" I shrug them off and reach for Revenge's shoulder without thinking.

He steps back, and my hand limply falls to my side. "Never mind," he says through his teeth. His fists keep clenching and unclenching, clenching and unclenching. He concentrates on a picture on the wall—a framed image of a horse that Mom gave me—as if it holds some deeper meaning for him.

Maybe it does. Remembering the phone, I glance down at it. The grainy face of the woman, frozen in passion, stares back. "If… if this is about the picture, I'm going to do something with it. Really. I just haven't had—"

"This isn't about the damn picture, Alex."

Before I can ask anything else, Disbelief speaks, startling both of us. "You can't really be jealous," she states. She raises her golden brows at Revenge. "Not you. Not with this… " The Emotion trails off, examining me skeptically like there must be something she missed.

"Don't you dare insult her."

"But—"

Revenge says something else that I don't hear; I'm still mulling over what he first spat at me. *You have no idea what you've done to me, do you? All I can think about are your lips. Do you see how wrong this is?* It's what I've been hoping for. It's what I've been wanting. But it wasn't supposed to happen like this. The moment wasn't meant to be marred by anger or resistance. I may not be a girl who daydreams about getting flowers or some happily-ever-after... but I did imagine it being more.

Still, he feels the same way. He's here. Even if he'll be gone soon, that doesn't mean—

My room is empty.

Revenge, Surprise, Disbelief, they're all gone. I look at the place where he stood for what feels like hours. Angus shatters the stillness with a knock. I blink, and suddenly the need to *move* consumes me again. My first instinct is to go to Briana's, as it usually is when something happens that doesn't make sense or I can't carry the weight of it on my own. I knock a sloppy good night back to Angus and hurry to pull on a hoodie. Missy is watching TV in the living room and I can hear Saul down in the shop.

"Mind if I go to Briana's?" I ask in a rush, the words tripping over each other to get out of my mouth. Missy presses mute on the remote, hesitating. We both know I don't deserve to go anywhere. "Please," I whisper.

My aunt must see something off in my expression, because she nods. Grabbing my keys off the hook by the door, I run down the stairs to my wrecked car. I blink, and suddenly I'm already at Briana's house.

The outside lightbulb hasn't been replaced in months, so it takes a few seconds in the darkness for me to discern that her father's and brother's cars are gone. It's just Briana and Francis. I get out, not bothering to take the keys with me, and go up to the door. Slam the side of my fist into the screen. *Bam-bam-bam*. There's the faint sound of voices within. As I listen, they get louder. Then the door flies open and Briana comes out, her appearance oddly haphazard. "Alex, it's not a good time," she says, trying to walk me back to the car. Her palm is clammy against my elbow. "I'll call you later, okay?"

"What's going on?" Worry walks with us. I crane my neck to look back.

She waves a hand dismissively, the gesture forced. There's a bead of sweat sliding down the side of her neck. "Nothing. Mom's just having an episode. I can handle it."

From the house I hear Francis thunder, *"Where are my cigarettes?"* A moment later she appears, wearing a frayed robe and no shoes as she stomps outside. Her eyes are red-rimmed and it's obvious she's been drinking. Briana hurries to her side, murmuring soothing nothings, and Francis swings at her. Briana ducks just in time.

Jolting into motion, I cross the yard again. Suddenly Francis's shouts turn into wails. It's a sound so desolate, so piercing that I feel it in my chest. Briana manages to catch hold of her mother's right hand, and I come up to take her left. My friend looks at me and we pull Francis to the house in silent agreement. She fights us, but barely, as though she knows there's no point but she has to try anyway.

Once we reach the threshold I pause, wondering if Briana still wants me to go. A mosquito hums past my ear. Briana guides Francis into the living room. She's still mumbling about cigarettes.

"We don't have any," Briana says gently, helping lower her to the chair. She kneels and adjusts the blanket so it's over Francis's boney knees. "You quit when I was born, remember? You told me the story, about how—"

"I don't care about some damn story," Francis mutters. Abruptly, she stands and wrenches free. She runs to the china hutch along the far wall and yanks a drawer open. The contents inside rattle. "I want my fucking cigarettes!" She swears again, her fingers trembling. She keeps opening drawers and cupboards.

Briana follows but doesn't try to stop her this time. "Why don't you sit down, and I'll run to the store?" she suggests, helpless. "Maybe I can get Ian to unlock the door." Francis responds with more words that are hot and foul. Greasy hair falls into her eyes as she searches for something that she won't find. But I know she won't stop, give up, acknowledge the futility of it. This is what it is to want something that's wrong or impossible.

So we trail Francis from room to room, watching her tear them apart. Throwing clothes to the floor and upheaving furniture and shattering anything that's made of glass. All the while Briana pleads and coaxes, mentioning rest or a new flower or talking to Bill. But it isn't until Francis shoves the garbage bin over and a potted plant falls out that she finally shatters. She drops to the tiles, her skin making a slapping sound on the cool surface, and crawls to it. Touches it with the tip of her finger. The leaves are withered and brown. She doesn't cry, doesn't sob, doesn't speak. She just looks down at the dead flower.

Slowly, Briana kneels next to her mother. "Let's get you into bed," she says. Francis doesn't argue, and she lets Briana pull her up. Together they walk down the hallway and into the bedroom at the very end. I can hear my friend singing to her, as if Francis is the child and Briana is the one with the responsibility. We should be consumed with things like college applications and growing up, yet here we are, tucking mothers in and holding guns. Life isn't fair. If I've learned anything, it's this.

To pass the time until Briana comes out, I tidy up the living room. There are plates with crusted food on the coffee table, a broken picture frame on the floor, a sticky substance dripping down the glowing television screen. I get a washcloth and the trash bin from the kitchen and fix what I can. The sounds of a *Jeopardy* rerun drown out the noise of my thoughts. Minutes pass, or maybe an hour, I don't know.

Eventually, feeling eyes on me, I straighten. Briana stands in the doorway, watching me with a fathomless expression. There are no Emotions around her to give away what she's feeling, but I can guess.

"What happened?" I ask quietly, pausing with the trash in my hands. Something clinks.

This seems to pull her out of her reverie. Briana folds her

arms and hunches her shoulders, moving to sit on the couch. I put the trash bag down and settle on the cushion closest to her. "We fought," she mumbles. "When I came home, she was already upset about that stupid flower. I just exploded, Alex. I told her she was a shitty mother and that she cared more about her plants than me. She didn't say anything. So, wanting to hurt Mom just as badly as she'd hurt me, I blurted out the truth that she's always pretended not to see. Even then, she wouldn't speak. I told her I hated her and stomped off. By the time I came back out, she was like this. Mom doesn't do well with confrontation or change."

There's a shocked pause as I take this in. All these years, Briana has never told her parents? Georgie and I thought they knew. We thought everyone knew. Suddenly, all the strain and resentment between Briana and her mother makes sense. How could I have missed it?

"Why tonight?" I finally whisper, brushing a strand of hair away from her face.

"Because I'm leaving." A bitter smile curves her lips. "Because I was running out of time, and I wanted to be heard." I've never seen her smile like that, not once in our entire lives. It frightens me.

At a loss of what to say, I wrap my arm around her. She's stiff at first, but then she relaxes into my side. "Where's your dad?" I ask next, putting my temple against hers.

"On his way."

Silence. We both look at the TV but don't really see it. Briana sniffs. I hold her close, wishing the world were simpler. More seconds pass us by, making me feel like we're two kids stranded on the highway with all these cars whizzing past and refusing to stop. Now Love and Sorrow haunt Briana, beautiful specters that linger longer than most. Some might think it strange, these two Emotions coming together, but I've seen it so many times in the course of my life. Sorrow accompanies Love just as often as Joy does. That's the thing about love; it may be permanent, but it's never the same. One day it brings light and smiles, and the next it becomes pain and shadow. Yet we still risk it, letting love into our lives. Because that light is worth facing the darkness.

Suddenly Briana sobs. I hold her even tighter and kiss her cheek. My friend tastes like salt and anguish. She shakes. And finally, after so many years of being silent and enduring, she cries. I stay there and keep my arms around her, as if that's the only thing keeping her together. Every sob makes me wince, and Revenge's words are lyrics to the music of Briana's pain. Pain I never realized the depths of until now.

I have never met anyone so blind.

And here I thought I saw everything, even what no one else could. Turns out, Revenge was right.

He was right about everything.

TWENTY

The beam of my headlights sweeps across the shop and the stairs. Near them, a pair of eyes glows in the dim. At first I think it's a raccoon. Then the animal wags a tail, and I know. Eggs. I cut the engine and get out, approaching deliberately. She pins her ears to her head, but she doesn't run. I squat. When she remains sitting, I run my hands over her. My palms brush her protruding ribs, mindless of the brambles in her fur. She makes a sound of pleasure deep in her throat. I realize that I'm smiling through a sheen of tears. "Come on," I murmur, flattening my palms against my thighs to stand. It feels like I've gained a thousand pounds in the last twenty minutes.

But Eggs won't follow, no matter how much I coax her. Hoping she'll stay, I slip into the apartment and open the fridge. Find a plate of roast beef covered in tin foil that was probably meant for me. I ease back down the stairs and pinch a piece of meat between my fingers. Eggs cocks her head, interest in her wide gaze. I wave it beneath her nose. She tries to snatch it from me, but I retreat, one step at a time. She creeps up the stairs in pursuit. "That's it. Good girl," I whisper.

The doorway gives us the most trouble. Eggs stops and peers inside, fearful, as if monsters might be lurking in the shadows. I know the feeling. "There's nothing there," I say soothingly, scratching one floppy ear. She leans into the touch and catches the scent of the meat again. "That's it." I ease into the entryway. After another hesitation, Eggs follows. I give her the meat and move around her to shut the door. She scarfs it down so quickly she probably doesn't even taste it. Praying that Saul and Missy don't hear something and get out of bed to investigate, I now herd Eggs toward the bathroom. Whatever reservations she had must have been abandoned at the door, because she doesn't struggle. I shut this door, too, and twist the faucet on the bathtub. The pipes shudder and groan in the wall. "Please don't wake up, please don't wake up … " I mutter, testing the temperature of the water with my hand. Once it's warm, I shove the plug into the drain and turn to Eggs.

She's already figured out my intentions and is pressed in the corner, whimpering. I croon empty words meant to comfort. Eggs resists, and I end up dragging her across the floor and lifting her into the tub. Immediately the front of my shirt is soaked. Eggs tries to jump out every five seconds. I keep one hand firmly on her neck while the other manages to get my shampoo off the ledge, open it, and apply it everywhere. I can feel tiny bumps burrowed into her skin—wood ticks. Some are just knots. Those will have to be taken care of later.

Someone clears their throat.

I jump and turn around with a sinking feeling in my chest. Eggs seizes the opportunity and leaps out of the water. Puddles form on the floor as Missy and I stare at each other. The dog makes it worse by shaking herself off and completely spraying us, the mirror, the walls. Though there's no possible way to cover this up, I still try to come up with something, but all that leaves my mouth is a strange croak.

Missy ends the silence by rubbing her eye with the heel of her hand. She's never looked more exhausted. "Alex, what is that?" she asks me groggily. There's a hint of resignation in the question.

"Uh ... " I clear my throat. "It's a dog."

"I see that. What is it doing in the apartment?"

I look from Eggs's timid eyes to Missy's tired ones. Though I know it's wrong to put another burden on my aunt's shoulders, I can't help it. "She needs us," I say simply. Behind me, the faucet leaks. *Drip. Drip. Drip.* Missy doesn't reply. She looks long and hard at Eggs, who cowers into my side. Petting her head, I don't say what I'm really thinking: that we need her, too.

"We'll talk about this in the morning," Missy finally mutters. She shuffles back to bed.

Telling Eggs to stay, despite the fact that she probably doesn't know any commands, I quickly clean up the mess with a towel and drain the water. It gurgles. Then I step into the hallway, and Eggs eagerly accompanies me. After we get to my room, I dig some scissors out of the desk drawer. Once again I pin the dog into place while I attempt to get rid of the forest tangled in her coat. Chunks of brown-black hair fall onto the rug. She looks vaguely ridiculous when we're done, like she lost a battle with a drunk barber, but she's probably cleaner than she's ever been in her life.

It's even later by the time I take a shower of my own, brush my teeth, and get into some sweats. I fall into bed, willing Dream to stay away.

Eggs paces for a few minutes, her claws clicking against the floor. She keeps looking at the door, me, the window. I lie on my side and wait. My patience is rewarded when the dog finally dares to jump up on the bed—the springs creak—and settles onto her stomach, heaving a sigh. The scent of my tropical shampoo surrounds us, seeps into the sheets. Eggs closes her eyes, and I've never seen an expression so content.

Envy and a sense of satisfaction stab my heart, like someone is curling their finger around it and digging their nail into the tender, beating flesh of it. Pretending not to see the Emotion sitting next to me, I enjoy the sight of Eggs for a moment, then close my eyes too. I put my hands under my pillow.

Something crinkles. Frowning, I pull it out. A piece of paper? It's too dark to see, so I lean over and switch the lamp on. When I see what it really is, my breathing becomes ragged and my pulse ricochets; Fear is already sitting beside me, studying it with curiosity.

It's a picture... of me. I'm swimming in the lake, and the image was captured mid-laugh. The camera wasn't able to see Revenge, so I'm completely alone in the water.

On the back someone has scribbled the words, *I LIKE TO TAKE PICTURES TOO.*

The painkillers Dr. Norris prescribed for my head do keep Dream away. Still, I sleep fitfully, tossing and turning until the blankets are twisted around me. It's one of those nights you're trapped halfway between slumber and reality, semi-aware of each realm. Random images flicker through my mind like one of those old black-and-white movies. A footprint in the mud. The branches of a tree. A silhouette in the entrance to the mines. All the while some distant part of me is aware of a solid weight on top of my left foot, the glow of moonlight across my bedroom floor, the bottle of pills on the nightstand.

Something pulls me completely awake, though. A familiar voice.

Alexandra.

My eyes fly open, and I sit upright, blinking rapidly. *Alexandra,* he whispers again. The room is empty and the window is closed, yet I can still *feel* him nearby. No, this can't be happening again. I clutch my head and focus on breathing. "You're not real, you're not real."

The clock reads 2:42 a.m. Eggs is still at the end of the bed, wide awake. She looks at me and whines. I peel the covers aside—they're damp with my sweat—and rub my eyes. Maybe I'm not really awake yet. I lean forward to rest my elbows on my knees. Something squishes. Frowning, I glance down. What ... ? Dumb horror clouds my mind. I gag, and it's so violent it hurts. Oh, God. Oh, God.

My legs are covered in mud. All the way up to the edges of my shorts. Leaves cling to the brown cake on my skin, some twigs as well. And there's a wood tick on my foot. There are probably dozens more, their heads buried in me. Sucking, sucking. Is that a leech on my knee? Tears spring to my eyes again. I stumble to the bathroom, mindless of Saul or Missy seeing this. All I can think is, *Oh, God. Oh, God. Oh, God.*

Somehow I manage to twist the knobs in the shower. The water shoots free of the spout, freezing. I don't care. My fist wraps in the shower curtain as I haul myself under the steady stream. Needles of cold stab every part of me that the water touches. Oh, God. Oh, God. Sobbing, I scrub at the mud, at the mess of ticks and leeches and horror. It comes off in chunks. Plops to the porcelain floor. I gag again and again.

The drain is clogged now. The filthy water is up to my ankles. I don't care. It needs to come off, it needs to come off. I don't count how many wood ticks I rip free. I can see my skin finally, stained but visible. My frenzy only increases. In my desperation I slip on my heel and I'm not quick enough grabbing the curtain. I slam down. Pain spurts through my hip. I just keep scrubbing, scrubbing, scrubbing. Sitting there in that dirty water.

Years go by, and eventually I drag myself out of the tub and collapse on the rug, a broken heap of flesh and searing shock. Eggs is huddled next to me. How long has she been there? But I lose track of time again. I don't know how long I stay in that tiny ball. And I don't wonder how I got all that mud on me, not yet. I have to keep concentrating on pulling and pushing air through my lungs.

Outside, it's still night. Through the tiny window, the moon observes my pain without sympathy. That pale, round face inexplicably makes my mind flash back to that moment on the road, when the man in the ski mask laughed at my fear. His teeth had glinted as brightly as that moon. The thought revives me, renews the ever-present urge to move and escape. Somehow I push myself up, clean the bathroom for a second time that day, and go back into my room. Eggs clicks after me. The sight of the sheets is almost my undoing again. But I force my insides to transform into something hard and unfeeling. I bundle the sheets up and put them in the laundry hamper. Then, adjusting my legs so Eggs has room, I curl into a clean blanket. I can't bring myself to turn the light off.

And I swallow three more pills.

On Sunday morning, it rains.

Saul is at the kitchen table, drinking his coffee. It's been days since I've really seen him, and I wince when his eyes narrow at Eggs. Missy is curiously absent. Sitting in my usual chair, I fidget and mentally prepare for another argument. Which is why Surprise pops into existence when my uncle just sets his cup down and leans sideways to get closer to Eggs. "Hey, old girl." He bends and scratches the spot beneath her chin. Her foot taps in ecstasy. "Are you the one who's been going through the trash?"

Neither of us answers. The town clock erupts into the silence. "I'm going to take her for a walk," I say. Then I hastily add, "I mean, if that's all right with you."

He's still looking at Eggs. "It's fine. Later you might want to go to Ian's and pick up some dog food."

A lump swells in my throat. Surprise grins at me. He's a nondescript Emotion except for his hair, which resembles an especially eccentric Albert Einstein; it sticks out in every direction. As I watch, he runs his fingers through the strands. It doesn't help.

"Well, have a good day," I say to Saul, sliding out of the chair and standing. Saul mumbles something unintelligible. His forgiveness won't be so easily earned. Only this time, I don't think I want it.

Eggs looks reluctant to leave, but she bolts when I open the front door. We leave Saul to his coffee, and a gust of wind slams into me the instant I step into the open. It has teeth that sink into my bones. I reach back to grab my jacket off the hook. Eggs thunders down the stairs as I shrug it on and reach to firmly shut the door. When I turn back, our new dog is vanishing into the trees.

"Eggs, wait—" I call. Too late. She's so excited that I can hear her crashing through the woods, until the sounds fade completely.

She'll come back, I tell myself. She'll get hungry. But doubt blooms in the back of my head like some poisonous flower. Experience has taught me that most things don't come back. And Eggs doesn't belong to me, not after one bath and one night. She belongs to the mountain.

For a few minutes I stand at the edge of the brush, hands shoved in my jacket pockets. Unable to let go of hope. An empty soup can rolls over the ground and touches the side of my shoe. I glance down at it . . . and my stomach drops. There's a clear imprint of a bare foot in the dirt. *My* foot, obvious in how the second toe is longer than the first. Suddenly last night makes sense—waking up with the forest caked to my legs. Those sleepy images that I thought were random, all the times I wondered why my bedroom window was open . . . I must have been sleepwalking. But where did I go?

The answer comes to me even before I've finished asking myself the question.

Birds sing to the morning and the sky writhes, but there's no sign of a dog with a bad haircut. Finally, giving the soup can a violent kick, I walk away. I hear it *clink* as it lands. Since Saul has given me permission to leave, I get into my car and go. The engine barely starts, hacking and coughing and wheezing like Loretta Roan after she's had too many cigarettes. It does start, though, and I tear down the slope, taking the twists and curves at a dangerous speed. Fear hooks his arm around my neck, putting his other arm out the window and grinning. Memories of the accident pound at me. I just go faster.

In the face of all that's happened—the attacks, the picture, Revenge—all I can think about now is my father and how even in sleep he haunts me. So I head back to the mines. I have to know. Was it real, or am I really going insane?

The mountain is vibrant, bright hues of green and brown everywhere I look. The instant I see that chain stretching over the road I squeal to a stop and get out, leaving the engine idling. I duck beneath it and run toward that looming mouth. He's nowhere in sight.

Like last time, I don't let that deter me. "Daddy?" I whisper, venturing into the darkness. It's dry in here, and dust stirs with each step. "Daddy, are you here?" Hope and Sorrow and Confusion follow me, their touches all gentle. My calls echo and the cavern swallows them whole. I turn around and around, trying to catch a glimpse, just a glimpse, of *something*. His voice had been so tangible, every single time. And I couldn't have just imagined seeing him. Now Frustration and Resentment are here, shoving me and squeezing my arms so tightly my blood stops. "Dad, *answer* me, goddamn it!" I scream, halting.

"Alexandra."

I scream again, spinning.

Dad stands near the elevator.

The Emotions crowd closer around me while I drink him in. He's shrouded in shadow, but it's undeniably my father. The eyes that I inherited stare back. He's wearing the plaid shirt that's hidden beneath the covers of my bed at home. There are bruises and cuts all over his skin, and the head wound that killed him gapes and bleeds. Not a figment of my imagination. Not a dream or a thought or a wish.

Reacting on instinct, I dive to embrace him. He evades me, stepping out of the way just in time, and I stumble, grabbing a stone jutting out of the dirt wall to stop my fall. Before I can recover or demand answers Dad says, "I miss you, sweetheart."

That voice. It brings back so many memories. A flash of pain. Brakes squealing. Straightening, I squeeze my eyes shut to keep the images out. I have to pause and take a few gulps of air in order to speak again. Questions have been living on the end of my tongue, and they've gone so long unanswered that they've begun to build homes and settle into a thing of permanence.

When I finally manage to ask one of them, it's not the one I'm thinking of, the one I intend to say. "Do you remember what you used to tell me about the mountain?" I ask shakily, wiping a tear off the edge of my jaw.

His expression sags into one of pain and regret as he answers, "I do remember, Alex. But I'm here for a reason. There isn't any time to relive the past."

"What reason?" I take a step closer, aching to touch him. He counters this by taking a step back. Hurt appears and hugs me, burying her nose in my hair. She's a tiny creature with the strength of a grown man. Dad's next words, though, make her vanish.

"Nate Foster is leaving."

I freeze, wondering if I'd heard him correctly. "What?"

"Someone made an offer on his house. They're leaving within the month." He doesn't say it matter-of-factly—he says it with barely suppressed fury. With unrelenting agony. The same way I must sound to others.

In the quiet that follows, I become aware of a distant sound. It's begun to rain. "H-how do you know that?" I ask Dad, meeting his gaze. He doesn't respond. I notice the wound again, and nothing has ever seemed so red and so deep. "Is this a dream?"

Slowly, my father shakes his head. "No. Not this time."

Despite everything else I need to know, I can't stop

myself from asking, "Is … is Mom here? Or Hunter?" My eyes seek the darkness around him as if they might be there, hidden and just waiting for me to notice.

Another silence spreads through this tiny hole in the earth, and it feels as heavy and substantial as if the walls gave way and buried us. Dad studies me with tears in his eyes, and I start to think he's not going to answer. But then he says, "We're all here, honey."

The breath catches in my throat, and suddenly Dad's form starts to go transparent. Already I can see through him to the elevator behind. "Wait," I cry, running to him again. "I still have so many—"

He's gone.

The twelve-year-old girl that still exists inside of me refuses to leave. She makes us wait for him to return, for one more word or glimpse to feed our starving soul. But there's nothing. There's only the dirt and the dark. Finally, mindless of the rain, I drift back to my car. Shift gears. Drive home. Walk up the steps. Go inside. Shut the door.

Missy is sitting at the kitchen table. She looks up from a magazine she's reading. "I made pancakes for lunch," she announces. "And I didn't burn them. That's always a plus, right? Hey, where's your little friend?"

I shrug in response, unable to speak after what happened in the mines. My aunt frowns, probably sensing something amiss, but doesn't pursue it. Part of my brain processes that she's telling me to get some food off the stove and eat with her. Feeling like an automaton or a doll, a thing just made of flesh and bones, I obey. I sit. The chair creaks, as it always does. Nothing has changed, yet everything has changed.

Seconds—at least it feels like seconds—pass. Missy is saying something again, pointing to my plate. Following the tongs of her fork, I look down. Somehow, the pancakes have become soggy lumps, bloated with syrup and butter. Cold to the touch. Indifferent, I turn to look out the window and lose myself in the gray sky. Right now there are no questions to avoid and no voices to disturb the stillness. There is only the rain.

TWENTY-ONE

On the way home from school I stop at both the mines and the Fosters'. Neither visit brings me any peace or satisfaction, so I don't linger. Once I get to the apartment I go to my room and sit at the desk, immersing myself in the mystery of the flash drive. If I don't focus on something, I might lose what little sanity I have left.

Someone is in the shop with Saul, buying one of the abandoned pianos he repaired. The thuds and clunks of the move reach my ears through the floor as I browse the files. I've been through everything at least twice already, and I barely understand any of the information. I open SUBJECTS and review the list of names, remembering the urgency in Dad's voice when he said, *I know you took the kids, and I know you lied to me and Stern.* And how does Sammy Thorn tie into all this? Suddenly I stiffen, leaning closer to the screen with interest.

There are profiles for each of the names. Phone numbers, addresses, physical details, and often photos for each subject. There are even descriptions of what drew the attention of the researcher. My heart struggles against the confines of my chest when I see words like *other plane* and *sight*. One story in particular stands out, about a girl with hazel eyes. Christine Masterson.

Four days ago, a report reached me about a young girl in a town approximately one hundred and sixty-three miles east of here. According to local residents she has always talked about things that no one else can see. She comes from a religious background, and her parents came to believe that she is being possessed. After interviewing her family further, however, I have deduced that these "demons" Miss Masterson sees are the focus of my studies. Her descriptions are too accurate and too detailed. Her parents willingly granted me custody, but Miss Masterson was not so compliant. Nonetheless, she has contributed to the serums.

It's such a strange realization, to know that I'm not as alone as I've always felt. There are similar themes in the other subjects' backgrounds, but something about the way Christine gazes into the camera makes me return to her again and again. I scroll to find her address, and my pulse quickens when I see that she lives just forty minutes away, in Kennewick. One of the boys, Travis Bardeen, isn't as convenient but still possible. There's no picture for him. I write their information down and keep looking. The others are farther out, too far. They're spread across the country. Some are even overseas.

As I read, one question returns to me over and over,

like the ringing of the town clock: What were these experiments trying to accomplish?

If I can't get the answers from Andrew or Dr. Stern or Dad, maybe the kids in these profiles will tell me.

The sky has deepened to the color of rust by the time I reach Kennewick. It takes me too much time to find Christine's house—the GPS signal on my phone keeps fading in and out—but eventually my car rattles down the right back road and a faded mailbox comes up on my left. No name, just numbers. Ignoring the flutters in my stomach and the Emotion in the passenger seat, I turn into the driveway. It's riddled with potholes, and I grit my teeth for a mile until the house comes into view. It's in worse shape than Briana's. The roof looks a moment away from caving in, and the yard is a landfill. I see an ancient dryer and an even older pickup truck among all the junk.

People in these mountains tend to open their doors with sawed-off shotguns in their hands, so I pull out my eyebrow ring in an effort to look less menacing. I glance in the rearview mirror. Two tiny holes glare back at me, red and aching. It might be worse than having the ring in, but I don't want to be here a second longer than I have to be. I get out, Apprehension fretting around me all the way up to the door. The air smells fetid, like there's a dead animal under the porch. There probably is. I force myself to lift my hand and knock on the side of the screen door.

Minutes pass. No one answers. Holding my breath against the stench, I knock again. Something stirs inside, then a crash. Someone curses. Footsteps. A woman opens the door and squints at me through the holey screen. She has stringy brown hair and wears a T-shirt so big it hangs off one boney shoulder. But the most noticeable thing about her—though I do my best not to stare—are the jagged scars running down her cheeks and neck. As if something with claws tried to rip her face off.

"What do you want?" she snaps. "I ain't got no money and I don't need no religion, you got it?" She swipes at her nose and starts to close the door.

"Does Christine Masterson live here?" I blurt.

She pauses. Opens the door wide again. "What?"

"Does—"

"Yeah, I heard you the first time. Is this some kind of joke? Do you think it's funny?" Anger and Sorrow are behind her now. She grips the edge of the screen and glares at me. *Danger*, my instincts whisper.

"I-I'm sorry. This isn't a joke. My father died a while ago, and I just found out that he and Christine may have known each other. I was hoping to talk to her, to see if she knew anything about him."

Pause. "You really don't know?" she asks, the fire in her eyes fading. I shake my head. The woman purses her lips, and Anger departs. She still doesn't emerge from behind the screen, but she tells me, "Christine disappeared six years ago. No one's seen her since. Police think she's probably dead. Hell, so do I."

Instantly I see that it was stupid to come here. I wasn't looking for Christine; I wanted something else. More about her Sight, her experiences, how she kept the madness at bay.

What the purpose of the experiments actually was. Stupid, stupid, stupid. I'm not going to get anything from these people.

"Why do you think she's dead?" I ask finally, reluctant to let go of one last shred of hope. Stalling. Delaying the inevitable.

The woman's gaze becomes as distant as her answer. "Someone came and took her away. A doctor. No one raised a finger to stop him. They thought she had a demon in her; they wanted her gone. But I never did. She still called me every day after she left. She always sounded scared. Then the call didn't come one morning, and later I was attacked by a guy who kept asking me where she was. I never heard from her again, even when I was in the hospital."

There's a wealth of feeling in her voice, obvious even if the Emotions weren't hovering around her. Suddenly, watching her, I see it. They have the same gold flecks around their irises. "You're her sister," I say softly.

She doesn't deny it. Instead she retreats again, her face falling into shadow. "You better go before the folks come home," she mutters. "They don't take too kindly to strangers on our land."

But still I hesitate. I step forward, a board moaning beneath my foot, and reach out as though to touch the door. When she tenses, I falter. Maybe she doesn't feel it, the connection between us, forged from the white-hot pain of loss. "What's your name?" I hear myself ask. A bead of sweat slides down the small of my back, and I wonder if somehow one of the creatures from the other plane reached up into the sky and fanned the flames of the sun.

Another palpable silence forms after I've spoken. At first I think the woman is not going to answer. She keeps staring into the trees, her features tight and distrusting. Something buzzes past my ear and it feels like the only thing in motion in this tiny space. Relenting, I slowly pull away.

Then the woman surprises me by meeting my gaze, looking at me like Christine looked into the camera. With uncertainty and a strange imploring. "I'm Nora."

I try to smile. "I'm—"

"I don't care who you are, girl. You have to go. *Now*. And don't come back." With that, she slams the door.

It doesn't faze me much; I'm getting used to having doors shut in my face. Sighing, I trudge back to my car and slide behind the wheel. Before the engine has finished rolling over there's a shimmer out of the corner of my eye, and I know I'm no longer alone.

Part of me expected—hoped—it would be Revenge. We haven't spoken since he threw his feelings at me. There's so much to figure out, so much to think on. But that minty fragrance prepares me, and when I turn to face Forgiveness, I've buried my disappointment so deep that the Emotion doesn't even feel my call. My knee bumps the keys dangling from the ignition and they clink into the stillness.

Forgiveness studies the run-down house, interest in his eyes. "Why are you here?" he questions.

It's a reminder that Nora told me to go, and I wouldn't put it past her to stomp onto the porch with a gun in her hands. Quickly I reverse onto the road and start the drive back home. *Home*. The word is so weighted it's a piece of iron in my head. I don't respond to Forgiveness and he doesn't press me. Revenge wouldn't do that. He would demand and prod and tease until he knew everything.

We're nearly halfway there—thundering past a sign that reads *FRANKLIN 20 MILES*—when the quiet becomes unbearable. It reminds me too much of the night Forgiveness read to me and I fell asleep to the sound of his voice. "Why do you care so much?" I say abruptly. He turns his head toward me, and his soft curls brush the collar of his T-shirt. "Why are you trying so hard to save me?" I add. The words are uneven. I clench the wheel and my knuckles go white.

The Choice twists away again, watching the passing landscape with an expression that almost seems weary. "You're so young, Alex. Your world is so small. You think it will always be like this, but you're wrong. If you would just give it some more time…"

"That's not an answer."

A cloud moves in front of the sun, and the world fades to gray. "I knew your father," Forgiveness states after a brief hesitation. His long fingers fold between his legs, and though his stance appears relaxed, I sense tension emanating from him.

"You did?" Surprise joins us.

"I did. He struggled with anger, too. He summoned me once, on the night you were born." Forgiveness stops and I want to snap at him, order him to tell me everything. Why has he kept this a secret until now? But that isn't the way to get answers from the other plane, so I force myself to wait. My restraint is rewarded, and Forgiveness angles his body toward me. His eyes are sad but resolved. "The first thing you should know—though you already do, I hope—is that your parents loved you. More than anything. But before you came along, your father had plans to go to college. He'd been accepted to a state school and he was weeks away from leaving this place behind for good."

I blink. Dad had almost left Franklin? I'd known it was his dream, of course, but I'd always thought he hadn't had a choice in the matter. If he had a way out, why didn't he...

Realization hits. Of course. "Then Mom told him she was pregnant," I finish. A sour taste fills my mouth.

Forgiveness nods. "He decided to stay. He got a job at the mines to support you both. And he never said one word to your mother about how much he regretted those missed opportunities. Secretly, though, he struggled with anger. Part of him blamed your mother for it." Forgiveness doesn't give me a chance to absorb this. "But on the night of your birth, everything changed. He took one look at you, and he made a choice."

Tears sting in my eyes. I'm grateful that I have the road to focus on, since it takes me a few moments to regain my composure. "Why didn't you tell me?" I manage.

A deer runs in front of us, far enough ahead that I'm not startled. It vanishes into the trees, a blur of brown fur and long legs and elegant movement.

In another odd moment of indecision, he doesn't answer my question right away. He rakes his hair back. But eventually he says, careful not to meet my gaze, "I didn't want you to think that the past is the only reason I'm here." He loses himself in the rushing trees as if this is his purpose, rather than redemption.

Suddenly I'm fascinated by the scenery, too. The richness of the dirt, the height of the treetops, the brightness of the sky. It burns in a simmering shade of orange, making the entire mountain feel like an inferno and we're only ashes. "What other reason is there?" I ask quietly.

I can feel Forgiveness staring at me now. "You know why, Alex." His voice has softened too, and, unable to resist, I glance at him. Something in his expression turns the anger within me into butterflies. They take wing, all colors and forbidden things. Forgetting the danger, I flounder in the ocean of his eyes. He's nothing like what I expected him to be, and I wish he was. I wish he didn't read books or see me or have such a kindness about him. Because it would make the choice so much easier.

Again, I'm the one to look away. We don't speak again until I'm pulling into my parking spot in front of the apartment. Neither of us moves. Birds call to each other and flutter on the power line over our heads. The smell of Forgiveness is overwhelming, coating my skin and the seats and the air. I breathe it in for a minute. Then I surprise myself once more, this time by blurting, "Do you have a name? I mean, a real one?"

I've astonished him, too; I can see it in the way he goes still. But I can't take it back. For what feels like the hundredth time in the last hour, Forgiveness doesn't immediately respond. It soon becomes apparent that he isn't going to, and it's even more apparent that it's because he doesn't have a name. Something I said to Eggs that day on the step comes back to me: *Everyone needs a name.*

I shift in the seat, clearing my throat. "Well, the next time you introduce yourself to someone and don't want to use Forgiveness . . . you seem like an Atticus. For the record." I get out of the car.

"Atticus," he echoes, almost to himself. A smile touches his lips. I shut the door, thinking he'll follow. But when I look back, he's gone. Saul is playing one of the pianos, and I stand on the sidewalk to listen. From this spot I can see through a break in the trees, to the high ridge of another peak. Mist swirls over the moss and rocks.

What's the right choice? I ask silently.

The mountain doesn't answer.

TWENTY-TWO

I'm in art class when he calls.

The number on the caller ID isn't labeled, but I know it by heart. The instant I see those digits I stop breathing. Recovering—my phone keeps buzzing, but I know it'll stop in a few seconds—I raise my hand. "Mr. Kim? I have to run to the bathroom. It's an emergency." Our teacher looks up from helping Yelena Prichard with her clay candle and nods his assent. Georgie and Briana give me questioning looks, which I ignore. Abandoning my sad attempt at a sculpture of the mountain, I slide off the stool and rush to the door.

"Dr. Stern?" I say, breathless and low. I tuck my hair behind my ear and hurry to the privacy of the girls' bathroom. The scent of unwashed toilets greets me. I grab the edge of the sink—water clings to my palm—and stare at my reflection, willing him to respond. *Don't let this be another fluke.*

His accented voice is terse and urgent. "Meet me in the campus library at three o'clock."

"What—"

"Bring the flash drive. And don't tell anyone."

Click.

There's no time to wonder how he knows I have the flash drive, nor about his sudden change of heart or the need for such secrecy. All that matters is that a window has finally opened when everything has been shut so tightly around me. Bolting from the sink, I sprint to my locker to retrieve my keys. Just as I reach it someone passes me, a man. His shoulder slams into mine. "Hey, watch it!" I snap.

He doesn't apologize or look at me, and I glimpse his face briefly before he walks away. I resist the urge to retaliate. Keys in hand, I turn toward the front doors... and time stops completely.

"You can't be here," I whisper. Surprise and Disbelief once again fly to Franklin at my call, both of them gaping. They murmur to each other as their hands grip me, and their words are as meaningless as the wind. My entire body trembles. My mind races, struggles to accept what my eyes see. I'm in school. We're not alone. There are no shadows. It's impossible.

Like our last encounter, my father's expression is solemn and hard. Something is different, though. He's not as mournful as he was in the mines. I can't discern what it is now shining from his eyes. I start to speak again, strange urges ripping through me like wolves over a carcass: the desire to be with him regardless of where we are, and the instinct to deny any of this is happening.

He cuts me off, quickly and curtly. "You've let yourself forget," he growls. "Your feelings for that creature are clouding your judgment."

Suddenly I know what emotion glints in his gaze. Anger. It's anger.

And he's talking about Forgiveness. Somehow he knows about my struggle, my unfulfilled promise, how I keep pushing Revenge away. Shame blinks into existence. His essence is strong, and I try to swallow the lump swelling in my throat and reach out a hand toward my dead feather. "Daddy, I swear I haven't forgotten anything. I've been trying—"

"Remember, Alex." He steps back, unrelenting. When I frown, he says it again. "Remember."

At first I don't know what he means. But then the Emotions around us vanish until only one is left. I twist to face it, and I recognize him as he draws nearer, so near I can hear the moans and sobs and wails that cling to him. Though I retreat, my back hitting the wall of lockers, he doesn't stop. Images waver all around—someone on her knees cradling a boy covered in blood, a wraith of a girl in a hospital bed, a family standing in front of a casket. More and more and more, a planet's worth of pain coming at me and threatening to undo me.

"No. Don't do this. Please. *Please.*" I'm on the floor now and I can't see Dad. Sorrow huddles next to me, his lips pursed in a way that's almost apologetic or reluctant. Before I can plead or run, he embraces me. His grip is so tight it hurts, as though his fingers have sprouted tiny blades that dig into my shoulders.

This touch is different than the other times he's visited me. I can't fight against it, not even for a moment. My eyes roll back in my head and my body convulses with the violence of the memory I've tried so hard to keep at bay all these years. I'm falling into it, descending into darkness and cackling shadows until I'm opening my eyes . . . and it's starting again.

I huddle next to my bedroom door. Lightning flashes, making the white material of my T-shirt glow white. I feel like a spirit. Then the sound of my mother's gasp makes my heart seize in my chest, and for a wild moment I really do believe that I'm dying. "Is that . . . blood on your shirt? Will, what happened?" she asks, the words urgent and low so I won't hear. They don't know that I always hear.

Dad doesn't reply to her question, and Mom doesn't say anything either for a long, long time. I don't move. The storm howls for all of us, raging at the windows and walls that contain so many secrets and quiet agonies. Eventually Mom says, "If we're really going to do this, then I want them to go to Andrew's. That way they won't hear anything or try to come over." Her voice wavers. It frightens me more than all the rest; I've never known her to be anything but strong.

"Yes, fine, okay. Let's go." Dad sounds just as desperate as I feel. There's the sound of footsteps now, coming down the hallway and closer to my door.

I run back to bed and pretend to be asleep. The sheets are freezing. Then Mom is coming in, gently urging me awake, telling me to get dressed. As I hurry to obey she goes into Hunter's room. She comes out with my brother, who's in her arms and blinking blearily. We walk past Dad, who's standing by the apartment door with the keys to the truck in his hand. He doesn't look at me, but I look at him so hard my eyes burn.

There's a speckle of red by the collar of his shirt, a color that doesn't belong among the blues and greens and yellows of the plaid he's wearing. My alarm grows. What's happening?

Something stops me from asking. Together we all go down the damp stairs. Mom shields me as best she can from the wetness, and she watches me get into the back. Next she circles the truck to buckle Hunter into his car seat, and he starts to cry. She soothes him but it doesn't help. Dad climbs in behind the wheel, tapping his fingers restlessly, and it's time to go so Mom leaves Hunter to get into the front. He keeps screaming, and I scoot over to comfort him. He swings his arm up and his little fist connects with my nose. Pain slices through the bone, but I don't leave him. I stay. Because that's what Mom told me to do. Stay. It doesn't matter where; all that matters is that I'm doing it.

The truck lurches into motion and Dad drives fast, tearing onto the road and away from our home. It's raining so hard now that the world seems to be made of tears. The windshield wipers whip back and forth, back and forth, steady as a heartbeat. Thump-thump. Thump-thump. With each movement water sloshes off the glass. Worry sits between Mom and Dad, blocking my view of her as she murmurs, "Will, I really don't think you should be driving—"

"I'm fine."

She keeps arguing with him, but it's hard to hear with Hunter and the thunder. I find a toy airplane on the floor and swoop it through the air in front of my brother, hoping it will distract him. It does. He forgets to cry and stares at the plane, hiccupping. The trails on his plump cheeks begin to dry. I smile and make engine sounds, gliding and soaring the tiny thing through its tiny sky.

"Will!" Mom suddenly screams.

He jerks the wheel to the right, but it's too late. Too late.

I drop the plane, and there's an instant of absolute silence. My wide eyes see the headlights coming for us, the vein in my father's temple, the horrified way my mother raises her hands in front of her face as if that alone will stop it. I see the brightness of the radio buttons and hear Elvis bellow even as the tires screech and the storm rages and my little brother wails again.

And I see him. The man in the other car. Our eyes meet just before everything explodes.

My world goes white. As I've done so often these last few months, I listen. I listen to metal tearing and my family's screams cut off and the thud of the vehicle rolling and hitting the ground over and over. There's more pain, but I don't know where it is and it doesn't matter anyway. My eyes are squeezed shut so tight it feels like they won't ever open again.

Then everything is still.

Mom and Dad aren't fighting anymore, and Hunter isn't crying. They aren't doing anything. I don't want to open my eyes and look, but we're upside down and my head is tingling. I have to move. So I look.

I don't scream. I don't recoil. I don't sob. Blood pools on the ceiling, just next to my head. My family is utterly broken, and I know without touching them that I've been left behind. Hunter is still strapped in his car seat, within reaching distance. I can't bring myself to touch him, though. I just stare. Can't look away. Can't understand how he was smiling moments ago and now he's that thing that vaguely resembles my brother. There's a strange smell in the air, not rain or soaked earth. Almost... rusty.

Suddenly I want out. I want out, I want out, I want out! I flatten my hands against the ceiling, mindless of the blood, and finally scream. No words, just a sound that isn't even human. And someone does come.

Gradually I realize that I'm not as alone as I thought.

There's movement out of the corner of my eye, and I turn my head so fast it hurts, thinking I was wrong and Hunter is alive. But this being has no trace of dimples or toothless grins. Instead, Death gazes at me with cold eyes. I have never met him before, yet I know it's him. I shiver, unable to look away. He's kneeling beside the truck, his coat dragging through the mud and his knees dampening from the puddle. Somehow it's not demeaning. It only makes him more surreal and horrible. I know he's here for my family.

This is the moment I begin to hate the creatures from the other plane.

Unable to meet those eyes anymore, I focus on my mother. She's still so beautiful. Even though she's silent and she'll never speak again, her frantic whisper from earlier in the night fills my entire being until it's my blood, my bones, my veins. I'm made of it. Stay, stay, stay.

"I don't want to go," I whimper, looking at Death again. I don't know if it's the truth. All I know is that I don't want those pale hands to touch me.

His expression is fathomless. He doesn't move. After a few unbearable seconds, he says in a voice that the darkness and the silence is made out of, "It's not your time yet, little one."

I blink, and he's gone. So is everything else that mattered.

I come back to myself, drenched in sweat. Dad is gone,

along with Sorrow and any lingering doubts I had about what I truly want. I sit against the lockers for hours, days, years, staring at a poster on the wall depicting a girl looking at college applications, preparing for a future I will never have. Suddenly, the meeting with Dr. Stern is insignificant. My search for answers, irrelevant.

I push myself up from the floor, somehow still holding my keys. There are bloody ridges in my palms from where I must have held them too tight. I drift down the hall, out the doors, to my car. I don't think about where I'm going, and when the car stops I lift my head and see that I'm back at the apartment. Saul and Missy aren't here.

When I climb up the steps, I see my mother rushing down them with plastered hair and wide eyes, her fear obvious. Then she disappears. Something twists inside me, and I pause with my hand on the railing, concentrating. But the pain doesn't fade, and my insides don't turn to stone no matter how hard I try. The sun keeps shining, oblivious to the fact that it shouldn't be allowed to illuminate a place where things like this happen. Giving up, I drift to my room and shut the door. I sit on my bed and see myself, six years earlier, kneeling on the floor with my ear pressed to the crack between door and wall.

"Alex?"

I blink, and for a moment the face across the room is blurred. Dread takes root in the pit of my stomach and becomes a weed that threatens to grow into my throat and choke me. Forgiveness? After everything I've seen? But then my vision clears, and I see that it's Revenge—not Forgiveness—who watches me. He's standing in front of the window, a black-silver silhouette outlined in moonlight. How did it become night? When I say nothing in response, he turns to gaze through the window, as if the world out there is so much more interesting than this one.

For a few seconds I just look at him. That bittersweet scent of chocolate surrounds us. And I feel it. All of this, ending. It's almost audible, like glass breaking or a page turning.

I've finally made my choice.

TWENTY-THREE

"Alex, don't do this."

Silence.

Then, "Alex. Look at me."

Still I don't react. Ignoring Forgiveness and his grating voice has suddenly become easy, and I watch the picture slide out of the printer. Over and over and over. Nate Foster and his whore, entwined and oblivious to the fact that they're not alone. No one is ever alone, even when they are. I've seen the image so many times now that it's ingrained on the insides of my eyelids, there whenever I close my eyes. Revenge is behind me, strangely silent. But he's here, even if he hasn't touched me yet. It must be only a matter of time, because I'm not going to change my mind again. The choice is made.

It's become a mantra: the choice is made. And now I actually believe it.

Making a sound in his throat, Forgiveness comes closer,

probably to plead with me again or help me find reason. I don't look up as I mutter, "Get the fuck out of my face, or I won't stop with the flyers." This makes him pause, and I know we're both thinking of the gun in Uncle Saul's glove box.

Now Revenge steps in front of me, blocking Forgiveness from view. His fists are clenched. I don't intervene. Mint clashes with chocolate and they glare at each other. "Nate Foster deserves it," Revenge growls.

"Ruining his life won't make anything better," Forgiveness snaps back, the first time I've ever heard his voice rise. "It won't change what happened, and it won't give you any sense of peace, Alex. It will only—"

"Save the speech about my own self-destruction, please." I keep my attention glued to the printer.

Gilbert, the librarian, doesn't even look up from the book in front of him. He has that glaze in his eyes that gives away the fact he's high as a kite. Ironic that he's one of the smartest people in this town. He doesn't ask questions, like what it is I'm printing so many copies of or what class I'm supposed to be in. He just bends over some pages, dirty hair hanging into his eyes, and reads the words intently. It makes me think of Angus and his strange, empty jars. Odd how people find meaning in simple objects, when the real meaning is something they can't even see.

Involuntarily, my eyes meet Forgiveness's. He doesn't speak, but his eyes are screaming. *Stop. Don't do this. You'll regret it. Please.*

The choice is made. The choice is made. The choice is made.

But Forgiveness won't give up. He sends his memories to me, wistful moments of release or reunion. Just when I feel myself begin to waver, Revenge steps closer and I see a flash. A memory of my own. My little brother in his car seat, bloody and broken and gone. My resolve hardens like it's a clay sculpture that's been in the oven just long enough. Finished with the printer, I take my stack of inky retribution and walk away. It's a relief to put my back to the Choices. "Bye, Gil," I say as I pass the lanky librarian. He flaps a hand at me.

Desperate, Forgiveness calls my name, and there are sounds suspiciously like a struggle. I don't look back, but I hear Revenge say, "Let her go." He doesn't sound as smug as I thought he would. He doesn't follow me, and I'm glad, because there's something I want to do without anyone hovering over my shoulder. I drift through the school hallways, memorizing everything even though it's already been memorized, and enter the girls' bathroom.

Light pours in through the grates over the window. Setting the flyers on the edge of the sink, mindless of the dampness, I take a sharpie out of my pocket and go into the big stall. I squat. Next to my mother's declaration of love I write, *ALEX WAS HERE*. Because I was, no matter how it begins or ends. I stayed when everyone else left, I walked these halls and laughed and lived when all I could think about was death. My hand shakes slightly. For once, though, I've created something legible. I lean back, trying to avoid touching the toilet, and study the plastic wall, the things that kids thought worthy enough of forever remembering. Love, hate, hope, pain. My parents. And me.

Finished with this, too, I leave that familiar and reeking bathroom for the last time. Flyers in hand, I walk two doors down to the office. A fan blows in the corner and the air smells like stale cigarette smoke. Julia Stork, our receptionist and nurse, looks up from her rickety desk. Her cat-eye glasses glint purple in the florescent light. "Hi, Alex." Unaware of my purpose for being here, she smiles.

I don't smile back. The old me would hesitate, think, reconsider, but I'm past all of that. The choice is made. And it seems significant that there are no Emotions around me when I say it.

"I'm dropping out."

Crows take flight as I turn onto Sanderson Road. In their wake they leave a mutilated deer lying in the ditch. Beside me, Revenge hums under his breath. He taps his thumbs on his thighs and his green eyes are sharp. Tonight he's wearing a cowboy outfit, complete with hat and spurs. Normally I would comment, but not now. The house comes up on our right, and though it's not huge, it's a mansion in a place like Franklin. Just one more thing to resent them for. From one glance I know that the Fosters aren't home. Lights off, cars gone, everything closed. As if locks can keep me out. I kill the engine and quiet descends. The trees stir in the breeze, making a gentle rustling sound.

Before getting out, I turn to look at Revenge, asking

him the question with my expression since I can't bring myself to say it aloud: *Is it time?*

A muscle twitches in his jaw. He shakes his head.

Frustration appears behind me, wrapping his fist in my hair. The force of his grip makes my head snap back against the headrest. "How can that be?" he growls for us. I grimace. "Will this not alter the course of their lives?"

"Not enough, apparently," Revenge snaps.

The revelation makes me want to scream. Even now, after everything, I haven't truly decided?

Frustration unlatches his fingers and leaves. For the first time I notice his scent, something that resembles burnt rubber. It lingers in the confined space of my car.

Revenge and I stare at each other. Just as I did with the school, I commit everything about him to memory. His features are so sharp and pale, like strange scissors. That tarnished hair isn't so artfully gelled today. It's mussed and wild, as though he's been raking his hand through it every time I'm not paying attention. Neither of us looks away. My heart aches, I want him so badly. It's always been Revenge, even when everything else got in the way. I was just weak. No more, though. No more. I've made my choice—apparently my head or my heart just need to catch up.

Maybe Revenge can hear my thoughts. I've always wondered. "What do you want, Alexandra Tate?" he murmurs suddenly. Our pulses beat into the silence. Then, as an answer, I grab the stack of flyers off the floor, along with a roll of tape, and swing up and out of the Saturn. It doesn't matter if this won't seal the decision; the result will still hurt Nate Foster.

Revenge stays where he is, and I can feel him watching every moment, every movement. I march up to the front door. The color of it taunts me. As red as blood. With the ghosts of my family looking on, I slap a flyer to the center of it and tape it in place. Then another, and another. Over and over again until the whole thing is covered. There's no way Jennifer Foster will miss it. I go back to my car, get in, and wait. Revenge doesn't say anything. I don't either.

Like clockwork, she pulls into the driveway at six. Purse in hand, she totters up the sidewalk on high heels. Her hair flutters. She lifts the keys in her hand, prepared to put it into the lock … and then lifts her gaze. She freezes.

She doesn't see me, but I see her. I see everything. Every knife I've stabbed into her heart. Anger, Sorrow, Surprise, Denial. All of them appear around the woman and reach for her with invisible hands. She puts her hand against one of the pictures to cover it, or maybe convince herself that it's real, and bends over. The sound of her sobs echo. The Emotions are merciless and take their time drifting away.

There's a whisper of sensation in my stomach, the beginnings of some unwelcome feeling. I shove it down by closing my eyes and seeing their faces. Hearing their screams.

My nostrils flare and detect mint. There's a shimmer in the backseat. Revenge stiffens. "Is this what you wanted?" Forgiveness asks softly. There's pain in his eyes.

Comforting myself with the knowledge that he won't be able to come near me much longer, I smile and make myself watch Jennifer Foster. She's on her knees now, just as Death was when he peered in at my family on the night of the accident.

"No. I want more."

TWENTY-FOUR

I stand on the edge of the bridge.

Missy and Saul don't know about school yet—Julia agreed to let me tell them—and I had to make a pretense of going somewhere today. This was the first place I thought of. The water trickles below, brown and bloated from all the rain. The morning sun is painfully bright, reflecting off the silver of my eyebrow ring, and I squint. Though the weather has been deceptively cold this spring, a drop of sweat slides down my temple.

Minutes pass. I envision myself spreading my arms like some sort of bird, slowly tipping forward and falling onto those rocks. If I were to die now, would I end up with my family? For that matter, do people change in whatever afterlife exists... or do we take all our pain with us? I consider it for a few seconds, try to imagine what it would feel like to have my insides at peace, my mind at rest, my aches and wars gone.

Or existing with them forever.

And yet … if I leave now, I'll never speak to Briana or Georgie again. Saul and Missy. Revenge and even Forgiveness. Their faces haunt me, their shadowed eyes and fragile hopes. So much unfinished and so much barely begun. So much undiscovered and so much concealed. At the thought, Guilt materializes on my other side. And thinking of him must have been the encouragement he needed, because Forgiveness forms on the other. I focus on his beauty while Guilt touches me with her big, meaty hand.

"Do you regret what you did to Mrs. Foster?" Forgiveness asks after a moment. Today his voice reminds me of bells. Though still gentle, it's harsh and clanging to my ears. Just like the town clock, always ticking in the distance. Reminding me that there isn't much time left. Nate Foster is leaving and I still haven't kept my promise to Dad and Mom and Hunter. And myself.

"Yes," Guilt says. I scowl and shake her off. She smirks and disappears from view. I turn to stare at the creek again, but I know Forgiveness is watching me instead of the water, waiting for me to tell him.

If only there were some middle ground. There's no such thing as halfway or middle or between, though. There's only what is and isn't.

Forgiveness hesitates. "Alex—"

"You know, I missed the part where you became my therapist. Just leave it alone," I snap. If I let him say too much, he'll find a way through my resolve. He always does. Forgiveness starts to reply, of course, but the sound of my phone ringing slices through the tension. Probably Andrew or Missy. The man who betrayed me or the woman I betray every day.

In a burst of emotion I can't contain anymore, I yank the phone out of my pocket and throw it into the river. It's still ringing when it splashes into oblivion. Then I swing away from all the Emotions crowding the bridge and storm toward my car.

Only one of them follows me. His white T-shirt flutters against his torso. As I open the door, twisting to get in, I can't help but notice the ridges of muscles beneath that thin cotton. *Damn it,* I think, looking away too late. Lust and Longing surround me and their smothering embraces make escape difficult. The pause allows Forgiveness to catch up. He grips the door to stop me from shutting it, politely pretending not to notice the creatures giggling behind us.

"What?" I demand, hating how his proximity makes my heart pound. "What else do you have to say? What vague commentary, what soul-searching advice could you possibly offer that will make me change my mind? *Tell me.*"

The Choice remains calm as always, regarding me with his shuttered eyes. For the first time I long for an Emotion to visit, to turn the tables and show me what *he's* feeling. I breathe hard and glare up at him. Whatever I expected him to say, it's not, "You stopped looking too soon."

I blink. "What?"

"You should pay a visit to Travis Bardeen's house."

Lust gets bored and goes, but Longing stays. She observes me with an expression as inscrutable as Forgiveness's. The bridge is empty except for the three of us and the only sounds in the world are the birds, the creek, and my own traitorous pulse. "I know what you're doing," I say evenly. "It won't work." He won't distract me from my vendetta. Not this time.

I finally manage to get in the car. As I jam my keys into the ignition, a strand of hair slips into the corner of my mouth. Before I can impatiently pull it away, Forgiveness leans in and does it for me. His finger nearly brushes my skin, and I freeze. He has to hear my heart now. But once again Forgiveness takes me utterly by surprise. He leans even closer, so Longing doesn't hear, and murmurs, "Revenge made a promise to you, right?"

That minty scent is so distracting I can hardly think, much less remember a promise. Forgiveness doesn't wait for me to nod or make some semblance of a response. "I'm going to make the same promise, right now." His eyes hold me captive. "I will never give up on you, Alexandra Tate."

Then he leaves, stealing my chance to find my dignity or have the last word.

Damn it, I think again, glaring at the empty air. I'm intrigued by his mention of Travis Bardeen, no matter how much I try to avoid it. And there's nothing else to do while the Fosters are at work. So I take the paper with the addresses on it out of the glove box—studiously ignoring the gun. Remembering that I have no phone to guide me, I also dig for a map. If I'm quick, I can be back by dark, before Saul and Missy notice anything amiss.

Revenge must have messed with the radio last time we were in here, because it's on. Just as Joe begins to introduce Elvis for the millionth time, I turn it off. A sign whizzes past on the right, with faded and chipping letters: *YOU ARE NOW LEAVING FRANKLIN.* That's it. No goodbyes or good luck or wishes for return. Just those simple words. It may be the only simple thing in the midst of so much complexity. The entire drive, I think about the sign and how I wish it were true. *You are now leaving.* No, not really. I always go back.

But soon, I'll make it true.

Like on the trip to find Christine Masterson, I have trouble finding the address. As I navigate through woods and winding dirt roads, I try not to picture Saul and the way his brow creases when he studies a map. *I like knowing how things begin and end.* They'll be sad at first, he and Missy, but they'll carry on, burning food and playing piano and collecting maps as they always have. I have to believe that.

"What if they don't?" Worry whispers. Our eyes meet in the rearview mirror.

Luckily, there's no more time to wonder; I hit a dead end with a single driveway leading up into more trees. Though there are no signs or mailboxes to let me know I have the right one, something tells me I do. Trepidation surges through my veins like needles. I force myself to turn into the driveway. My car groans as I inch up the hill. There's junk and trash everywhere, and a flat tire is the last thing I need so I slow down even more.

Then, suddenly, signs start appearing in random intervals. *BEWARE OF DOG. KEEP OUT. NO TRESPASSING.* The next one isn't a written warning, yet it's a warning all the same: a strange, grotesque skin nailed to a piece of plaster leaning against an abandoned RV. A smart person would stop, reverse, and drive as fast as they could to get away from this place. But would Forgiveness really send me somewhere truly dangerous?

Of course he would, a tiny voice hisses. *He's one of them.*

I've come too far to go back now. And even if Dad doesn't want me to let any distractions in, all the new memories sprouting up demand answers. When I resolved to choose Revenge, I thought answers didn't matter, but they do. Courage touches my arm with gentle fingers and I keep going, until the trailer comes into view.

This place makes the Mastersons' house look like a palace. Two of the windows are broken, the door hangs off its hinges, and an enormous beehive thrives on the rusted siding. Deer antlers hang everywhere as morbid decoration. The sound of my approach brings a man to the door. He steps outside, barefoot, a cigarette between his thumb and forefinger. I can feel his stare, a sensation that makes me think of oil or insects. Shifting the gear into park, I glance at the glove box where the gun eagerly waits. Impulsively I lean over and take it out, hoping the man doesn't notice the movement of my arms as I tuck it—safety on—into the waistband of my jeans. Then I get out and walk up to the trailer. Here, it doesn't smell like rotting animals. It just smells like garbage.

"You're not Al," the man says when I'm close enough to hear. He takes a long pull on his cigarette and squints at me through the haze.

I hesitate, tempted to succumb to the urge to flee. A bug flits past me. I halt a yard away from where the man stands and do my best to seem undaunted. "No. Is Travis around?"

Slowly, the man's dull eyes scan me from head to toe. He wears a stained wifebeater and has a buzz cut. There's a large, visible scab on the side of his head. "Nope." He flicks the cigarette to the ground. Sparks scatter across the dirt.

"Do you know when he'll be back?" I press, clenching my fists. *Don't run, don't run, don't run...*

Now the man shrugs his bony shoulders. There's a wood pile next to the door, and he kicks a piece out of the way. "Your guess is as good as mine." He hocks and spits a brown glob to the ground, right next to my shoe.

Hearing this, my stomach suddenly sinks. "Travis is missing, isn't he?" I know the answer even before I've finished asking the question.

"... never reported it. I mean, is it considered missing if you don't want to be found?" the man counters, his drawl reaching through my reverie.

I frown. "What do you mean?"

"I mean, that kid was never around to begin with. He was always running off somewhere, usually that damn college. Probably screwing around with the female populace, if you know what I mean. Waste of space, that boy. Good riddance."

"Do you have a picture of him?" I blurt, driven by some unknown instinct. The man pauses, like he's thinking. It looks painful. Without a word he slams back into the trailer. I can hear him rummaging around. He comes back a few minutes later, a crumpled photo between his dirty fingers. He leans his hip against the doorjamb and appraises me again.

"What's your interest in my son, anyway?" he asks. I can't see the picture and he doesn't give it to me.

I attempt to sound casual. "I used to know him, is all."

"So, what, you want a picture to remember him by?" The man snorts. "Whatever. Here you go. Keep it. What am I going to do with it?" He hands the picture to me unceremoniously. While I take it he tilts his head and pushes his brown tongue through the gap in his front teeth. "So . . . you want to come inside?"

Some part of me knows he's speaking, is aware that words are coming out of his mouth. It's impossible to separate that distant hum into a language that makes sense, though, because the entire world has narrowed and shrunk until all that's left of it is this single image in my hand. A boy, looking away from the camera, a sly grin curving his lips. His profile is fuzzy, but I still recognize it. *Hey, watch it!*

Travis Bardeen isn't missing.

Because he's the man who bumped into me in the hallway at school.

Briana is sitting on the steps when I get back to the apartment.

Anger squats beside her, and the sight of him is what makes me pause. In the course of our lives, I have never seen him touch my friend. Sure, Briana gets mad. She's human. But she doesn't let it control her, and it's always so brief I'm not around to see it happen. But of course I would be the reason she's finally let him close.

Birds harmonize into the stillness as I approach. Regret and Sorrow walk with me, holding my sweaty hands. When we stop, Regret departs, wiping his palm on his slacks. Sorrow lingers, pressing his shoulder to mine. I don't look at him, yet I can still feel him as keenly as I do Revenge and Forgiveness. There's an eerie kinship between me and this Emotion, like an invisible string knotted around our souls. Forever binding, always tugging when the other takes a breath.

Anger lifts his head to glare at me. Briana doesn't move. She examines the cracks in the sidewalk as she says, "Missy called me. She begged me to talk to you. Said that if anyone could get through to you, it was me."

Of course she's talking about school. I lean back on my heels and heave a sigh. After everything that's happened today, all the revelations that are flying in circles within my head and cackling like witches on brooms, it's more obvious than ever before that I don't know what's right or wrong. What I do know is that Revenge is at the end of my story.

So instead of offering an explanation, I sit down beside her. Overhead, clouds drift across the sky with a detachment that I envy. My mind flashes back to when Briana and I were kids lying in the grass, staring up at them and claiming the fluffy whiteness resembled a train or a flower or a heart. We were both so innocent, so free. The girl sitting beside me now is someone I barely recognize. How did I miss this pain, this struggle?

Because you were so focused on your own, that vicious voice answers.

Shame kneels before us, gripping my ankle. His baby face is pointed to the ground, where he isn't forced to see what it means to realize your own shortcomings or how much you've disappointed. It occurs to me yet again that I don't deserve someone like Briana Brinkman. She's still waiting for me to respond, and I curse all my inadequacies. If I could make one wish right now, it would be having those perfect words on the tip of my tongue. Not to take away the battles or the wounds—we need them to make us strong.

This isn't a place where wishes come true, though, and Briana stops waiting for me. "You're not the only one suffering, Alex," she says.

Finally I speak. "I know."

Watching me, Briana's voice softens. As always, she sees my own struggles. "I still love you." Her shoulder bumps mine, and it must be true, since Love appears. Usually I don't let myself look at her too closely, but in this moment it's unavoidable. The Emotion is so beautiful it's difficult to breathe. With a single graceful movement, she bends and kisses first my temple, then Briana's. The images come. An old couple in a garden, their wrinkled hands brushing as they pack the earth down around a seed. Two children beneath a blanket, giggling as they make finger shadows on the lamp-lit wall. A woman cradling a baby so young its countenance is still pink and scrunched.

"Why?" I sigh, knowing it would be easier if one of us let go.

She tilts her head. "Even though it can be hopeless, or unhealthy, or just stupid—we love anyway. Because that's what love is. Choosing to give it, especially when you shouldn't."

The way she puts it resonates with me. The idea that love is a choice. In my mind, it was something so inevitable, burning bright and hot until only ashes are left. That was just another lie. After a moment I say, "Your parents will come around, Bri."

Pause. Then she laughs. It's a sound made entirely of knives and razors. "No one comes out of the closet in Franklin, Alex. You know that. We're not as progressive as the rest of the world. We still play Elvis every day, for God's sake. Girls like me and Rachel Porter are either ignored or treated like dirt."

Now she sounds like me, and that's more frightening than making a choice or voicing what I'm really feeling. What was it Forgiveness said? As if I could forget. "Our worlds are so small," I murmur. I wonder if we can ever find our way back to those girls who studied the clouds.

"I have to go home. I'll talk to you... well, guess I won't be seeing you in school anymore, huh?" With that, Briana gets up and walks to her car. Once again I commit everything to memory. How she always moves like a dancer, the way her hair brushes the tips of her shoulders. Her frame is so short and thin, I worry that a gust of wind will blow her over or whisk her into that looming sky. Then she's getting in the car, the engine is rolling over, and she's driving away. Gone. Maybe I should have tried to stop her... but what good is trying to stop someone when they're determined to go?

The smell of grease suddenly permeates the air. I blink and Guilt towers over me. She extends her dirty fingers toward my face. It already feels like someone has rubbed me raw through my skin and under my bones, right to my soul. "No, don't touch me! Don't!" I cry. Without thinking, I jump up and stumble down the sidewalk. Guilt appears in front of me with a wolfish grin. Recoiling, I slam against the window of Saul's shop. She comes near again, running the back of her knuckles along my jaw. Her breath makes me retch. Immediately remorse consumes me in every possible way. For my weakness, my cowardice, my selfishness. The memory of what I did to Jennifer Foster crowds as close as an Emotion. Briana's expression when I didn't reassure her that I would survive this. The lines deepening beneath Missy's eyes every day. The sound of Saul's fraught piano playing.

And the look in Forgiveness's eyes when I made it clear who I would choose.

A new scent combines with Guilt's, this one rich, cloying, tempting. Just like him. It's the oddest combination, chocolate and lard. Revenge says something to Guilt, low and sharp, and a moment later we're alone. When I don't move or react, he says my name. Stricken, I stay where I am. He stands in front of me, stooping to peer into my eyes. "Alex."

"Don't," I repeat, softly this time. This isn't something Revenge would understand. I'm not sure he even knows what guilt is. My fingers press against the window behind me, and it feels as if this single sheet of glass is the only thing keeping me upright.

He frowns. "Okay."

That's it. The simplicity of it is so unexpected that I open my eyes and look at him. I'd been bracing myself for questions. That's when I notice what he's wearing. His lithe body is draped in a frock, a red waistcoat, and a top hat. Square-toed boots and black trousers complete the ensemble.

"You look ridiculous," I observe flatly. My glance flicks to his fist, which is clutching the handle of a walking stick. "Scratch that. You look *completely* ridiculous."

"Oh, good. For a minute there I was worried I'd only accomplished partial absurdity." His tone is dry. I touch my lips to hide a smile, and one corner of Revenge's mouth tilts up in an uncertain smile of his own. A dimple deepens in his cheek. "Anyway, you know I'm impervious to insults," he adds.

Forgetting that I have no right to laugh or tease after all that's happened, I lift a brow in challenge. "You're also annoying."

"Well, that's true," he concedes.

"And infuriating."

"That too."

My lips form another insult, but music suddenly drifts into the space between us. The despondent tones of *Swan Lake*. Again. We both turn to focus on Saul. My uncle is sitting at one of the pianos in the back, creases lining his forehead while he plays. He doesn't notice me at the window, staring. The sight brings me back to reality, to what I've done and what must be done.

"I have a plan, Revenge," I whisper, almost unconsciously. But I don't elaborate, and though I don't look, I feel my friend's frown returning. I can't tell him that this new plan, woven thread by thread as I came to my decision, involves the bottle of pills that live in my pocket. I can't let on that the moment Revenge is gone, I'm going to disappear, too. And it's not because I'm unable to exist in a world without him, or because of the consequences of what I'm going to do. It's because—despite what Death said—I should have died that night, with my family. I stayed because I was frightened. But I'm not anymore. I think I stopped being afraid that moment in the cave, when my father told me they were all there. Waiting. Watching.

"Alex! Supper is ready!"

Saul's playing halts and he slides off the bench. He still doesn't notice me, and for a wild instant I wonder if I'm really here. Missy calls for me again, and I pull away from the window. Drift up the stairs. Revenge follows me, and it's reminiscent of how things used to be. The apartment doesn't reek of burning food, which is promising. Shutting the door, I kick my shoes off and face the kitchen table, making an attempt to seem cheerful. Whatever façade of mirth I achieve, however, wilts immediately once I glimpse Saul and Missy's faces.

Taking a breath, I sit in my usual spot. And it begins. Emotions come and go, words rise and fall. The food in front of us is untouched. "... can't support you forever ... get a job ... back to school ... " While my aunt and uncle are talking, something flashes and sways in the window, drawing my attention. Missy must have hung a bird feeder outside. I didn't even notice, and I nearly ask her how long it's been there before I remember that they aren't thinking about feeders or birds, they're thinking about futures and fears. Neither of which I hold on to now. As I watch, a hummingbird darts toward the feeder. Its wings are a green blur and its beak long and slender. It takes a quick sip of the red liquid and before I can blink, it's gone again.

"Alex? Are you listening?" Something clinks. A fork against a plate.

Blinking, I look at Missy. She clearly expects a response of some kind, so I just nod. Nothing comes out of my mouth, though. What can I offer that they'll accept? Her jaw clenches, and it's so hard for her to say what she says next. "We want you to start seeing a therapist again."

Both of them tense, clearly expecting a battle. And the old me would have argued that people in Franklin don't talk about their problems; we act like they don't exist. Besides that, they can't afford therapy bills. Now, though, I only nod again, sitting there with my hands limp in my lap. Revenge watches me from his perch on the edge of the countertop. I gaze at his lips and imagine how they'll feel on my skin. It's easier than facing Missy and Saul.

But apparently we're done. Saul heaves himself up to refill his glass with milk, and Missy takes a bite of her meatloaf. When Saul sits down none of us try to start a new, different conversation. Eight minutes pass. The planet keeps on turning even when it should at least hesitate, and somehow the light outside is gone.

Once again Missy is the one to venture into the bleak land of silence. "We're going to the cemetery tomorrow," she says. "Are you coming with us?"

Tomorrow is the last day, a time for goodbyes and last chances. If she'd asked me two weeks ago, I would have said yes. I'll go with you to the cemetery to see them. Say the words there was no time to say the night of the accident. But now? I know where my family is, and they're not in those graves.

"No, thank you," I say. To be polite, though my appetite is nonexistent, I take a bite of the food she made. It should taste like ketchup or have a faint taint of something overcooked. Instead, it's a lump of nothing in my mouth.

Neither of them is surprised. Missy hauls herself to her feet, taking Saul's plate and stacking it on hers. "Almost done, sweetheart?" She sounds so, so tired.

Watching her, I know I should have been a better niece. I should have been a better everything. "Almost," I whisper.

TWENTY-FIVE

After dinner, I pay a visit to the sheriff's station. Saul and Missy don't try to stop me from leaving; they've finally realized it's inevitable. I walk through the glass front doors of the station and enjoy the air conditioning on my skin. This is one of the nicest buildings in the county, even with its stained tiles and scuffed walls. The woman manning the phone—Belinda, Marty Paulson's mother—smiles at me kindly. "Hi, Alex," she says. "It's finally getting warm, huh?"

"About time, too. Is Frederick here?"

She inclines her head to the office behind her. "Back there. Go right in; he's not doing anything important. Hey, we got the water fountain fixed. You should try it on your way out."

I manage a smile. "Don't worry, I will."

Skirting around the desk and attempting to ignore the smell of menthol cigarettes rolling off Belinda, I open the door. Frederick doesn't seem to hear my entrance, because he doesn't look up or move from his chair. He moves his finger around the pad of a laptop. I lift my own hand to rap on the inside of the doorway, but find myself pausing to watch for a second. According to Saul, Frederick DeLauro is the youngest sheriff in our county's history. He's in his mid-thirties, already balding, and still lives with his mother. Most people underestimate him when they meet him.

"Damn it," Frederick grumbles suddenly, continuing to be oblivious to my presence. His glasses glint in the lamplight. "Stupid, cocky, cheating … "

"That German kid kicking your butt again?"

The sheriff jumps and simultaneously slams the laptop shut. "Oh, Alex. Uh, I don't know what you're talking about."

At this, my mouth twitches. Everyone knows that Frederick's one goal in life is to be a chess champion. He may be the only person I know that has a dream and still clings to it, pursues it day after day. And I genuinely hope he achieves it. Someone should.

Trying to regain his composure, Frederick adjusts his collar. His badge flashes. "What can I do for you, Alex? If this is about the guy that broke your car mirror, I don't have anything yet."

"How many people know that Andrew Lomenta is really Andrew Thorn?"

His eyes go wide. His reaction is the answer I already knew; I just needed a confirmation. Or maybe a quiet part of me wanted someone to say that it isn't true, that the man who had my family's trust isn't a monster.

Stalling, Frederick plays with his shirt collar again. His mother must have put too much starch on it. "Not many," he admits after a few seconds, probably realizing that there's no way to avoid the truth. "He left town when he was young, and most people have forgotten that Sammy Thorn even had a son."

There's something else I need to know. My gaze drops to Frederick's feet, and his shoes become all that exists. A tiny world of leather and laces and simplicity. "Did my father know?"

"Yes." He appraises me, and Compassion makes an appearance. The Emotion touches his back and, as most of them do, stares at me while she does it. What does Frederick pity me for? My family's stupidity? Or the fact that they're no longer alive to trust the wrong people? I'm about to ask him more, but Frederick isn't finished. "People in town were mighty vicious," he tells me. "Especially Erskine, since he was the kid they found at the Thorn place. But your father defended Andrew. He said that the blood you inherit doesn't make the man."

The revelation about Erskine is drowned out by this last part. It sounds like something Dad would say. A lump swells in my throat. "Then what does?" I mutter, resisting the urge to shrug off whatever Emotion is putting a hand on my shoulder.

Frederick's brow creases. "What?"

The weight on my shoulder dissipates. "Never mind. Were there any other disappearances reported? Say . . . around the time of my family's accident?"

"Why don't you leave that to the adults, Alex. We know what we're doing." To soften the words, he winks. I glance at the holstered gun against his hip and think, *So do I.*

An awkward silence falls, and I shove my hands into my pockets. For a moment I consider telling Frederick everything. About the attacks, the note beneath my pillow, my findings from the flash drive. But that threat haunts every thought and action I make: *Tell anyone about this, we go after your precious Saul and Missy next.* When I leave this world, I want more than anything for those I love to be all right. And I also don't have the time to sit in this tiny office and answer whatever questions my revelations will spur on.

"Well, guess I better get going," I say eventually. "Thanks for your time."

"No problem. Say hi to your aunt and uncle for me."

I move back to the door. "Will do. And also . . . good luck."

The man tilts his head in confusion, and I cast a meaningful look toward the computer. He rubs the back of his neck sheepishly. "Oh, right. Thanks. Bye, Alex."

On my way out, I make sure to try the newly fixed water fountain. Belinda beams, and I tell her it's great. The water tastes like rust.

The moment I step outside, a new voice calls out. When I see who it is, dread coils in my stomach: Mrs. Warren, mother-in-law to Ian, the owner of the general store. Ian's always complaining about how she'll never die, because that would mean she'd have to stop talking. Today she's wearing waist-high pants and a flowered top, with permed gray hair and oval-shaped glasses.

She hurries up to me, panting. "It's going to rain tomorrow. I can feel it in my old bones," she manages to say.

There's no chance to respond. She goes on and on and on. Eventually I cut into her rampage on the state of Franklin's economy, or rather, the nonexistence of it. "It was really nice to see you, Mrs. Warren, but I need to go home. Missy probably needs help in the kitchen. You know how it is."

"Oh, I certainly do. Remember that church picnic when you were twelve? She brought a ham, but it looked like a pig that died in a barn fire! Tasted okay, though. I mean, you can't *really* ruin ham—"

I hurry away.

Next, I drive to Nate Foster's. Not to use the gun or contrive more ways to ruin his life; just to observe. The entire way to the house I keep thinking how tomorrow is the anniversary of the accident. It seems fitting—even poetic—that everything should end on the same day it all began.

As if my vengeful thoughts are a beacon, deafening and exhilarating, Revenge arrives in his usual seat. He smiles at me through the dimness. I'm opening my mouth to greet him when headlights flare behind me, a white flash that makes the rearview mirror so bright it hurts.

Fear quivers into view, already grinning. "Revenge," he drawls, wrapping his arm across my neck. The instant he makes contact, my spine goes rigid and memories of the Taurus taunt me.

"What is it?" Revenge murmurs. He doesn't even bother to respond to Fear. I don't—can't—answer. The skin on my palms goes numb from gripping the steering wheel so tightly. When the headlights don't fade or retreat, I push down on the gas pedal. Revenge twists around. "Do you know who that is?" he asks sharply, glaring at the car that's too close to our bumper.

Mutely I shake my head. The speed needle inches further and further around the circular gauge. Before I can attempt to explain to Revenge what's been happening, he vanishes. Fear leans forward again, his near-white hair glowing from the green numbers on the radio. His eyes are as bright as the headlights, eager and excited.

"I know how to drive," he announces. "Move over."

"Go to hell," I say through my teeth.

Clearly affronted, Fear starts to retort. Revenge comes back, thankfully, and my heart sinks when I see his scowl. "It's no one we know. Just a guy." He glances back at Fear. "Don't you have somewhere to be?"

Once again Fear has no opportunity to respond, because at that moment the car behind us turns. The light fades. All the breath leaves my body in a *whoosh* and Relief sags against me.

"False alarm," I manage. Fear rolls his eyes and leaves. *Get it together*, my instincts hiss. Sanderson Road is close. There's the tree that fell during the last thunderstorm. I concentrate on breathing normally, and Revenge appraises me.

"You've changed," he says. It's not a question or a barb. Just an observation. I don't ask him if that's a good or a bad thing, because I don't want to know. We go the rest of the way in complete silence. He doesn't disappear again, though, and that says more than words ever could.

The mailbox appears on the right, and then the house. It stands on the hill, no longer untouchable or majestic. Tonight it looks... ill. As though cancer has invaded and infected everything within and around those walls. There are no lights, no meals in the dining room, no music drifting through the windows. I get out and tiptoe across the lawn. Even if her car wasn't gone, I would know that Jennifer left. Because the kitchen is a mess. Shattered glass glitters on the floor. Satisfaction fills me, and I almost don't mind the fact that the Emotion has his hand on my chest like he's trying to find my heart. He won't find it. With each passing day it's been shrinking and shriveling, until nothing remains but a husk and the memory of what used to be.

Movement startles me, and I comprehend that I'm looking right at Nate Foster. He's sitting on the floor in the hallway, a bottle clenched in one hand. A belch shudders through his body. Seeing how he's deteriorated, I don't feel remorse or compassion or regret. Revenge comes to stand beside me. I can't tell what he's thinking, but we must be thinking the same thing.

He's lost his wife. Now he needs to lose everything else.

A figure strolls along the edge of the woods.

The moon is a faded crescent above the mountain, but the mist surrounding him emanates a light all its own. It swirls and thickens. His hands hover, palm-down, in the air next to his narrow hips. I park in front of the apartments and turn to watch Fog finish his work, the leather cushion beneath me creaking with the movement. Revenge watches, too. The Element keeps walking until the mist swallows him completely. When I face the windshield again, I catch sight of another figure. This one hunches on the steps, smaller and infinitely more human. "Angus," I sigh. Shadows move on the gravel. His parents are fighting in front of the window.

Our worlds are so small.

I angle my body toward Revenge. "I'll see you tomorrow, okay?"

"Tomorrow," he repeats, like it's a promise. I can't help but notice the absence of light in his eyes, the lack of anticipation and excitement and fervor. He reaches for my face, and I tense in surprise. His skin doesn't make contact. His thumb hovers along the edge of my jaw. I close my eyes and imagine what it will be like when it really does happen. It will be so brief, so cruelly brief. Will it be worth all of this? *Yes*. When I open my eyes again, Revenge is gone. Swallowing a sigh, I pull the keys from the ignition and get out.

My young neighbor looks up at the sound of my approach. "Wait here," I say as a greeting, as if he has somewhere else to go. "I have something for you." Angus remains silent. I hurry up the rest of the stairs and into the apartment. Missy and Saul have gone to bed. His snores and her fan blend together in an odd harmony. I fetch the jar I've been saving from my room and go back outside, settling next to Angus. Crickets sing into the stillness. "Here." I put it into his small hands.

His profile is unreadable. It strikes me, in that moment, that we've both changed. Somehow, Angus grew without my noticing. His voice is a little deeper, his limbs a little longer, his scars a little darker. Even in a place that does its best to keep him tiny and broken. With the tip of his finger, Angus traces the ridges that holds the lid in place. He runs it down the side of the glass. Around the curve at the bottom. "Want to take a walk?" I ask him, watching.

As an answer, Angus slides off the step, clutching the jar as if he's afraid he'll drop it. I head for the woods, and he doesn't protest. Neither of us speaks. This time, it's not because we need a wall to knock on or the wall between us is too thick. Words just don't belong here.

Old leaves and branches crackle underfoot. My gaze keeps returning to the treetops, hoping for a glimpse of the rocket that's been lost for so many years. I skim the bushes and underbrush, too, yearning to catch sight of a swishing tail or those familiar floppy ears. There are only shadows and the flickering lights of fireflies in the distance. The stars are out, but they're locked in a fierce battle with the clouds, making them difficult to see.

We don't go too far from the apartments. I listen carefully every time we draw near, and when I finally can't hear his parents arguing anymore, I bring Angus back. He trails after me up the stairs to his front door, all the while staring at his new jar.

I squat so I can see his too-wise eyes. He transfers his gaze from the jar to me. "I want you to remember something, no matter what happens," I say. Angus nods, and I purse my lips before continuing, thinking of Los Angeles and dead flowers. "Some things change, but so many don't. There comes a time when you have to stop waiting for it. Okay?"

He blinks slowly, absorbing this. "Okay."

"Bye, Angus." Hoping he won't notice the wobble in my smile, I touch his back as he slips inside. The latch clicks, and I know I won't see Angus again. Not in this lifetime, at least. For a moment I study the dented doorknob that leads to him and his fragmented world, thinking I should ask Saul to replace it. Then I turn away.

It's getting late. I should go to bed. Really, there's so much I should be doing. Calling Georgie, telling my aunt and uncle that none of this is their fault. What I do in the end, though, is drift to my room and take out the present that's been waiting in my nightstand for weeks. And finally, I open it.

The paper tears easily. A note flutters down into my lap and I pick it up, scanning it briefly. Missy's handwriting: *A place to keep your secrets.* The gift is a wooden box, with exquisite, swirling carvings all around the edges. The latch is simple, a golden clasp, and I finger it gently, just as Angus did with his jar. Impulsively, I dig the flash drive out of my bra and put it inside. Nestled in the red velvet, it doesn't look like an object of unanswered questions or mysterious pasts.

On the desk, my laptop suddenly begins to hum. I lift my head. Everything in my room is so familiar, so safe. The striped wallpaper, the cluttered floor, the tilted ceiling light. Everything the opposite of what my other room was, a few yards to my left. That was a space of light and order and futures. I wish I could walk over to that place, to see it one last time. Strength is easier to imagine than to achieve, though.

It's strange to think that all of this will be here tomorrow even when I'm gone. I study the stain above me. A muscle ticks in my jaw. "What are you doing here?" I ask without glancing away from it.

Forgiveness sets something down next to my feet. It makes a soft thud. He straightens, and I see that his sleeves are pushed up his elbows, exposing the hard tendons in his arms. "I brought you something," he tells me. Curious in spite of myself, I lean over to peer inside the cardboard box. It's ... tapes. Dozens and dozens of tapes.

He doesn't wait for me to ask. "You can listen to them in the car instead of Elvis. Maybe when you leave Franklin." A ghost of a smile haunts his lips.

Words stick in my throat. I'm never leaving Franklin. I swing my legs to the side of the bed and crane my neck to admire Forgiveness's face. He's so kind, so good, so painfully out of reach. His legs are close enough to my knees that it would only take a slight shift to touch him. I don't try, though. I keep staring, and I wonder why we push people away. There are a thousand reasons, really, but I think the biggest one—the most important one—is that if we don't, they get close. And then they can see.

Forgiveness abruptly looks away and walks to the window. His stance reminds me of Revenge. Tomorrow. Choices.

"Forgiveness?" I say his name in a whisper. He doesn't respond, but I know he's listening. I fix my gaze on the tapes he brought and wish I could forget the night he read to me. "Don't come tomorrow, okay?"

No response. A moment later, he disappears. I crawl into bed, clothes and all. My eyes shut, and sleep descends within minutes.

Dream comes in the night. And this time my slumber isn't rife with pain or storms or twisting metal; it's filled with mockingbirds and mysterious houses next door and noble, unflinching beliefs in freedom.

A sound wakes me. Something ringing in the distance. A phone? The sunlight pouring through the window makes the insides of my eyelids bright red, forcing me to open them. Morning streams across the floors in hues of orange and pink. Before I have a chance to glance at my alarm clock, there's a tap at the door. "Alex? Someone calling for you. Are you up?" Missy's voice.

It's early. Who would be calling me at this hour? My friends know better, and Andrew always tries my cell . . . which is now rotting at the bottom of the creek. Frowning, I leave the warmth of my bed. "Coming, Missy." I throw a zip-up black sweatshirt over my tank top but don't bother changing my sweatpants.

Missy is standing in the hallway, hair dripping and holding the phone out. Her eyes don't meet mine as I take it from her, and I pretend not to see Worry standing in the shadows of the hallway. "Thanks," I mutter, turning away. "Hello?"

"Alexandra Tate?"

The accent is an immediate giveaway. "Dr. Stern." I pinch the bridge of my nose. In all the commotion of discovering the profiles and making the choice, I'd completely forgotten that he called about wanting to see me. "I'm sorry I missed our meeting."

He sounds just as harried and urgent as the last time we spoke. "Are you alone?"

"Hold on." Though I know Missy wouldn't eavesdrop, my instincts tell me to have this conversation far away. The floor creaks as I leave my room. The apartment smells like coconuts, Missy's shampoo. A second after I notice this, the sound of a hair dryer comes on. Quickly I head outside, where there's nothing but the trees and the clouds to hear me. My feet are bare against the wooden steps. Despite the bright sky, the mountain air is surprisingly cold, and a vicious wind numbs my nose and the tips of my ears. "Okay," I say into the phone, wrapping one arm around my waist in a vain attempt to keep the chill at bay. "I'm alone. What's—"

"Alex."

That voice makes my head snap up. Andrew is standing on the sidewalk, flanked by two Emotions like soldiers.

"Stay away from me," I hiss, taking a step back. Fear and Anger wrap their hands around my upper arms, a small army of my own.

Andrew begins to say something, but his words are drowned out by Dr. Stern, who's still pressed against my ear. "Is that Professor Lomenta?" he demands, his voice so sharp it threatens to slice the phone in half. "Alexandra, do not talk to him. Run, do you understand me? *Run.*"

My father's best friend extends a hand toward me, palm-down, trying to make me see reason with a small thing made of flesh and bones. There's a bandage over his nose where I punched him. "Alex, please, just listen to—"

"I know who you really are." I glare at him. Stumbling back another step, I drop the phone. Anger spits at Andrew's feet, though he doesn't see it.

At my words, he goes still. "What do you mean?" But it's evident in his eyes and voice that he knows.

"You're Sammy Thorn's son. You lied to everyone. You lie about a lot, actually. Who knows what else you're hiding?" My car is behind him. There's no way I can get to the glove box.

"Yes, Sammy was my father," Andrew says bluntly, recovering. He doesn't seem to notice how I keep eyeing my car. "I was going to tell you someday, when the time was right. But that's irrelevant right now."

"Irrelevant?" I repeat in disbelief, focusing on him again. "How is that irrelevant? Your father took children from their beds. Then, after he disappeared off the face of the earth, it started happening again, to Christine Masterson and the others. In fact, most of them disappeared just before the accident. No, I'm not finished. I don't know what experiments you guys were performing on those kids or why my dad was involved, but I do know it can't be a coincidence that you're tied to all of it."

I stop, out of breath, and Andrew looks at me for a long,

long time. His face is ashen, and his nostrils keep flaring like there's a foul smell in the air. At some point during my speech, Fear appeared at his side.

"You unlocked the flash drive," Andrew says finally.

"You didn't!" Fear gasps, in my direction. Normally I would flip him the bird. Now, though, there's an awful feeling blooming in the pit of my stomach, like a toxic rose. In a burst of clarity—even if the reasons aren't clear—I know I've made a mistake.

Spinning away, Andrew rakes his hair back. It's the first time I've ever seen a strand out of place. He stares at the trees, then turns back to me, wild and desperate. "Please tell me you didn't contact any of them," he says. There's a tremor in his voice. "Please."

"I talked to Dr. Stern."

He closes his eyes. "Alex, you have no idea what you've done."

"Then *tell* me," I snap, hating the feeling of being closed in by all our Emotions. Fear, Anger, Desperation, Regret. But Andrew still says nothing. I grit my teeth, glancing up at the apartment window to make sure Missy hasn't overheard us. She must still be doing her hair. "Dr. Stern told me to stay away from you. I saw you in some videos, standing next to those missing kids. Then I heard the voicemail Dad left—"

"You what?" Andrew stares at me.

Suddenly my cheeks are on fire. Shame and Defiance join the fold, laying their hands on me like they're praying for healing. "I listened to your messages," I state, refusing to sound apologetic. "I heard my dad accusing you."

Pause. Then Andrew asks, his voice tight, "Did you listen to the whole thing?"

What?

My expression is all the answer he needs. Wordlessly he pulls his phone out and taps it a few times. A moment later my father's voice emerges from the tiny speaker, gravelly and frantic. "Andrew, something happened today," he says. Dimly I recall him saying the same thing to my mother on the night of the accident. "Stern couldn't find Christine, and he lost it. He sent Travis after her family. I didn't know, I swear it. When the boy came back, he was covered in blood. He wouldn't tell me whose it was, and when I pressed him, he attacked me. I see it now, what we've done. You were right about everything.

"I know you took the kids, and I know you lied to me and Stern. But if you think he can't find them, you're wrong. He's put cameras everywhere. Your office, our houses, theirs. You need to change their identities and get them far away from here, understand? I got onto his computer and stole every piece of research I could find—I have it on a flash drive—but it won't be enough if he can get to them again. I'm heading home to move Tracey and the children. I don't want them caught in any crossfire. Don't—"

Static.

Three seconds pass. Five seconds. Ten. In a daze, I tear my eyes away from the phone and meet Andrew's. "I... you didn't... "

"I'm not finished," he cuts in, using my earlier words. His finger moves over the screen again. He waits. Then he tilts it toward me. "Hello?" a new, younger voice warbles, this one undeniably feminine. A face appears there, in what must be a video chat program, and all the breath leaves my body when I see who it is.

There's no need for Andrew to introduce us. I recognize her from the profile picture.

Christine Masterson.

TWENTY-SIX

Andrew asks her if she has enough groceries and if her cough has gone away. She's polite and maybe a little confused when she answers yes, she has enough groceries and yes, her cough is better. She asks Andrew who I am, and he tells her I'm his best friend's daughter. "You can trust her," he says, looking at me, and I want her to believe it because it's true.

After they've hung up and the screen is empty again, I sit down on the bench in front of the window, putting my hands beneath my thighs. Andrew settles next to me and I let out a breath. "Tell me," I say.

He squints at the rising sun, and he does. He tells me everything. "You were five years old. You were playing with some toys in the living room and a cartoon came on. Joy appeared and touched your shoulder. Will was standing in the doorway, and he watched as you looked right at her and smiled. He didn't want this life for you."

Shock vibrates through me at this—not only from hearing Andrew mention an Emotion, but at the fact that my father knew about my Sight. Andrew goes on without giving me a chance to absorb it or react. "Will was determined to find some kind of cure," he says. "I didn't believe him at first, about the Emotions and Elements. But he wouldn't stop badgering me until I helped him. So we worked together. We did research. We found a chemist, a Dr. Felix Stern. He's been mocked for his theories about the existence of another plane and he's a laughingstock in most scientific circles. When your dad told him about his Sight, he relocated to this area. And the first thing he did was find more test subjects." A muscle in his jaw tightens.

"Christine? And the others?" A flash of memory, the video of Christine holding a towel to her arm from where someone had drawn blood.

"There's a part of your brain that works differently, allowing you to see these creatures," Andrew explains. "It can be inherited, which is why there are more people with the Sight here than anywhere else. You know how it is." He gives me a look. I do know. People don't call us hicks and white trash for nothing; around these parts, there's a good chance the person you're with could be a second cousin twice removed. "Anyway, we eventually came up with a serum. It doesn't work on everyone. Some of the kids had bad reactions and... didn't make it."

While Andrew struggles to go on, my mind goes back to the files on the flash drive. Those words next to some of the names. *Found. Failed.*

"Your dad and I didn't know that to find the antidote, Felix had to first find the poison," Andrew continues. "He didn't want to be a joke anymore, so he found a way to *give* people the Sight, in addition to taking it away. It's how he can see them himself, now. If this information were released to the public, it would be catastrophic. Which was another reason to hide the remaining children and halt the research."

A bird swoops toward the ground. "Was my dad taking the antidote?" I already know the answer, but I need to ask anyway. I need to hear him say it.

Andrew hesitates. He's already told me so much, though, that there's no point in hiding this. "By the end, Will was addicted," he admits. "We knew there would be side effects, of course, but we didn't know how severe they would be. It changed the test subjects, made them violent and unpredictable. See, the serum attacks the part of your brain that allows you to see the other plane, yes, but at the same time it attacks your primitive vertebrate nervous systems. Then it started to evolve. It eventually spread to prefrontal cortex, the deep limbic system, anterior cingulated gyrus, temporal lobes—"

The words are completely foreign, and Frustration and Impatience scowl with me. "So, every part of the brain," I interrupt. "I get it. But if you knew the serum was so bad and kids were dying, why didn't you *do* something?" My hands clench into fists and my knuckles dig into the tender parts of my legs. Resentment kneels by the bench and pats my knee. Any uncertainty about whether or not Andrew has the Sight dissolves; he doesn't even blink when we're surrounded.

"... did, Alex," he's saying. "I couldn't turn Felix in for the study—I'd been a part of it, and I was as guilty as him—but I tried to convince your dad to stop. When he wouldn't listen, I talked to the kids, and some of them were willing to leave the study and go into hiding. It wasn't until Travis Bardeen attacked Nora that Will finally saw what I'd been seeing for weeks, and he decided to stop taking the serum and no longer participate in the experiments. That same night, you had the accident."

The accident. No, I can't think about that. If I do, I won't be able to deny that maybe—just maybe—Nate Foster isn't entirely the one to blame for what happened that night. Nothing would have been set into motion if it weren't for my Sight.

"Dad did all of it for me," I whisper, remembering his words. This truth can't be put into any wooden boxes. Andrew doesn't confirm or deny it, which makes the realization worse, somehow.

Distantly I'm aware that Andrew is saying my name, prying, wanting to know more. One insight rises above the rest, soft and devastating: my father was out of control the night of the accident, and if it's not Nate Foster's fault, everything I've done is for nothing. An Emotion is leaning over me, and the only reason I know which one is because of the stench emanating from her. Guilt.

I need to change the subject. Have new thoughts. Ask any questions not about the accident. Shaking myself, I look at Andrew. "So, that day in your office, when you wanted us to go outside so badly...?" I prompt, grasping for a topic we haven't covered yet. And this is something that's been plaguing me since he nearly assaulted me.

Now Andrew's cheeks redden. Guilt and Shame saunter over to him, drape themselves on each side, and force me to scoot away. "Because of your dad's warning, I knew Stern had bugged my office. I didn't remove the device after I found it, though—I figured it was better to control what he knew. Keeping your enemy close and all that." His countenance darkens.

There are more questions I want to ask, more things I need to know, but the sun is rising higher and higher and my last day shouldn't be this. It should be more. So I stand up and look at my father's best friend, thinking of Dad's response to Frederick: *the blood you inherit doesn't make the man*. Shrugging off an Emotion's hand, I extend my own to Andrew. "Thank you for telling me all this. And… I'm sorry. For making such a mess out of everything."

Startled, Andrew gets to his feet, too. Of course he fixes his rumpled shirt and slicks his hair back. Then he takes my hand and doesn't let go. "It's not safe for you to be alone," he replies, disregarding the apology. "Stern knows you have the flash drive, and he knows that you're Will's daughter. That's something your dad and I always kept from him. If he hasn't come for you already, he will."

Come for you. The Taurus trying to ram me off the road, the intruder in our apartment, the note under my pillow. I knew someone was trying to find the flash drive, but it had never occurred to me that I was a target, too. But Dr. Stern is short and pudgy, and fairly old. The man in the apartment was tall and gangly. Who…

Suddenly I make the connection. Of course.

Travis Bardeen.

How has it taken me so long to put it together? He's been stalking me under Dr. Stern's orders, even at school. From the sound of his history, Travis enjoys violence. A shudder wracks my body when I remember Nora Masterson's face. That was his work, too. Good thing that after tonight, I won't have to be afraid of him anymore. I won't be afraid of anything.

"…you hear me? I need you to promise me that you'll be careful. Make sure you're always with someone."

I blink and the blurred world comes into focus. How long has Andrew been talking? He's staring now, waiting for a promise. My conscious flicks at me, but what's more empty words? "I promise," I say, giving him a fake smile. "Call you later, okay? From our home number, since mine is sort of out of commission."

Andrew finally releases his hold and murmurs a goodbye. Then he goes to his car, expecting a call that will never come. I watch him drive away and the dust fade. When I turn back to the stairs, I'm surprised to see Missy standing there. She's picked up the phone from the ground. "Did you two get everything figured out?" she asks, brushing a strand of black-gray hair off her forehead with her free hand.

I start to answer, but the phone rings. Missy jumps. Then she presses *TALK*. "Hello?" Her brows rise and she holds it out to me a second time. "It's for you again. Someone's popular."

Since she's smiling at me and expecting a normal response, I do my best to mask my terror. It has to be Dr. Stern calling back. *Be smart about this,* my instincts urge. *If he thinks you're cooperating and still on his side, it'll buy you some time.* Once again, I take the phone from Missy and put it to my ear.

She climbs the steps to give me some privacy. As soon as I hear the door close I breathe for a few moments, willing my voice not to tremble. Then I rush to say, "Sorry about that, Dr. Stern, it was—"

"Hello, Alex."

Whoever is on the line is most definitely not Dr. Stern. His drawl throws me. "Who is this?" I snap, clutching the phone tightly. I put my back to the window above so Missy won't see my face.

"It hurts that you don't remember me. I thought we were so close. After all, you did try to kill me."

In that instant, I recognize it. He isn't hushed now or shoving me against a wall, so his mountain twang is more prominent. Brazen.

"I think you've got that the other way around," I say unevenly, walking toward the tree line just to fill the need to move. The cool wind surges, stirring every leaf. Mrs. Warren must have been right about a storm coming…

Travis Bardeen makes a sound his throat, part-laugh, part-indignation. I remember what Andrew said about the injections: *It changed the subjects, made them violent and unpredictable.* "You're wrong, Alex. I was never trying to kill you. I was just trying to have a little fun."

"Attacking me and threatening my family is fun?" I counter. The phone crackles and I know I'm going too far from the base. I can't stop moving, though, can't stop trying to escape from this.

"Yeah, actually, it is. But our time together has come to an end. You've made my employer very unhappy, and it's time for all of us to have a little chat. A *tête-à-tête*, if you will. Okay, confession, I've always wanted to use that word." The man giggles.

It sends a shiver down my spine. Hoping to disconcert him with what I know, I ask, "Your employer? You mean Dr. Stern." Silence. I listen to the sound of Travis's breathing. "I saw your father, Travis," I add. "He didn't look good. You should go home. I think he'd be happy to see you."

Lies, so many lies. More crackling erupts in my ear and I relent, whirling to head back to the apartment. A twig snaps under my foot.

It elicits a reaction. "Why don't you mind your own business, you little bitch," Travis hisses. Hatred drips from his voice now, and as I press my back to a tree Fear flattens his palm on the bark beside my head and leans close. His cheek brushes my temple and his essence rips through me, rendering breathing impossible and coherence implausible. All I can think of now is Nora Masterson's jagged scars. Travis is still talking. "... can't wait to get my hands on you. Just wait. I'm going to take my knife and cut you up and make you beg for me to end it. I'll—"

"I'm not going anywhere," I manage, shoving at Fear's hard chest. He smirks but allows the distance between us. The scent of fruit is overwhelming.

"Shame. Your aunt and uncle are all you have left, right?"

I freeze. The apartment. He could be up there right now. I left Missy all alone. Lurching into a run, I do nothing to disguise my approach. "If you touch them, I'll—"

"Good, so we're in agreement." He's smiling. I can't see him, but I hear it. "I'll see you in a little bit. Oh, and I don't think I need to mention that you should come to our little meeting alone. Call anyone else, and I have permission to tear your limbs off your body the next time we cross paths."

The threat hardly touches me; I'm in the apartment now and Missy is there, standing in front of the window. Waiting for me. Unbroken and unaware. "Where?" I growl, bending to catch my breath. A rock digs into my heel but I don't even feel it.

"Sit tight. I'll bring you a note with the location on it. This'll be fun, trust me! And I have your belated birthday gift, too. Sorry, I'm horrible at remembering those kinds of things. And before you say I didn't have to, just know that I wanted to. From the bottom of my heart. I feel like we've gotten so close these past few weeks. Am I right?"

I hang up.

Clouds gather over the mountain. It's nearing sunset now, and still no word from Travis. My stomach is a mass of knots, and Emotions have been pacing with me all day. It's the anniversary of the night that Nate Foster collided into my family and killed them all, and I had a plan, but now I don't know who to blame or where to go. Revenge and Forgiveness don't appear. Maybe there's no longer a choice to make and I'll never see them again.

Another knot forms in my gut.

Missy is worried too. Saul was supposed to come back from Ian's hours ago, for the visit to the cemetery. "I can't get your uncle on his cell," she mutters, hitting the buttons harder than necessary as she calls him yet again. "Maybe the storm is messing with the reception."

"That's probably it," I say to the roiling sky. "I'm sure he'll be home soon." I don't tell her not to worry, though, because it would be like telling that sky to rain fire instead of water. Missy leaves a third voicemail for Saul and I don't move from the window. When Travis arrives with his note, I want to know. The gun, hidden in the waistband of my pants, is hot against my skin.

Suddenly there's a scratching at the door, loud and unmistakable. Missy pokes her head out of the kitchen. "Is that the dog?" she calls. A dark sense of foreboding stretches into every corner of me, as if the spider outside my window is weaving its webs from within. Damn it, damn it, damn it! Travis must have parked down the road and approached the building from the back, where I wouldn't spot him. Why didn't I think of that? Swearing, I hurry to open the door before Missy does. The hinges groan and the wind instantly swoops in, making my eyes water and my hair fly back . . . and there's no one outside.

But that doesn't mean he isn't here.

"Be right back!" I shout to Missy, blinking rapidly. "I need to check something!" Her response is drowned out by another zealous gust of wind. I slam the door behind me. Thunder rumbles as I rush down the stairs. Rain seeps through my shirt, small pinpricks of cold. There's something lying by the bottom step. I squint. Is that fur . . . ?

Then I get closer, and I see. "No!" someone screams. Me. "*No!*"

It's Eggs.

He must have broken her neck—it's bent at a wrong angle. Her eyes, once so bright and cautious, are unblinking and dull. She did come back. And this was her reward for daring to trust me. Sorrow and Regret come to touch my shoulders, then Regret and I watch as the dark-haired Emotion kneels to close Eggs's eyes.

All my instincts go against looking at her, and I'm about to turn away when a flash of white catches my eye. There's a piece of paper sticking out of the dog's gaping mouth. With trembling fingers I pull it out. A string of slobber comes with it. Dimly I note that the handwriting matches the message he left under my pillow. *HAPPY BIRTHDAY*, it says. *I HAVE WHAT YOU WANT MOST. YOU HAVE WHAT I WANT MOST. MEET ME AT THE MINES.*

What I want most? I almost vomit then and there, thinking he's taken Briana or Georgie. But then I think of the one person I haven't heard from today, the person who isn't answering his calls or coming home when he should.

Saul. He's taken Saul.

For a moment all I see is red. Hate and Anger run with me up the stairs and into the apartment. The entire way I mentally chant, *Revenge. Revenge. Revenge.* He must be too far away or too preoccupied to answer. *Forgiveness. Forgiveness. Forgiveness.* But I've pushed him away too hard. He doesn't hear, or he chooses not to answer. I go in and grab my keys off the counter. Panic swells in my throat and chest as I hurry to the door again.

"Alex, did I hear you shouting?" Missy asks. She's turned away from the window, her hands cupping her elbows. Thankfully she can't see Eggs from her vantage point. "Where are you going?"

The question stops me in my tracks. She won't believe I'm going to the lake on a night like this. I just saw Andrew this morning. Saul was getting us food and gas. She knows I'm distant from my friends…

"To the cemetery," I say, swallowing. "I'm going to the cemetery."

My aunt believes this. Sympathy and Sorrow surround her, looking like angels from the flashes of lightning behind them. She doesn't tell me it's not safe, or offer to accompany me. "Take an umbrella" is all she says. *I'm going to get him back*, I want to tell her. Instead, I leave her there, waiting for someone who can't come home. Eggs is still at the bottom of the stairs, and I force myself to drag her beneath them so Missy won't see. Afterwards, I brush my hands off on my shorts and leave her there. I feel my aunt's eyes follow me as I get into my car and speed off down the dusty road.

The drive to the mines has never felt so long. When I pass the fork that leads to the sheriff's station, to Frederick, I'm torn. Then I remember yet again what happened to Christine's family when she dared to defy Dr. Stern. So I keep going, and after hours and years the entrance looms up and swallows me whole. It's the first time I want to heed all the warning signs. The mines beckon, though. Saul needs me. There is nothing so terrible and wonderful as being needed.

Stopping where the chain dangles across the road, I kill the engine and swing up and out. I leave the door open so the slam doesn't alert them—pointless, since they probably already heard me coming from a mile away. It occurs to me that I should figure out how to handle this. The treetops rustle and quiver, making a sound like television static. I imagine they're speaking to me, trying to warn me away. But in this, there is no choice. "Will I survive?" I whisper to Courage, who laces his fingers through mine.

"Do you want to?" he asks right back. The wind lifts the hair off his forehead. He doesn't look at me. I tear my attention away and follow his gaze to that black mouth. Terror is a strong, fruity taste in my mouth. I know better than to ask the Emotion if he can tell me what's waiting inside; interfering and all that. There's nothing left to do but face this. Face them.

It takes twenty-two steps. Each one is louder than the one before it. Courage doesn't come with me, and it's strange, actually wanting an Emotion to stay. He doesn't, though, and when I reach the entrance I don't let myself pause or hesitate. The storm illuminates the tunnel in erratic flashes.

My pulse skips a beat when I see Dr. Stern sitting near the elevator, watching my approach with a shrewdness he didn't possess before. They actually brought chairs in for this. Travis stands beside him, grinning. He looks exactly like his picture: mischievous and big-nosed and dirty.

"Drop the gun, please," Dr. Stern commands in a way that makes it clear he's used to being obeyed. When I don't, his eyes narrow. "Or you'll never find out where we're keeping him," he adds.

Urgency makes my tongue thick and dry. "Where is he?" I put my finger on the trigger, tempted to shoot him in the knee just to make that confidence disappear.

"All in good time," he replies, infuriatingly calm. "I want to speak with you first."

Still, my eyes scan the shadows. There's only the three of us. When I continue to hesitate, impatience flickers behind those glasses. The old man waves a hand to the chair across from him. "Sit."

He wants to talk? Fine. I plop down into the chair—air whooshes out of the cushion—and toss my gun at his feet. Travis picks it up.

"Why the charade?" I spit. "Why make me think you were so terrified of Andrew?" Maybe once we get all of the questions out of the way, he'll be willing to make a trade. Me for Saul.

Dr. Stern leans forward, forming a steeple with his fingers. "I hoped to gain your trust, in order to obtain the flash drive," he answers simply. "What is that American saying? You catch more flies with honey than vinegar?"

"You'll never find it," I snarl, clutching the armrests to restrain myself. I wish it were true. The box Missy gave me is in plain sight, just waiting for someone to lift the lid and discover its contents.

This doesn't concern Dr. Stern. The only Emotion present is Excitement, and she doesn't look pleased to be next to Travis. The old man eases back again, expressionless. "I imagine not. But you'll tell us where it is in due time." Before I can ask him what he intends to do, Dr. Stern gestures to the man standing behind him. "This is Mr. Bardeen. He's going to take care of you tonight."

Take care of you. The words make me want to dive for the gun. My eyes meet Travis's, and I clench my jaw so tightly pain radiates through it. "We've met."

At this, Dr. Stern falls silent. He inclines his head slightly. Travis looks rueful now. "Aw, I couldn't help myself, doc," he whines. "I kept an eye on her like you said. I just played with her a little, too."

"You tried to ram me off the road."

Travis laughs, the same laugh he made when I shot at him.

Irritation shimmers into existence—an Emotion that looks like a child, strangely enough—and taps Dr. Stern on the shoulder. He sighs and looks at him. "Not so hard, little one," he admonishes. I blink in surprise. Then he focuses on me again. "I do apologize for those incidents. The injections have made Mr. Bardeen unstable, like the others, but he follows orders well enough that I decided to keep him around. As you've probably discerned, he enjoys the work he does for me. Now, before he takes you back to the lab, I believe there is some unfinished business for you to attend to. A deal is a deal, after all."

"You'll let him go?" I breathe, digging my nails into the chair again as I wait for his response. It doesn't matter that they've lured me out here to kill me or take me. All that matters is Saul walking through the door of our apartment tonight, and Missy running from the window to embrace him and lecture him for being so late.

Dr. Stern rises and tugs at his vest in a manner eerily similar to Andrew. "Letting him go is entirely up to you, Miss Tate." He nods at Travis.

I frown. "Wait, what—"

My head explodes. The force of Travis's blow makes my chair tilt, and a second later I slam into the dirt. A moan echoes off the walls. I see stars and colors. Some part of me is aware of retreating footsteps—Dr. Stern is getting away—but I'm helpless to stop him. Travis leers over me. I steel myself for a kick that doesn't come. Outside, Dr. Stern starts a car. The engine purrs, then slinks away. He's gone.

As soon as the quiet wraps around us, Travis reaches down and helps me up. I try to snatch my hand back but his grip only tightens. "We have to climb down the ladder," he tells me, winking. I sway on my feet. "Think you're up for it?

Hell, what am I saying? You're tougher than any other chick I know." He swings away, whistling through his teeth. My gun is tucked into his belt.

Wheezing, I manage to follow him to the hole that leads down, down, down into the ground. Everything inside me writhes and recoils at the idea of going deeper into the mines, but this choice has been taken from me. I didn't realize how valuable decisions are until I no longer had one. Without glancing back to make sure I'm coming, Travis puts his feet on the rungs and descends. He vanishes into the darkness. I'm frozen, staring into the hole and trapped in the memory of the last time I was here.

Daddy, take me back up! I'm scared.

It's all right, honey. We'll go back up. Just put your arms around my neck and I'll carry you, okay?

Warmth. A lullaby. Then air. But my father isn't here this time to save me. This time I'm not the one that needs saving.

Breathing raggedly, I clamp the sides of the ladder in my hands and inch down until my heel touches a rung. *Go back up!* instinct shrieks. Somehow I ignore it and shuffle to the next step. Then the next. My stomach quakes. I do this again and again and again with all the swiftness of Georgie reading a book. That is, extremely slowly. "Sometime today!" Travis shouts, his voice bouncing off the walls. Suddenly light reaches for me, showing the way, and I dare to peek toward the ground. There's an electric lantern waiting at the bottom of the ladder. Travis must have carried it down earlier. It makes me braver, and I eventually reach the end.

The instant my feet touch ground I collapse, catching my breath. My fingers brush against something hard—a rock.

"Finally," Travis mutters, stalking down the tunnel to our left. "Let's get this show on the road."

My hand wraps around the rock. Picking it up, I break into a run to keep up with his long-legged strides, desperate to stay within the circle of light despite how close it brings me to Travis. There's a swagger to his walk that tells me this isn't his first time in these tunnels. Soon we're so far underground I can't hear the rain anymore. Every time thunder sounds, though, my heart leaps into my mouth and I'm terrified that the ceiling will come down on us. It begins to feel like the mines are closing in, burying me alive, and Travis just keeps turning and walking and whistling. I try to keep count of every step and memorize each turn. Right, right, left, right, right. Twenty-two, twenty-three, twenty-four...

Somewhere in the fifth passageway, my endurance snaps.

"This is far enough," I hiss, trying to keep hysteria at bay. My nonexistent nails leave indents in my palms. "*Where is Saul?*"

Travis twists around and walks backward. His face looks like a Halloween mask in the lantern's glow. "Saul?" he echoes with raised brows. He chortles. "We don't have Saul!"

He's still retreating, but I jerk to a stop and stare at how the light glints off his crooked teeth. This was all a ploy. No one knows where I am, and Travis has my gun. When I thought I was making the sacrifice for Saul, it was worth it, but now?

I want a choice.

Which is why I raise the rock and bash it into Travis's head.

He crumples instantly, and something warm and sticky coats my fingers. Without waiting to see if he'll recover, I stumble in the direction we just came from. The light doesn't stretch far and soon I'm plunging into complete darkness again. The only sounds are my wild gasps and Travis's groans, and it all echoes together to form a soundtrack of horror. The walls are uneven and unmerciful and I keep slamming into them. By the time I reach the next tunnel my entire body aches, my lungs burn, my ribs scream. I pause for an instant—just an instant—to listen. *Nothing*, that tiny voice whispers. But then comes the sound I've been dreading.

Footsteps.

"Oh, Alex!" Travis singsongs. My veins burst in terror and adrenaline. I shove away from the wall and keep going. Travis waits a beat. When I don't answer, he bellows, "*Alex!*" His voice is too close. There's a manic abandon to the way he says my name, and I know that he's a predator and I'm the prey. If I can just beat him to the ladder, get to my car…

No. That's what he'll be expecting. *Be smarter than him.* I push myself harder and try to ignore the way my head is throbbing. My hand trails alongside the wall now to adjust my steps to the dips and curves. Once again I'm counting, struggling to remember the number of steps it took and the twists we made to get to here. Thirty-seven, thirty-eight, thirty-nine. My palm scrapes over an angle and I breathe as quietly as I can, shuffling forward and feeling out the secrets of the mines. Yes, this is the first turn. He took us right, which means that the left would take me back to the ladder.

All my instincts are howling to dive, to go, to flee toward the certainty of light and air and life. Shuddering, I force myself to step back. Then I shuffle along the wall until I find a gap big enough to tuck myself inside.

Not a moment too soon. Travis thunders past, seething. Every pore of my skin is twitching, anxious, eager to crawl away. But I force myself to be still and wait. His mutterings become fainter. I begin to relax, thinking I've outsmarted him and there's distance between us . . . until he whispers in my ear, "I know you're here."

A scream ricochets up my throat and it's just about to emerge when I comprehend that Travis is moving away again. "I can smell your pretty sweat!" he shouts. My muscles are locked into place, so rigid that one twitch will shatter everything. There's a thud, like a fist meeting packed dirt. Travis lets out a deafening scream. The darkness watches me cower, and I know it's smiling. The salty taste of tears slips inside my mouth and my heart sounds like a chorus of bombs in my ears. That's when I realize the rock is no longer clutched in my shaking fingers. Panic sears through me, and I try to tell myself it doesn't matter. I won't be able to surprise him again, and he has the gun. What could I use that would—

The pick.

If I can get to it, find it, I won't be so helpless. Purpose surges through me, and after listening a few seconds more, I leave the safety of my hiding place. Nothing happens. To keep the fear at arm's length, I focus on everything my father said about the pick. It's in the very first tunnel, which would mean it's near the very first entrance. Closer to the surface.

I'm going in the wrong direction.

But I can't go back; there's a very real possibility of slamming into Travis. The only option is finding the tunnels no one has ventured into for years. Tunnels my father told me nothing about. It's them or Travis. Picturing Nora's ruined face, I run.

Dad's voice follows me through each blind turn. *They hung it on the wall, as a way to remember where we've come from and where we're going.* The floor starts to slope upward. Once the surface feels close I thrust my hand over my head to feel the wall, alert for anything man-made or out of place. Suddenly my foot catches on something jutting out of the ground and I go sprawling. A tree root. Did he hear that? Biting my lip to trap a cry of pain, I'm just about to push myself up when my name booms through the darkness again.

"Alex!" a different voice calls, young and frightened and out of place beneath the ground. I freeze. That doesn't sound like Travis.

"Hello?" I shout-whisper, terrified that he will hear and come.

No answer. Stupid, stupid, stupid! It has to be Travis. No one else is down here. Some part of me doesn't believe it, though, and I stay where I am. Watching. Waiting. Even if it's a trick, I can't leave this place wondering if I've abandoned someone to a fate that was supposed to be mine.

Somehow he finds me. The lantern bobs into view, held aloft by one hand. A moment later, Travis himself. I tense, about to bolt, but then I see he's not alone. Whoever he's dragging behind him is short and painfully small, shrouded in shadow so the identity remains a mystery. Every organ inside me droops, as if it knows anyway. Knows before my mind fully does.

"Looks like you have a shadow," Travis pants, eyes gleaming with triumph as he wrenches someone forward. The light falls over the newcomer's face, and I want to sob.

Angus.

TWENTY-SEVEN

Dirt sprinkles down on our heads as thunder growls above. Angus stands there, his shirt wrinkled and the laces on one shoe undone. Before this I kept thinking how much he'd grown, how old he seemed, but now all I see is a scared little boy. "He has nothing to do with this," I manage after a choking silence, clenching my fists. "Let him go."

Mocking me, Travis taps his chin as if in deep contemplation. His hairline is clotted with blood. "I don't think so," he decides. "See, I think this kid will keep you in line."

Possibilities tear through me. Pretending Angus means nothing to me, throwing myself at Travis, trying to cut another deal. In the end, Travis makes yet another decision for me. He yanks the gun out of his belt and puts it to Angus's head. "Walk," he instructs. Helplessly, I start to edge around him.

Quick as a flash of lightning, Angus finds my wrist in

the dark and begins to tap, tap, tap in our language. There's no time to figure out what he's trying to say.

As I move forward, Travis doesn't try to hide the fact that he's inhaling my hair. The same moment his nostrils flare, a pale hand reaches for me from the shadows. I shriek and recoil. Without pausing, Travis swings the gun and the lantern toward it—Disgust's eyes go wide, and I realize that he must have been answering his summons—and pulls the trigger. Angus screams and the wall explodes. There's a ringing in my ears.

Before the dust settles I recover and rush toward Angus, pull him after me down the tunnel. We don't even get ten seconds of freedom before Travis's hand wraps around my arm and hauls me back with such force that I lose my footing and fall. "You want to make this harder?" he shouts. A glob of spit lands on my cheek as he leans over me. "Fine! I like a challenge." Agony radiates through my face yet again from the strength of his fist.

Angus's frightened face swims into view. "Run!" I try to tell him, coughing. Something hot and wet dribbles down my chin. A rusty taste slips into my mouth. Smirking, Travis straightens and gives me a kick in the ribs. I hit the wall and cry out. He says something that I don't bother listening to. Angus is no longer hovering in the background, and somehow I push myself up, wanting to know if he's escaped.

Relief squats in front of me when I see that he's gone. The Emotion's expression is tight as he touches the cut on my lip. Out of the corner of my eye, I see that Hope is standing behind him.

"What do you have to be relieved about?" Travis demands, looking in the Emotions' direction. Right. He can see them. They vanish but I still bask in their essences. It's the strangest thing, reveling in the other plane's power. With a jolt, I comprehend that I'm smiling. Travis notices this the same time I do, and he scowls. Tightens his fingers on the gun. From this angle his face looks like a skinless skull. "Dr. Stern doesn't have to know," he says, almost to himself. "I could tell him something went wrong. I could tell him it's your fault. Which it is, isn't it? You just wouldn't cooperate. All you want to do is play."

Play? Laughter bubbles up and bursts out of my mouth. Enraged at the sound, Travis flies at me and shoves the barrel against my forehead. Suddenly nothing is funny, and the mines are so quiet I can hear the rain again.

The surface. It must be close.

"I've never seen a face explode before," Travis whispers. His breath reeks of death and decay. "This should be interesting."

The urge to fight and survive rises up again, but there's no place for it to go. Travis's finger is closing in on the trigger, about to pull. Any moment Death will come ... this is the end he saw when our eyes met that night. As I wait for the inevitable rupture of light and pain, it occurs to me that I'll never see Briana's smile again, never hear Georgie's rambunctious laugh, never taste my aunt's burned eggs, never listen to my uncle play those forgotten pianos. And I'll never have another chance to touch Revenge or argue with Forgiveness. Somehow, I thought it wouldn't be so hard to leave it all behind.

Not wanting the last thing I see in this world to be the twisted face of Travis Bardeen, I close my eyes. There, in the darkness, is my family. Mom, Dad, and Hunter ... along with everyone else. The people I let down and tried to let go. And I know now, more certainly than I've known anything, that I wouldn't have been able to swallow those pills tonight. To say goodbye. Forgiveness was wrong; the most difficult choice wasn't him. It was living on when my family didn't.

The sound I'm expecting—a bullet bursting from the chamber—doesn't come. Instead, the stillness is shattered by Travis's ear-splitting screech. Something snaps. My eyes pop open, and for a moment they don't accept the sight before me. The image of Hope standing over Travis, watching coldly while he cradles his limp wrist. Then I notice the gun resting in the dirt. Instinct takes over and I lunge for it. Travis glances up, realizing what's happening, and dives for it at the same time. He beats me to the gun and lifts it with his good hand. Just as he's about to put his finger on the trigger again I grab his broken wrist and yank it with all the strength I have left. Travis howls and I try to grapple the gun from him.

"You *bitch*!" he snarls, leaning away and kicking at me. I hold on like a pit bull, feeling something inside me crack when his heel makes contact. I can't hold back a scream of my own, but I don't relent. When it becomes apparent his hold on the gun isn't going to break, I put all my body weight into the struggle and take the gun in both fists, slowly turning it toward him. Travis fights it—though he's weakened—and for a minute we're locked together, straining and trembling and grunting. My middle finger travels from the handle to the trigger, just barely brushing it. Travis's elbow knocks my jaw and I grit my teeth and push harder. Stretching and reaching … reaching …

The tunnel detonates in a blend of white and soundlessness.

Blood splatters my face, and I'm easing away from Travis. The air around us becomes considerably cooler as something approaches. Travis isn't moving now, and his eyes are as glassy as Eggs's were when I found her at the bottom of the stairs. A shadow moves. Death. This time he doesn't address me. He just leaves, taking Travis's soul with him.

Some part of me is aware that I'm pressing my back to the far wall, putting distance between me and the dark pool leaking out of the body. The body. Dead body. I killed someone. Travis is dead, dead, dead.

Minutes or hours pass—I'm not sure which—and my brain registers that a voice is coming from a long distance. It's telling me I can put the gun down, so my hands open and something falls out of them. Hits the earth with a soft sound. A face looms close and I blink. Again and again, until Hope's blurred features come into focus. Eventually I figure it out—she was the one who broke Travis's wrist and made it possible for me to claim the life I didn't realize I wanted.

"Thought you couldn't interfere?" I rasp.

The Emotion's eyes take in my dirty hands, my torn clothes, my battered face. "It was worth it," she says. With that, she vanishes. And I'm alone.

No, wait. I tilt my head and my breathing quickens. Maybe I'm wrong again, because a new sound echoes through the tunnels. Not a footstep or a voice. I don't know what it is. Is there a chance this still isn't over? Using the wall for support, I stand on shaky legs. The circle of light goes fuzzy for a moment and it seems like I've died and entered a realm made entirely of muted color and sharp sensation. One of my ribs feels broken. All I want to do now is lie down and let the darkness take me for the rest of the night, but I resist the urge. I've allowed it to have me for too long. So I pick up the lantern, ignoring the jarring voices of my wounds. After a long hesitation I get the gun, too. Pretend that it's not wet and cold and sticky. Then I make my way through the mines again. With each step the sound gets louder, human and strangely muffled. "Angus?" I call, wincing.

The sound answers, more frantic and adamant. Up ahead, another light appears. It spills out of a tunnel opening to the right. I falter in surprise, and Emotions join me in the tunnel. I lick my lips and take comfort in their presence; they're proof that I've survived. Cautiously, I round the corner. Their hands slip off my shoulders as I walk toward the brightness. And when I realize who it is making the sounds, his eyes glinting with a sheen of terrified tears, I stop. My grip on the gun, out of habit or pure instinct, tightens.

"You," I whisper.

He's tied to a chair, secured by layers and layers of duct tape. Even his mouth is covered, preventing him from shouting for help. I stand there, gaping, and Travis's words suddenly make sense. *We don't have Saul,* he'd said. I thought that meant they had no one, but I hadn't let him finish. And the note. *I have what you want most.*

Nate Foster stares up at me.

His gaze begs me to help him. Feeling as though the tunnel has collapsed and I'm walking through rocks and dirt, I slowly approach. Of its own volition, my hand reaches out and peels the tape off his face. The second it's gone Foster gasps, his chest expanding and contracting violently. "Thank y-you," he says. Nothing else. It makes my blood run cold, that these are the first words he's spoken to me. An expression of gratitude.

I study him, noting details I hadn't been able to see when there was so much distance between us. One of his front teeth is chipped. There's a splotchy birthmark hovering just above his jawline. His hair is receding to the point that it's hardly more than fuzz. He's ugly in every sense, which makes sense; only an ugly person could murder an entire family.

It occurs to me that Foster is completely silent now. He sits in that chair and, though fear still lingers in his countenance, there's also an eerie calm. Like he recognizes me. My skin prickles and I set the lantern down next to the one already here. "Do you know who I am?" I ask him quietly. The time for silence has passed. The gun has never been steadier in my palm.

"You're Alexandra Tate," Foster replies. And then he makes time stop when he says, "Go ahead. End it."

This can't be happening. I'm hallucinating or dreaming. "Do you know why—"

"Of course I do. I see their faces in my sleep. Every night.

Just like I saw you sitting outside my house. I can never escape it . . . and I don't deserve to. So just finish it, please. Now." His Adam's apple bobs, and Foster actually leans his head closer to the gun. His eyes flutter shut.

Shock roots me in place, until I'm a tree made of flesh and everything unresolved. "Y-you saw me?" I manage.

Guilt crouches next to Foster, and she touches the birthmark on his cheek with familiarity, like she's done it thousands of times before. He looks up. Tears fall out of those eyes now, leaving streaks down his crusty cheeks. "Many times," he answers hoarsely. "When you were in your car, when you stood outside the window. Each time, I hoped you would finally come inside and end it. But you never did." He pauses, and Guilt is joined by Sorrow and Resentment. Strangely, it feels like a betrayal that they're going to him. Then I realize that despite my new doubts, Nate Foster doesn't have any. He believes it was his fault. He wants to be punished. Doesn't that mean something?

"It means he's a good man, in spite of what happened the night of the accident," Forgiveness murmurs.

"I thought I told you not to come." I keep my attention trained on Foster, even when the Choice steps so close that his minty scent blocks the ones of blood and sweat. My insides quiver and the gun handle becomes slick.

Forgiveness disregards this, of course. "I know that you made a promise to your family, to honor them," he says. "And I know that every day is a struggle for you. Even though the people in your life don't know it, you're constantly fighting the urge to give up. But do you know how you can really honor them, Alex? *Keep fighting*. Lead the lives they should have had, would have wanted for you to have. Do you really believe they wanted *this* for you?" He gestures to Foster, who's staring at me in utter confusion. He can't hear Forgiveness; he only hears what seems like nonsensical babbling pouring out of me.

"I'm just so tired," I sob, uncaring. The gun begins to slip and I adjust my hold again. "I-I don't want to die . . . but I don't know how to live, either."

"No one does, Alex. That's what makes it so beautiful." Forgiveness says it tenderly, and the intensity of his gaze makes me feel like something beautiful, too.

"It's ugly," I say through my teeth, shuddering. "Just like him." Nate Foster becomes the center of my universe again, fading in and out of focus. Forgiveness responds, but the words are overpowered by the ringing in my head, piercing and painful.

"You can do it, honey."

This voice brings me back, and the sight of my father is the motivation I needed. He stands next to Foster's chair, smiling sadly. "Dad?" I say, searching his face for some sort of affirmation that he's real and this is what he wants.

His eyes are warm. They don't waver. "Go ahead," he urges. As if there's any doubt to his meaning, he raises his hand and points at Nate Foster. "Come on, honey. I know you can. Pull the trigger. Do it."

"*Do it*," Nate cries.

But now I'm staring at something else. When my father lifted his arm, his shirt rode up, exposing a strip of pale skin.

Even after the shirt covers it again, I keep looking, knowing that something isn't right. Like a missing piece in a large puzzle.

Then it comes to me in a quiet burst. The piece falls into place, and I begin to see the patterns and the meaning. "Dad... where's your scar?"

My father frowns. "What scar, baby?"

"It's supposed to be on your stomach, from your appendix surgery."

He steps into the shadows and his tone is unexpectedly terse. "I'm dead, Alex. I don't have scars anymore."

Wrong, my instincts whisper. Everything about him is so detailed, down to the injuries that caused his death. The crow's feet around his eyes, his unshaven cheeks, the way his smile always pulls to one side. Why should his scar be any different?

"You're not my father," I realize, slowly, devastatingly. There's another pause, and I wait for him to deny it.

In the silence that follows, we all hear a commotion, people shouting and calling my name. Frederick must be here. He'll find us any moment. But I don't react.

Forgiveness shifts, like he's about to touch me. Instead he steps close to the thing wearing my dad's face and snaps, "She knows now. You can stop."

The imposter continues to hesitate. No one speaks or moves or breathes. The search party gets closer. Then, as I watch, every feature that created my dad melts away. His floppy ears, his brown eyes, his big hands... until Revenge is all that's left. He looks at me with those green eyes, completely detached, as though none of this touches him.

A myriad of emotions tear through me, making me bleed and die and darken. Shock, disbelief, confusion, fury, denial. A hundred screaming words ricochet up my throat and fill my mouth, and yet all that emerges is, "You *did* rip that book up, didn't you?" I'm not sure why it matters. It just does.

Revenge doesn't answer. And in that instant, I know I'm right. He lied to me. Just like he lied about everything else. "You bastard," I breathe. It feels like he's carving out my insides with a dull hunting knife. "You psychotic bastard."

How did I not see it? Everything falls into place, and it makes perfect sense. It wasn't until the night Nate Foster was released that I heard the voice in my head, calling my name. And again the next day, when I was torn between hiding in my safe little bubble and going back to face him. Essentially, whenever I was unguarded or vulnerable, I heard my father. No, not my father. Him. Revenge. The creature I fooled myself into thinking was my friend, was idiot enough to wish for something more with. And every time I got close to Forgiveness, Revenge was there, whispering in my father's voice and toying with my sanity as if it were one of the dolls I used to love.

For what seems like an eternity we both stand there. A moth dares to flutter into the frozen space. "I should have known," I say bleakly. "My dad would never have done that to me."

Finally, he tries to explain. "Alex, I—"

"You know what I keep forgetting about that day? When

you let me climb the tree?" I demand. To the others, it probably seems odd that this is what I think of. But that memory meant so much to me. Every time I needed strength or an affirmation that I wasn't utterly broken, I thought of it. Remembered that there are some people in the world who don't think it's impossible to touch the sky. This time, I don't wait for Revenge to respond. "I *fell.*"

Wailing, I collapse to my knees. Forgiveness is beside me in an instant. He still doesn't touch me—he won't—but I lower the gun anyway. A deputy bursts into the tunnel and spots us. He calls to the others.

It's over. It's finally over.

TWENTY-EIGHT

YOU ARE NOW LEAVING FRANKLIN.

I look at the sign, unblinking, until it rushes past and disappears behind us. Elvis sings in the background while I search for something else to focus on. A hawk lands on the power line high above. The bird flaps its wings as though it's about to lose balance. And when that disappears, my eyes seek out other simple things and identify them. Tree. Sign. Mailbox.

"Are you sure you're up for this?" Missy asks me. I turn and catch her worrying her bottom lip. "We would understand if you need more time, Alex. Really. After everything."

After everything. There's so much that it's nearly impossible to select one incident and define it as the one that caused the most damage. My mind goes back to that night a week ago—the night in the mines, the aftermath of killing Travis and letting Nate Foster live. Of discovering that it was my best friend who'd hurt me the most.

Moments after the men found us, Nate Foster saved me from having to come up with any explanations for why he was still tied up and why there was a gun at his feet. "She's hysterical," he blurted. "A man left me here, and later I heard voices and shots. This girl found me and tried to help, but she didn't want to put down the gun, and she couldn't untie me with one hand. Then she heard you guys and dropped it."

Why he chose to save me, I don't know. Maybe he'd made some promises of his own. Or maybe he's not the monster I made him to be. Maybe he's just human, with light and darkness like the rest of us.

When I told Frederick about Dr. Stern's part in what happened, he sent out an APB. But Dr. Stern hadn't run; he was at his house, cooking dinner as if it were every other night. During the initial questioning about his involvement, he denied everything. He didn't know that Angus, hiding behind a tree, had seen him leaving the mines and was able to describe both him and his car. He faces kidnapping charges now, along with attempted murder. Especially in light of the information Christine and Nora Masterson gave about their own experiences with him.

All I can really think about, though, is the fact I haven't seen Revenge or Forgiveness since that night.

"I want to do this," I say to Missy. For once, it's nothing but truth. She nods and concentrates on the road, still fretting. It will take some time, but eventually she'll see that things have changed yet again. This time for the good. And it's a change of my choosing.

An hour later we're here. Missy offers to walk me in. I

smile and shake my head, trying not to cringe when I get out of the car and my injured rib protests. She watches me all the way to the doors, and I know she'll be right there waiting for me when I'm done.

"My name is Alexandra Tate. I have an appointment," I say to the receptionist at the front desk. With a kind light in her eyes, she directs me to an open doorway at my back. I go in only after a brief hesitation.

"You can shut that," the man says. I do. Then I sit down without any convincing.

His office is cheerful. The walls are yellow, and a picture of a rainbow hangs on the wall. Under the rainbow it says in cursive lettering, *YOU ARE THE CREATOR OF YOUR OWN DESTINY*. Dr. Goodwin is just sitting there watching me, his hands folded. He has white hair and a layer of fat under his chin. He seems entirely normal, like someone you'd see sitting in a coffee shop reading a newspaper. "Hi, Alex." He smiles. "Why are you here today?"

I have no control over my hands, and they twist in my lap until they look malformed, a pile of skin and fingers. It feels like talking will make me shatter into a million pieces. There are already so many cracks that I'm not sure I can take another one in the delicate glass that forms me. But that's not true. My bruises are fading and my ribs are healing. Here I am, alive, when I've faced death so many times. It's not because of fate or what my family wanted. It's because of what I wanted ... even if I didn't know it.

My eyes meet Dr. Goodwin's, and I'm not glass anymore. I'm steel. "I made a choice."

When we pull up in front of the apartment, Revenge is waiting. And he's not alone. Seeing this, my heart pounds harder and Disbelief hovers in the backseat.

My aunt twists the key and climbs out. She doesn't see Revenge's visible companion, since the railing conceals them. She just starts for the stairs, then realizes I'm not following. "Are you okay?" Worry appears, rolling his eyes.

Though it's the hundredth time Missy has asked me this over the past week, I don't snap. "I'm fine. Just want to enjoy the fresh air for a little bit, if that's all right."

She swallows and walks over to touch my cheek. "Don't stay out here too long. You shouldn't be standing so much." I nod. She pulls away and heads up the stairs. Then comes the sound of a door closing.

The moment it echoes through the clearing, Revenge releases her. Eggs bolts toward me. Her damp nose sniffs my hands, my legs, my arms. Joy leaks through my chest as if my heart has exploded, and I lower myself to the ground to hug the dog I thought I would never see again. When I got back from the hospital two days ago and her body wasn't under the stairs, I just assumed Saul had found and buried it.

Eggs whines happily and licks my face. I gag, jerking back. "Oh my God, Eggs, you *reek*."

But I keep stroking and petting her. She's warm and solid in a way my father never was during our encounters. *This* is real. Finally I look at Revenge. "How—"

He shrugs, hands shoved in his pockets. "Called in a

favor. It's not like we're breaking any rules, right? I didn't interfere in *human* affairs." He flashes me a shadow of that grin I know so well.

At a loss of what to say, I settle for the same words Nate Foster did in the tunnel. "Thank you."

"You're welcome." Revenge rocks on his heels, and it's easy to imagine a white flag over the two of us. We're both painfully aware, especially now, how much things have changed. I open my mouth, to ask why or what happens next. But then Revenge blurts, "I'm not human, Alex."

I frown, turning slightly when Eggs tries to lick my mouth again. "I know..."

"No, you don't. And it's my fault, really." He purses his lips, focusing on his shoes. That gelled mane of his looks like liquid fire in the twilight. "I've lived so long and met so many of your kind. I've been there through so much destruction. And I enjoyed every second of it. Until you." He still doesn't look at me, and my heart is pounding so hard he must be able to hear it. "At first, you were just another game. I waited and put ideas in your head. But along the way, you grew up, and I forgot to keep my distance. I forgot to love the game. Instead, I just loved you."

For a moment, I stop breathing. We stare at each other now, me and this creature who I once considered my best friend, once believed myself to be in love with. Then I tear my eyes from his and take two steps away. Emotions touch me with gentle hands, but I won't let myself look at them. Eggs is the only one that matters among all this warmth and summer oblivion. She cocks her head. Her attention is quickly diverted when a dragonfly zips past her nose. When she runs into the trees I'm not afraid, though, because some things come back.

Suddenly I swing around to face him again. "You don't do that to someone you love, Revenge."

He doesn't react like he usually would, like I expect him to. He stays calm, and his voice is subdued when he counters, "Didn't you do the same thing to the people you love?"

Silence. Birds chirp. An airplane soars overhead. In that silence I realize that Revenge is right. In the ways that matter, it is the same. I know better than anyone that love encompasses everything it means to be human. Laughter, pain, shadows, suns. To love is to stay when it's hard and leave when it's necessary. Sometimes it's wrong and unhealthy and doomed. Sometimes it isn't. And sometimes it makes us do things no other emotion would. "Revenge—"

"I fought it. I tried to ignore it and push it away. The trick with your father? That was nothing compared to what I've done in the past. At least, it should have been nothing." Agitated now, he starts to turn away.

I move so he can't. He glares at his shoes again and I want to touch him so badly. Not a kiss or anything romantic. Just a touch—like when Missy brushed my cheek—to let him know that even when everything seems ruined, there's always something to salvage in the wreckage. "You don't have to explain any more. I understand," I say.

At this, he looks up. His expression is so anguished that the cold stranger in the mines seems like a distant memory. "Do you know why I fell in love with you, Alex? Out of all the mortal women on this earth, why you were the one to make me forget what I am?"

Sniffing, I shake my head. Revenge smiles a little. "You're so *alive*. A part of you has always thought that you died the day of the accident, right? But that was the biggest lie of all. When I was supposed to be on the other side of the world, focused on retribution, I just wanted to be near you."

He falls silent, and so do I. Does he expect me to feel the same way? I might understand the reasons for his actions, and I might even be able to forgive him eventually, but that part of us did die in the mines. I open my mouth to stumble over a response and Revenge shakes his head to stop me. He's not smiling anymore. There's still a softness in his gaze, though. "One day you'll get off this mountain," he tells me quietly. "You'll leave all this behind. You'll meet new people and see new places. Maybe even fall in love." He pauses. "And I want that for you. Because you deserve it."

It's the most I've ever heard Revenge say, which is considerable since he's never been the sort to hold back. There's nothing else to add, really—he knows me better than anyone. He probably knows my thoughts before I do. Like now, because he turns away again. And this time I let him.

He starts toward the woods on soundless feet. Just as he's about to walk out of my life, I realize that there's one more thing to say. "Revenge," I call. He faces me. Eggs darts around him and prances toward me. Kneeling to pet her, I keep my focus on him and swallow. "For what it's worth . . . you made me forget, too."

The Choice smiles. His shirt flutters in the breeze. Watching him, I remember when Eggs ran from me—after I'd bathed her and fallen asleep with her warmth against my back—and I'd realized that some things can never be truly tamed. Revenge doesn't belong to just one person. He belongs to everyone lost or bound or broken.

I bury my fingers in Eggs's thick fur and watch him vanish in the trees.

TWENTY-NINE

The bell rings overhead. It's the last day of school, and the Emotions following my former classmates around are Relief and Excitement and Joy. I stand in a corner and wait for the tide to slow. At the end of the hallway I can see Georgie and Briana. It's as if nothing has changed: Georgie talks without taking a breath and Briana listens intently, nodding and smiling in the right places. They're the reason I'm here—I wanted to experience this last day with them, even if I ruined my chance to be part of it. The sight of my friends brings Regret to our tiny school. He leans his hip against a locker and folds his arms. He observes Briana and Georgie with a pinched mouth.

"You know what I've learned?" I ask abruptly. Georgie slings her arm around Briana and they head for the doors. Neither of them looks back.

Regret focuses on me now, and he actually seems curious. "What?"

"I may regret what I've done, but I regret what I didn't do more." The Emotion stays where he is, even after I've pushed away from the wall. I can feel his eyes on me as I walk away, and then I'm the one that's gone.

On my way out, a couple kids wave at me. They say *have a good summer* or *I'll see you soon* as they pass each other, and I think of what Forgiveness said about time. It's always moving even when we feel like it's stopped completely.

Dong. Dong. Dong. Bag in hand, I halt on the front steps and listen to that damn clock boom over the mountain. It stands there so piously next to the school, like it's all-powerful and untouchable. Acting on impulse, I march toward it. There's a small door around the back, right at its base, and after testing the knob to find out whether it's locked, I go inside. I climb the stairs and enter the tiny room that's awash with the gold of sunset. One wall is entirely overtaken by the face of the clock, and the shadows of the hour and second hands fall over me. The air is so stifling in here, the heat so overwhelming, that I open the tiny window beside the door. For a moment I watch the seconds tick by. Then my stomach twists and, dropping the bag, I grab the giant hand.

"What are you doing?"

His voice makes me jump, and I spin around to face him. Even though I knew I would see him again, even though I've been expecting him, the sight of Forgiveness is terrible and exhilarating. Like watching lightning streak across the sky and then getting struck by one of the bolts.

"Turning back the clock," I answer, wishing he wasn't

so beautiful. I take hold of the hand again, pushing and pushing and pushing. My muscles bulge with the effort.

"Why are you turning back the clock, Alex?" He asks this as though I do it every day.

I laugh. "Because maybe, just maybe, it'll actually work."

Forgiveness is silent now. That's okay. I have enough words. Too many words, actually. They pour out of me like blood from a wound. The clock moans and grinds as I force it backwards. "Of course, it probably won't. This isn't a fairy tale. It's Franklin. But you never know if you don't try, right?" I free one hand to swipe at my nose. "All I'll accomplish is confusing the hell out of the people in town. That'll be funny, though. Worth it." Another laugh.

"Alex."

"I hate when you say my name like that!" I snap, letting the hand go again to glare at him. *Dong. Dong. Dong.*

"Like what?"

All his questions. I hate his questions. I want them to stop forever. "Like you *know* me," I hiss. This time when I move to face the clock, Forgiveness is in my way. His eyes are gentle but unrelenting.

"You didn't love him, Alex," he tells me.

"Now you're telling me how I feel?"

"Think about it. Did you ever seen her when you were together? Love?" He takes a step closer and I instantly retreat. My back hits the wall, and since there's no plaster, a piece of wood digs into my spine. Forgiveness invades the space around me, infecting the air and my breath and my thoughts. "It's okay to be afraid. It's normal. You've never let yourself wonder about your future before because you always assumed you wouldn't have one." Then he shocks me by wrapping his fingers around my wrists. "Let the clock keep going, Alex."

Alarm slams through me. I'm not ready for this. "Let go of me! Let go!" I try to wrench away, but Forgiveness only brings me toward him. His skin is warmer than I thought it would be, and, like him, his touch is kind and devastating. Calming, I hiccup and stare at his chin so I don't have to meet his eyes. "I don't want to forgive Nate Foster," I whisper brokenly.

"Yes, you do." He says it against my temple. His lips are how I imagine clouds would feel.

As always, Forgiveness is right. Ever since the night in the mines, when I put the gun down, the choice has been obvious. I close my eyes, relaxing against him. And then—for the first time since I can remember—I go completely, utterly, incandescently still.

Nate Foster's face fills me up. His sad, drooping eyes. *I see their faces in my sleep. Every night. I can never escape it… and I don't deserve to.* He made a choice to get in his car drunk one night, and he changed the course of my life forever. But some of the fault could belong to my father. Some of it could belong to me. It doesn't matter anymore.

"I forgive you," I breathe.

But it's not finished yet, not yet. One more person lingers in my head, and I can smell chocolate. A tear falls down my cheek and off the edge of my jaw. "Revenge." The name slips out, soft. The breeze carries it away. Forgiveness still hears. He follows the direction of my gaze, out the window. Standing in the middle of the street, looking back up at us, Revenge lifts one hand in a solemn wave.

Then he's gone.

It's the easiest and hardest thing I've ever done. To let go. To not need him anymore. It's difficult to imagine a world without Revenge in it, without that fierce ache for reckoning that has existed inside of me since the accident. He may have been the cause of it, but he never would have been able to haunt me if I hadn't wanted him there.

Now the only one left is Forgiveness. I focus on his face again, and he's so, so careful. His hands cup my face as if I'm something precious and breakable. He gives me time to turn away or stop him, but I don't. His lips brush mine. He tastes fresh and overwhelming as his essence continues to sweep through me, a sensation akin to falling. All too soon he's pulling back, putting distance between us, and I hit the ground. I open my eyes.

Forgiveness doesn't move, doesn't speak, doesn't even breathe. This time, he's the one who's turned to stone. He almost looks... lost. Trembling, I rise and step closer. And I put my hand on his chest.

He makes the smallest of sounds, almost a sigh. He's been waiting for this, too. Wanting it, too. I come alive when I hear it, and there's no more hesitation.

I rise on my tiptoes and wrap my arms around his neck. His palms skim up my sides, leaving a trail of goose bumps. He tries to be gentle with me at first, like before, but my desire for him is too fierce. I open my mouth and the kiss deepens.

We stumble into the wall again. Our ragged gasps are deafening and frantic. Forgiveness is everywhere, everything. For a few minutes I'm only aware of him. His hands, his heat, his skin against mine. Then we're slowing down, and he's pulling back. I let him. Our eyes meet again, and I absorb his expression, fighting the urge to pretend that this can have a happy ending. That nothing will change.

"I'm not going to see you again, am I?" But it doesn't sound like a question. He doesn't answer. Really, he doesn't need to. We could say all the things we're supposed to say in a moment like this. Goodbye, love, live. So I just smile and say, "Thanks, Forgiveness."

He brushes a strand of hair away with the tip of his finger. "Actually, it's Atticus."

Unable to resist, I lean into him again. Our foreheads press together. It's the most beautiful-hideous thing, choice. It doesn't define us... it reveals us. Who we are, who we've been, who we'll become. All we can do is try to make the right ones.

Suddenly the warmth against my skin is gone. The room is empty save for the clock. Blinking rapidly, I approach it and put the hands back to where they're supposed to be. *Dong. Dong. Dong.* Outside, the sun is a sliver on the horizon. This is the only place on the entire mountain that anyone can watch it disappear. I shuffle to the window and pull myself up on the sill. Eleven minutes pass, and eventually the sun leaves our half of the world to go light the next. The sky darkens into a blend of black and purple. It feels permanent, in a way, and impossible that it could be bright again. Morning will come, though, as it always does.

We just have to wait for it.

Almost the entire town turns out for the graduation ceremony. Which isn't considerable, granted, but there are enough people that half the folding chairs in the gym are full. Missy, Saul, and I manage to snag spots one row behind the students.

I lean my chin on the back of my hand, which rests on the edge of the metal chair in front of me. Georgie talks out of the corner of her mouth. "I can't believe you dropped out when we were so close to graduating," she hisses. The tassel dangling off her cap sways.

Regret pushes his shoulder against mine. I ignore him. "Just add it to the long list of mistakes I'll make throughout my life."

She scowls. "Well, are you going to fix it?" Yelena Prichard glares at us and Georgie's arm moves. I suspect she's giving her the finger.

We watch Briana walk across the platform. She takes the diploma from Principal Bracken. "I'm going to try," I say. Georgie's turn comes shortly after. Then Yelena's. Then Rachel Porter's. There are some that dropped out, like me, who sit in the small crowd. It happens so fast. Soon they all have their diplomas and we're all standing, cheering while they file out the door and toward their futures. The moment the last kid is gone everyone moves, off to make their celebratory dinners or go back to business as usual. I stand there for a second, people parting around me like I'm a stone in a river. Part of something and forever separate.

Then someone's arm is wrapping around me and a voice is saying, against my ear, "Come on, then." Georgie. I hesitate, though, and search for my aunt and uncle. Saul and Missy wave at me, giving permission even as Worry holds both their hands.

So we all go to the last bonfire. Since I'm driving myself, I make a stop at the apartment. By the time I get to the lake the party is well underway. Georgie greets me with her usual flair and soon flounces off to be with Billy. Briana is there, talking to Rachel Porter. Smiling, I move to stand by the fire. I toy with the bundle in my hands.

It takes me a while, but eventually I throw my father's shirt onto the pile and watch it catch the flames.

Georgie comes to stand beside me. The shadows dance and quiver over her perfect skin. "I think I'm going to stay here for a while," she murmurs.

Now I look at her. "What about California?"

She shrugs. "Some dreams are just that, Alex. Dreams. They're fun, they keep us going, they're what make us human. And they change. I'm okay with that."

I face the fire again and watch the remains of the shirt become ash. Then I say, "Bullshit."

"What?" Georgie turns to me and frowns.

"You heard me. Bullshit. You're scared."

Anger quivers into view and puts his hand on her back.

"You're one to talk," my friend snaps, her eyes bright and defiant. "You didn't even finish high school."

"That's right. I didn't. And I regret some of my choices. But I'm making new ones."

For once, Georgie doesn't press for more or try to argue a point. She just absorbs this, then clears her throat. She's still angry, still frightened, but there's nothing I can do about that. Our emotions and our choices are our own. "So what's next for you, then?" she asks awkwardly. "Mark texted me. He said he was tutoring you."

I let her change the subject. "He is, since I'm so behind. Andrew pulled some strings, and I'll be able to finish school at Green River this summer. After that, who knows?" That's the most terrifying part about life, I think; not knowing how things will turn out. But I'm learning that it's also the best part. I have a life to live, to fear, to discover. I think of that night I went to the lake with Revenge, leaping into those freezing waters without hesitation.

Someone turns on a radio, and Elvis sings over the crickets. Groans erupt down the beach. "Turn it off!" Marty Paulson shouts. Briana flinches from her place next to him. She must feel my stare, because our eyes meet across the fire. Our last conversation plays in my head: *No one comes out of the closet in Franklin. We're not as progressive as the rest of the world. We still play Elvis every day, for God's sake.*

During all of this, I was so convinced that things had to change. And I was right. I'd just been pursuing the wrong things. Suddenly I know what I have to do. "Georgie, make sure they don't turn off the radio," I say in a rush, moving away. Frowning, she calls after me, but I just take my keys out. "Make sure!" I jump into my car and tear off.

Our local—and only—radio station on the mountain stands next to Ian's store. All the lights are on and I can see Joe through the front window, drinking out of a coffee mug. He's an old man with peppery hair and a penchant for bulky vests. Rapping on the edge of the screen door, I wait for him to look up before going inside.

"Alexandra Tate," he greets in that throaty voice everyone knows so well. "To what do I owe the pleasure?" There's a book resting on a stool, one of the romance novels he pretends aren't his. They're the reason he sometimes tries to talk like he's British.

I drop into the chair across from him and lean forward, resting my elbows on my knees. Without warning I say, "Joe, I know this is your station and you have the right to play whatever you want. And I respect that, I do. But don't you think Elvis would want you to play other music, too? I mean, so many of his songs were about love and experiences. Shouldn't we be able to learn about that through someone else?"

The old man blinks, as though this is incomprehensible. "Elvis was king, Alex." He adjusts one of the knobs. "And anyway, I've been running this place for over twenty years. No one's been able to change my mind about this. They've offered me every bribe known to man, to no avail. Why should I make an exception for you?"

The song playing finishes. I twist my lips, thinking of Briana. Change. Some of them come naturally, and some we have to force into being. My mother did tell me that I would change the world. We just have to start with small pieces of it.

"Okay, let me put it this way," I say slowly. "If I have to listen to one more Elvis song, I'm going to get violent."

Surprise flickers in Joe's gaze ... and a little wariness. Though he tries to hide it, the Emotions give it away. Fear winks at me, his near-white hair glowing in the dim lighting. My eyes narrow in response.

"You remind me of your mother," Joe mutters after an obvious pause. He doesn't sound happy about it. His finger taps the counter beside him. *Tap-tap-tap-tap-tap*. I wait again. Then Joe swings around and switches the microphone on. "All right, folks. We're going to do something a little different tonight, per request of the ... feisty Alexandra Tate." He swivels toward me. "Any requests, kid?"

My heart leaps, and I hurry to tell him the song.

The DJ sighs, reaching for a CD among the stacks in front of him. "Write this down, because it's a historic moment. I'm going to play 'You Get What You Give' by New Radicals. This one's for you, Briana."

THIRTY

The next day I find Saul in his office. There are papers in front of him, numbers and words typed across the white spaces, but he isn't looking at them. Instead he's staring at the container of pens next to his hand. Probably worrying or regretting something, as we're prone to do. Entering without invitation, I set the gun down in front of him. "I stole this from your nightstand."

My uncle takes it wordlessly, and we both study the angles and edges of the gun like it's one of his maps. Something that, even after exploration and discovery, still doesn't make sense. "I'm sorry," I add. Still he doesn't respond. He doesn't tell me it's okay or ask me why I took it—it isn't, and maybe he's afraid to know—so I find a lifeline for both of us and grab it with both hands. "I was wondering... do you think you could teach me? How to play piano, I mean?"

From behind the desk, Hope grins at me. As her hand

settles on Saul's shoulder I remember how she saved my life in the tunnels. I wonder if she has one more miracle to give.

"I can do that," my uncle says after a breathless pause. He tucks the gun into a drawer and finally smiles.

I nod. "Good."

We keep looking at each other like we're people with a wonderful shared secret. Then Saul glances down at the papers, and I step away. "Okay, well, Missy is making spaghetti. So I'll see you in a little bit."

"I'll bring the fire extinguisher."

I leave him to those pieces of paper. They don't seem so meaningless now. I weave through the pianos, aiming for the stairs that lead up into our apartment. Movement outside the window makes me pause. Angus. He sits on the bench, holding yet another jar. With my hand on the rail I watch him. My first instinct is to go out there and thank him for what he did that night. Something tells me, though, that Angus wants to be alone; the sounds of his parents' latest argument drifts through the ceiling. Listening to them, I realize that some promises have to be broken … and some never should have been made in the first place.

Sunlight reflects off the glass in his hands. For the first time it occurs to me that maybe those jars were never empty. Maybe they hold all his invisible pain. Everyone has to put it somewhere. Someday Angus will have to break those jars and find a new place for it. Someday. Not now.

Missy is standing in front of the stove when I enter the kitchen. She's watching the noodles bubble with rapt attention, and I wonder how long it's been since she dared to blink. Just as I'm about to speak, brakes squeal outside. Missy doesn't move. "Who is that?" she mumbles at the pot.

"It's probably Mark. He's coming over to tutor me, remember?" I go to the window. He's getting out of his truck, shoes crunching on the gravel. As I watch, Mark wipes his palms off on his jeans. His gaze flicks up to the glass, but the sunlight must hide me from view. I hurry to grab a notebook and pen.

"Bring him up for supper!" Missy calls on my way out the door.

The stairs shudder beneath my weight. Hearing my approach, Mark lifts his head, already smiling. The sinking sun reaches for his eyes. Strange that I've never noticed how blue they are before. "Hey," I say.

"Hey," he says. "Are you ready?" An Emotion fills the space beside him. There's a pause, and I let my glance flick to her. Hope smiles at me.

I smile back. "Ready."

Eggs pants in the passenger seat.

As we wind down Briana's driveway, she raises her hind leg to scratch her neck. "You better not have fleas," I tell her. She just leans out the window to watch our progress.

When we reach the house, I see that there are no other cars besides mine and my friend's. "Stay here." I shift gears and twist the key in the ignition. My dog snaps at the air, distracted by a fly, and I get out. The soft material of the dress

I'm wearing whispers against my skin. Birdsong follows me to the door, which is propped wide open. "Hello?" I call. A fan purrs in the corner. Cautiously I step inside.

"Alex. Come and look."

Francis. She's in the living room, hunched over something resting on the windowsill. The floor creaks as I approach. She moves so I can see, and there, bursting from the soil, is a white flower. Alive and vibrant and growing. "It's a Peace Lily," Francis tells me, touching the white petal. "Isn't it beautiful?"

"Yeah, it is." I study her and think of how many meanings that word has.

There's a sound from the hall, and I glance up. Briana stands in the doorway, watching us. Her hair is damp from the shower. All my carefully rehearsed apologies about the kind of friend I've been fly away. I can almost hear wings flapping. After a beat of uncomfortable silence, Briana inclines her head. I stand and join her. When I reach her side I start to utter those ridiculous words, since they're all I have. "Briana, I just wanted to say that I'm—"

"What if it dies?" she interrupts, her voice sharp.

The flower, she means. I turn to Francis, who's still staring at it. Even after every plant she's watched wither and fade, she still has hope that things can be different. I face Briana again, my own voice soft. "What if it doesn't?"

Briana doesn't respond, and her hand clenches and unclenches. Worry grabs it with both of his, and forces it to go still.

Suddenly Francis whirls, startling us. Leaving the window, she brings the lily over to Briana and kisses her forehead.

"I want you to have this," she says and presses it into her daughter's grasp. Stunned, Briana takes it. Without another word, Francis creaks down the hallway and into her room. The door closes.

There's a long, long pause. When it becomes evident that Briana isn't going to talk about what just happened or what it means, I ask, "Were you listening to Joe's station last night?"

She tears her attention away from the door to look at me. Her grip is white on the potted flower. "Yes. Georgie didn't really give us any choice." Another Emotion joins us in this small space, but I don't let myself see who it is. I want to ask her what she thought, if it changed anything, if it helped at all. Maybe it was just a song, even if it felt like more.

"Well . . . " I clear my throat. "You know I'm not good at, uh, expressing myself. So just know that I'm so glad you're going to college, and I'll think about you every day. And I hope you find a radio station that doesn't play a single Elvis song." When she doesn't smile back, I make a vague gesture. "Okay, then. Bye, I guess. Good luck with everything. Not that you need luck, you're so good at everything." *You're rambling*, that inner voice nudges. Right. I swing around and clatter down the steps.

"Alex."

I turn. Briana smiles, a thing just as fragile as all those flowers. "I kissed Rachel yesterday. Right when we threw our caps into the air."

A lump forms in my throat. "That's good," I say. "You'll have to give me the details before you leave."

Briana nods, still smiling and clutching that lily. "See

you soon. And . . . you look beautiful." She retreats into the house again, but that doesn't matter. It's a beginning, and beginnings are just as important as the endings. I linger for a moment, fingering the skirt of my mother's favorite dress. It still smells like the attic I finally removed it from.

Eggs prances impatiently and I slide behind the wheel. *Home?* her expression seems to ask. "Not yet," I say. "There's one more stop I have to make." The engine rolls over after a few tries, and then we're thundering down the road, dust flying up all around. Overhead the clouds are thin wisps, so delicate that one gust of wind could wipe them away forever. Eggs hangs her head out the window, her long tongue flopping out of the corner of her mouth. Slobber splats the seats behind ours, but I don't care. We pass the lake, the general store, the radio station, the school. Until there's nothing but trees and a single sign on the right.

FRANKLIN CEMETERY.

The instant I stop and open the door, Eggs tumbles out in a flurry of legs and gleaming fur. I stretch my arm toward the backseat and grab the box Missy gave me. Butterflies flit through the air and long, golden grass tickles my knees as I trek away from the rest of the headstones, toward a row that stands apart. A huge oak tree towers over my family's graves, the branches twisted and ancient in their wisdom. Kneeling, I dig a hole with my bare hands. Dirt cakes beneath my nails. Once it's big enough, I bury the box containing the flash drive, laying it to rest along with everything else. There. Finished.

I flatten my filthy hands on my thighs and they all gaze

back at me. *WILLIAM TATE. TRACEY TATE. HUNTER TATE.* "Love you," I whisper, my vision blurred with tears. The scents of chocolate and mint drift past, carried by a breeze.

Suddenly Eggs barks, an urgent sound. She stands on her hind legs and claws at the tree trunk. A squirrel titters angrily from the leaves. I glance up at it and start to smile. But then something glints. I frown, looking closer . . . and the oxygen leaves my lungs.

There it is. Rusted with age, cracked down the middle, so brittle that it looks like it'll never fly again. But it will. Because my father built it, and he made things to last. I jump to my feet and haul myself up the unyielding branches. Each one brings me into the blue, unending sky. The squirrel scurries into hiding, thinking that my outstretched hand is reaching in its direction.

I pull the rocket free, smiling.

2009 Olivia Wagner Photography

About the Author

Kelsey Sutton has done everything from training dogs and making cheeseburgers to selling yellow page ads and cleaning hotel rooms. She received a BA in English from Bemidji State University and lives in northern Minnesota. When Kelsey is not writing or trying out a new career, she can be found in the park with her dogs, ordering a drink at the coffee shop, or browsing a bookstore. *Where Silence Gathers* is her second novel with Flux.